The Quick End

For Kathy Acker

Michael Bracewell was born in London in 1958 and educated at Epsom College and Nottingham University. His first novel, *The Crypto-Amnesia Club*, was published in 1988 and deals with celebrity victims.

Don Watson was born in Glasgow. He was educated but is much better now and is currently still living.

Mark Edwards was born in 1963. He was raised in Hampshire and now lives in London.

She lifted the lobster clear of the table. It had about thirty seconds to live.

Well, thought Bolacqua, it's a quick death, God help us all.

It is not.

From Dante and the Lobster *by Samuel Beckett*

THE QUICK END

Three Novellas

Fourth Estate · London

First published in Great Britain by
Fourth Estate Limited
113 Westbourne Grove
London W2 4UP

British Library Cataloguing in Publication Data

The quick end: three novellas.
1. English fiction — 20th century
I. Bracewell, Michael II. Watson, Don
III. Edwards, Mark
823'9'4'08 PR1307

ISBN 0-947795-52-9

Typeset in Palatino by York House Typographic, London W7
Printed and bound in Great Britain by
Richard Clay Ltd, Bungay, Suffolk

Contents

Missing Margate

by

Michael Bracewell

For Michael Woods and Susan Martin

Andy – I am not here anymore but I am fine.

Love, Billy

(Farewell note to Andy Warhol from Billy Name)

Beside the Queen's Highcliffe now rank grows the vetch,
Now dark is the terrace, a storm-battered stretch;
And I think, as the fairy-lit sights I recall,
It is those we are fighting for, foremost of all.
(Sir John Betjeman, 'Margate 1940')

1 The Hesitation of Empedocles
One: No One Knows Your Name
Two: Her New CD

2 Psychowhizziology
One: Party Games from New Manderley
Two: Pacman Software plc

3 'Broken Lute Strings and Pet Monkeys'
One: Top Man of Nothing
Two: Max de Winter's Apostasy

Introduction

As one New York analyst wrote recently apropos this new frenzied consumer conciousness, there is now a 'new type of patient' who is presenting himself. The classical neurotic for whom psychoanalysis was invented suffered from symptoms which were lodged in a self that was otherwise intact. By contrast, the 'new patient' of the post-modern period has not even progressed to the point where a stable identity structure has coalesced. 'Typically he or she suffers from feelings of emptiness, isolation and futility, pre-Oedipal rage and primitive separation . . . which are masked by grandiose narcissistic fantasies', fuelled by 'the marked intensification of the pursuit of material success, power and status; an increased preoccupation with youth, health and glamour, accompanied by difficulty in forming relationships with emotional depth.' Excessive alienated narcissism frequently masked by social adaptability has come to dominate our era, according to this perception, just as hysteria and (later) neurosis did Freud's.

(Brandon Taylor, 'After Post-Modernism', with reference to J. Whitebrook, 'Reason and Happiness: Some Psychoanalytic Themes in Critical Theory', in R. J. Bernstein (ed), 'Habermas and Modernity', 1985, p. 150.)

1
The Hesitation of Empedocles

One: No One Knows Your Name

The bleached pavement rose up to Max de Winter's undefended eyes as he stumbled out of Duchess Street W1 and then stopped, wavering a little despite its solidity because Max wasn't feeling very well. On the freshly scrubbed façade of the BBC building that Max proceeded to lean spitting and cursing against, red-faced and breathless, the slogan

NATION SHALL SPEAK PEACE UNTO NATION

seemed – despite the authority of its sans-serif, no-nonsense capitals – somehow inappropriate.

The early-afternoon sun made Max's eyes ache terribly, and he squinted nastily at a passing Arts Administrator before wiping some excess saliva from the corner of his mouth with the back of his hand. He had left his sunglasses on a bistro table in New Cavendish Street, and was predicting their subsequent theft and destruction at the hands of the professionally rude waiter. His thought patterns were laced with the tearfully self-righteous suspicion and oath-laden outrage that frequently attach themselves to a self-pitying, physically uncertain and hopelessly drunk young man. The sunglasses were important to Max, his only mask to advance behind, and life seemed unbearable without them.

As he swayed like a tall building in the slipstream of Hurricane Rayban the glasses took on a totemistic significance, and their loss seemed to verify that in some underhand, insidious kind of way his right to have any say at all in his destiny had been taken away from him.

Max clasped the sides of his head and moaned quietly, his extravagant emotion giving rise to much twitching of net curtains in the windows of the office across the street which had been cunningly degentrified to make it look like an office.

The traffic moved on across the lights and Max crouched sobbing on the pavement, his hunched and defeated aspect being gradually obscured by a mist of russet exhaust. It was, one could say, operatic.

It was also the day of The Big Launch, and the atmosphere around Fitzrovia, along Cleveland Street, along Goodge and Mortimer Streets, gusting beside the Diuretic Unit of Middlesex Hospital, sneaking down Tottenham Mews and emerging with a self-conscious flourish – 'There!' – into the electronics retail end of Tottenham Court Road had driven this section of West One quite rigid with indifference.

It was the day of the Big Launch of *Designate* magazine: a new and exciting look at the future style of tomorrow yesterday – or today, or next week. Last year, possibly – the definition is irrelevant; the point of the thing is style, and *Designate* magazine had wide enough margins to make anything stylish.

Max de Winter walked into one of Wren's elegant pillars which support the soaring needle spire of All Souls and was by that time past caring whether the future was here today or gone the day before. His past and his future no longer seemed to meet in his present and the style of this confusion was of little interest to him. He wasn't there. Not really.

Max de Winter wasn't there either when Malcolm Houston, the new and exciting editor of *Designate*, was addressing his staff with the same mixture of generosity and weariness with which one addresses Christmas cards on the subject of young blood, old wood and fresh pastures.

This was at the big planning meeting. A room had been appointed with a view of the car park of the neighbouring television headquarters, and coffee was poured from a triangular stainless steel coffee pot with a parrot-yellow handle and a spout the hue of July blue. As the coffee was drunk – ritualistically, one might say – the clever triangular beakers were scattered with precision among dunes of forward profiling sheets, advertising copy and provocatively opened diaries.

Rough sketches were made in moments of wild inspiration on the backs of proof sheets, and the illegible crudity of these illustrations remained in the centre of the table as evidence of their intention to attract favour from the editor as opposed to demonstrate a point. Black fibre-tip pens were sucked and fiddled with. Telephone numbers were seized with religious fervour out of the heated wardrobes of fame-hungry brains, and repeated litany-like by their captor until noted down as 'interesting'.

It was feeding time at the latest glossy.

Malcolm was very frank about the cut of his jib, the tightness of his ship and the passenger-hostile persuasion that he expected of his crew. Heads nodded fervently at the mention of 'commitment', and watery smiles swam magically across tense faces when evening and weekend input was stressed. Knuckles crackled with the urge to impress and not one knuckle crackled more urgently than those belonging to Arabella Cloth, the exciting new Assistant Editor (Features) who sat on Malcolm's left.

Sitting on Malcolm's left was a way of not looking at Malcolm, and thus subordination could coexist with Individual Flair by virtue of the lack of eye contact. Arabella looked hard at the table top and nodded when Malcolm outlined the market gap that *Designate* hoped to fill. She shook her head when Malcolm suggested (by way of proving himself open to criticism) that they might have made some errors in their brand-profiling age-group-wise. It was vital to commence both the venture and the planning meeting with a ritual of self-questioning. The admission of possible error (although not for one moment believed) served a vital role in establishing a backdrop of bogus maturity and clear-headedness against which the team could then act out their wildest schemes without fear of seeming any less than professional.

An oriental dissonance filled the air when Malcolm said: 'Are we ready to go for this one? If we're not – we should say so.' And it was at this point that Arabella shook her head. She just shook her head without moving her lips or looking at anybody. She shook her henna'd ringlets and Soviet ceramics ear-rings by way of a token genuflection to ward off the evil spirits of Marketing Doubt and Product Insecurity, those gremlins within the periodical publishing machine. She was silently saying (as she shook her head), 'No Malcolm – we will not let you down. We are ready to go for this one.' Arabella was itching to shine and knew that one moment's misplaced visible or vocal enthusiasm could eclipse her rising star with its cloud of unprofessional effervescence.

Max de Winter was lying on his back in the Chelsea Physic Garden when Gemma Danvers (Deputy Editor 'In and Out' section and Advertising) choked on a piece of chewing gum whilst trying to make herself heard during the debate on a projected feature entitled 'New City Men: Who Are They?'

Max de Winter was inhaling verbena by the stone lip of a fountain and thinking how, given just a little strength, he would simply press a button and disappear whilst the *Designate* team turned their media-sodden gaze to him and decided that he would make a splendid feature.

Knowing his little army to march on sycophancy as well as fear, Malcolm had shared a joke with the troops in order to win their support for this his best (and only) idea for an in-depth *Designate* styled feature.

'You know when Bill Wilson over at Channel 8 – the new late-late independent cable – ah, told me about their profiling of Max de Winter Associates, I have to tell you I thought he was crazy. And I'm telling you that. I thought he was crazy. I said "Bill, you must be out of your mind. De Winter is just – not – fucking – famous enough." ' (laughter) ' "He's not even a potential revival." ' (Hysterical laughter, the team are in stitches. Gemma used the general moment of shared hilarity as a cover for pouring herself another cup of coffee out of the terrifyingly awkward-to-lift coffee pot which was just out of reach; others lit cigarettes as they laughed – all these actions thus doubling as guarantees that the laughter was quite genuine and uncontrollable because it continued even as they did other things. It was therefore a moment of regrouping and rearming disguised as applause for Malcolm's anecdote.)

And now it must be said that Max de Winter and Max de Winter Associates were names to respect, for the very same Max de Winter whom we discovered unwell at the junction of Duchess Street and Portland Place (and who subsequently has been observed inhaling soft scent in the Chelsea Physic Garden) is the most brilliant young architect in England – he who shaped the new London skyline into an aphorism that summed up the age in architectural language and then underlined it with glorious style by marrying the beautiful Rebecca Walters, erstwhile child-neurotic turned Cork Street Fine Art dealer *par excellence* whose glamorous gallery is the International launch pad of the effortlessly uncommercial.

Malcolm looked around the table for a minute and then continued: 'So then I got to thinking – and I'm telling you this now – then I got to thinking, "Well, it's a strange world, and maybe there's a story in this architect after all." ' He leaned forward slightly, a man just testing ideas, a man just – running a few things up the flagpole to see if anyone salutes.

'De Winter is just turned thirty. He's responsible for some of the most controversial office buildings in the City. London Wall will never be the same – but he's a bit of a mystery. So I think, mystery – Howard Hughes – gothic – meetings in car parks – sudden departures from restaurants – receiving the Hands On Design Award *in absentia* – a place out of town. He's so public . . .'

'Yet so private?' suggested Gemma, hopefully.

'Possibly, Gemma, possibly. But what I was thinking of was this: we do a feature on de Winter buildings and stress the anonymity of their architect by implication. We stress the 'Corporate Structuring: What Is It?' angle. We do a late-seventies Fritz Laing/Art School throwback, but new. I want the visuals to say 'Desire' and I want them to say 'Power' – the romance of the post-bang Career/Aesthetics interface when investment consultants have that kind of David Bowie, photochromatic-glasses, glamour. I want to make Eurobond dealers screen-dump finance projections in a way that would look good in *Designate*. The de Winter buildings are a feature of New City Youth – pan-financial, slick, colourful – a little sinister. So what's the guy like who built them? What does he wear? How's his marriage? What's his aftershave? What's his opinion on religion? Does he eat out a lot? I'm putting you on this one, Arabella, issue five, the *Designate* Finance Supplement.

Max de Winter was lying in the long grass of a small London garden when *Designate* decided to feature him. It was an evening in June, threatening thunder above the dulled roar of the traffic, and sentimentalists would have noted the brevity of the lilac that year. He watched the evening airliners glinting in the sun, their silver underbellies shining like magnesium fish drifting through tinted water. He kept falling asleep. In the middle distance, across the river from Chelsea – the conservatory of London – some youths were vandalising the peace temple. Max wrote letters to himself in his head.

'If I were to see the components of my life from without, would I envy the owner who is by titular right alone myself?'

And the tone of his questions reminded him of the ludicrous and stupid rantings to be found in the London evening papers.

'Why, oh why, oh why . . . I, for one . . . .'

He felt drowsy. 'I never share anything, and thus I never possess or colonise anything – I don't own anything. I am a vagrant, a venture vagrant. I should have got into property, not designed it. I can't stand this dot matrix of bits of a life that I wander around, unable to stand back and see the picture, or self-portrait, that their combined number – hopefully – creates.'

And then he fell asleep, vivid and various dreams stealing out of the shrubs and flowering alpines of Chelsea to torment him with their fidelity to the real-life originators of their teasing characters. He kept seeing his beautiful wife Rebecca, only as she was once, not as she was now, and then seeing the garden at New Manderley, their place in the country.

In Max de Winter's dream, lunch had raised Rebecca and him above the animals. For the first, second or last time, he was standing on the steps of St Paul's listening to the sound of a wasp trapped behind the blinds of a summer's morning. There was also a waltz-time in progress, wafting on baked breeze from the Croissant Express in Leadenhall Market. With rings on her fingers and bells on her toes the bells of St Paul's chimed out across the city whilst Max de Winter waited for his wife.

For the first, second or third Mrs de Winter. Max had only married once but been separated three times and reunited twice. Away from Rebecca his work suffered and his physical condition grew steadily worse, but married or separated they loved one another and that was the basis of the problem.

Max dreamt of the rain pouring over the fields and black leaves gusting across the stubble, a heavy scent coming off the greasy shoots and damp earth. A whisper of autumn in spring.

And then there was Rebecca, who had returned to him Persephone-like last spring and then gone away again whilst he was designing the Historic Invoices Library for the Museum of Corporate Finance. He had waited for her to come back to him again, this spring, and she hadn't, so he just kind of waited around, scratching his ear from time to time and staring moodily into shop windows in St Christopher's Place. When she was last with him she had seemed different; those loved features had changed and she was no longer the glamorous blend of despot and doll, suffragette and usherette that had confused the gossip columnists of three continents. And he, Max de Winter, the most celebrated young architect in England! Was nothing good enough?

But lying on his back in the grass, now that he could no longer feel anything, and now that he'd more or less given up being an architect, now, – now it was difficult to imagine a better evening for giving up everything, the weather being ideal.

In his dream he was standing on the Whispering Gallery of St Paul's. He looked like Leslie Howard. He was wearing a raincoat and smoking a pipe, leaning forward slightly to smile in a fatherly way at four Tommies. It was the Second World War . . .

Max was never really sure where the four Tommies had originally come from, but he was always pleased to see them. AWOL, lost, or legitimately Doing The Town, these four cheery privates would materialise in Max's mind with all the ruddy vigour and down-to-earth decency that one would expect from a quartet of the nation's finest. It was his relationship with them that was . . . odd. Rebecca used to comment on it. 'Max!' she would whisper, urgently looking into his eyes for a glimmer of recognition, 'Max! Darling! What do you see? Is it the squaddies again? Tell me – it's Rebecca darling, your wife . . . ' And then she would shake him by the wrists, several minutes generally passing until he slowly turned his head to her with curious robotic jerks to look at her in total bewilderment before coming to. As his marriage failed and his hatred of his career increased he saw more and more of these sons of Britain for whom the empire was a sunnier, more purposeful place.

When Max dreamt of St Paul's, and when he encountered the Tommies upon it or within it, he was filled with a new energy that communicated itself as a faith in something. He took on the facial expression of Leslie Howard, and his hock-spritzer-stained architect's raincoat became a goodly pristine weather-proof. His eyes twinkled with knowing patriotism as he turned against the wind to light his pipe, and England, his England, became a place totally unlike the one his conscious hours of existence were troubled by.

The first time he met the Tommies they were all Lending A Hand in the making of a short film. Max joined in. The enthusiastic young man from Cambridge who had worked for the Varsity film unit before the war was only too pleased to work with 'real chaps'.

'This is even better than Mass Observation!' he chortled, busily arranging his little crew into a prototype of the documentary goon-squads who would race round the capital on the amphetamine of pure self-importance some fifty years later. Together Max and the Tommies made a twenty-minute propaganda film. It was called 'Going Our Way?' and involved much use of the thumbs-up salute on the part of the Tommies and even more cheerful discussion on the part of Max about the notion of Commonwealth democracy that was being defended by Those Who Served. It was a very worthwhile film.

The trouble was that Max never knew what drew him into the period and company of the Tommies. Was it a longing for something to fight for and believe in? Was it simply that he needed friends and found his own age surprisingly hostile? Or was it some deep-rooted and outraged sense of patriotism that found solace only within a subconscious recreation of the Blitz Spirit? All of these options were unlikely. St Paul's, the Battle of Britain, the Tommies – all of these archaic phenomena were nothing more than the point at which the strands of Max's neurosis met. They were the point of visualisation. It could have been anything – a department store or spring on the Rive Gauche, any mental landscape that took over when anxiety reached overload. As it was it was the Tommies, and they were a decent enough bunch of blokes. Max knew he would never really go their way, but the pretence of beginning a journey with them afforded him some kind of exhausted comfort before his everyday self crawled wearily back into the jostling nervousness of reality.

When awake, Max de Winter had been feeling tired for nearly fourteen months. It was always important to him to be somewhere else, to be somewhere different from wherever he happened to be. This involved a lot of travel. He was always trying to find The Other Place, and never could. He ran out of conferences on Brushed Aluminium and Decorative Lagging at the Building Design Centre, desperate for some Cool Alley by the river or a cemetery near Leicester. He would arrive at his office in the mid-morning and bark suggestions to his incredulous staff with a crazed enthusiasm that utterly belied the fact that by lunch time he would have gone away again, his mind a stroboscopic chamber of meaningless images, each one hinged to its neighbour with the touch-welding adhesive of liquid panic that was secreted daily out of his crushed subconscious.

Even as the *Designate* profile research team were thumbing through the Royal Institute of British Architects Directory in search of a contact number for their prey, the subject of their research was stumbling around London in an ankle-length raincoat and increasingly dusty suit. Added to this organic vagrancy was a new pair of sunglasses – tortoiseshell frames and gold rims, the lenses a stagnant mill-pond green.

Back at *Designate* the interview sheet was being drawn up amidst much 'Oh yes, that would be interesting' and 'Let's save that one.'

They would ask:

'What does success mean to you?'

'Are you interested in designing for the Chicago Art Fair as rumoured in *The Urbanist*?'

'How do Rebecca and yourself relax?'

'What advice would you give to a young architect?'

But Max de Winter had just one question, and this he addressed to himself all the time:

'How do I stop being Max de Winter?'

His dreams were moulded to the venue and circumstances of the cerebral pot-holing that he was forced to call sleep, but more and more frequently, dreaming whilst awake, he reinvented himself as a traditionalist, an Englishman, and a professional – one of those whose efforts were now paying back their toil with an insight into the philosophy of the Greater Game.

But what was the Greater Game? It should not, he reasoned, be a sport played simply for the sake of winning. Only the vulgar young lions for whom success was a matter of competitive remuneration played merely to win. Max de Winter despised the new City citizens who danced upon the grave of reason in celebration of the redundancy of the Eternal Horologist who had tended to his cogs and chains with something more than the liquid grease of textbook executive management.

Even as Max sank deeper and deeper into despair he knew that it was those sycophants to fashionable business sophistry who had the ownership of tomorrow. Tomorrow most probably belonged to them by virtue of a shrewd down payment the previous fiscal.

Oh yes, they knew the ropes, they knew their way around. Buy in Hackney before it goes through the roof! Too late! Buy in Oval whilst it's still stable. Too late again! Ever thought of the Home Counties? Henley, perhaps, or the nice bit of St Albans? Anticipate the spread of the commuter belt, wait for the waistline of London to bulge out a little more in the direction of cheaper property. Wait for it, then wait for it, then – Coronary Now! Big Bang! A nation of shopkeepers and stylists. Then take advantage of the convalescence of the heart, watch it growing stronger daily in your little bit of England. Never mind the flutter, go for serious speculations, and then relax, in the Fulham Palace Road, with clever rustic cooking from somewhere your grandmother had never heard of and a bit of pompous chat about tax shelters and the market. Be smart, get with it – think of the Pecking Order and the Company Ladder.

And this was when Max de Winter saw well dressed corpses in rusting company Saabs as he sketched in obsessive Rotring on thin architectural paper the Mahlerian moods of his nightmare corporations.

In his dreams Max knew an older England. The pictures of faded postcards brought tears to his eyes as he travelled up and down in the lift in Heal's. He was permitted this eccentricity by the prerogative due to a shopper's account holder and the ownership of a gold charge card. Occasionally he would get out and buy something – a carpet perhaps, or a dinner service. These would be sent down to New Manderley on the instruction of the cheerful assistant from Highgate and then Max would haughtily return to his lift, disappearing upwards or downwards depending on which way the lift arrived. This would go on for maybe two hours.

Unshaven, his dull eyes hidden behind green glasses, Max spent his days on the move because to stop was to sleep was to dream.

St Paul's, June 1940, the azure above Wren's dome a wreath of dogfight curls. The four Tommies were always there at the start of the dream. Sometimes they were journalists dressed as Tommies and other times they were Building Fabric representatives. Max told them why they were Dying for Their Country and they were respectfully grateful for having had their fate explained to them by a gentleman.

He would point from the dome of St Paul's in the direction of Stratford-upon-Avon and then muse reverently about Shakespeare for the Tommies' general good. He told them about their history, about Raleigh and Pitt, Wellington and Robin Hood. He was really talking to them about Rebecca, only he couldn't bring himself to say her name.

In his sleep this all made perfect sense, but the glue of dreams makes flypapers of us all and in the slightest breeze we tangle. Max de Winter, a projected feature in exciting new *Designate* magazine, was knotting in the wind.

Whether Max de Winter's dreams were the result of continued

inhalation of the potent ozone of pure self-criticism was not a Problem To Be Solved noted in grey fibre-tip on the 24 June a.m. page of Arabella Cloth's Personal Organiser as she walked briskly down Oxford Street from Marble Arch en route to her working breakfast in Soho.

Arabella loved getting up and going to work. Most of all she loved ringing people up before she left her flat to tell them how busy she was. This happy generalisation, when underlined by the all-important Deadline of a working breakfast, was all that Arabella needed to put on for the day by way of accessory to her armour-like uniform of black clothing.

The morning was cool and overcast, Oxford Street not yet a cattle drive. Here and there a chemist was open, and postcard racks of happy topless girls and florid pop stars stood rakishly outside on the pavement, chained to the wall.

Arabella made a mental note to write a small item for the 'In and Out' section of *Designate* about the colonisation of West One by the working population of the outer suburbs. Oxford Street was, after all, the High Street of England, indistinguishable in its cast of shops from Norwich, say, or even Croydon. This was the worn out oesophagus of London, where massive mouthfuls of money were lubricated by the saliva of retail design in order to slip effortlessly into the stomach of business. The money was then broken down by all the little enzymes employed by business corporations to keep the process working. Shopping in Oxford Street is the only organic junk food to satisfy the massive hunger of England for a healthy diet.

This, however, was not a process that people like Arabella had to participate in. Arabella was clothed and shod on a strictly one-to-one basis.

She turned down Argyll Street, where the slower air smelt of stale fruit, and allowed herself a sideways glance into one of the smaller shops. This was research, not window shopping. Then she paused at the newspaper stand opposite Liberty's to buy *Business* and *Ceramics* and noted with pride that *Designate* had nearly sold out. She had reached that peak of achievement in magazine buying as art form and compulsory professional skill where hunting for change in her rubber purse actually cheered the news-vendor up, so elegant and articulate was it in uniting the designer of the periodical machine with its mechanic's oily rag. The news-vendor waited respectfully for the inevitable twenty-pound note with the cheerful patience of an old and trusted family servant, his print-darkened fingers flexing with an eagerness to please in the depths of his change apron. Arabella would use the useful tenner and brace of pound coins that she received back from him to pay for her breakfast (reclaimable) and a taxi back to the office.

Past poor Shelley's house in Poland Street and so into Soho, the cosmetically embalmed corpse of sleaze where builders' skips are both the cross on the door and the tombstone of those buildings condemned to make way for the import of period fittings. Soho, the graveyard of frolic. Busy ghosts flitted across the set of this depressing musical, film directors all, and longing to be the subject of their own documentaries. If Arabella's business ego were to grow any larger as the result of her working breakfast in Soho it would have to apply for planning permission.

Morning spread over London like a broken egg, and some, like Max de Winter, were drowning in the yolk. Arabella turned into Old Compton Street and bought some more magazines for the hell of it so that by the time she reached her favourite patisserie where the working breakfast was scheduled to take place the black leather strap of her black leather rucksack was biting into her white shoulder and sending shivers all the way down to her black heart.

Max de Winter was colouring in the Arts page of his morning paper. He too was on his way to work, but there was little point in it. His studio was based on the edge of the City, the semimirrored glazing of its windows hanging like plastic raindrops in the fringe of London Wall. Max de Winter will never design another building. He can no longer see the structures in his mind or visualise their components. He can no longer envisage the frame, the omniplatz, the lift shafts, the cooling ducts, the mezzanine cloakroom or the subterranean squash court. He used to be able to visit these places in his mind, transcribing his patrols onto drawing paper. Now he can't. He can no longer see anything, or look forward to anything. His imagination puts all energy into his dreams.

There is one early-morning dream which he sees in the mirror of his office washroom. In it the brief midwinter twilight hangs low over Bankside and nobody will ever tell a joke again. The Battle of Britain is over, and the Tommies are all dead. They never lived to hear about George Baselitz, the Café Pelican, or the Pet Shop Boys. Times have changed, and there are different needs. Max dreamt that after the death of the Tommies another battle began, The Battle of London, and this was the one in which Max de Winter attacked the Capital. As yet there was merely an abrogation of the uneasy peace treaty that existed between Max and the City, and the air around Carter Lane was heavy with cordite, the stench of guns that had merely cleared their throats in polite anticipation of a war.

Arabella, unaware of these hostilities, ordered hot chocolate and counted her magazines. This passed the time until Paul Vince, the Press Officer to Max de Winter Associates, arrived with a slightly chiselled look in his eyes to explain to Arabella that Max de Winter would not be available for interview in *Designate*.

'Of course de Winter Associates is swiftly becoming one of the leading corporate business building practices in the UK,' he whispered, 'and of course Max himself has become one of the leading lights of the architectural scene and something of a celebrity . . . ' A shower of brochures and press releases were offered to the professionally disappointed but personally relieved Arabella.

'All his main buildings are described in these – D'Arblays Trust, Pacman Software, the Self & Assurance . . . Ah, here's one you might find interesting for your magazine, Max de Winter's unique design for the Church of God the Truth in Tower Hill. Oddball sect but a brilliant use of slate.'

Arabella looked carefully at the brochures, inwardly calculating how long she ought to look at each one in order to give the impression that she was reading the complex columns of building data as opposed to simply looking at the dramatic pictures.

'But we are very keen to talk to Max,' she said. 'I was rather hoping we could set up a meeting.'

Paul Vince tensed.

'He's extremely busy right now; the Historic Invoices Library is really taking up time and of course it's July soon . . .'

'July?'

'The Urban Ergonomics conference in Sâo Paulo. Max will be speaking, of course, unless the Paris Community Housing seminar is set back yet again – you know how it is.'

'We'd only want him for an afternoon – for lunch?'

'I'm sorry. Max did ask me to tell you that he will be most happy to give you access to drawings, architectural models, etcetera, but an interview – so sorry.'

Somewhere in the back of her mind Arabella could see greedy black vultures circling over the dying body of her first *Designate* profile feature. She began to worry.

'Could we talk to Rebecca? Is she still in Cork Street?'

'She was the last time we heard. They're separated, you know.'

'Again?' squeaked Arabella.

Paul looked at the table cloth and nodded sadly.

'Is that why Max won't be interviewed – depression?'

'I'd leave the dirt to the dailies,' said Paul. 'And now I must dash. It's the same again at Channel 8 in twenty minutes and I can't spend too long on each refusal. Nice to have met you, anyway.' And then he was gone.

Arabella wondered whether it was worth pretending to resign in order to prove her commitment in the wake of her failure. She decided it wasn't, but felt almost interested in Max de Winter.

The Friday when Arabella had her working breakfast with Paul Vince was the tense last act of an anxious week for Max de Winter. As he waited for Vince to report back to him he stood with his face pressed against the window of his office and thought about the garden at New Manderley. At New Manderley, in the evening, you could hear the peacocks scream and watch the somnambulistic progress of a pollen-gorged bee as it hovered round a flower. In the twilight you could sometimes see a peacock perching high on the ancient wall that surrounded the garden, its black eyes fixed on the reddening sky.

All of Max de Winter's buildings in London, the five that crowned his success, seemed to be forming a circle around him in the hope of discovering a truth. They were like inquisitive journalists, and there was shoving at the back. Max de Winter did not want anyone to know his name. He didn't want to leave anything behind him after he'd gone. It was as simple as that.

Paul Vince was soon back in the office, and Max turned slowly to look at him.

'Well?'

'I don't think they're going to follow up,' said Paul. 'They're looking for stylists, figureheads of the New London. The usual lifestyle design commentary thing.'

'I see,' said Max, playing with the tungsten stapler, 'they want to know whether I'm excited or busy, and then take a photograph of me in a room with a charcoal carpet.'

'That kind of thing,' agreed Vince.

'Well, my head will never be on their pike, never, ever.'

Paul Vince sat down and opened his mouth, a little speech preparing itself in his mind.

Max continued, 'Why do people make chairs out of old motorbikes?' he asked, interview style.

'Image profile?' suggested Paul, brightly.

'No I don't think so,' murmured Max.

A dark-grey moment wandered slowly across the room like a well bred secretary looking for a biro.

'Are there any imminent commissions?' asked Max. 'Or bad debts, or lawsuits, or press conferences?'

'You're all clear,' replied Paul. 'The Invoice Library is in fact ahead of schedule except for the Swedes and their energy-saving ionisers that are causing the boys in Finishing a bit of a headache, but other than that' (he checked his notes) . . . 'It's seminar time, Paris, Sâo Paulo, and Herr Greutchen faxed in a positive structuring leaflet from Düsseldorf – he wants you to talk about the omniplatz at Pacman Software.'

Max groaned. 'Why?'

Paul checked his notes again. 'It's . . . radical.'

'It's horrible,' said Max. 'Four thousand square feet of compressed rubber holding down a triple layer of service ducts. If a pipe bursts the thing'll go off like a bomb.' He was quiet for a moment. 'Imagine . . . '

Paul looked back at his notes. 'Our client response questionnaire found that 78 per cent of the Pacman workforce found the building a major contribution to de-stress. The 28 per cent of those who are also at management or executive level reported that absenteeism due to boredom-spiral has dropped significantly.' He paused. 'But they don't like the colour.'

'It's white,' said Max.

Paul checked his notes again. 'Surgical, hostile . . . effeminate, cold, hot, boring, alien, too bright, pretentious . . . unprofessional . . . '

'And Spain,' said Max, 'Is so cheap once you've got there.'

Paul blinked and looked at the laces of his shoes. He put the Pacman file down very carefully and then drew a deep breath. 'Max,' he announced, 'I've known you for a long time now and I think I can say that in those four months I've never seen you as in need of a long holiday as you are now.'

'Thank you, Paul. Go away.'

Paul stood up, pretending to want to argue. It was Friday, the day of the long lunches, so he left the room anyway.

And then Max was alone.

As Max de Winter left the office by a side exit, a rhomboid of yellow sunlight fell sharply across his back and followed him down the metal staircase. Max knew he would never return to the office, so he left the side door open.

The dusk of his Badoit and Babycham days had surely come. He had only to count the thousand silver milk churns in which he was storing for some inexplicable purpose the gallons of tears and spilt milk that he had accumulated during his career and his marriage.

Pacman Software, D'Arblay's, Self & Assurance, The Historic Invoices Library of the Museum of Corporate Finance, and the Church of the God of Truth, Tower Hill. Those were his five greatest buildings, and they were all in the City of London. Those were the things that he loved and must kill.

Walking up Fish Street in the sun, he could see the scarlet wigwam water tank that stood high on the roof of his Self & Assurance building. It was maybe two streets away. He made his way down a dark alley and came out into a dazzling white piazza. There was nobody around and the breeze brought the sound of a distant rustling, the litter of a thousand sandwich lunches, the thought of all those paper bags. Max stood in front of the twenty storeys of blue glass that were the Self & Assurance London headquarters.

'Movement 5', a work in steel salvaged from the debris of the building that used to occupy the piazza, stood forlornly on a little concrete plinth to Max's right. It cast a jagged shadow in the murk of which a lolly stick could be seen.

Max ran his finger sadly across the brass plate that was fastened to the wall of Self & Assurance in a little mock-classical alcove. 'Max de Winter Associates 1986' it read.

Rubbing the 6 thoughtfully, Max formed some words in his head. The plan he decided upon can be articulated as follows:

'As the architect of this building and its four brothers in the neighbourhood I reclaim the right to destroy my own work. I do not suppose this right exists but I reclaim it nonetheless. I hereby exchange the theodolite for dynamite and the slide rule for a bomb. I will take out all five of the buildings that I have designed. There will be nothing left. These buildings were my signature, my name on the horizon, and I shall cross them out. I want to know that no one knows my name. Maybe no one does. Rebecca does – in the sunny corridors of her complex – but she always was an obsessive note taker. However, I want nothing but rubble, no sense, no meaning, and no name.'

As he left the Self & Assurance piazza he remembered his very first commission. Not so much a house as a hacienda, in Margate. It had paid for the wheels on his E-Type, that hacienda in Margate. He would commit no acts of terrorism in Margate.

'He's called Max de Winter,' said Arabella with growing impatience as she hurried along to Malcolm Houston's office with little time to waste on the slow-witted Gemma Danvers who trotted along beside her, pearls bouncing about the lace collar of her blouse, 'and he won't give us an interview. Malcolm will be furious.' Gemma agreed that he probably would be.

But Malcolm was strangely calm as Arabella sat in one of his low office chairs with her face a mask of total commitment and mature responsibility.

'Call up Rupert Goodwyn for the photographs,' said Malcolm. 'He's very exciting. And then have a meeting with Betty about the fashion coverage and blend the two. I know that Betty's a collection behind for the Finance Supplement and the buildings and the clothes will look very good together. Forget the interview. He's probably really boring and, anyway, who's going to know him? Just put backdrops in – 'Buildings: de Winter Associates', like they were an accessory. And use some catchy words – 'SkyHigh', 'Dare!', 'Money Walks', that kind of thing. And hey – don't worry'.

So Arabella – a ready-bottled cocktail of emotions and shaken, if not stirred, by her meeting – walked slowly back to her office and marvelled at the capriciousness of creative management whose ways are sometimes strange but generally for the best.

Max de Winter looked at his reflection in the windows of a passing taxi on the Strand and thought he could see the slightly widening eyes of a diver whose pool had just transformed into a parquet of tessellating television screens. Trafalgar Square was baking, and London drowsed heat-stupid through the silent overture to Max de Winter's funniest lines in that brief comedy, his life.

Two: Her New CD

Gemma Danvers emerged from a precocious Chelsea childhood spent in a Sydney Street cottage surrounded by expensive cornflower-blue bric-à-brac to learn the necessity of involvement. Not being of a philanthropic inclination, she avoided the organising of charity balls in favour of becoming a creative consultant to the media set. Her greatest work of art was her diary, which bulged with useful telephone numbers, the correct arrangement of which could see her through one hectic day to the next, and so on, until one day she would either get married, become her own boss, or die.

The result of all this involvement was difficult to quantify. Gemma was not like Arabella for she possessed neither the clever ear-rings made of coat hangers nor the dynamo of a careerist hysteria to make Malcolm Houston take her seriously. What she did have, other than her job on *Designate*, was a mantelpiece obscured by invitations and a greater degree of self-confidence than many people of her age, which was nineteen. It was a combination of her age, self-confidence, and fluency in business-speak as a second language that attracted Paul Vince, the fast-lane publicity person of Max de Winter Associates.

Once Gemma had jilted the muscle-bound synthesist of a well-known and generally disliked pop group, who had been paying her some attention for the previous three months, she and Paul commenced to eat their way across London. There were few weekends between May and October when the sedimentary hours of daylight were not washing the bonnet of Paul's BMW as it drifted between Maida Vale and Chelsea to pick up Gemma and nose back into twinkling Knightsbridge for a few hours serious eating.

The weekday routine was slightly different, weekdays being work-based and week evenings being the nutritious dessert to the main course of nine-to-six involvement.

It was by way of a social dessert that Paul and Gemma came to be at the eagerly anticipated private view of Dane Aston's New Works in Bronze at Rebecca de Winter Fine Art Ltd in Cork Street.

By six thirty that evening the three spacious galleries were temporary workbench, weapon and tomb to nearly three hundred of the People Who Thought They Counted and about one hundred and fifty of their 'friends'. Here and there amongst the crowd some spaces were found to exhibit the spindly and esoteric New Works in Bronze that were the excuse for all the fuss. The bronzes themselves brought mixed comment – when they provoked any – and this uncertainty of opinion was due to some doubt over the generosity of their Meaning. The debt to Caro was generally considered immense.

Rebecca de Winter herself was thought to be fetching in

watered silk, but having disturbed the rhythm of her Boston Fibre Diet with several glasses of Spanish champagne and two tranquillisers she looked on moodily as the bombastic and overdressed Aston became more and more noisily grateful for the nasal whoops of insincere congratulation that were being showered upon him by London's cognoscenti.

Around the slightly bow legs of *Autonomon 3* (1985) a small cluster of elderly painters were shouting tactless comments about both the artist and his work before turning round as one to beam roguishly into the white flare of a society reporter's camera flash.

Discovering that the white sauce in his vol-au-vent contained anchovies, the publicly vegetarian critic from *Art Digest* wedged its offensive remains between the narrow angles of what he later described as one of Aston's delicately shifting planes. Having wiped some crumbs out of his beard he wondered whether it was boredom or wine that was making his eyes water as he listened to an enthusiastic young sculptor explain to him how long he had been looking at lines and what excitement they caused him.

Angus Fythe-Brown (Grindlay's – Old Bond Street; Aquarelles and XIXth Century Fine Drawings) retired injured after being elbowed into the lethal corner of *Piece 5* (1986) by the wildly gesticulating Berta Hilsop, a Dutch buyer of little self-control who was engaged in a tearful and sisterly reconciliation with Andrea Hodgson of Sotheby's after nearly five months' unpleasantness over Paul Whitely's photolithographs.

The girl with the crudités cried quietly to herself in a corner subsequent to a suggestion put forward to her by the only person in the room who could claim to having known Cocteau.

Rebecca felt as though she were drowning. Her head ached and her arms were puckered with nervous shivering. She smiled weakly at Dane and then went into her office.

Just as she was groping for the door handle she overheard the triumphant roars of merriment coming from Paul Vince as he explained with the use of *Twin Locking Piece 2* (1985) that the enormous bronze hemispheres that were the hallmark of Aston's later work in fact displaced their centre of gravity to within a centimetre of collapse.

'Bloody thing can hardly stand up!' he crowed, the wine inspiring him to a devil-may-care irreverence for his surroundings.

As Rebecca looked anxiously at the trembling structure of several thousand pounds worth of unsold art – that least stable of commodities – she happened to catch Gemma's eye, and Gemma, not being a girl to miss a professional opportunity, immediately snatched at the chance of a chat.

'I hear you've left your husband again,' boomed the jovial Gemma with a tactlessness that echoed all the way to the Royal Academy.

'I hardly think that's any of your business,' replied Rebecca, dipping the barbs of her words into the liquid poison of pure politeness – a technique entirely wasted on the cast-iron sensibilities of the self-assured Chelsea-bred Gemma Danvers.

'Well, he won't let *Designate* interview him, which you can imagine is perfectly bloody ghastly for poor old Arabella who got landed with the feature. Seems rather odd to me – rude not to, I'd have thought, but the editor's more or less lost interest now anyway. Is he still designing those weird buildings? My sister's boyfriend used to arbitrate in one of them or something and he's a real laugh. I'm completely useless with anything to do with money. Where did you get your shoes? I've been looking for some like that for ages.'

'You must excuse me,' said Rebecca, 'I'm very busy this evening.'

'Is it drugs?' queried Gemma as the office door closed. 'I mean, one hears so much about drugs these days, and . . . '

Rebecca retired into her office, and Gemma giggled as Paul bit her neck. Together they descended the steps of Rebecca de Winter Fine Art and stumbled off down Cork Street, returning art to its customary place between Lifestyle and Contacts on the priority scale of their professional requirements.

Closing the door on the clamour in the gallery, Rebecca lay down on the floor of her office, a worn-out mermaid beached on watered silk. She picked up the telephone and dialled New Manderley, gently massaging the back of her neck with her free hand as she listened to the ringing tone. There was no reply.

Maybe it was too early, or maybe Max was still in London. There had been a rumour that he was about to design a night club and Rebecca recalled the three notices that were hanging above premises in New Burlington Street. One sign said (in gold): 'The Al Hambara Club'. Beneath that sign a further notice said: 'The Most Exclusive Wining and Dining Nightspot in London' and beneath that a smaller, slightly shabby sign said: 'Lease For Sale'. It would be like Max for him to be prowling around the dark and dusty innards of a closed-down nightspot working out how to rebuild it. But Max would never design another building. She felt sure of it. And what was a 'nightspot' anyway? It sounded like an ugly blemish that appears on the face of a city that lives unhealthily after dark.

Rebecca hung up and poured herself some sour coffee from the percolator in her secretary's office. Then she got her cigarettes out of her desk drawer and lay down on the floor again. Outside she could hear the private-view guests saying things they didn't mean, like 'See you later on!' and 'Hope you can make it!'

She stared at the telephone, the room cool and dark around her. She had locked the door.

Her office felt like a sepulchre made out of tungsten, and she wanted only for a griffin, or a journalist, to curl up with a Bible at her feet to enable her to do an imitation of a lady by her knight in a tomb.

The side chapel of the Collegiate Church of St Jude in the village of Ashby-cum-Manderley contained such a pair of eternally resting aristocrats. Sixteenth-century. Max adored that church. In a niche in the adjacent wall of the chapel, hollowed out of the kindly sandstone, there was another smaller tomb underlined with memorial verse where was laid the departed earl's noble impe. Apparently impes were lucky in the sixteenth century, an ancient precursor of having a hairdresser you can trust.

Max and Rebecca de Winter had never been very good at the Country Life, despite Max's increasing obsession with the Glorious Heritage of England. Watching his interrogation of English History was like watching someone trying to cook on ice. The greater the fire of his passion for the subject, the more the subject itself dissolved, and his meditations by hedgerows and riverbanks seemed to bring nothing but frustration and sadness.

Soon after they were married Max and Rebecca de Winter had decided to have an 'At Home'. On the appointed day the rain poured down across the garden, and through the open windows you could hear the cedar drip. The sun came out. It started raining again. The guests were amused to see the perfect couple so unprepared for the reality of their quaint idea.

In the evening, after the guests had gone, Max and Rebecca left the house to let some air blow the perfume and cigar smoke away and went for a walk along the cliff tops. Max was in thoughtful mood, calculating the height of a ceiling or the depth of a lift shaft. Leaving him to his own thoughts, Rebecca had wandered off on her own down the cliff path that led to a little cove.

Max was inexplicably angry with her for doing this.

'I told you not to go down there,' he snapped. 'It's just a stretch of sand – an old boat house. There's nothing to see.'

Rebecca tensed at his outburst, slipping her fingers through the collar of their labrador. 'I'm sorry darling,' she replied, her eyes bright with tears. 'I was looking for a rope for Jasper. I didn't mean to annoy you.'

Max de Winter was a difficult man.

A crimson sunset fell across the wet lawn, drawing long black shadows from the house and the trees. The garden walk dripped and the apple blossom hung low under its heavy cargo of rainwater. Down on the beach wet shells lay warming in the last of the sun, their tiny serrated edges tracing delicate patterns in the surf-hammered sand. Max de Winter was wondering just how many wrong trees there were for a dog to bark itself hoarse beside, and saw in this canine error a ventriloquism of his own situation. Confused architect put on trial by the purpose of his profession. Architect unsettled by love, buildings, London and his times. Architect takes horrible revenge by quitting – wife and colleagues upset and confused. A salt breeze flicked at his hair; he took off his jacket and rolled up his sleeves before turning to smile at Rebecca, and ask her forgiveness for his temper. But Rebecca had gone, walking along quickly ahead of him to go and sit by herself somewhere and consider what kind of a life she was living.

Max de Winter's fame after the success of his Pacman Software building had been considerable. The nylon touch of cruel irony was on the fact that it was to be his penultimate building.

The following morning, on the tube to his office so far away from the seabord garden of the previous evening, Max considered the stickiness of his fame. Silent fame for a silent profession. Nobody ever heard architects speak. Not really. 'Max de Winter,' he said to himself. 'Spray it on dry hair and the style will stay there; spray it on wet hair . . . and one supposes that nothing much will happen.' He repeated these absurdities to himself, litany-like, all the way to Mansion House station.

Rebecca realised that she was still staring at the telephone and dialled New Manderley again, lighting a cigarette and balancing her shallow white coffee cup from the Contemporary Crafts Gallery on the bevelled edge of her compressed-rubber studio table.

At the other end of the call, at New Manderley, Max was writing a list. It read:

D'Arblays Trust
Self & Assurance
Pacman Software plc
The Museum of Corporate Finance
The Church of God the Truth (Tower Hill)
Margate (?)

He was sitting at a little table in the billiard room of New Manderley. The furniture was covered in dust sheets. Outside it was threatening thunder again.

Max stared at the list and numbered his buildings from one to five. He felt sentimental about the hacienda in Margate. A door slammed upstairs, caught in the draught from an open window. Rain began to thud against the windows. Max realised that if he took off his dark glasses he would be able to see better. He left them on.

A dream lay waiting in the out-tray of his mind. He pictured Rebecca, his pretty young wife, running her fingers through her hair. She is sitting on the ancestral hearth, there at New

Manderley, and she is wearing a ball gown. She rubs the front of her legs, staring into the fire that is heating her taffeta.

'I'm so confused,' she says, her chin trembling slightly but her soft voice bravely even.

Max feels a hot sensation in his stomach. He lights a pipe, pressing the hot tobacco down with his thumb. He exhales some smoke, looks at the ceiling, and coughs. The newspaper slips off his knees and he goes over to turn the wireless down. Rebecca is crying softly by the fire. Sobbing. Her tears are dissolving her eyeliner.

Max says, 'I can't bear to see you crying on the hearth again.' Rebecca desperately wants to run into his arms. Somehow she can't. She wants Max to comfort her, but he looks so far away, he looks like a stranger! He wants to do something helpful. If he comes any closer to her she'll scream.

'L'Amour Fou,' Rebecca whispers, despite herself, 'Lee Miller . . .'

'Darling, don't cry. Please don't . . . '

Rebecca buries her face in her hands. The firelight glows in her hair. She is so terribly alone. So terribly misunderstood. She is the victim of so many cruel sensations that obscure the way between happiness and herself. Max panics, uncertain of how to calm her. He tries changing the subject.

'I've decided to blow up my complete works, darling,' he says in the same tone of voice one would use to say 'We're going to move to Tuscany.'

Anticipating incomprehension, the dream flicks a succession of images through Max's mind: Lincoln's Inn Fields, chocolate croissants, a jar of moisturiser, a painting by Steven Campbell. Then the dream refocused, disaster threatening.

'Oh Max!' Rebecca wails, twisting the hot hem of her dress. Her voice is husky and confused. Max can feel his heart knotting with grief and self-loathing. A nervous nausea creeps through his system like a mini cab lost in south London. He wants to love her so much, to take her tiredness home, kinder than God . . . He whistles noiselessly.

'My Bonny lies over the sea . . . '

There is thunder directly overhead.

And then everything happens at double speed. There is a

sudden crack and the high-pitched war cry of a low-flying cinder as it hurls itself into the folds of Rebecca's ball-gown. The dress catches fire.

Max leaps up in his dream and throws his pipe into a far corner of the hall, cursing Jasper for going off obediently to retrieve it.

He drags Rebecca from the blazing wreckage of her dress, beating off quadrants of smoking taffeta before the flames can reach her lingerie.

As he carries her up the moonlit staircase to her room he despises himself for announcing his vandalistic intentions towards his buildings. Why can't he control himself? That this should happen! It must be a sign, the gods drumming their fingers on the conference table by way of an omen of imminent tragedy.

The dream slinks darkly off, throwing a spiteful glance over its shoulder to the waking Max. The telephone was ringing in the next room.

Answering it, Max nearly wept to hear Rebecca's tired voice.

'I was having such a strange dream,' he said, 'and I must tell you about it. Please – will you come down?' There was a pause.

'I'm rather busy,' replied Rebecca. 'It's the opening of Dane's show and I ought to be here.'

'I'm not going back to the office, Rebecca. I'm giving up . . . architecture.' There was another pause.

'Why?'

'I'm simply finished. With it. Someone wanted to interview me. It broke something. I don't want to be here any more. I don't want to leave my buildings behind either.'

'What do you mean?'

'Please come back, Rebecca. If only for a day. I don't want you to hate me any more.'

'I don't hate you.'

'I don't want you to be indifferent to me. I want you to be happy. I know I can't make you happy but I wish we could understand one another again. Just once. We once said we loved one another more than we loved life itself . . .'

' . . . and now we're going to die anyway,' finished Rebecca.

The rain was hammering on the windows as Max de Winter

sat hunched over the phone. In the garden the magnolia was luminous against the night.

'Will you come down?' asked Max.

'Not now,' said Rebecca, 'but I still love you . . . in some ways. Maybe when things are a bit quieter here in a month or two. I'd better go. Are you all right?'

'No,' replied Max.

And they hung up, their conversation terminated by the planned obsolescence clause that was written into their marriage contract. This was the clause of poetry, and poetry is the soul's dartboard, the place where the feelings stick in. Never theirs the door jamb to varnish or the bird-table to mend.

Estrangement, anxiety and terrorism crept silently into the service of Max and Rebecca de Winter's ambitions for a happy marriage.

Rebecca sighed and wondered whether she should, after all, go down and see Max. She decided against it. She looked in her bag for a lighter and a receipt fluttered out on to the floor. She remembered that she had bought a compact disc player at lunch time.

2
Psychowhizziology

One: Party Games from New Manderley

The cement dust and petrol fumes of an August afternoon in Charlotte Street mingled with the scent of Arabella Cloth's Rhubarb and Jojoba Midday Tone-Up Lotion as the *Designate* profile team grouped earnestly round the conference table to discuss their feature on Max de Winter.

Malcolm Houston was in a particularly creative mood, having just lunched around the corner with an exciting and new ceramicist from the RCA. Although largely monosyllabic in her conversation Debbi Tring could do radical things with glaze, and her latest 'holocaust' breakfast china was causing quite a stir in artistic and commercial circles alike. Picking moodily at her devilled mushroom mousse, Debbi had given Malcolm all that he needed for an enthusiastic paragraph in the *Designate* 'Next Up' pages.

On the subject of de Winter he addressed the meeting as follows: 'You people – ah – have maybe been aware that we've not had much – that is not 100 per cent co-operation from de Winter Associates – on this – ah – one, and I – ah – must admit that my gut hunch was to ah – drop it.'

As one the *Designate* team looked concerned about the hunch but simultaneously optimistic about the replacement suggestion that their editor's raised eyebrows were forcing them to anticipate.

'It would seem,' he continued, 'that we alone are left to tell the tale, but I'll ask Arabella to fill you in on the background.' There was a low fizz like pressurised bilge-water being squirted out of the side of a ship as Gemma opened a bottle of Perrier.

'Thanks, Malcolm,' whispered Arabella, in a committed kind of way. 'As you have probably heard, Max de Winter is not available for an interview so we're going to be relying on the visuals as both a comment on Max the man and as a backdrop for the fashion that Betty's putting together. As regards the shoot, we're going to begin at D'Arblays Trust in Moorgate. The main arbitration floor and home accounts offices. I have some pictures here of the interiors and as you can see they're really very new and exciting.' Some glossy prints of what looked like the back of a clock and some carpet squares were circulated to the meeting. Murmurs of interest, enthusiasm, commitment, optimism, and excitement were duly forthcoming.

'We're using the same model agency that we had for the Soho Facelift feature, and Betty has got winter collections from MythMyth, Henry Kong and Margot Jones. The shoot is next Tuesday' (a noise like a house falling down accompanied the opening of thirteen diaries), 'and it's at nine in the evening. From D'Arblays we're doing Self & Assurance on Thursday night; the Church of God the Truth – that'll be a sportswear spread – in Tower Hill on Friday after evening purification; Pacman Software plc over the weekend; and the Historic Invoices Library the following Monday – that's almost in the Docklands so Gemma's checking we're not double-booked with anyone else.' She paused, sucking the end of her mapping pen thoughtfully. 'Malcolm?'

'Thanks, Arabella. Now, cover stars. We've finally got hold of one old picture of Max de Winter that we think is really good. It's old but it looks – archaic. He held up a black-and-white photograph of Max taken some years before. He is standing on the steps of an office block wearing a long gaberdine trench coat. His face is smiling and his hair is short and neat for the mid-seventies. He is wearing a pair of dark glasses.

The meeting dispersed.

The following evening Max de Winter was sitting on the steps of the Royal Exchange. His hair was uncombed, greased back behind his ears, and his face was drawn and tired. Lukewarm drizzle gusted across the street and his raincoat was flecked with little black spots. One of his shoes was unlaced. Hovering overhead, the sun was too red, and as a car sped by, its wheels hissing on the wet road, Max looked at the City as one would study a putrefying piece of fruit. It was eight forty-five.

He grimaced, and then got up carefully. His chest was aching even more than usual and as usual he ascribed the pain to nerves.

His car, an old Ford Granada bought for cash that afternoon, was parked down a side street. Inside it was a large quantity of high explosive.

Very gently he got into the car and turned on the ignition, waiting for a moment before driving off slowly into the gathering darkness wherein the Self & Assurance London headquarters was towering.

The windscreen wipers pulled across the windscreen making a horrible rubbing noise. Max felt lonely. He thought of the crowds that happily filled these streets during the day, and of how he had never been of their number, not even when he used to meet Rebecca for lunch at St Paul's.

Soon he was opposite the building that had won him a medal from his colleagues. He was just twenty-six when some Captain of Industry snipped the ribbon, and he still hated him for it.

'Welcome to the Labelling Conference,' whispered Max to the night as he got out of the car and tiptoed over to the darkened doorway of a newsagents from where there was a good view of the edifice of white metal and granite that was to be his first victim.

Leaning against the shop door, Max remembered with a lump in his throat how Rebecca and he had co-designed the tiles for the men's room of the banking section. Fishbones and Mexican eyes, quaint hieroglyphs that meant nothing at all to the staff who used the facilities they decorated. Why, Max and Rebecca had even supervised the grouting. It had been a labour of love. And then there were the directors' rooms on the twelfth floor, the brickwork faced with specially corroded metal sheets and rusted bolts salvaged from old ships cleverly adapted as light fittings. 'Ruins in Action', the *Urbanist* critique had stated. 'The

Triumph of Trashing', roared an American commentary.

Then darker thoughts came into Max's mind, and it was hard to know in the fading twilight whether the walls of the Self & Assurance were exhaust-stained or in shadow. Once they had been white, tinted anniversary silver that time mellowed into a slightly sluttish daughter of pearl. But now these white walls were definitely brown, turning to a teak of mediocrity that recalled the tragic bridal suite where Rebecca and he had attempted a second honeymoon. On the second night Max had smashed an aftershave bottle against the flock on the wall and then sunk slowly to the foot of the enormous bed on which Rebecca lay with her tear-brimming eyes wide open. They had drowned on land at that coastal resort because of architecture and neurosis and some insidious bad magic that always put them out of one another's reach, incapable of giving happi-nenss, or strength, or confidence, or support.

A cold breeze whipped around the corner of Self & Assurance and dark clouds billowed into the summer sky. The moon was new and exciting, a brilliant star twinkling to one side of it.

Lighting a cigarette, Max dreamt for a moment of how the eyes and head and heart could roam these streets with nothing but vandalism in mind. Let his terrorism, he thought, though empty of compassion, not be devoid of meaning. After the scarlet of evening had turned into the purple prose of night and all around was sleep or sleeplessness, Max wanted the Self & Assurance building to become some kind of ship of the line, pitched between the horns of a dilemma by force. And in an upstairs room somewhere, by candlelight, under beams or rafters, tarred or scented, Max knew that the unbelievably ghostly She would be sleeping on the hearth rug again. It was during these short aromatic nights that Max might very well die, and seeing how he had lost his way and his wife, separated from silk by suit, he hoped she would quickly forget him. And with that thought he quickly walked back over to the car, turned on the ignition and wedged the accelerator down. Then he ran for cover.

Ten seconds later a sheet of flame spat former building through the roar of a massive explosion. Windows blew out in all directions and the shattered ergonomic fixtures of a major financial institution arched fitfully into the street. The first three floors were gutted and, as the main frame of the building weakened, whole panels of plaster, steel, brick and rubber plant came tumbling down into the charred remains of the foyer.

Feeling in his raincoat pocket, Max took out two grenades and hurled them into the rubble. One blew the mailing room apart and the second transformed a vending machine into so much powdered plastic. Shards of open plan screening came fluttering down from a great height, some still trailing memos or holiday postcards. The lift shafts were ablaze and scarlet flames licked lasciviously out of many of the windows. On the roof the wigwam water tank was steaming.

As sirens and bells began to fill the air Max climbed neatly over a wall down the street and dropped into the car park of a neighbouring office.

Getting into his E-Type, his mind was full of nothing. He felt bored, or numb, or nothing at all. He drove west towards the Strand, then parked in Covent Garden to try and find somewhere to have a cup of coffee amongst the purgatorial Piazza hell-hole cafés and wine bars. Above the merry lights of Covent Garden hung the life of indecision like broken veins, and the bloodshot crescent of the moon, staring moodily into the middle distance, was brooding on red.

The emergency services were still finding pulped box files and buckled work stations amongst the smoking ruins of the Self & Assurance London headquarters as Arabella Cloth, forced into a peculiar mood by the speed with which a magazine feature could be transformed into an omelette of broken masonry, locked herself into her office to have a lonely and unprofessional little cry.

She wasn't sure what had prompted her tears or why they should fall in such profusion. She changed her multi-vitamin course and finally stopped drinking coffee. She looked with a kinder eye upon the socially dyslexic Gemma. She softened.

'I think maybe I'm not getting enough zinc,' she said in a broken voice to her gay flatmate, Jim.

'I thought that it was iron that made people moody,' he answered, brewing her a beaker of parsnip and privet tea, the paper label on the bag of which contained a thousand-word history of herbal nerve tonics, beginning with Saxon root infusions and then passing glibly over Victorian patent medicine, acknowledging the discovery of hysteria with a respectful nod before admitting with shy pride that the tea about to be drunk had been blended with the massed herb research of the last eight hundred years. Arabella would have to, surely, benefit.

Arabella swallowed a mouthful of the orange boiling liquid and her lips puckered, her cheeks sucked in and her throat fizzed viciously, the delicate flooring of her stomach buckling in panic by way of warning to the bowel.

'Oh God, that's good!' she croaked, and lit a cigarette.

Arabella had stopped by the cordoned-off bomb site earlier that afternoon. It was raining. In the shallow crater a few policemen in high-visibility vests had been picking their way through the bureaucratic entrails that the explosion had thrown up.

She asked if she could take some pictures and this had been refused. Not having the strength to argue, she had thanked them anyway in very slow English and pretended to be a tourist. From the papers and the television it was clear that nobody had accepted responsibility for the 'outrage'.

They rescheduled the fashion shoot. They would delay publication of the de Winter feature. They would try to interview some terrorists and maybe run their findings across the camouflage textiles and swimwear photographs that they had been trying to place.

Nobody could get through to de Winter Associates. A secretary – or it could have been an ansafone – patiently explained to callers in a soft American accent that there was nobody there right now but, hey, thanks for calling anyway. There was no tone, and no invitation to leave a message. The spectral secretary just kept on showing you the door with a smile.

Gemma had not heard from Paul Vince either. She didn't really mind that much because she had recently decided that she didn't really like him anyway and furthermore she had met Rupert D'Oyle ffookes, currently in his second term at Sandhurst and a real laugh in the chukka. Through the oily Rupert Gemma had learned her new expression, 'Bloody funny', followed by an appreciative widening of the facial muscles, and it was this habit that caused Malcolm Houston to pause in the middle of picking fluff out of the turn-ups of his Japanese trousers and consider giving Gemma the boot. He decided against it.

It was about a week later, when Malcolm and Arabella were sifting through the hundreds of CVs that *Designate* received every week from hopeful contributors, that a newsflash on Malcolm's Watchman alerted them to a new tragedy in the City of London.

'. . . and read Combined Media and Communication Studies at Grimsby Polytechnic from 1985 to . . .' Malcolm read in a weary voice like one condemned to memorise the Yellow Pages. His reading was interrupted by the urgent voice of the newsflash.

'Reports are coming in of a further attack on one of the City's leading investment agencies. D'Arblay's Trust, a brokerage house on London Wall, was severely damaged earlier this evening by what the police are calling a copy-cat attack of the crude car bomb that destroyed the Self & Assurance headquarters in the City earlier this week. There have only been a few minor injuries and this the police are describing as "miraculous".'

Malcolm looked at Arabella, the carefully typed CV hanging limply in his hand. 'Another of de Winter's,' he said slowly, and then Arabella burst into tears again.

Whilst Arabella wrung a boutique tissue between her fingers and Malcolm Houston rang some friends in the City, Max de Winter sat quietly on the river wall by Traitor's Gate and felt no remorse at all about his latest attack on his career. He had no doubts at all about the bastard yuppies whom he had just made homeless; they were stinking vagrant zombies for whom he felt neither sympathy nor compassion. They just got in the way, but would survive, regardless of the ferocity of the de Winter campaign of violence.

'I should leave London for good,' thought Max, 'leave for some provincial town this autumn, some place of historic interest and natural beauty that is the loose change rattling about in history's charity box. To Manderley perhaps, and the Collegiate Church of St Jude, by way of 'B' roads and dual carriageways under white expressionless skies, fringed with August bracken.

'Here lies Max de Winter
Architect, Husband and Terrorist.
We by example are warned and mourn
His Going on Ahead to a Higher Choir.'

A twenty-one gun tone from a battery of desk-top PCs, crossed *RIBA Journals* at dawn, the futile vigil, the insincere hymns and the golden gargoyles – the stupid image and ridiculous fancy. It had been easier to blow up D'Arblay's than he had thought. A fire alarm set off, the assembling of a few late workers in the car park and their ho-ho decision to go to the Chip and Cheese for a few drinks . . . The ease with which Max had parked a brand-new Golf under the smoked-glass porch with the bronze finishing that had been called 'provocative'. The time bomb amongst the packs of explosives on the back seat, the run for cover. The discovery – at last – of an issue of *Designate* amongst the dustbins where Max had hidden. He was halfway through the Rome supplement when D'Arblay's went up a few minutes later. A small explosion, then an enormous one; a waterfall of glass and a few screams. Max finished the Nightlife paragraph and then peered out to inspect the damage. The explosives had been supplied by a no-questions man who demolished old council flats during the day. It must have been extremely powerful. Max was amazed when he saw that the fourth floor – Overseas Accounts and Direct Budgeting – had shifted in more or less one piece some fifty metres down the street and crushed several small shops and a Rocco sandwich bar upon landing. This meant that the fifth and sixth floors, concertinaing the lift shafts, had become as one with the lobby, and the intervening floors were therefore compressed into a kind of layer cake out of which electric cables spat sparks and little fires flickered through the dust. Further baby explosions puffed clouds of black smoke into the night. Here and there a desk slid out of a window or a filing cabinet crashed through a wall.

As the moment hung stretched and dazed, Max lay full

length behind his dustbin. Night was falling when the police arrived, the blue lights on their vans and cars washing in circles around the street. The bomb squad, ambulances, the press – all the relevant bodies gathered Lilliputian around the wrecked financial institution, and Max cracked a grin. The grin soon went and Max followed after it, going down to the river to sit by Traitor's Gate and ponder the success of his attack.

He considered the mess left over on history's palette by the vigorous and neurotic process of keeping the masterpiece of the urban centre alive with these inspired acts of terrorism. He walked through Lincoln's Inn Fields, smoking a cigarette and feeling his invisibility. He was fading a little more with each building destroyed, crossing out his signature on the skyline with his bare hands, the same bare hands with which he had built a glittering career and sculpted an envied marriage. Irony, the liquid engineering within the machinery that drove Max de Winter as myth, leant a pleasing symmetry to the otherwise arbitrary and chaotic bombardment of man by phenomena that was the reality of Max the Man.

At one in the morning, dozing in front of a glass of vodka in the conservatory at New Manderley, Max turned his clouded mind to the destruction of Pacman Software plc, but was aware only of a palm frond fluttering in the sea breeze that stroked his jungle logic – the life after love and success, the melodrama of an everyday failure whose imagination was teaching emotional karate to be used for self-destructive purposes. What a way to go.

Despite the upper and lower case 'i's, life goes on regardless. This may be annoying in itself, the individual determined to beg a crisis or statement off the general indifference of Time to a lonely and bitter old soul. Whatever it is that psychology does – knocking down buildings or selling magazines, marrying people or murdering them – it would seem that the universe shrugs. All this high drama, the tiny details in pink and grey or black and white that cluster like summer insects about the slow afternoon of memories – in all this is the meaningless statement, the difficult to translate. And so strenuous singles are played after tea at New Manderley, house-party games going on and on amongst laughter or silent rage. Happy families, whist and vandalism, the endless charade of watching the roof fall in, and finally, before dinner, or before sleep, or raising a ragged cheer as in some inexplicably hilarious way we witness the house falling down – with or without the aid of explosives.

Two: Pacman Software plc

'There's a Ghost in My House'

It was early afternoon, the second Friday in August. From the upstairs windows of New Manderley, the yellowing fields were shimmering under a heat haze and the trees in the middle distance appeared cross-hatched by sunlight and shadows. A heavy stillness filled the air, the only sounds being a dove that cooed beneath the eaves and the far-off booming of the sea. Fleshy pink roses hung limply around the windows, and after Max had breathed in their scent he exhaled with an expressive sigh that combined immense longing with deep regret, the respiratory equivalent of a requiem.

This was the weekend that Max had set aside to blow up his finest building. These were the leisure hours during which Pacman Software plc, that symphony in polished granite, was destined to reach its final crescendo, the dusk of Sunday evening set to play host to the last few echoing chords of the explosion, a handful of delicate arpeggios in shattered glass playing out the emotional coda.

Pacman Software was the building that Max de Winter considered to be the Bride of All Loveliness, the girl he never married and could therefore never leave. In its thirty-five floors of carefully designed workspace, from the lyrical Italian marble of the lobby to the Californian aluminium cladding of its roof-top solar panels, Max saw only beauty, and when he gazed into the smoky sheets of windows it was his soul that he saw reflected there.

Designate magazine was also scheduled to work over the weekend of 10 and 11 August – booked into Pacman Software to take some fashion photographs.

By Friday lunch time the heat was in residence, and the streets around Cannon Street were soon bursting at their wine bars with relaxed City workers all loosening their striped collars and looking forward to the weekend. From the Buying Department of Pacman Software about twenty of the younger staff had congregated outside The Olde Lampe and Firkin to generally have a bit of a laugh. By 1 p.m. most things were 'bloody funny', 'you know really', and laughter began to spill out at the slightest joke as jackets were taken off and sleeves rolled up to the fierce heat of the sun.

Angus Treadleigh, fired with a passion for Diana in Shipping over at Lampwert Beazeley, the marine insurance people, gazed happily around at his laughing colleagues and thought with pleasure about the interest his well invested money was earning him even as he laughed. He had just bought a two-bedroomed flat down river and things were looking set for a weekend of suntan oil and sex on the secluded oven of a balcony that his brilliantly negotiated mortgage had secured for him as a feature of his purchase.

The depth of the pleasure came from imagining just the merest hints of what might swim across his week-end. A fridge door swinging open to catch Diana's face with a blast of light and watercress-scented cool, the darkness of a shadow off a new concrete wall at five in the afternoon with a clear sky above it, the lazy drowse of passing pleasure boats in the evening . . .

At New Manderley Max de Winter sweated as he loaded dynamite into the back of his car. He would sleep in his old office on Friday night and wire up Pacman early Saturday morning. He was going to pretend to be doing a structural survey of the building – as its architect this seemed only natural.

Friday's dusk was particularly idyllic, a bunch of black grapes being slowly burst in the mouth of London. Early evening was a harmony of brakelights and relaxed pedestrians, the golden blue of the West End washing gently against the white cliffs of Bloomsbury. Arabella Cloth strolled down Charlotte Street with nothing in mind but a dinner *à deux* with her boyfriend Nick, a sandy-haired sculptor of immense talent whom the system had forced to be a pushbike messenger, complete with greased pony-tail and shoulder-high walkie-talkie. They would dine in silence, surrounded by the orange-blossom tenting of her bed, all curiosity about media, art and exploding buildings pushed to one side with the ice bucket.

Rupert would spend the evening alone in his darkroom, flipping the channels on a two-inch-screen TV and rereading Lyotard as an intellectual work-out. Gemma was powdering her neck in preparation for a South Kensington ball, Paul Vince's orchids already filed in the pedal-bin and her grandmother's engagement brooch demurely pinned to her dress.

Angus of Pacman Buying (International) was cleaning his bath and watching the cable. His New Age CD plinked and plunked with a suitably ambient eeriness in his minimalist living room and beside the *Investor's Chronicle* a copy of *Easy Money*, a novel by Steven Hinksmith, lay open at a raunchy bit. Glancing at a page as he passed by to Windolene his mirror Angus read: 'He saw her nipples hardening beneath the soft silkiness of her blouse, suddenly the helicopter exploded . . .'. It was a fast-paced action thriller, all right for just before bed but a definite step down from *Dubrovsky's Chessmen*, the Kremlin exposé that Angus kept by for the tube.

Angus wondered long and hard about what Diana's nipples were like and then went to look in the fridge. He was a success.

Of all this cast of characters the only two left unoccupied were the two who linked them together, Max and Rebecca de Winter. Max was sitting in his old office, at his old desk, in his old desk chair. He felt old. He felt like a ghost. He could read the impression of his last memo on the charcoal-grey blotter on his desk – he just had to hold it up to the desk lamp:

'Burn the Files.'

Across the street, beneath the neo-Gothic minarets and cupola of a disciple of Pugin's attempt at Camelot, the windows of Wheatley & Vernham (Solicitors) glowed bronze in the twilight. The dusty offices were blind to Max's illicit presence, the mirror-glazing of the de Winter building keeping any onlookers out. This was a good thing, lending as it did, an element of tactical anticipation to the design of Fortress Max.

Back in Cork Street Rebecca de Winter was alone in her gallery. A large oil painting was propped up against the wall in front of her, and she walked up and down with a cigarette in her hand, stopping occasionally to look at it. It was *Pineapple Causality for Defoe* (1986) by Lawrence Crane, a new and exciting painter from Oxford whose art school attendance stretched halfway round the world from his foundation year at Athens Technical College to a divided Master's from the Slade in London and the Kunstschule in Hamburg. Twenty-six years of eclectic cultural influence was written into the deceptively easeful cartoon of chaos that the massive canvas depicted.

The painting took as its focal point a self-portrait of Crane. By applying the irony of Schwitters to the agony of Bacon and stirring in a hint of the Glasgow School Crane had depicted himself seated at a blue grand piano, the strings of which were cascading serpentine into the stagnant green foreground wherein they converted to long-stemmed roses, florid of petal and vicious of thorn. The face of the 'pianist' was a mask of wild despair, brown eyes fixed psychotically upon the white and nervous fingers that were splayed across the red and purple keyboard. In the background a parade of jungle animals lurched, powder-blue elephants jostling yellow pelicans and wild snow tigers bounding hysterically into a paradoxically arctic sunset. Their highly comic forms were offset against a drape of blue velvet above which hung a shining motorbike, spokes like moonbeams and the gas tank buffed to a dull maroon. In the right-hand corner a country churchyard stood surrounded by verdant foliage. To the left an elegant ship passed away into tropical azure.

Rebecca tried to determine – in her own mind, for her sake – whether it was the role of nature that Crane was discussing in this allegory or the role of painting itself. She was sure, at any rate, that it was the quintessential Crane, and would certainly fetch the demanded thousands. There were no less than three requests to reserve it, and *FlashArt* was doing an interview. A Star was being Born, and everyone wanted a cut of the nutritional afterbirth.

Rebecca remembered the exploding sun that had been the birth of Max's stardom, the ceaseless attention and flattery, the 'he-can't-put-a-foot-wrong-everything-he-does-is-art' legend. All for being good-looking and an architect. All for being a person, moreover, who used to be happy – until the spotlight gave him sunstroke and changed into an inquisitor's blinding torch.

London never tires of success stories and why should it? Living as she had in the Green Room of Triumph, Rebecca knew by heart the discourse of Success and could follow the vapid annotations to Glamour like a script. The circuitry of Fame, the Souvenir Issue – the intellectually italicised portfolio that was rushed out by the backers at the merest sniff of serious money.

In the absence of carefully marketed talent and the industry that thrived within its hinterland one could always consider the alternative option of the patronising classes which is the profession of banking. A boy with whom Rebecca had hidden in the back of a wardrobe at a children's party for her ninth birthday was now a commodity broker living in West Surrey. Perhaps that vivid incident of her pre-pubescent years had driven her to see only the madness of art-pimping or the madness of money-pimping as ways to a comfortable lifestyle. She was past caring anyhow and wondered with a quiet smile which bank her crazed genius husband was likely to vandalise next.

As Saturday dawned Pacman Software was wrapped in a deep warm mist, and high above its lightning conductors the golden sphere of the sun was destined to burn the sky into clear blue by mid-morning. Beside St Paul's a window slammed and the pigeons on the cathedral steps scattered up into a wheeling crescent that soon dispersed into the masonry beneath the dome. It was going to be a very hot day.

The air was thickening in the deserted streets, and by nine a.m. the heat was enough to give the impression of late afternoon. It was a day of permanent sunset, the eternal summer evening.

A helicopter touched down on the landing barge opposite Bankside Power Station, the heat muffling the noise of its blades. The pilot in short sleeves was obscured by the dancing white lights that dazzled on the surface of the water. From the air the City would have looked like desert canyons, the irregular slopes and plateaux of golden and silver roofing breaking off into black chasms of shadow in the depths of which were the streets, the piazzas, the squares and the alleys.

The west façade of Pacman Software was gently humming in the heat. The steel-caged air-conditioning units that stretched at regular intervals beneath the thirteenth floor windows looked like basking lizards, and as Max de Winter stood beside a green security door and squinted up at the summit of his building there was something malevolent about the presence of these wall-hanging fixtures. It was curious, he thought, that in order to win his personal war he was forced to lose every battle. For Max the loss of each building was a defeat – he had wanted his buildings to glorify the financial centre of the UK. He had wanted them to be architectural jewels in the crown of England, their design offsetting the virtues of a green and pleasant land, their aesthetic references intended to echo a proud historic legacy of English tradition. He had wanted to stay at New Manderley, his garden palace, safe in the knowlege that London carried on in his absence growing prosperous and noble within the buildings that he had designed before his thirty-second birthday. How pitifully naive. A sickness chilled him and a dread of the work he had done and the role that it played in New England as the kinky dungeon of London Style City and the Money Brothel of Britain where all the young executives smelt of stale fish and the sweat of progressive greed.

Downstream, Angus was dreaming of a swimming pool beside the black-sanded desert, only it was his old school again and he was getting all the answers right by simply memorising the possible answers and underlining them in red.

Carrying a heavy suitcase that contained a number of powerful small bombs that could be detonated individually or collectively by a thing like a TV control unit, Max let himself into Pacman Software.

The security men, two of them, had been informed the previous day that Max would be calling – informed, that is, by Max himself pretending to be a Personal Assistant. Checking their appointment book, they respectfully tipped their hats, suspicious for merely the look of the thing. Security men must look suspicious at all times yet are generally so bored that one can catch them out.

Max felt sure that he was virtually invisible anyway. Even as he stood in front of the wide reception desk and said 'I'm Max de Winter, the architect, you should have a note of my visit' he felt that he could be neither seen nor heard.

'We thought you were one of the other lot,' said the smaller guard by way of conversation. 'You look like a fashion person.'

Max turned back, puzzled. 'What fashion people?' But the guard was laughing, doubtless at the peculiar things that fashion people do, and so Max assumed that he was merely telling a security-guard-style joke.

First of all Max went into the mezzanine cloakroom. In the lilac-scented air and purple lighting he felt his head clear a little and carefully planted one of his bombs, or 'leeches' as they are known in Mafia circles, behind a roller towel unit. Pausing to wash his hands and water back his hair, he then pulled on some surgical gloves and made his way to the lift.

Getting out at the third floor he planted four more leeches at either end of the corridor, two in the office of J.K. Cartwright (Assistant Director Exhibitions) and two more around the base of a cheese plant in the Display Department typing pool.

On the sixth floor he carefully unscrewed a panel off one of the cooling ducts. The sun was savage by now against the windows and Max noted with pride the efficiency of the air conditioning. He was disoriented, however, by the mesmeric stripes of shadow that fell from the vertical fabric blinds, and looking down at his ankle-length cement-coloured raincoat he felt like a zebra in a cage. Lighting a cigarette, he taped two leeches inside the service box of the cooling duct and screwed the panel back on.

Feeling a little cavalier, he sauntered down to the large conference room that occupied the entire width of the east end of the sixth floor. On the large back wall hung a painting by Tom Vreeland, one of the lesser known but highly collectable members of the London School. It depicted Commerce in London, a twilit city scene of bus tops and umbrellas against the buildings of London. In the foreground a hunch-shouldered businessman stared accusingly out of the canvas and peered at Max from under the brim of his hat, round wire-framed glasses lending a trace of menace to his painted eyes. The painting was dated 1958, and its predominant collaging of grey and yellow was fragmented by snail-trails of white that were the beginnings of a Great British Downpour.

Max looked out of the window at the unnatural heat bouncing watery distortions off the rooftops of London and then fastened a bomb to either side of the Vreeland's frame and shrugged.

'What the discovery of oil painting was to the Venetians,' he whispered to himself through a cloud of cigarette smoke, 'let dynamite and remote control be to the Art of Max de Winter. And I'm not really sorry about the Vreeland.'

Three floors down the *Designate* team were setting up lights and breakfasting on fruit juice and tubs of Greek yoghurt. Over by the windows the models were being carefully installed in the MythMyth winter collection. Catching three of her twenty-seven bracelets in the wild foam of her newly acquired peroxide perm, Betty the fashion editor was having the Compulsory Professional Crisis, her skewer-like personality making kebabs out of the sensitive natures of those she so enjoyed to supervise.

Much moving and removing of people, lights, clothes and props later, the first fifty photographs were pronounced a mess. Three tall girls with the standard-issue white crewcuts had been photographed over and over lolling moodily against door-frames and marching with serious looks on their faces up and down the geometrical playground of the famous de Winter fourth-floor corridor with its lime green pillars and triangular scarlet floor tiles.

Dressed in short black denim skirts and stretched-out jersey jackets, three more girls were beginning to pose themselves in arrangements of business-surreality as assistants various threw cashmere overcoats and accounts ledgers at them for nearly two hours.

And then it was lunch, a short professional break for all the committed professional people before taking to the roof to do the Margot Jones leather leggings and topcoats. Soon the *Designate* team were standing in the ruins of a salad that had been their lunch.

Max de Winter was working fast now, running from floor to floor depositing bombs in any and every available space – under desks, in wastepaper baskets, between books, under sinks and behind filing cabinets. Pacman Software plc was alive with dynamite.

Soon he was on the roof. Leaning over the low metal balustrade he could see the whole of London bask beneath the afternoon sun. The river curled slowly into the heat haze, and the peaks of Centre Point, the Euston Tower, the London Hilton and the funnels of Battersea Power Station were all clearly visible despite their one tone of powdered gun-metal blue. Just down the street Max could see the grooved façade of the NatWest tower, and behind him – sinking, he felt, into the warm asphalt – stood the complex steel knitting of the new Lloyds Building, pods a-quivering in the desolate heat as though they were fruits getting ready to drop.

The aluminium cladding of the solar panels could not be approached directly, so Max left his last four bombs on the cast-iron cradle that supported them. A hot wind buffeted off the roof structures and Max had to steady himself with one hand as he closed his terrorist's suitcase.

Hearing the giggles, whoops and severely uttered little cries of warning of the approaching *Designate* team, Max quietly slid behind a water tank and then took the service lift down to the ground floor.

Nodding to the security guards as he signed himself out, Max casually strolled through the lobby and then went down to the street, suitcase empty and raincoat flapping in a sudden gust from the pavement air vents.

When to press the button? It didn't really matter – or did it? Did he want to massacre the innocent fashion victims playing on the roof of his greatest building? Dancing on his grave? Somehow he had not got the stomach for killing them knowingly. He sat in his car and left the primed detonator unit winking silently on the seat beside him. He felt tired and the car was warm and airless. He dreamt.

Rebecca and he were children, playing in the garden of Rebecca's house. It seemed important that the house was Rebecca's house, not his house, or their house, and Max was most definitely a guest.

Rebecca was like a little princess from a children's picture book, and Max was the idiot boy in love with her. He loved her desperately but there was something, some fact that he knew about himself but could not tell her, that prevented him from loving her honestly, or openly. She loved him desperately in return, and was tortured by the fact that he could not really love her. Held apart by this discrepancy, Max and she still played together, loving one another as much as they could, in the garden of Rebecca's house.

It was a law of the dream that if Max ever got into Rebecca's house she would never be free of him, so they had to play in the garden.

To entertain her Max had put on a big bearskin, the bear's head over his head and the flat skin over his back. He plodded up the garden path, pretending to be a bear. The skin was terribly heavy, but it made Rebecca laugh so much to see him shuffling along that she helped carry the skin to ease its weight on him, dancing for joy at the game.

Finally they reached the door of Rebecca's house, Max's head and the bear's head resting on the step. And then Rebecca remembered that she must not let him into her house or she would never be free of him and his tormenting non-love. She said, 'Oh no you don't, if once you get inside I'll never be free of you' and dropped the skin back onto Max so that it crushed him to the path. The skin was hard like pine needles.

So then they played some more in the garden until, standing on the over-green lawn, Rebecca put her hands to her cheeks and said, 'I don't feel well. I feel ill . . . '.

And Max said, 'I'll get you a glass of water' and ran off to fetch it.

Rebecca shouted, 'Don't go into my house! It isn't water that I want anyway, it's love!' And Max replied, squirming uncomfortably, 'But *I* love you!'

Rebecca's anger and distress worked her little girl's face into awkward shapes. She screamed 'But you *don't* love me!' and then stooped down in her little long dress to pick three stones out of the flower-bed – hard, sharp, flat stones. She hurled them with all her strength at Max's face.

The first he caught, and then the second, but at the third he screamed, 'But you'll kill me . . . '.

Waking, Max looked out of the car window and decided to leave the detonation until the building was empty. On Sunday morning there wouldn't even be security people there, just a few hot lines from the burglar alarms and smoke detectors to the nearest police station.

Waiting for the bomb to go off – that is, waiting to push the button . . . In these twelve hours the malignant chemicals that had been harassing Max de Winter for the previous God knows how many years began to finally coagulate into a horrific compound, Gothic in its inventiveness to prophesy, depict and scare. From the moment when he awoke in his E-Type Max was aware of the seconds ticking by like a dripping narcotic; they brought nocturne, lullaby and nightmare, the dusk, night and dawn all gathering about Pacman Software and Max's soul to bring the two of them down.

Late on Saturday evening Max thought about his afternoon, and of the activities traditionally set aside for other people's Saturday afternoons. Other people – decent, ordinary, healthy, prosperous citizens, those whose troubles, even tragedies, were contained by the standard social machinery of sympathy, celebration over adversity and thanksgiving for deliverance. Other people. Other fucking people. The handsome groom and the nervous bride, those proud parents happy to announce and the privately reacting friends there gathered, so public in their approval. The highway is well lit, the stops ahead pre-planned. The nervous bride as Lovely in White as Rebecca had been – those who had attended any of Max and Rebecca's weddings could confirm the latter's Loveliness in White. The bride's spirit was maybe leaning against the hot side of the hired Daimler, eyes vacant, or piercing, and smoking a Senior Service untipped right down to the stub. On a Saturday afternoon of intense heat, with dust dropping off the sandstone steeples of Surrey or Kent, so many other people could be happily getting on with the business of living whilst Max was waiting to destroy his tallest building, at the height, as it were, of his creative powers.

There was also the consideration of all those people whose careers and self-images had maybe been founded on a glimpse at Pacman Software. The aspirant young executives' first post-graduate yearnings for a Good Life in the City. Dreams of brilliant financial coups on Thursday afternoons whilst the dramatic weather bounced off the windows and the head of a financial wizard was bent inspired over the screen of his desk-top terminal.

Max de Winter resented his inability to continue, and doubly resented the perversity of his monied despair. True despair is supposedly the property of the damned have-nots – it was galling as a have who did not want to be considered a fake.

He wondered whether time erases experience or underlines it: experience, mistakes, desires, impressions – the ingredients of a palatable or an indigestable life, depending on the arrangement. We ought to reject arrangement, thought Max, not wait for the abstract to make figurative sense.

On Sunday the City was –

Empty.

One or two cars, a sunbaked cathedral like an old piece of pottery in some Byzantine town just waiting to crack or be reversed into, the gathering of crisp and dirty newspapers against traffic island railings. The heat continued, stronger than ever, and the river glided slowly by, a glacier of diamonds.

Rather too nonchalantly for the severity of the occasion, Max leant against the side of his car in the early morning heat. He was parked down a cool alley between a clearing house and an Australasian bank. Directly ahead he could see the Pacman Software building, and behind the bulk of that was nothing but blue sky.

He felt like an advert for a course in decision-making; one hand resting on the passenger door of his car and the other holding a remote-control detonator unit. He was wearing a blue and white striped shirt, cement-coloured linen trousers and a pair of Italian shoes. His fringe flicked elegantly over his dark glasses. During his campaign of violence he had got quite a tan.

Pacman hummed in the early morning stillness, its many floors and windows letting out a single tone into the heat. Max strained to listen for any activity in the neighbourhood – there was none.

Except,
the Four Tommies.

They were loitering inquisitively on the corner by the Bank of Tunisia, looking over at Max with their thumbs pushed into their green webbing belts and their toecaps glinting in the sun.

'I say, you blokes,' said one of them, 'he looks like a likely customer . . . '

Max assumed his friendly yet paternal persona, the ghost of Leslie Howard possessing him.

'Morning, you chaps!' he called out cheerfully to them 'Taking in a few of the historic sites of the old City whilst you're on leave, I'll be bound. Well, there's plenty to see, and all of it's got a tale to tell, straight off the pages of English history.'

The Tommies wandered politely over, the one who had spoken looking around to the others for their support in his trusting this gentleman as a bloke who didn't mind a chat.

'It's like this, sir, see. Me and my mates here – that's Alf and Georgie, and the big ugly bastard (laughter) at the back, that's Bill – we all thought we'd see a bit of old Blighty but now we're blowed if we can find our way back to Paddington. If we're not back by noon the CO's going to have our guts for garters and no mistake. Slept last night on a bench by the river but we was all a bit the worse for wear, you might say . . . '

Max laughed approvingly. 'Well, you chaps have certainly picked a hot morning for sight-seeing, but if Rommel's men are sweating in the desert there's a thing or two we could show them on a fine English day like this!'

The City towered over Max. He was standing alone in the street, his eyes dull and his face drawn, shoulderblades fluttering like summer-blown petals and his mind picking thoughts as a maniac picks bluebells with a monkey wrench. Thousands of miles of telecommunication systems surrounded him, yet still he couldn't make himself clear.

He gave each of the Tommies a cold bottle of beer and had one himself. 'Yes,' he said, with respectful warmth, 'There's a quality in England that will always shine, no matter what dirty tricks Johnny Banker may stoop to. Be you commoner or earl, rich or poor, Mrs Simpson or petrol pump attendant, there's always a place in England to do your bit. To be a part of our . . . heritage, and traditions, a continuation of Arthur, Shakespeare and the song of the Sweet Swan of Avon. Let it never be said – and here Max rammed his thumb down on the detonator button – that an Englishman refused his country the very best that he has to offer.'

Max's last words were drowned by the sound of forty leech-bombs simultaneously exploding. The Tommies evaporated into the heat haze and everything went into slow motion as Max turned his face from the slipstream of the blast.

A cacophony of shattering glass laced with strident alarm bells, the screech of rupturing water pipes and the muffled thud of collapsing walls and flexible partitions. A sheet of fire swept quickly down the carpet in the foyer and behind the blistering paintwork on the window frames a roar announced the lift shafts alight.

Two years of basic designing and hundreds of man-hours of planning negotiations were put out of service in a quarter of an hour.

Max began to ramble, waving his detonator over his head like a pageant flag. 'Saw the lone Lancaster, radioed for help, saw a boat adrift, down there in the cove, near the rocks . . . a waved headscarf in the terrible storm that night, and all stations to London Bridge, to Godless January, the eye of the architect . . . '.

Sirens moaned and cars screamed into the City. Coming to with a nervous jolt, Max got quickly into his car and dodged the police cordon by minutes. He drove out of London towards New Manderley and the sea. He had spared *Designate* at least – let them be grateful for that.

Within the hour Malcolm Houston had left another message on the de Winter Associates ansafone. 'Given the recent and not altogether unexpected destruction of de Winter's tallest building, would it be possible for *Designate* to stage the West One Fashion Week Show on a catwalk across the rubble? He'd be grateful if someone could get back to him on that one.

3
'Broken Lute Strings and Pet Monkeys'

One: Top Man of Nothing

Summer was drawing to a close, the heat of August nearly spent. There was a chill in the clear mornings, and at noon a pale sun gilded the tops of the trees as their fluttering leaves were tossed in the quickening wind. Dusk was a cusp of moonlight traced with cider gold. Max knew that he would not survive the winter.

In London the squares of Bloomsbury – Gordon, Russell and Bedford – were three dusty pitches overhung with powdering foliage, and beyond the Euston Road, in Regent's Park, the sunshine spread moodily up the broad garden walks to convert into a rolling wilderness of bleached grass. The shabby white houses tumbled down their mysterious suburban escarpments on the foothills of north London, and down by the side of the dark canal a few of the furthest-tumbling of these stood silently in the afternoon shadows. Time stood still in this basin, the dregs of summer gathered in the bottom of a shallow garden urn. Max de Winter sat on the bottom step of summer and saw only the sea for a winter, the breakers off the beach at New Manderley perhaps, as his button hole converted to a foppish technicolour and he mused on matters of Life and Death. He had maybe a fortnight in which to conclude his career.

He felt tired, and incapable of the effort required to reason. This lassitude was complicit with the concluding moves of his mission; he had only to destroy two more buildings and then wait for the floodtide of the loosened Thames that flowed past his targets to rise up and sweep him away on a blast-severed security door, then to spiral delicate circles into the waterlogged meadows of Surrey. He would finally find himself out to sea, a crashed fighter pilot drowning in sight of his native England.

Let us consider the garden at New Manderley. In the morning, the heavy dew of late August made the grass a carpet of sparkling water; by lunch time the heat of the sun was barely enough to evaporate it. The borders were overgrown, and the thick furred stems of the larger plants had grown coarse and brittle during the summer that had burnt their sap away. The last few petals on the roses hung bronze and rusty over their darkly folded underleaves. The sky stayed cloudless from mid-morning to tea time, but in the very early morning and the late afternoon an aromatic mist hung loosely in the sparse pine trees at the edge of the cliffs. All day long the air smelt of woodsmoke and dried wallflowers. The cracks in the garden paths were dry river beds brushed with a crimson dust. The Judas-tree cast a long shadow, and at the very tip of this long shadow sat Max de Winter on an old garden chair. He brooded on his life whilst the garden bled to death.

He knew that he had treated Rebecca badly. His moods had hung around on the street corners of her life, sometimes smiling and trying to look handsome, at other times peevish and nasty, a hint of a threat in their presence. Whilst never losing sight of her beauty, Max de Winter had sat in the swivel chair of confusion with his elbows firmly planted on the desk of paradox whilst he contemplated her personality. He adored her, his adoration becoming all the more inarticulate as he realised the slenderness of the vocabulary they had in common. Their Greater Game was as devoid of team spirit as it was of prizes.

And so finally, on September the fourth, Max knew that it was time to leave the darkening garden. In London his fists would whiten in the darkness of shop doorways, all the flowers that he might bring up with him from the country would turn to tinder, and eventually, in the blast, an asphalt perfume would rise to wrap up the finale of his blighted marriage and pass it on into the indiscriminate care of history.

The Museum of Corporate Finance stood low beside the river, three pyramidal roofs of lead-welded glass under which a variety of museum precincts housed a permanent collection of exhibits related to the history of banking. These were annotated by a succession of temporary displays that depicted methods, dramas, and follies from the world of financial record keeping – the freak shows of data processing. There were flow diagrams, touch-operated displays, a talking bank manager courtesy of Tussauds, and a hand that gave out money in real bank notes at the precise speeds it would take various graduations of income earners to receive it. Part of the interest of the latter lay in the detailed description of the security measures taken to display it. Children gaped and fathers nodded with stern approval; it was, after all, real money.

Max de Winter stood alone in the foyer, looking at the postcards of historic invoices, oven gloves depicting legendary account numbers and washable kitchen charts with basic accounting practices printed on them. It was a successful museum, horrid too, with its gift shop and no-smoking restaurant, its lecture rooms and crêche. The light filtered down in tropical pools, the great moments of financial history mottled by tiny spotlights.

Max de Winter's recent annexe to the museum, the Historic Invoices Library, still smelt of plaster and paint. It was a white space with ladderax shelving, a more lucid environment for the serious student of the balance sheet to extend his scholarship within.

Above all Max knew that he must not stop now, must not be dragged screaming into debate with anyone about what exactly he was doing with all these carloads of explosives and highly peculiar dreams. A sunny autumn day closed in around the last English architect, Max de Winter, and at 5 p.m. precisely the museum would close for the day. In possession of an intimate knowledge of the building, Max sneaked down one of the administrative offices corridors and hid in a photo-copying room. On the wall there was a witty cartoon clipped from the *Guardian* about photocopiers. He locked the door from the inside.

Soon he heard the air conditioning groan to a halt, and then the lights were turned off. A few footsteps, some resigned and forlorn 'goodnights', then silence.

The Museum of Corporate Finance was his.

He sat on a box of Infotech paper and closed his eyes. His father had been a wing commander, his mother a keen gardener.

All around him the gathered invoices cried out their spectral balances due. From Pooby Trust Ltd 1926 to the bill for Concorde's cockpit, the history of purchase in its documented form was represented in various styles: the illuminated manuscript of the demand, the delicacy of serrated edges where bills are torn off the invoice pad. A higher choir of fiscal chanting filled the air with its muted Miserere. The light was failing, the skylights turning blue, and a single star played overhead by the moon. From Basingstoke to Birmingham, from New Cross Gate to New Manderley the invoices fluttered like angels in the young dusk.

Max rested his head against the thin partition wall and closed his eyes. Rebecca had been using Grapefruit and Seagrass washing granules whilst he was drawing up the final plans for the Historic Invoices Library. The relationship between love and creative inspiration had always struck Max as being a stormy one. He had been well paid for his work, however; a Nation of Shopkeepers – disgusting.

He pondered the uselessness of all financial systems, his memories diverting to the time that Rebecca had climbed up the stairs to their London flat one hot afternoon years ago with a box of houseplants in her arms.

You have to bash out sense, hack it from chaos, that's the trick – but even then . . . To build is to demolish chaos, therefore to demolish buildings is – thoughtful chaos? Who cares anyway, thought Max.

For Max, surrounded by the paper tombstones of Transactions Past, there was the sense that he was watching, or thinking, an elderly public information film, from maybe 1947. As he wondered why it looked as though the ceiling of his photocopier room was made entirely out of heavily starched aertex blouses, he could almost hear an urgent fanfare announcing 'The Voyage of an Invoice'.

The voyage of an invoice through the mind of an employee, a budget director from Crawley or somewhere with Burridge Plan (1949) housing estates – an old church steeple and a pub with roses about its door and a wishing well just outside the butcher's.

Max thought, 'I think I'm getting a stomach upset . . .' There was Rebecca, having tea in Heal's, her gentle hands pouring out and stirring, a scone, and jam, and cream – the little laugh of self-reproach. That she might put on weight – Oh sylph, Oh love, Oh Rebecca!

And now I must blow up this monument to economic appetite, thought Max, drop a depth charge into the stomach of London's only public financial archive. Would a budget director from Crawley think twice about a mislaid file? Yes. Would history mourn the prejudiced termination of the Historic Invoice Library? What priests defend this shrine? What eunuchs of the digital watch and thin wrist, brown-suited and photochromatically bespectacled, would leap to defend this sacred place, this arbour of PR, the power behind the drone?

The invoice would appear – like writing and summer – out of nowhere, whizzed from a pre-process womb on to the stage of a freshly cleared desk. Touched down in the in-tray, it would want only out, a desperate document tattooed like a Messerschmidt or Spitfire with a number and a legend, waiting to scramble to its doom, to its encoding with PAID and the date, to when it simply wouldn't mean anything any more – when it was PAID IN FULL and dated, its demand met and its power defused, it dead (and dated), en route from the file to the dear old shredder, without any due rights or solemnity but just a number, a justification for its originator to retire to Surrey and have a beech hedge and a white gate with children swinging upon it and a rather exceptional buddleia . . . .

Ought Max to light a candle in his local Collegiate Church for the unknown invoice, strewing a petal or two onto the ancient slate? It would be a pathos pact for the invoice that died for its country – that country being a queer place, a long way from Max's exotic England.

In London the meetings never end; the curiously stylised self-importance that patinas the fundamental banality of their careerist participants must be endlessly serviced by ritual, an egomania masquerading as the exchange of information. At de Winter Associates, at Rebecca de Winter Fine Art, at *Designate* where Arabella is endlessly underlining things, like she did at school, at college and in bed.

And speaking of underlining things, as Max underlined his brilliant career by marrying Rebecca and therefore bringing attention to his brilliance by liaising it with beauty, let us follow Max through his office opiates and paper-scented reverie to the Bloodye Battles and Historye of one piece of paper he is about to blow up.

Once upon a time there was a photocopier, and above the photocopier was a sign that said 'Photocopier'. Beneath this sign was another sign that said 'DO NOT OVEREXPOSE THE DRUM' and this written sign was generally accompanied *sotto voce* by the advice 'Never, ever, whatever you do, look directly into the light source'. It is very bad luck to look directly into the light source, and office superstition amongst the lower clerical grades stipulates in no uncertain terms just what tragedy can befall a member of staff who tries to *witness with his own eyes* the process of copying. And, therefore, great magicians, and budget directors, sighing to themselves as they pass by, whisper *Beware of Magic* to the curious or just plain lazy who will not put the cover down before making a copy.

The photocopier stood in an old palace that had been renovated in the middle of the nineteenth century to house the original Self & Assurance company. By 1984 the photocopier was a disgrace, being both overused – as it was – and abused – as it never should have been. The touch-sensitive buttons had long since ceased to activate the copy functions that their user symbols denoted, and the Interrupt Copy button, for instance, now released the paper feeder. The Copies Made counter ran, blasphemously, backwards, and the Cancel button made fifty copies without stopping. The right forward castor was missing – possibly stolen – and the paper cabinet beneath the copy unit itself was locked for good. Someone, some highwayman or terrorist, had had a go at the paper cabinet door lock with a wrench and missed. A dent recorded this deed.

At the other end of the corridor to where the photocopier stood there was a door. The door was always firmly closed. Mr Read, to whom the door belonged during office hours, had been frequently heard to say: 'And remember, Joan (Bill, Jonathan, Helen, Marjorie, Peter), my door is always open – even when it's closed.'

Members of staff frequently repeated this bit of news to one another, their features widening with mirth as they marvelled at its self-contradiction.

'How can a door be open – even when it's closed?' they said to one another. They attributed the paradoxical qualities of the statement to whatever facet of Mr Read's personality they had decided to dislike, regardless of whether or not they believed their diagnosis to be true.

Mr Read sat on the other side of the door, his head bent over a large green file with 'Budget Accounts' written on it in felt-tip. The file never changed, it was always 'Budget Accounts'. At about three o'clock most afternoons Mr Read would walk the length of his little office and consult the Sasco Year Planner. He looked at the number of the year, the month and the day with a smug, proprietorial look. Then he nodded once or twice.

Michelle, a clerk typist, sometimes had to make fifty copies of a 'document' for Derek Fish, Assistant Director Accounts Department, who worked at the other end of the corridor. She would go to the photocopier and lay the original down upon the correction-fluid-scarred surface of the glass, and then put the cover into the down position, prior to copying.

On one occasion she was wearing metallic purple nail varnish as she made her copies. She had done her nails on a Saturday evening, because she was going out, and it was Monday when she made her copies for Mr Fish. On Saturday night, at Roscoe's in Essex, under ultra-violet lights, her nails had looked white. Her friend Sally had screamed when she saw them whilst they were dancing.

'Why are your nails white, Michelle?' she had asked above the sampler drumbeats and deadpan vocals.

'Because I painted them purple,' Michelle had replied. And they continued dancing.

Later on, holding her cocktail in the warm crimson light of

Roscoe's Dive, Michelle had noticed with satisfaction that her nails now appeared the electric purple she had wanted them to be.

'Look Sally,' she said, 'my nails aren't white.'

'What's the colour called?' asked Sally.

'Seventh Heaven,' replied Michelle.

Having put the cover down on the photocopier, Michelle then pressed the Cancel button in order to make the fifty copies more quickly. She tried to walk the entire length of the corridor and back before the copies were made.

She spread her hands out in front of her, palms down. She looked at her chipped, purple nails.

'Not the sixth and not the eighth,' she thought. 'The Seventh.'

Heaven.

Mr Fish sat behind his desk and waited for the document to be returned to him with its copies. He was thinking about Michelle. Could an eighteen-year-old like Michelle with a boyfriend at university possibly find him attractive? It was pathetic how lovely he found her. Although on the short side, she had firm legs. He liked the black ski-pants she wore. He liked the black polo-neck tops she wore. He wondered how they made them these days to pull down so tightly over the bust. Maybe . . . it was a leotard! and he sighed.

'It must be so soft,' he thought, with a mounting sadness. He did not know what exactly must be so soft. It didn't matter. Michelle, her ski-pants, her black polo-neck top, the fabric of these garments, her lips, her body, everything – must be so soft. His eyes watered slightly. He felt comforted by the presence of an emotion. He knew that he wasn't all bad. He knew that he would never take Michelle out, although sometimes at lunch time he would walk past the little Greek restaurant in Farringdon that he had always imagined would be a suitable rendezvous.

He would be forty-eight in July. His daughter left home the previous September. In two years time she would be a classicist. The library at her university was made entirely out of glass and contained over four million items including microfilms and fiches. It also contained the Harding Collection of Illuminated

Manuscripts. It was a good university and a fine library. June, his daughter, was happy there.

The previous week, on Wednesday evening, June had driven from the campus to the town where Phil, her boyfriend, lived. He lived in a house with some people. They had meals.

June parked her Ford Escort outside Phil's house. It was the first week of the summer term and everyone was talking about their exams. Phil came out of the house, pulling on his leather jacket. After June had kissed him they drove into the centre of town to meet their friends Bob and Rob and Cosmo and Mitch for a drink.

The clouds were purple over Leicester (the town). The centre of Leicester was orange; the white taller buildings a cupric shade of red. The friends went to the Marquis of Grimsby, or 'The Grim', a pub.

They talked about work and jobs and travel, the latter being something they had all done a little of but would like to do much more of. One would extol the exotica of Peru, another the need to do Europe in one go, on a train. They made an excitable and implausible plan to all go to Spain together for the summer because Spain is so cheap once you've got there.

Mitch wondered whether Jan would finally ditch Phil and pay him some attention if they ever all went to Spain. Mitch had a Greek restaurant too. Two phone calls unreturned last vacation, later ascribed to an abundance of weddings. He readily forgave her. He could never hold on beyond the point in his fantasy when she stood in front of the television set.

June and Phil had decided not to sleep together during exams. They talked a lot, marvelling at the way that sometimes things don't work out, which is strange, and sad, but usually for the best.

June Fish's father sat in his office and tried not to look up when Michelle came in with the document and its copies. She didn't say anything either and put the copies on the front of his desk and placed the top copy on top of them. She was neither friendly nor impolite, having no need to be either. Despite himself, Mr Fish looked at her bottom as she left the room. On his tiled windowsill a spider plant dangled brown leaves into a saucer of dust and cracked mud.

He looked at the document, a standard letter format for Mortgage Enquiries. It was drafted for people who were improving the value of their property. The letterhead read: 'Self & Assurance Estd. 1867.' The address followed: 'Investment House, 58–62 Bishopsgate, London. He closed his eyes. After twelve years he still could not remember the post-code. This was a nuisance when people rang up and he had to give them the address.

'And the post-code?' they would ask, despite his hoping that they wouldn't. And then he would have to lean over awkwardly to look at the piece of headed note paper he kept especially for when people rang up and asked him the post-code.

He was pleased with the pile of standard-letter copies that the blessed Michelle had put on his desk. They were all ready for Internal Circulation to Heads of Sections prior to the monthly Financial Systems Meeting at which their contents would be discussed and he would be acknowledged as their author.

It was a quiet afternoon. Typewriters tapped and beeped in the distance. A window was opened and a blind lowered; soon it would be summer.

Mr Fish picked up the telephone receiver and dialled Mr Read's extension. He heard the phone ringing down the corridor. He knew that Mr Read would be in because his door was closed.

'Hello. Mr Read's extension.'

'Oh. Is he there please?'

'I'll just get him.'

Mr Fish was now worried in case he was disturbing Mr Read. 'Hello, Richard Read here.' (That gruff yet approachable voice, always ready for new ideas if not new activity, always keen to sound out new blood. A lot of new blood had been sounded out in the twelve years that Mr Fish had been ringing Mr Read.)

'Oh, hello Richard, Derek here. I thought you might like to look over the letter for the Finance Meeting. I've just received the copies.'

'Oh, good. Bring them down.'

Mr Fish was pleased. Being in Mr Read's office meant not actually having to do any work, or rather it was the most work (in visible terms) that one could be seen to be doing.

He put down the phone. He looked at the top copy and read it through. He thought about a racing bicycle with Michelle on it. The last line said 'Yours sincerenely'.

The sky was brilliant blue above the buildings across the street.

The lights were going out all over Bishopsgate. Mr Read sat behind his technically open door and read computer print-outs. He wanted to lose himself in his work as one might lose oneself in Hampton Court maze, finding pleasure in the struggle to escape. He also wanted to be free of desires, and regrets and memories. He wanted to have only the least demanding of ambitions. He wished that he wasn't alone, and was troubled by the remembrance of things that were made visible to him during his brief brushes with romance – gorse, for instance, and a particular flying club in Kent where it was always September even in March.

The old Self & Assurance building was falling down, and Mr Read found it difficult to come into the office with a sense of pride. Working late on winter evenings he had heard slates falling off the roof, and rumour had it that the west wing of the building had been known to attack birds. The ceilings were riddled with damp and asbestos, the lift shaft leaked. The gentlemen's toilet was more or less open to the elements.

He had often wondered what colour the carpets were.

But if only he could lose himself in his work! Simple, blissful routine . . . Beneath his executive exterior Mr Read was susceptible to the slightest emotional shock. Little things left permanent scars and at night the light on his radio alarm clock seemed to wink at him mockingly whilst adverts for soap and certain late-night chat shows made him cry. It was surprising that he was the director of a firm, given his emotional instability, his complete and utter inability to communicate with people and his increasing fondness for drink. Success, however, is largely a matter of appearances, and Mr Read did look like a director.

Whilst he talked to himself in a sing-song whisper, Michelle listened to her friend Christine talking about the distraction being currently thrown in the path of her engagement to be married soon by a friend of a friend of hers who is now 'arty'. Christine had been proud of her boyfriend Kevin until she met Sean, and now there is something glamorous about the ragged state of Sean's black jeans that makes her say to Michelle: 'It's people like Sean who sort of shape the way that people like Kevin think.'

Kevin had been working hard at his business studies diploma for nearly fourteen months; he could not, however, paint, and his trousers were in a banal and conventional state of repair. For Christine there is something, some glorious, clandestine, passionate something about the way Sean says 'Really?' Also there is something mysterious and sexy about a person who can talk to a famous art critic about how long they've been looking at lines and how interesting they find them.

Kathy was working for the Self & Assurance as a SuperSec Temp with w/pr, s/h and skills. She saw the advert for the job in *Working Girl* magazine on 20 September 198-, an orange, blustery day, during the cleaning of the north side of St Paul's. She had always known that she wanted to be a super audio sec, possibly legal, with w/pr, s/h and skills, even as a child, and when she read about the great office and terrific perks she knew in her heart of hearts that ere the sun had set over West One again she would have convinced the personnel department that she could cope with a busy director and have a sense of humour – even under pressure.

It was her mistake, but she would never admit it.

All that Michelle is interested in is finding her seventh heaven; neither the sixth nor the eighth will do – it has to be the seventh.

Mr Read looked through his old diary. He noticed that on 25 June of the previous fiscal he had made a note to kill himself. He went over to the Sasco Year Planner and looked at it carefully before saying 'Drat' very quietly.

Max de Winter Associates were commissioned in September 198-, to design the new Self & Assurance headquarters. The shareholders were pleased, the board was pleased, and the staff were pleased.

Mr Fish sat at his desk in his shirt-sleeves, a broad oblong of yellow sunlight turning mandarin across his back. He thought about Michelle wearing a pair of blue jeans and a black bra, cupping his leathery face in her soft brown hands. There were tears in his eyes.

June Fish sat at her little desk in front of the window in Room 6 of Merksham Hall of Residence. She had a cup of tea in a white mug with part of the *Times* crossword printed upon it. The only word filled in on the design was 'coffee'.

Her brown hair fell lifelessly across her face. She placed the longest strand behind her ear and then reapplied herself to a translation:

'Utinam populus Romanus unam cervicem haberet.'

It is Suetonius, *The Life of Caligula*. In her conscientious blue-biro handwriting she wrote:

'Would that the Roman People had but one neck.

And then she underlined it in red, because it was the answer to the question.

Max de Winter underlined the Museum of Corporate Finance by lacing it with sixteen gallons of petrol and dropping a match. Not one single invoice remained, just a few scraps of greasy black paper that settled like snow on the river.

The Voyage of the Invoice ended as ash in the Thames, and Max could not help but feel convinced that nobody would miss the offices through which the invoice had sailed that much.

He exploded myths. There were no hanging baskets on the platforms of Max's last stop. There were no dates in his diary either, just a few old photographs that became more and more of a body-temperature problem. The life of an open book.

To disown a life, to break it first, then go.

Two: Max de Winter's Apostasy

'Because We're Living in a Material World'

In Margate there were elderly advertisements fading in shop

windows for soft drinks and beers that no one wanted to buy any more. Summer Fizz, for instance, and Tucky, an American root beer.

Max de Winter never revisited Margate after the completion of his jazz-hacienda in its seaside suburb all those years ago. Someone once said it was beautiful. Some things are.

Malcolm Houston summoned his team to the meeting. 'It's just a brief one,' he said whilst they were taking their places.

'The November issue, "Season of myths and mellow . . . "; shopping guide, "Who has not seen thee oft amidst thy stores . . . " – no more puns; I think we can leave it this month. Features – Korean Holidays: "Seoul'd", Korea generally; men's underwear; Loose Grooves; Martin Caleman's new novel *PictureFright* and interview with Lawrence Crane: 'Carry That Weight". Ah – "In and Out": this month's TV, Quiz Shows, "Do as You Would Be Done By", cable selection, Michael Caine on video choice . . . Yachting feature, everglades fashion, child pornography . . . Arabella?'

'Just a mention, Malcolm, about follow-up on de Winter.' (General laughter, lowering of eyes to table whilst smiling.) 'As you know, there's been quite a lot of letters in about our use of de Winter sites, and an awful lot of 'How-could-we-do-it-someone-might-have-been-killed-terrorism-isn't-funny', but on the other hand the clothes were very popular . . . '

'I wonder if de Winter's done a bunk,' chimed in Gemma unprofessionally; 'I mean, it's a bit bloody funny that he hasn't been arrested or something, isn't it?'

Arabella frowned. 'I believe that there's only that church thing left now – they're hardly likely to blow that up, are they?'

'I wonder who's doing it?' said Gemma. 'And incidentally, why don't we do a feature on churches? You know, the ones to be seen in, who worships where, the one's with the celebrity vicars, that kind of thing . . . ?

Malcolm noted down the idea in very small handwriting on his grey note pad. 'Churches,' he wrote and then '(Gemma?)'.

'Thanks Gem,' he whispered, nodding and flicked the point of his pen at her slightly by way of grateful acknowledgement for her input. Gemma immediately looked serious.

The meeting gradually broke up. A few people made suggestions as to the identity of the de Winter building bomber but fairly soon the attempts to be witty outweighed the educated guesses. As the team drifted back towards their offices their conversation slipstreamed back into the empty meeting room. 'I hear Dave Blax has started casting for the de Winter biopic . . . They want Terence Stamp and that girl with the hair who was in thingy . . . .'

Arabella sat down at her desk and ate a handful of seeds from the Seed Shop down the street. The little white plastic bag had 'Seed Shop' printed on it in black capital letters.

Malcolm went to Basta Manica in Percy Street to have lunch with a woman from the Victoria and Albert Museum who knew of an opening in design exhibitions. He was tired of trying to stay awake for long enough to keep London's diary, and even more tired of writing about the future of tomorrow last week or whatever it was that *Designate* used as an excuse. A few months in the job had kindled his ambition to be taken seriously by his friends in Holland Park. He would go for art history or documentaries perhaps. Something solid. There were only so many plausible moves in the arguments In Defence of Ephemera and most of those were in French and largely incomprehensible. A book was a possibility. He knew that Stefan Durand were looking for books on something artistic. Wide margins, hushed chatty text with footnotes and the all-important beautiful printing. The literary equivalent of being chatted up by a well-dressed librarian with a colourful past. Maybe that's what he would do. There had never been a decent history of aftershave, for example – a pan-cultural jog down the trail of the scent, the history of the hunk from Romeo to Rambo . . . . He'd maybe go to Minos and write a synopsis. He felt that back issues of *Designate* were tossed like unwanted bouquets onto the nearest grave. He wanted to contribute something serious. The future was such a lovely thing.

The Church of God the Truth (Tower Hill) was closed.

A black magnetic sign board with clip-on metal letraset announced the times of services, the hours of private consultation, and the last orders for the restaurant. Max de Winter watched the sun going down in the black glass of the front doors. He could see brakelights reflected in the windows. On the other side of the glass was a hedge of houseplants and potted moss.

Peering inside, he could see the Church of God the Truth bookshop. Large posters advertising holidays to India and curious roots were interspersed with garish depictions of the Holy Deity, who bore a striking resemblance to an elderly hairdresser or a second-division centre forward. His hands were outstretched from billowing white sleeves and he had a soft-core perm where the crown of thorns is generally supposed to be. Max wished all the faithful of this church could be sent on a one-way canalling holiday.

The church had been commissioned and paid for in cash by an American concern. Max was delighted to realise that he had blown up the receipt that survived from the transaction. But at the time it had all been conducted through property consultants in East Cheap – perfectly legal and the chance to do something sacred in teak. Laminated concrete, black glass and semiprecious metals had been the other desired materials. The money had probably been supplied by the wealthy and stupid youth of America and Europe who stood around in airports and places of historic interest looking for something to outrage their business-class parents with. Some put crazy-colour in their healthy bleached hair and others ran away to join an alternative religion. Max had no sympathy with them either – they just wanted to feel important or something. Who cares?

On Thursdays the church closed at six p.m. after evening purification. Thursday evening it would be, then – but how? The unused anniversary present of two Gucci suitcases could be utilised as bomb casing for light explosives. The rest could be simple arson. Max had not the slightest interest in doing his buildings in with a skilled technique – just as long as they were written off.

In the early hours of Thursday morning Max and Rebecca were talking on the telephone. Max was crammed between the side of his desk and a wall, cigarette ends heaped in the ashtray beside him, and Rebecca was lying on the mysteriously uncomfortable emotional fouton that she begrudgingly accepted as her mind.

'This mobile economy that goes up for young people', said Rebecca, 'seems to hinge largely upon a thinly disguised solipsistic stupidity punctuated with occasional flashes of animal cunning. They drift around expensive shops like the deranged predators that they are, picking lurid berries off the better bushes of London. They're humourless, like poems, they're sick.' Her voice was strained and breathless, her words coming in uneven bursts like the calypso beat of a hypochondriac's pulse. Her arm ached from holding the phone for so long. It was three in the morning.

'Above all', said Max, 'it's the need to be in company, to be in a meeting, to be on the phone. I can't sleep until I've made a call but there are very few people whom I would wish to speak to. I want an ansafone that will only play back messages when I'm out . . . .'

Rebecca stifled a yawn. She felt suddenly faint and drained. She thought about the windows in a modern flat in Chiswick, rain streaming down them during the night and a comforting cool smell of grass wafting peacefully into the blue bedroom that two anonymous friends were sleeping in. 'You were born too late, Max. You've chosen a life that is like the hardest building in London to find, right at the heart of a labyrinth, the labyrinth.'

'It's not that the building was hard to find, it's the roads that are so complicated . . . '.

Max was talking slowly, his phrases dropping heavily into the receiver like an old carpet being repeatedly hurled into the same canal. He knew he was inarticulate, and he was ever so slightly bored with the struggle to make his words servant to his meaning. He said, 'There was an orgy of social and business intercourse that surrounded de Winter Associates and surrounded every other concept, character and corporation that we came into contact with. I contracted syphilis from all that intercourse years ago, and now I'm left here raving *in extremis* in the late 1980s. There's a skip on every corner that I pass by and they're full of either builders' junk or *objets trouvés*, depending on the postal district and my mood. Outside all the little houses and across all the waiting sites, beside dual carriageways and down dark alleys. Maybe they are the body bags of some authorised war, the collected dead of the mass gentrification of the future. Now that my war is finishing I can see the future as a city of catalogue design against a backdrop of ruins. The strange thing is that after love there are fewer funnier topics than outraged dissent. I suppose that one day the skips will be taken away and the rubbish they contain pulped into transporter wagons to be dumped on an estuary in Essex. Even the seagulls will think twice before they dip down into the dumps of Dartford to pick for bugs amongst the debris.'

He hung up. The night stretched ahead, empty. Fewer topics funnier than love . . . . If Max was ever to deliver a final sermon – and there was little chance of that now – it was love that he would take as his theme, not vandalism, and he would speak with reference to those of the yellow polka dot sash whose perfect legs never caught the rough end of anything. Those with possession of a hero to cheer them up when their muscles are tired in some little night spot that caters for their sort. When strange doorways open in the life of some Donna or Diamanda – bit of a farce played out with lip gloss and shimmer cheeks, and it's not cheap but it seems so cool and desirable . . . perhaps. Love, thought Max, was a pastoral conceit, but he knew that his lawns were made of concrete and his flower-beds were of ice-rimed anthracite. Beneath the drowsing chestnut trees of previous summers someone had poured turpentine onto the crustless sandwiches of his lonely and emotional picnic.

In front of the car park of the Church of God the Truth there was a small acreage of wasteland. This battered oblong of stone-filled white mud, an urban field, was caramelised by the autumn sunshine and bordered on three sides by Bitterness, Anger and Loneliness. These non-fluid commodities were fixed by market forces, their joint effect not-negotiable within any deal of real-estate.

A petroleum slick spread its dusty violet palm across the surface of a muddied puddle next to Anger, and a platoon of adolescent nettles leant wearily against Loneliness. On Bitterness there hung a stone-scuffed notice, its message scrawled by an unknown copy writer in childish capitals, each letter painstakingly drawn out with a stick dipped in creosote:

Our padre is an old sky pilot,
Severely now they've clipped his wings . . .
Good Old Padre! God for the Services!
Row like smoke . . . !

In the past this melancholy zone had been where the Council Daughters of Bermondsey and New Cross would meet to hear the steel breeze playing through some wire. In the summer, when the dusty trees wore their blouses open, one could hear romantic lyrics like textbook Latin, the sweet voices of the girls – 'Do you, do you, do you, do you like our eyes? Our eyes are sixteen years old. Do you like them? Do you want them? Do you know about our eyes?' Ghosts.

Now, in September, this area enclosed by three strange fences contained a showroom-new Mercedes minus its windscreen and a complicated freestanding structure made out of an old ironing board and a classroom map of the political geography of the world. The coast of South America had twisted itself inelegantly around the steel strut of the legs, whilst the ripped surface of the board was covered with the sky-blue fabric that denoted the Central Atlantic. Europe, the Soviet Union and the greater part of Australasia hung heavily over the other side. There was a gash in the map between Nanking and the northern tip of Borneo into which some roguish or simply distracted passer-by had slipped a neatly folded advertisement. The capital letters on the protruding fold announced 'BREATH TA' with an unremitting confidence in their legibility.

The Mercedes belonged to Max de Winter and the loss of its windscreen to some junior vandal was of no importance to him. The sculpture – for sculpture the map and ironing board were – had been purchased by Max for many thousands that same Thursday morning from Rebecca de Winter Fine Art Ltd, Cork Street W1. He had had it placed on the little area of wasteland as a permanent loan from de Winter Associates to the City of London.

But things must mean something, however confusing their

initial appearance, and translation – unseen – is difficult. There are so many attempts to be crossed out before a fair copy can be nervously handed in to history, a friend of England. The working out in the margin – that which winds up in the skip – is confusion, the by-product of translation: artificial roses dripping under artificial spring showers in a department store, modern art stacked in a builders' yard in south London – what truth value does the ambiguous product of looking for the right answer have in artistic terms? It is the Art of The Great Crossing Out, and Max de Winter's gift to the City of London was a modern masterpiece of this genre, skip-junk art and priceless rubbish.

There was a brief talk about reincarnation after Evening Purification. That particular Thursday evening found a number of the Church of God the Truth congregation sitting with little cups of fruit juice as they listened to an official of the church explain about the various stages of the Life Eternal. During the progress of the soul from one body to the next, it was dictated by the Church of God the Truth that the spirit – or 'Truth', as they called it – never in fact changed. Leslie or Janet in 1758 were the same Leslie or Janet in 1958, it was simply the body that changed. God suppressed memory at the start of each new body-tenancy and it was only to a Chosen Few, high up in the administration of the Church of God the Truth, that a kind of spiritual season ticket was made available to allow commuting at will through a succession of lives in order to return to the present and tell the faithful about God's intentions, world plan and immediate financial problems. The Church of God the Truth did terribly well out of the money raised by these tele-theological sponsored walks.

The problem was one of moral purity, and the Church of God the Truth had exclusive rights to the TCP of the soul. They annexed this programme of expensive spiritual hygiene to a lot of pseudopolitical lifestyling, the backbone of which seemed to be enforced cheerfulness – the proof of which was singing, laughing and physically threatening The Uncheerful.

As Max de Winter leant quietly against a fire extinguisher he could not help but smile at the thought that he, a man who had doubtless been reincarnated into his present life some twenty minutes too late and was therefore cursed for ever with a complete awareness of his history and that of his context, should be the chosen assassin to blow this phoney temple of evangelical conmen half way to the Elephant and Castle. He could only hope that those who attended it would not be permitted the luxury of martyrdom. They would be – it was inevitable – but he would at least have done his bit by destroying the one structure that associated his name with theirs, like the banks, insurance companies and software firms that he sought to have no relation with.

After the little talk Max left with the rest of the congregation and went to sit in his car whilst the church was locked up. A cold wind blew through the smashed windscreen and so he put a cassette of English poetry reading on the in-car stereo. Betjeman's wavering voice filled the car with a poem that Max knew by heart:

I used to stand by intersecting lanes
Among the silent offices, and wait,
Choosing which bell to follow: not a peal
For that meant somewhere active; not at St Paul's,
For that was too well-known. I like things dim –
Some lazy rector living in Bexhill
Who most unwillingly on Sunday came
To take the statutory services . . .

Soon it was time to commence the attack. He trudged through the chill air up to the main doors of the church and, shrugging, smashed the glass with a spanner and let himself in. Checking that the building was empty, he made his way back to the car and took out his detonator, coil of fuse wire and the two Gucci suitcases packed full of explosives. Like a travelling salesman crawling wearily up to the lobby of a motorway motel near Leeds, Max heaved the machinery of his vandalism into the foyer of the Church of God the Truth. He began to feel quite humorous – there was an end-of-term feeling to the exercise, the terrorist's equivalent of being allowed to bring in games.

He made his way to the congregation area where a pool of moonlight was washing around the legs of the stacked chairs. His plan was quite simple: the two suitcases contained explosives and detonators. He would connect the suitcases up to the main detonator with fuse wire and then put one at either end of the hall. Before he set them off he would douse the rest of the place with petrol.

Having placed one suitcase beneath a poster of some flamingos flying into a tropical sunset with 'Life' written underneath them in sentimental italics, he put the other one beneath the entrance to the hall. He began to wire them up, whistling 'Jerusalem' to himself in a workmanlike manner. His good humour continued; as he walked stealthily backwards with the reel of fuse wire he began singing quietly to himself:

'I'll build a stairway to Paradise . . .
I'm going to get there at any price . . .'

Max suddenly heard a noise behind him, the tinkling and crunching of someone walking softly over broken glass. He held his breath for a second and inwardly cursed all those he had known in the past who might possibly have a reason to rumble him. A second later he realised that retrospective threats are amongst the most pathetic of all so he abandoned himself wholeheartedly to whatever drastic measures the present moment might require. He stood up and slowly turned around. It was Rebecca. She walked slowly towards him, and even in the darkness of the church hall he could make out her face. Her eyes were fixed upon him and she had been crying. Her mouth couldn't smile but Max knew that in some posthumous kind of way she still loved him. Her hair was longer than it had been when he last saw her getting into her car on the drive at New Manderley one fine April morning earlier that year. She hadn't been smiling then either; she had simply told him that it wasn't working and driven away. That was the day that Max walked down the cliff path and threw their wedding album into the sea. Once thrown it lay open face down in the surf, and hunched upon each foaming bar in a tireless attempt to lurch back onto the shore. The soft coda of the tide had sentimentalised this blind progress, making melodrama out of rubbish.

The pages of the album had separated into two distinct hemispheres of compressed pulp beneath the laminated surface of their covers. An equatorial line of rotten stitching was all that had secured that old world to its spine, and soon the corroding ribs of brittle glue broke with the back of the book to make a final divide. As the sea flashed under the passage of a cloud the individual pages floated away, offering the loosening photographs to be christened with new meanings in the endless manoeuvres of a vast and indifferent font.

He took Rebecca in his arms, and felt her tense and nervous against him as he always had done. After a moment she relaxed, put her hands up to his face and kissed him.

'How did you know I was here?' Max asked, more out of curiosity than a fear of discovery.

'Some girl called Arabella rang me up from a magazine. She wasn't very coherent. Do you know her?'

Max shook his head. 'She's from *Designate*. They wanted to do a feature on me . . . '

Rebecca was silent. They walked over to a little stage that ran along the back wall of the hall.

'Does this go up tonight?' Rebecca asked. Max nodded.

The church was becoming darker. The fading parenthesis of detail that the moonlight had picked out was now little more than a wistful afterthought. Rebecca's road to this wired-up church had been a curious one but, having arrived, what was she to do? Who would she talk to now? What does a girl do when her hem is too high or too low, when her husband is a socially fêted architect who decides to turn to terrorism, when there is graffiti on her pedestal and a long drop to the plinth? *Designate* built pedestals out of balsa wood and Rebecca knew all about profile features and the weight they carried. If only she had been an arbitrator, or an arbitrator's wife . . . .

There was little need now, in the Church of God the Truth, for a guiding voice to lead her through the gathering darkness. 'I am not a guide,' the voice would say. The boat of Max and Rebecca de Winter's life together was now ready to push out into the night, indifferent to its course beyond the harbour wall. For them, the perfect couple, any time, any place, anywhere, astronomical navigation was simply a game of chance, with the stars strewn like diamonds across a gambler's velvet.

Max lit a sacred candle without leaving his Visa card number and brought it over to where they were sitting. Rebecca's head inclined into the little shell of light and Max recalled the rest of the poem he had been listening to:

All silvery on frosty Sunday nights
Were City steeples white against the Stars.
And narrowly the chasms wound between
Italianate counting houses – Roman Banks
To this Church and to that. Huge office doors
Their granite thresholds worn by weekday feet
(Now far away in slippered ease at Penge),
Stood locked. St Botolph this, St Mary that
Alone stood out resplendent in the dark.

What would Society have made of this meeting? There was always someone ready to comment, some rattler in the *Tatler*, some maggot. The City slept around them. They did not know whether it was indifference that surrounded them or the massive silence of an artificial intelligence that they had become too tired, or too confused, to find stupid. Max pondered the future's assessment of his campaign of violence. Evidence would be sifted at artistic and clerical levels in an attempt to find the truth but it would never be found. There is nothing like a determination to see things clearly for bringing on a spiritual myopia. Every time a journalist passed by an accident they might think of Max de Winter, that was all. Even if Max were to step forward and remove the mask that he had worn during his disguised advance it would only reveal the plastic surgery underneath.

Across the street the vagrants were coming out of nowhere to sleep on the site in front of the church where Max de Winter's art loan to the City was standing. By the glow of a dozen arc lamps which hung from the gallows-like scaffolding in one corner it was possible to see the parcels of cardboard and dumps of plastic carrier bags being corralled about home fires of street debris. The vagrants were an army camped out on manoeuvres, a transit camp between the nothing and nowhere of London UK where the track-furrowed mud made loam lips that winter would silence with frozen water.

The vagrants quickly dismantled the sculpture, finding more

practical uses for its medium of classroom map and ironing board. They harvested daily from the tidemark of rubbish that collected around the edges of the site: sherry-soaked newsprint, sex magazines and back issues of *Designate* burst out of plastic bin liners, and features on Hair Gel and Italian furniture were half read in the cold whilst Sandra or Angie, Yvonne or Bibette spread her legs to the sleet off other faded pages that flapped over all night in the wind.

The vagrants began to bed down on mattresses of cardboard, others sitting up on broken stack chairs or blue milk crates to drink in little groups around the litter fires whose lights could be seen from the Church of God the Truth two hundred metres away.

One day a new crown would be skilfully balanced by some future architect on the edges of this prime-site abcess in the City. It would rise up elegantly on the rotten gums of dirt that held together this barren plate of land.

Inside the church Max and Rebecca had wired up the suitcases of explosives to the detonator. The floor was soaked with petrol. They sat side by side by the light of their candle in front of what they took to be an altar. It could have been their final marriage.

All that remained was to push down the button on the detonator. Very gently they both rested their hands upon it, united at last. The candle suddenly wavered for a moment, throwing up huge shadows and a bright light. Max turned to Rebecca and then there was darkness.

'Why – the candle's out . . . ' he said.

Rebecca softly pushed her hand down on his.

'Twas I who blew it,' she whispered, 'Dear . . . '

The Fear of Heaven

by

Don Watson

1 Rollercoaster
2 Wake
3 Silvered Shadows
4 A Cold Plunge
5 Undertow
6 Eurydice in Mirrors
7 The Scars of Memory (1)
8 A Network of Recall
9 Mnemosyne, goddess of the Railway
10 Memory Spotting
11 Sirens over Lake Geneva
12 Stillness over the Rails
13 In Transit Veritas
14 Force
15 Cipher (1)
16 Eurydice in Ruins
17 Diving
18 Dawning
19 Prey (1)
20 Cipher (2)
21 Sweet Sickness
22 Drifing
23 The Wings of Morpheus
24 Cloister
25 Poppy Fields

Rollercoaster

And over the hill once more, the coiled spring of anticipated speed clenched in his stomach . . . .

Ghosts of cities pursue J through the final dark cycles of his sleep, motorway intersections meeting in a vanishing point of tail-lights. Liquid sodium dances in the flickering gaps of the railway bridge. In the distance, the yellow glare of a distant constellation of street lights wheels past, its light made brighter by the action of motion immaculate.

Perched once more on the brow, hovering, a predatory bird in the lull before the rush of the descent . . . .

Alien spires pierce the horizon. In the glittering edifice of mirrors rising slowly in the light, the reflections of tower blocks ripple with the lazy distortion of a heat haze.

Before this carriage there was a platform and the line of the roof across the rails scored black against the sky. The framework of the roof was broken, revealing the eroded bones of rusted stanchions like the skeleton of a leaf, and allowing a few weak beams of sunlight to fall on the far end of the dust of the platform surface. Two small children held a precarious balance in the rays, their cries rising and ringing with the iron above them.

From the hole in the roof, its edges curled and soft, a wound in decaying fruit, burst a flutter of small birds, spiralling, twittering and scattering, leaving the station haunted by nothing but the sounds of the ghosts in the wires.

Before this platform there was an entrance hall, lined with curling and cancelled timetables; there were the lines around the eyes of the station's sole attendant, seams packed with the dust that settled by the second on the peak of his hat, on the single rusted mail trolley.

Sometimes it fell so dense that vision became impossible. And, after the dust settled, there was nothing but visions of the railways.

A harshly illuminated waiting room glowing in the darkness, footsteps falling slowly as the drizzle, J's reflection imposed on the harsh image of the slumped figure inside on the bench.

Passenger or derelict? Or something in between, a gentleman not of the road but of the railway café, a wanderer across the lines. Was this the end of J's own addiction? Half asleep somewhere in the wastelands of analogue culture, alien cells blinking all around him, lower lip jutting and the neon shine of dribble glittering, silver wisps of hair floating in the flecked artificial light.

Sometimes sounds filtered through the memories – a symphony of silicon from a distant new town, concrete forms lurking in the darkness, the discordant chorus of synthesised blips grating through the cold air and the soot. The sound of one digital watch alarm, followed by another on a different tone, and a deeper, lower sound, like a warning tone, the sound of an electronic siren in the distance, cries from the electronic abattoir.

He could hear it all filtering through the moisture. He could feel them out there in the dark, plotting, cloning and regenerating. He remembered windows flashing past, a series of single travellers, a couple, a group of soldiers. Like flicking through TV channels.

Sitting on the brow once more, the halt of a moment's silence, the splendour of the landscape stretched out before him.

And before the entrance hall there was – nothing but the dust, thick as television static.

As J watches, the ripple of the images judders to a halt before his eyes, leaving a frozen screen flooded with mercury, hardening to a mirror's surface, leaving him with his own reflection. Looking deep into the eyes for a trace of past or future, he sees only the reflection of movement, a gaze that reveals no past behind the rushing landscape of the present. The reflection rises in the distance, looming over a carriage now stripped of its outer casing.

He and his fellow passengers, the wind now playing in their hair, could feel the suffocating rush of acceleration deep within them, the air forced through open mouths straining lungs to the point of bursting, membranes stretched to a pale tension.

Across the aisle, a girl's hair explodes into a sandstorm of motion in front of her face, strands caught in the red line of her lipstick, her grimace stretched back by the acceleration, the hair flickering between her teeth. Her movements revealed in successive and discrete frames, a progression of still photographs:

CLICK – her face covered by a veil of dark hair.

CLICK – her neck arched against the movement, a line of teeth white against dark red lipstick. The frame bleeds elation.

CLICK – her head flung back, the lips stretched, their colour blanched. In her eyes a look of terror.

Somewhere behind these images crouched something terrible, something . . . nothing . . . before this journey there was . . . there could be . . . nothing.

Once more at the peak of the hill, suspended for a moment in stillness, looking down at the progression of the tracks towards the huge carnival head on the opposite hill, a grotesque parody of his own image. In the eyes, the ghosts of cities, dark-eyed ghouls prowling blank-faced through dismal back streets, their pallor luminous.

On the soundtrack the screams rise. J watches the features change, assuming the gaudy colours of a fairground prop, the lips and cheeks reddening, the face bleaching white and the area around the eyes exploding in colour. He could hear the yelps and shouts around him.

As he continued to look, the red brightened, its colour the ten cent revelation of a cheap religious icon. Reaching a glowing peak, it burst into flames, its substance flaring quickly into gaping holes, newspaper laid over a flame.

As he walked down the hillside, the light was fading, transforming the intricate frame that had held the face into a charred silhouette. As the light dipped lower, the glow of embers could be seen. One of the joints collapsed, leaving a gaping hole in the structure.

Wake

The twisted frames of derelict buildings intruded on the last spirals of J's sleep, memories of machinery clanking in their wake. The dull noise pursued him towards consciousness.

The jolt that finally woke him wasn't the sense of movement, rather the sensation of its absence. His neck jerking, he looked up, meeting the sight of a smeared windowpane.

Through each frame, the only thing that was visible was a blank whiteness, due either to the absence of the outside world or to the density of the brown-green film that seemed to have formed on the outside – or perhaps the inside – of the glass, lending an underwater calm to the scene. He ran a dry tongue round his mouth and noted the presence of a similar substance.

Achieving at last a minium mobility in his neck, he began to look around. In the corner a radiator encased in an iron cage was rattling piteously. J noted that some benevolent passer-by with large boots and a larger sense of indignation at the senseless confinement of dumb heating implements had made a gallant attempt to liberate the radiator, buckling the cage severely. This made J feel better about the human race, although it didn't do much for the throbbing pain that was beginning to afflict the bridge of his nose.

Through the window, vague outlines were beginning to etch themselves on the blankness.

A green bench stood across from the one that J had woken on, empty apart from a few crumpled lager cans. Lines of conversation began to cut through the mist that enveloped his memory, laughter shaking the radiator cage, shouts echoing around the concrete of the room.

Before this waiting room there was . . . what? His finger traced a figure of eight in the dust of the bench's surface. The sound of a muffled voice from beyond the window proved the continuing existence of the outside world.

Suddenly J was conscious of a dripping sound to his right. He turned quickly, regretting it immediately as he felt a sharp pain in the nerves at the back of his neck. Through the sunblindness of the pain, he recognised another presence in the room.

On the bench adjacent to his own sat a hunched figure, his hair flowing back from his receding hairline and tumbling over the greasy back of his tattered military jacket. His moustache was profuse, bordering on the surreal, drops of liquid still glistening in its burgeoning growth. By his side stood an upturned can of lager, its contents dripping off the bench and making slow and spider-like inroads into the dirt on the waiting-room floor.

'Morning,' said J, uncertain as he did so whether it was statement, enquiry or greeting. The dark irises swam through a bloodshot 180 degrees to fix an uncertain focus on him. J looked quickly away, not out of any innate shyness but because the undulation of the man's pupils was making him feel seasick. The man pulled out one of the two remaining cans by his side and proffered one to J.

J's eyes and stomach leapt simultaneously. Pulling the ring, he swallowed his stomach and hit it with a belt of lukewarm fizz to keep it down.

'Thanks,' he belched.

A small tear squeezed out of the reddened corner of the man's eye, running in a straight line until it hit the burst vein that bulged from a bulbous breakage in the enormous nose, running a streak across a cheek touched by the waiting room's dust and settled amidst the beer drops in the nicotine-streaked moustache.

'The walrus wept,' thought J to himself. The sour smell of vinegar wafted past his nostrils; he traced it back to a crumpled chip paper over in the corner of the room, settled amidst a small pile of things, many of which might at one time have been vaguely edible.

Even through the green smear, the outside world was begining to materialise through the clouds. J could see the opposite platform emerging in grey, the arches of the station pillars, iron dripping bilge green, and the rust of the corrugated roof. A sudden beam of sunlight bled down diagonally across the platform, freezing the form of a leonine black woman, her elegance ethereal and timeless amidst the trickling rot of the station. A streak of condensation ran across the windowpane, catching a glint as it went.

The hiss of a beer can opening dragged J back inside the stale smoke of the waiting room, the ring-pull releasing memories of the night before. The place before the waiting room still belonged to the mist. He didn't know how he got here, or indeed which one of a national chain of waiting rooms this was. He did remember that in the moments before unconsciousness caught him there had been quite a party here.

There had been the walrus, of course, he had been here before anybody, part of the furniture, coloured in the regulation slime green. He had sat silently, with an entire crate of beer, proffering one occasionally to J, but stubbornly meeting requests from others with silent, flinty stares. The rest of the time he peered directly through the opening of his can, held reverentially in two hands as if it contained his private oracle.

Then there were the soul boys, whose clothes accurately reflected the wide range of colours of vomit, from a relatively healthy two-tone yellow and green to a there-goes-my-stomach-lining shade of pink.

The company was completed by a pair of French au pair girls, who seemed to have travelled all the way from Paris, or so they claimed, for such exclusive pleasures as this – sharing a waiting room with the walrus, the sputum spectrum soul patrol and J himself, a dazed Orpheus unable to look back for fear of the sight of his Eurydice in flames.

The tear still glistened in the walrus's moustache, catching some of the light that now dared to cast a beam through the dank of the waiting room. With a single gesture he turned another half empty can upside down, bubbles bursting in the froth as it flooded the floor, the dust playing in patterns on its convex surface.

As the sound of the door shutting died away and J disappeared into the sunlight, its angry fizz did battle with the clanking from the radiator.

Silvered Shadows

J runs a hand through his hair, the strands falling back immediately across his forehead, coiling dark against pale skin.

'There is nothing in my memory but a twist of ugly dreams.'

Walking towards where the platform meets the mist, he is a shadowed figure, enfolded in blank white light.

The past doesn't creep up on you, it maintains a respectful distance; you may not feel it breathing down your neck, but you can hear its footsteps, or the sound of its voices, voices without echoes. You are the only echo.

His imagination whirred into motion, the sound of a old film projector, the dust of a generation of junk-shop storage spilling from its spools and hanging in its beam. Foreign memories flicker, the home movies of some stranger, long dead. Ghostly faces flare a livid white as they loom on the shaky camera.

The picture resolves to a scene of recent destruction, now calm, the dust settling, silent as snow, its carpet shining silver in the moonlight.

J can see his own image, his face a pale glare sliced diagonally by deep shadow, piles of rubble casting jagged shapes across his path. In his shadow, another identical image, pursued by another and yet another into infinite regress.

As the sunlight falls on his face, the vision evaporates, leaving him to stare down the platform, past the elegant parade of lamps and down towards the vanishing point where the rails fade into the mist that still hangs over the unseen realms beyond the station.

The past, he had heard it said, was a foreign country. It certainly was for him. J was proud to disavow himself of any claim of heritage on the England that he watched unfold beyond the train window. So why, he wondered, should the ghosts of this country pursue him, stepping through the rubble of its shattered beliefs? Perhaps the past had echoes after all.

Walking back past the waiting room, he peered in the window, catching sight of the walrus. His head lying on his hand, he was sleeping, huddled like a refugee on the bench. His face, which vacillated between the troubled and the threatening while awake, had relaxed into soft and peaceful folds. J walked past and left him.

It would never have occurred to J to ask the walrus who he was or where he was going, any more than it would to volunteer the information on his own behalf. The conceit which travellers employed to eradicate their hours in the station's vacuum was one which was foreign to him; he felt no need for the constant reference to the Utopian state of the destination, no need to imagine the world that supposedly lay beyond the limbo of the station.

The glowing light of the destination plays on the face of the traveller; J by contrast had become a wanderer, a face in the darkness of the window, illuminated only briefly by the flares of warfare. 'Fallen angels,' she'd said, 'afflicted by the fear of heaven.'

Her words pursued him from beyond the mist. J walking through the shadow of the platform was their only echo.

A Cold Plunge

As J passes a hand across his brow, dazzled by the clarity of the light, the gesture is replicated by a dark-haired girl, adrift in white sheets, somewhere in north London. Her window is paned with thick glass, lined with lead, ivy twining around the borders of its frame. The sun streams down towards the dark carpet, almost tangible.

Stretching her hand out to the beam, she opens and closes the fingers as if trying out a new limb. The hand drops, lying limp by the bed. Her eyelids are closed, her face expressionless, still softened by the shadows of sleep, yet on its silvered blankness thoughts flicker, monochrome, jerky movements.

Imagine the job of the tube train driver. Was it in the contract? she wondered – the employee will be expected, if necessary, to stare death in the face.

What could it be like to look right into the eyes of the living end of this unknown figure as it slumps off the platform? What is it like to see that pale face looking at you, and know that it is looking at death? Does a foreign life flash up in the tube train windscreen, a TV drama flickering at subliminal speed?

Do they see a last regret, a moment's fear, or helpless resignation in the suicide's face as the train flies towards them? Do they experience impossible pain as they feel the impact and hear the body break, or do they, in their private little cells at the front of the train, secretly glory in the elimination of another failure?

Karen fingered the last communication from her sister. It was a skilled, cartoonish representation of the two of them, drawn in biro. Karen was represented as a skewered doll, her sister as a triumphant, vengeful angel. AND CAIN SLEW ABEL. The words were streaked in red painter's ink. 'I care nothing', read the scrawl underneath, 'for ties of blood, or ties of shit.'

Down below she could hear the low moan of her mother wailing, the deep boom of her uncle's voice. She closed her eyes once more and saw a wall of screaming mouths.

Undertow

Wild cranes trace elegant spirals through the pre-storm stillness of J's imagination; their cries pursue the lost line of the horizon as the rattle of the rails indicates the train's approach.

The anticipation of motion rising within him, J watches his reflection flashing in each passing window. In the wild stare of his eyes, the after-image of the story lingers, dark circles shadowing the drama. In each of the gaps between the windows he reaches out towards the memory, then recoils once again into the refuge of his own reflection.

He knew that his appearance was disturbing to others. It was a revelation to discover just how quickly his face had taken on the mark of a lifestyle unacceptable to the world through which he passed. The mark of Cain, a restless wanderer on the face of the earth.

How long had he been this way? He struggled to recall. Recoil. Recall. His thoughts struggled through the cries of the cranes, but somehow the distance seemed impossible. Had he come too far already? Had he come too far already? Too many rows of blackened, broken windows, too many endless moments bathing in the rusted light that leaked from deserted junkyards.

Reality, the system of consecutive time, was bound by the orbit of commuters he occasionally found himself among. J for his part had amassed sufficient speed to break from the pattern. He was a random electron, hurtling off in a direction no longer bound by the rule.

How long?

Recall.

Recoil.

'And yet once more my own reflection, dusted by the mist of my own breath.'

Despite the glare from his eyes and the pallor that seemed to hang on his cheeks, J found his reflection a source of comfort. So often now it seemed to be the only thing he could cling to and lately even that seemed to be somehow shifting, a change that spread like the fur that now lined his mouth.

The train was slowing, the distance between the flashes of his image lengthening, the gaps now too long to be easily dismissed. As the after-image of his reflection decayed, it seemed to transform, slowly, its haunting difference seeping through, the sadness that seemed to shine from her skin.

His mind wheeled once more around the fact, a random orbit around the truth, the moth around the inevitable flame. Every time his thoughts reached out he allowed himself to be carried once more by the drift.

The train had now stopped. He reached for the door slowly, feeling himself trapped in a slow-motion sequence. The beer he had drunk was beginning to curdle in his empty stomach. As the train pulled away he felt the drift pulling, powerful as the motion.

He looked across the rails, catching sight of the children playing. Their cries rang in the iron of the station roof, plaintive, like the cries of wild cranes.

Eurydice in Mirrors

As the train snaked through the wastelands of a city's outskirts, J focused his eyes on his own reflection in the window. Beyond his cheekbones reeled a landscape of broken brick and splintered glass. A cluster of dark metal lay rotting, slow as the crawl of his thoughts. The ghost of his outline was thin against the sunlight that streamed through the train, the face indistinct.

J was drawn in his own image, drowning in the eyes; like some tragic Narcissus of the railways he watched his reflection on its way to death. Mythical figures flitted through the destruction of the landscape – Orpheus facing the ticket inspector. Sorry mate, the return on this ticket's out of date. A fallen water-tower passed beyond the shadow of his cheekbones. Still the image was haunted by the geometry of another face.

That look, which seemed somehow to burn its way through the retina, straight through to the senses. That look, as if some unfathomable tragedy were taking place behind her eyes. Her face was an expansion of the sadness, a golden section between beauty and pain.

Light burned liquid on a rush of reeded water, stabbing at the back of his eyes. In the golden glare he saw a figure, the obscenity of its gyration reflected back by a barrage of mirrors.

Even after the sunblind spots had settled, he could not excise her image. He recalled the doomed air she carried with her, how it seemed to soften the sharp lines of her angular face, as if a mist had somehow formed between its pale surface and the eye of the observer.

With the memory of her face came the memory of that feeling, the feeling he'd had at the first glimpse of her, like something inside him curling up and quietly giving up the ghost.

He remembered an article in an old newspaper he'd found in a waiting room somewhere – even into J's dimension the news from the outside world penetrated eventually. Its subject was the syndrome of death from an overdose of beauty – strange to read in a waiting room in the midst of the drizzle of English marshland.

It seemed that certain visitors to Italy, particularly middle-aged women travelling alone, were so overcome by the beauty of Renaissance paintings that they would simply gasp a last ecstatic breath and cease upon the chapel floors.

Petra's face seemed to shadow the image of these silent deaths. Like a Renaissance crucifixion, she too reeked of suffering and death, but so beautifully you could lose your breath to look at her.

The twisted shape of the fire escape leading from a broken-down warehouse pulled him into the battered vortex of memory, back towards the chromium staircase of a cellar night club. He remembered the bank of televisions flickering along one wall, each one of them seeming to reflect visions of a landscape of decay, like some twilight prediction of his current odyssey. But then his memory played so many tricks nowadays. Crucifixions seemed to shadow his dreams as he dozed on the rattle of the rails.

Memories do not unfold, they reel around like malfunctioning film shows, snatches of dialogue seeping through the white noise.

As J watched, the images on the televisions changed one by one, the momentum of the motion they reflected was maintained, translating itself into footage of a bombing raid. Seen from the point of view of the planes, the ground rushed below as the bombs were released. Their descent was slow and elegant, each contained in its own bubble of silence.

The air inside the club was a cacophony of electronic noise. Black figures flitted in front of the televisions. The bombs on the screen landed, casting red and orange shadows on the faces of the club's clientele.

Suddenly amidst the blur J had noticed Petra, walking down the spiral staircase by the entrance. Her pale face glared in a column of light descending from the ceiling. The mist hung around her like silence. She walked lightly through the glow, a figure licked by flames.

Her face possessed an ethereal blankness that seemed to place it in a different dimension from the narcoleptic flickering of the television screens. Her manner was distant, but not offhand, as if unaffected by J's presence. He offered to buy her a drink, and her face somehow broke, a weak smile recomposing itself from the fragments. There was a sad acknowledgement in her eyes.

'Why not?' she'd said. Her voice was perfect, untouched by an accent, but her words seemed full to bursting point. She ordered a vodka martini. Her hands were delicate and bony, a pinched pink; they shook slightly as she reached for the glass.

He could still feel now the energy that seemed to flood from her, a dizzying exhilaration that found its echo in the kick of motion. He watched the landscape passing behind the transparent screen of his memories, shattered frameworks and rubble. Addictions like energy never disappear, they only change in their form.

She held her drink in a greedy grip, looking deep into the glass, staring lovingly into the oblivion it offered. 'Inside me,' she'd said, 'there's nothing, just a hollow.' Her lip curled with a look of childish concentration. 'I want everything, I'll take everything to try and fill the emptiness, but I never will.'

He'd started to say something, cut off by a bitter laugh.

'And don't go thinking you can do it for me, you can't.'

On the screens, a man's hand hit a woman's face, her hair flicking across her features. She looked back towards the camera, resentment burning in her eyes. The sequence was repeated.

The Scars of Memory (1)

J watched the sequence flashing again and again on the train window, the impact of a hand on a pale and perfect cheek. Every time it recurred, he felt himself wince.

Beyond the shadows, the early brightness had given way to a heavy cloud, ruptured every now and then by a powerful beam of sunlight, a divine revelation reigning on a landscape of ruin. Razor-thin slashes of rain slowly filled the window, the occasional beam of sunlight bristling across their intersecting patterns.

There seemed now to be no escape; the touching of any sense set the pictures flowing, the flickering film show rolling on against its background of yellowed window frames, dingy rooms and smoke-dyed net curtains. He remembered the miniature bottles of brandy he'd stolen from an unattended buffet trolley, and reached into his bag. The spirit's dreamy texture sent him drifting back once more.

The razor cuts of rain lashed against his reflection in the window.

'I know about you,' he'd said, his mouth running on with the drink; 'I've seen your arms.' The sleeves of her simple black top had ridden up during the course of their conversation. She began to tug at one self-consciously, in an attempt to pull it back down.

Before she could move he had her by the wrist, twisting her arm back round to reveal the scars that stood livid against her skin. A face looms in towards the camera. The swoop of the bird is silent, its talons like razors.

She looked straight back at his gaze, her eyes flashing furiously. He felt all of a sudden as if he'd been discovered reading a private diary. Her mouth was pursed in indignation, opening out into a snarl. A wisp of fine black hair fell over her face and intersected with the twist of her lip. Her anger seemed to scorch through the clouds of her eyes.

Sitting in the train carriage, J could feel the memory cool, the feeling of the window against his forehead. 'I'm sorry' – the words fell through once more. 'It's not even just your face its written all over.' He'd let go of her wrist, the arm falling once more, its story written in criss-crossed cuts.

She looked back at her drink. When her gaze returned to him it seemed strangely misaligned. 'Oh sure,' she said, 'sure you know, I can feel those little beady eyes of yours staring straight through my flesh. But do you understand?'

'Perhaps more than you'd like to admit.' J looked straight back at her. He had the sensation for a second that she was falling away from him, flailing out for something to hold on to, just anything.

Then her eyes fell once more.

'I'm leaving.' she said.

'I'll come with you.'

'Don't expect much,' she countered.

'I never expect anything.'

As they left the screens were flaring a scarlet, luminescent red.

A Network of Recall

Time seemed to be a problem for J these days. It seemed as if the morning had still been with him only a few stops back along the line, and yet the light was already falling, pouring through the windows of deserted warehouses. Its beams pierced the train, leaving J suspended in the last rays.

He watched as the train passed the shell of yet another factory. The arches of its roof stood intact, lightshades still hanging from the empty frame, but the walls now lay in rubble, spare flesh shaken off. The dying light scorched J's eyes; in the patterns of the sunblindness he saw bleached bones in the sands of the Orient.

His reveries were interrupted as the door at the end of the carriage burst open. Through the shapes of dying cells falling across his vision J saw a pair of eyes on stalks entering at great speed. Blinking in alarm, he recognised the figure of the walrus lurching towards him.

'We're safe,' hissed the dishevelled creature, collapsing in the seat opposite J.

J looked blank. The walrus's eyes were bulging with enthusiasm.

'There's none of them on the train,' he continued.

'Them?' J asked the question tentatively; the last thing he wanted right now was to get embroiled in yet another paranoid fantasy. His fellow nomads were often a breeding ground for a particularly tedious strain of conspiracy theory. When you're on the move it's all the easier to see that everyone really is out to get you.

It wasn't the general principle that J disagreed with. A paranoid might very well, in the words of the popular witticism, be someone who really knows what's going on. Unfortunately he usually suffers delusions of knowing *why*, which is what makes him such poor conversational value.

'Surely by now,' the walrus continued, 'you've realised that it's a matter of us and them.' J had a terrible feeling of impending doom about this exchange. Looking into the walrus's eyes, he could see a monologue hatching.

'We regard travel around this marvellous country of theirs to be the inalienable right of the individual. They expect us to pay for the privilege.'

For the first time the walrus had strung enough words together to allow J to discern his Irish accent. So here was another Celtic wanderer, a stranger in a land much stranger than it seems. J looked towards the window once more – a radar dish drifted past, all floodlit luminous white and glowing green. It seemed to get stranger the more you saw of it.

'Us and them,' the walrus went on, now bouncing slightly in his seat. 'The eternal conflict.'

J just carried on looking blank.

'The ticket inspectors, boy, the ticket inspectors!'

He banged the table hard for emphasis, sending J's empty miniature bottle flying. Picking it up again, he studied it for a second, seeming to calm down.

'You wouldn't have another one of these now, would you?' he asked, almost quietly.

J rummaged around in his bag for a second and silently proffered the walrus another of the miniatures. The walrus gulped it down in a second and sighed.

'Anyhow, we're safe,' he repeated. J said nothing. The walrus shook a huge finger in his direction.

'Do you remember me?' he asked, his tone accusatory.

'How could I forget?'

'Is that a problem of yours?'

'What?'

'Forgetting.'

'Sometimes.' J looked back to where the light had almost died. Buildings lurked as indistinguishable black shapes in the grey. His words seemed to drift. 'Right now it's time that bothers me.'

'Forgive me for saying so,' replied the walrus, 'but isn't that the same thing?'

For the first time J's interest was aroused. 'Yes,' he replied thoughtfully, 'I suppose it is.'

'It's a terrible thing,' the walrus continued in a mourning tone, 'the inability to forget. I remember reading once about a man who couldn't forget the most trivial thing. He could have told you what he'd overheard at a bus-stop ten years ago. Worse still, he could remember every dream he'd ever had.'

'What happened to him?' J asked.

'Since the story took place such a long time ago, I assume he just went mad. Nowadays he'd have been plugged into an IBM system.'

'A sign of the time,' said J, the echoes of digital alarms still buzzing in his ears.

'Ah yes,' said the walrus, 'but the point is the same, you see. Once we can't forget, we're no longer human.' The walrus's face folded into a hundred wrinkles. He picked up the empty miniature, toyed with it briefly and shot a glance in J's direction.

'Just how many of these things would you have?' he asked.

What the hell, thought J, he sounded like he had a story or two to tell, besides which he remembered the walrus's generosity with all those cans of beer, back in a waiting room, somewhere, sometime.

He produced a handful of the miniatures and a couple of sandwiches he'd stolen from the last buffet.

'Just who are you, anyway?' he asked the walrus.

The walrus grinned.

'I could tell you that I can't remember,' he said, 'but I doubt you'd believe me. I could tell you that I can't forget, but that would only make you suspicious. Instead let's just say I'm trying.'

'Does this line stop at the French Foreign Legion?' asked J with a one-sided smile.

'Who needs the French Foreign Legion,' the walrus smiled back, 'when we have ' – he lowered his voice in imitation of wonder – 'the British Railway System?'

Mnemosyne, Goddess of the Railway

By now the darkness had closed in on them completely; its only shadow was a reef of grey, lining the black of the skyline. The sound of the train on the rails was circular and hypnotic, a vortex of echoes drawing J through successive visions of his own past. Was this the effect of travel drowsiness falling on him? Perhaps just the distant cries of the harpies that fluttered in the wake of the alcohol.

He had the unmistakable sensation, as the train began to pick up speed, that they were heading somewhere, the walrus and he, hurtling into the darkness.

The lights in the carriage showed no sign of coming on, leaving the walrus's face illuminated only irregularly by the weak yellow glare of the sodium lights as they wheeled past the window.

Us versus the ticket collectors – the eternal battle, the walrus called it. How often, thought J, have I been grateful for a darkened carriage like this in my flight? I have crouched beneath seats to avoid them, only my eyes flashing in the darkness like a rodent's. Sometimes I am the most wretched of creatures; sometimes, when I slip a barrier, when the motion takes effect, I am the most elevated of men.

He looked into the face of the walrus, as it flickered once more into yellow light. The after-image faded green. What should such creatures as you and I do, he mused, crawling between heaven and the carriage floor?

The walrus was talking, his words haunting the bleak landscape.

'What happens, you might ask, when memory gets fucked? Mnemosyne the goddess of memory was fucked by Jupiter, and the results were the muses – history, pastoral poetry, lyrical poetry, historical poetry and tragedy . . . .'

'All the things, in fact, which haunt the railway system,' J interrupted.

'Smart boy, smart boy,' nodded the walrus, the movement of his head frozen in sequence by the lights, 'and so the railway system . . . '

'Is memory.'

'Or at least the cobweb in which our memories are caught. People travel to and from their loved ones on the railway; they sit, and they pretend to look out of the window, and they remember, or reinvent, or they try to forget. The railway feeds on their memories; they soak the seats, rattle through the rails, hold the crumbling stations together. You must have noticed their smell, the waiting rooms are thick with it.'

The walrus turned towards the window, his face glowing as a cluster of lights drifted past.

'You see these places,' he said, indicating a craggy terrace, standing high and isolated above the lines, 'the places where no one could possibly live, and yet people clearly do. The railway drains the hopes and dreams from the rabbit-hutch housing; they disappear down the lines as memories of what might have been.'

'As nostalgia for a future now denied.'

'Exactly that!' replied the walrus. 'Every now and then the occupants band together and set off to reclaim their memories from the railway system. They stand in clusters on damp days, in pathways from where they can see the rails clearly. They cower at the sight of signs that read "Beware of Trains", but they persist, and bravely they write down the numbers of the trains which pass. They believe that somehow that knowledge gives them power, that somewhere in the depths of some dusty bureaucratic building they can exchange these numbers for their memories. But really all they're left with . . .'

'Is a list of numbers,' finished J.

The last glimpse that he caught of the walrus's face before it faded back into the darkness was irretrievably sad.

'A list of numbers,' he repeated, 'each one representing something that could somehow have taken them . . . somewhere . . . else.'

Memory Spotting

'The dimension that you and I inhabit', the walrus continued, 'is the dimension of memory which, perverse as it seems, is the best place to forget. You see we're so drenched in other people's memories that our own become diluted. Or perhaps not so much diluted as . . . invaded.

'Now, take me for example. I used to have a photographic memory; now I find that the photographs have bleached out. More than that, they've been invaded by shadows, shadows that I no longer recognise, I suspect that they're shadows that I never knew.'

'It's strange that you should say that,' J replied; 'some of my memories look like photgraphs, or films – the type that are all silver and darkness and they smell of old dust and cigarette ash.'

'I always distrust memories like that,' said the walrus,

shaking his head.

'So what sort do you trust?'

'The ones that smell of burning and human flesh.'

The walrus's eyes seemed to loom from the darkness for a second, then faded once more into the gloom of the carriage. J looked down the bank the train was riding; in the dereliction below a church stood alone amidst the wreckage, isolated in a pool of yellow light.

'Believe me, I have those as well,' J continued at last. The rattle of the rails juddered along the spine of the train. 'But those are the ones I've been trying to lose.'

Sirens over Lake Geneva

J speaks:

'We're perpetually trying to freeze the movement, capture it as a still image, because a still image is something we can possess; while something still moves it can slip through our fingers like sand.

'I remember once, a German girl I met, some time early in my travels. "For years," she told me, "I kept trying to take a photograph of Lake Geneva from a train. I always wanted just one photograph of Lake Geneva to put on my wall.

' "Somehow," she went on, "it never seemed to work the way I wanted; all I ever ended up with was a blur. Now I have a wall full of pictures, a grey blur at the top left corner which is the dawn over Lake Geneva, which changes slowly as you get closer to the bottom right hand corner into a red blur, which is sunset over Lake Geneva. Nowadays it seems as if that's the best way of seeing it anyway."

'When we got to the end of the line we got out. "I'll see you again," she said with absolute confidence. Of course she never will.'

Stillness over the Rails

This train has come from silence and is heading towards

silence. The only locus of noise is the one in which the train revolves. All around it is silence, the ultimate destination, the vacuum that remains after memory has gone, the irresistible force that sucks everything in.

In the darkened carriage, J's words cast shadows.

'What do I remember? I remember the way she looked, the way she seemed to transform the sadness within her into a combative weapon with which she threatened anyone who looked her way.

'I remember looking back at her, feeling somehow naked, but wondering. Everything seemed to go black, not so much the sight of black as the sense of black, the sort that you feel all around you as a child when a hot summer night closes in, the dark that usually is so threatening, somehow enfolding you as a friend. For some reason you are not afraid. For the first time you are struck by the full consciousness of being awake, while everybody else is asleep. Their dreams crackle in the air around you, playing on your cheek like static.

'In that moment she seemed like all my memories, dissolved in the warm black of forgetting. Warm as her skin, black as her hair. Curls. Spirals of forgetting.

'I remember looking at her arm and realising just how much she knew about memory and oblivion, the shadows of the scar tissue, paradoxical memories of moments you'd rather forget, like knots in handkerchiefs attached to the past and not the future, angry little notes reading whiter than white on pale skin. You forget to remember to forget.'

'Ah,' said the walrus, his face flaring briefly and fading once more, 'so she was fleeing Sodom and Gomorrah, holding your hand, but just couldn't help looking back?'

'No, she was the type who never looked back. You know the sort, past a blank, future an open book, but one with a stunningly familiar plot, or that was the way she saw it, at least. She looked down occasionally, sometimes when you met her gaze, but never back.

'I remember her laugh, the vicious type whose hooks had to be torn from her flesh, before they could engage in yours. "Memories?" she said. She laughed then as she pulled her arm from beneath my fingertips. "It isn't memory that bothers me."

'So what did?'

'Nostalgia, or so she said, nostalgia for the future.'

'By which she meant?'

'I'm not sure I know. It had something to do with a phobia she said she had – like claustrophobia is the fear of enclosed spaces and agoraphobia is the fear of the outside world, what she had was the fear of heaven.'

'Oh, I see,' said the walrus, 'another good Catholic, holy visions in nightmarish incarnations?'

'No. More a matter of other people spending their lives yearning for heaven, while she spent hers actively avoiding its every incarnation. Her nostalgia for the future was a sadness for the way things could have been.'

'If only she didn't appear in'the picture?'

'Something like that.'

J looked once more at the walrus. The hooked nose and knowing smile gave him a satyr-like appearance. There was something he distrusted about the walrus's acuity, his ability to crystallise a thought that drifted through J's words. Nevertheless, his thoughts continued to unfold, as if under their own momentum, as the drama proceeded to unravel in the visions beyond the train window.

'I was the one who looked back,' he continued. The words seemed to trail, like a train siren cast backwards into the dimension of silence.

The walrus sat a while and smiled. 'Poor Orpheus,' he said. A glimmer of irritation crossed J's face.

'What did you say?' he snapped, the question frozen for a second in a flash of light.

'Orpheus,' the walrus continued, 'who rescued the abused woman from hell, only to lose her in a look.'

'That wasn't the way it was,' J replied, 'I don't think. Sometimes my memories seem so fractured. They run around and around like films trapped in loops. But if you look for long enough the sequence of events begins to change.'

J looked beyond, into the darkness. Perhaps it was getting lighter. Vague forms could now be distinguished, crags of ruins emerging from the black. Perhaps it was his imagination.

'Some of them aren't even my memories.'

The words trailed.
The train crashed on through the silence.

In Transit Veritas

On the darkness beyond the window, J's imagination projected scenes from previous journeys, these visions of England, these reconaissance trips through the combat zones.

He remembered the sight once, surreal in its setting of the English countryside, of a floodlit, giant golf ball, looming in ghostly burning blue from a background of a sunset streaked like a blood-fed muscle.

He had been struck so forcibly by the image, he had actually returned to forage for information on the encampment. Walking around the area, he had heard a number of different stories. A farming community, suddenly finding they had a giant prop from some science-fiction fantasy landed on their doorsteps, had created their own fantasy around its function.

There were only two that had any plausibility – it was either something to do with the nuclear early warning system or an elaborate device for the monitoring of telephone calls.

War either way, J reflected, given that telephones are as much an instrument in private war as nuclear missiles are in public war. The telephone is the easiest way of inflicting violence on anyone, from a complete stranger to a loved one.

He remembered her silences as they leaked through the crackling line, dark and murderous late at night, his grip tight on the receiver.

Now that warfare under the guise of diplomacy is commonplace, now that nuclear missiles have placed us in the perpetual domain of total war, what more natural than that our private lives should imitate the social world that surrounds us? We soak up war in the atmosphere nowadays.

For our parents it was different. Warfare then was still something that broke out in identifiable rashes like the herpes that would wrack Petra's body once a month, transforming her face into a cold mask of pain. J's parents would exist in silent hostility most of the time, and engage in active combat only at times convenient to both of them. J on the contrary regarded himself as being at war all the time.

The scene recurred in his imagination, a hunched old man on a long train journey, through his life backwards, from the tatters of the system he'd built to the threatened citadel of the system he loathed, the system whose destruction had been his dream.

Now showing through the train window, beyond his own haggard reflection, somewhere between him and the sequential flash of yellow sodium, 'Scenes from the Life of Leon Trotsky'. Odysseus vanquished. Moving backwards at the speed of a Trans-European train. Through Trotsky's window the era of Total War approaches; through J's it continues.

Force

'I remember her standing in that street. "So," she said, "you'd like to take me home." The quiver of her voice vacillated between amusement and mockery. "Perhaps you'd like to take me for another drink first." I was skint by this time.

' "Perhaps you'd like to wait for five minutes while I find a brick to hit a rich American with," I answered.

' "Oh, don't worry about that," she replied, running a sharp nail just past the corner of my eye. "After all we wouldn't want you to scar your face. Not yet, at least." The gentle trail of the nail ended in a malicious, gouging scratch.

'Her taunting finally caused me to snap; without thinking, I lashed out with my hand, giving her a full, open-handed slap across the face. The force of it sent reverberations of shock pulsing through my veins. I looked after the motion, an action dropped into time. The ripples of resentment passed across her face. For a second I seemed to see a genuine expression of hurt float towards the surface of her face.

'Then suddenly she threw her head back and laughed, splendidly, guiltlessly. It was a laugh that carried everything with it, an upward and outward spiral; it echoed the shape of the mirrored stairway, coiled around the arched and vicious eyebrows of the bouncers attending the doorway and out into the street, where it dissipated amidst the falling paranoia, seeping through dimensional gaps and settling amidst my silent and persecuted memories.

'I see these scenes, floating like bubbles in the murky pools of my imagination. I am suspended in these pools, rarely able to sleep, scarcely capable of sleeping, suspended in a living state of nonsequential dream.

'Her words on a postcard, from a self-imposed exile she had undertaken in pursuit of her own sanity. "Finding myself unable to look at you, I walked through the valley where I once lay naked in my childhood beneath the rain. I looked for a pool the colour of your eyes and stared into it. It felt, as it always does, like drowning."

'And me? I was left suffocating in the blackness of her absence, as dark as a tube train tunnel, as dense in its dreams of destruction. The sound of electricity pulsing through the lines, the confirmation that the system has not yet collapsed in on itself.

'Outside her window, one of a few houses left in an area of reconstruction, stood a building site, its half-completed structure bathed in floodlights like the remnants of some classical ruin paraded for display. The birds, held spellbound in the delusion of some perpetual dawn, would herald the flaring neon in a chorus that lasted all night, lapsing into an exhausted silence just as the real dawn cast the girders into silhouette. Throughout the night, their spirals could be watched through her window as they spun in frenzy through the empty space between the building's framework.

'One time, as we sat in a tube station waiting for a train to carry us through the stupor, she had cast back her head in the golden luxury of the dreamy state of the heroin. "It sounds', she said, as the electricity chirped in the rails, "like the birds outside my window calling."'

Cipher (1)

J was awakened by the sound of a telephone, ringing from

somewhere in the darkness of his past. The gloom of the carriage somehow threw up an image of the corridor in his flat, high above the railway station that even now was glowing, isolated and surreal in the shadows of south-east London. He could hear the tones of an unanswered call ringing out over the flaking floorboards, travelling through to the empty kitchen, where the vibrations rattled the broken pane of the back window.

The ring multiplied in time, joining with the sounds of countless other telephone calls. Watching the scene, calm and dispassionate, J could see his own figure fighting sleep down the stairs towards the receiver.

Her early morning calls were usually implicit questions. The light that torched from her eyes went unseen; J could only imagine it as he held the dead unit in his hand. He could hear her dead voice, squeezed dry by the fear of emotion. Her syllables sounded cut up and reassembled to provide a reasonable imitation of the sound that sprang from her living and vulnerable throat, but all expression had bled away in the process.

The phone calls were like visitations from the other side of the grave. Irony flickered briefly across the face of J's reflection in the window. The sounds always seemed diffracted through incalculable dimensions of distortion, as though eaten away as they lived by the cancer of forgetting. Her voice, transformed through the electronic ciphers, crackled into his ear in a storm of nerve-splitting static – as cold, as ill sorted and as chilling as a love poem on a recorded information service.

J would talk back to the heart-broken machine inside the telephone, but still the first sounds of the tone would strike him dumb for long, static-crackling seconds. He felt as if, standing in some cold morgue, he was looking at her corpse, dead and white, held by surface tension from spilling all over the slab. He could almost see her body, covered with dry wounds, puckering, grotesque stigmata.

To watch a friend, coiled in pain, to see a lover dead and feel the blame.

The telephone ring sent J back through a series of waiting-rooms, ringing with the echo of his own howls. He could still hear it ringing, still see himself, his hand resting lifeless on the receiver. He could see his gaze, looking down his arm at the intersection of the veins, his finger tapping.

Eurydice in Ruins

'There was something impossible in her look, something I longed, somehow, to capture, to hold, to fix in some permanence, because everything about her seemed entirely lacking in any permanent substance.

'A friend who met her once came out with a peculiar comment: "If she were to disappear tomorrow, what would remain to prove her existence?" I don't know what prompted him to ask the question; perhaps he had noticed the tenuous hold she seemed to have on the world. The possibility of her image collapsing in on itself seemed so tangible, I could just picture her flickering suddenly into nothing, with nothing but the random epileptic gutterings of a malfunctioning neon light.'

As J spoke, he and the walrus waited for the dawn, waiting in the darkness for the rising of that grey, the colour of old stone, spreading cold against the sky. J's words were the only mark of the landscape of their journey, like the remnants of pillars, marking out the perimeters of some ruin.

'And what would have remained? A basement room with only two strange pictures to mark its ownership. Not even that would have lasted for long. I imagine if I went back now I'd find it invaded by some dowdy lumpenpunks, like some ugly little parasites come to live in my memories.'

'And there was no family?' asked the walrus.

'Only the one she'd been disowned by,' answered J. 'Oh, and then there was the sister, Karen. She seemed somehow like the inverse of Petra. If she seemed more at home in the world, in some way more *there*, it was a result of her own mental effort. Where Petra seemed to be dreaming herself to death, her imagination striking against her own existence, Karen was the reverse: she seemed always to be dreaming herself back to life. I suppose in a lot of ways she was the proof of Petra's existence.

'Perhaps that was why Petra hated her so much. She always

insisted on playing the caring sister, lecturing her about her drug habit, that sort of thing. She was the positive to Petra's negative – and if there's one thing Petra hated it was to be cancelled out.

'She was negative, not in the most obvious sense of the word but in the most profound way. Her very look was like being drawn into a repressed memory, somehow shared but never spoken, as if in the silence between us something dwelled, something that neither of us could acknowledge.

'I still find myself haunted by her look, the way that coil of hair fell over one eye, a spiral forever dragging you down. Nothing ultimately meant anything to her, and her look was the vortex of the meaningless dimension she inhabited, pulling you in to a soft, black-velvet oblivion.

'I remember that look the first time I noticed it, on the mirrored staircase at that accursed club. She stopped and cast a glance in my direction. It was like being enfolded in darkness. "Do you think you're like me?" she asked. It sounded like a challenge. I looked at her face and at my own reflection over her shoulder simultaneously. Between the two images whirred an endless sequence of calculations of the algebra of need.

'My immediate reaction was to answer no; I was for some reason rather scared by the question. But as I looked back at her I saw only the vacuum of my own face behind her. Both of us seemed to revolve around some ruin of classical splendour, a dark shadow to the eyes and a ravaged cynicism falling on the pouting, protested innocence that played around our lips.

'I saw that look so many times, that look of the hopelessly defiled Eurydice, looking at me with an expression that said "Can you look at me now? Can you dare to look back?"

I remember the time she returned from some trick or other, one side of her face bruised and swollen. "Not everyone is as gentle as you," she said and gave me that same look. My questions, as always, faded into black.'

Diving

J's words emerge from the darkness of the carriage.

'How far back can I remember? It seems to make no more sense than asking how far forward this train has progressed. Sometimes, in the sunshine, you can stare into the pool of memory and see the glinting of what seems to be the bottom. Other times, surrounded by the drizzle and dismal grey, it seems impossible to see beyond the texture of the surface, pock-marked in the rain; there is no more than the suggestion of shadowy and sinister submarine forms, weaving designs of their own amidst the deep, green dark.

'Sometimes the silt of memory looks like the grease and damp-stained patterns of the wallpaper in the tenement block where I was born; at other times its dense undergrowth of rotting leaves seems to betray a glimpse of something more behind, of a noble and wandering race, dispossessed and left to scavenge city streets. Sometimes their spirit is what I'm searching for, deep in the alcoholic mists of station waiting-rooms. Sometimes they are no more than further illusions, shadows flitting through the half-light on the other side of the train window.

'I remember that night, certainly, as we stumbled through the streets that echoed with her laughter, words tumbling through the drunkenness, cascading immediately into the realms of forgetting. I tried desperately to fix her image and her words in my mind; somewhere amidst that snake-infested labyrinth, my salvation depended on my ability to hold these moments somehow, and yet they poured through my fingers.

'We descended into yet another cellar, this time a seedier, subterranean world, where people came not to parade a superficial difference but to gain solace for an alienation that was so much more profound. In the corner smiling boys with flinty eyes fumbled around the corpulent figure of some minor drug baron and flashed gazes over towards their leader. Standing over by the stage, he smiled, sated and serpentine, while an old drag queen with a face like last year's Christmas decorations led a gaggle of skinheads in a chorus of 'There'll Always Be an England'.

'The boy on the door had his hair scaped close to his head and tied in a small pony-tail at the back. "Well, well," he said, twisting off his stool behind the cash register and greeting us with a deeply parodic theatrical bow. "If the princess hasn't found herself another pawn. And how is life behind the one-way mirror, my dear?"

'She could turn cold in a second. "Just swallow it, Martin," she snapped. "You ought to be good at that by now."

' "Now, now, darling," he droned, planting a noisy kiss on her lips, "let's not be like that." Pulling back, he draped an arm round me, allowing it to slide off slowly. "I'd kiss your new boyfriend too," he continued, "but he doesn't look like he's decided which way to go yet, and I wouldn't want to deprive you of whatever fun you might manage to squeeze from it."

' "Just ignore him," she said; "he's just another working-class boy who just can't cope with how he makes a living."

' "We can't all be born with silver dildos in our mouths," he shouted back after her as we headed for the bar. She looked at me and puffed out her cheeks in a gesture of indifference. As she blew out her breath, I expected to see bubbles rising.

Dawning

'That night we walked through the building site, our shadows forming stars under the floodlights. We'd jumped a taxi from the West End, diving in uninvited with three bemused south London lads, too much the victims of her strange charisma to suggest that if we were to share her ride perhaps we should contribute to the fare.

'She was well practised in the weaving of the cobweb of charm, she studied the intricacies of its design as she watched her own movements in the mirror.

' "It oftens seems to me,' she said later, 'as if I'm always looking at my own reflection. It's like that working in the peep show – I never see their faces as I draw them in; I'm watching my image in the mirror, pursuing the lines of my dance."

'Sometimes I wondered whether that wasn't precisely what she was doing with me, casting me as some three-dimensional reflection of herself. Perhaps that was what she meant by that strange question on the stairs of the club – "Do you think you're like me?", as in "Do you think you're my reflection?"

'And yet it's me who is left staring at myself. And the sound of the rails rattles on. Recall, Recoil, Recall, Recoil, Recall, Recoil.'

Outside the train window the landscape begins to etch itself on the blue-grey blur of the distance, the black extent of some giant bomb site. In the distance a red warning light winks on the top of an iron tower.

J's voice continues; the walrus blinks bleary eyes in greeting of the day.

'Sometimes the inevitability of her isolation seemed in question even to herself. When this occurred, she lost the will to hold the mirror in front of herself and it would fall and crash in fragments at her feet.'

Looking through the window, J sees a dark room in an old house, the falling light glinting off the sharp fragments of a broken mirror.

He has the sense that something inside of him has broken, he can feel the blood flowing through his veins as the detail floods the picture in his mind. The bleached monochrome bleeds into pastel colour.

'We had to break in through the window of her room. Petra had had a feud with some mad girl upstairs, who was now nursing six stitches in her face and an even bigger grievance. She had had to barricade her door from the inside.

'She flipped a catch on the window and climbed through first. At that time it might well have been the portal to paradise.

'Inside, the room was stark. Above the stone fireplace was a series of photographs of what seemed at first glance to be her. Although the faces were bleached out, it was her figure, her tangle of black curls. They'd been cleverly treated, the image superimposed with an old painting; from the back there seemed to burst a pair of angel's wings.

' "My sister." She spat the words with a bitterness that seemed out of place. "My guardian angel." She laughed. The sound, compared with that wonderful, guiltless bellow on the spiral staircase, sounded heavy and sour, curdled like the milk neglected on doorsteps, on a day when humid clouds hang heavy over London.'

Prey (1)

'On her wall there were two pictures, a crucifixion behind the bed, set on a marbled, pastel-coloured background, that proved on closer examination to be made of butterfly's wings. There was something haunting about it, as if that image of suffering was made somehow more real by the thought of a hundred wingless butterflies in their death throes.

'On the opposite wall hung a picture labelled 'Orpheus and Eurydice', although it bore more resemblance to the image of Salome. A woman, dark hair flowing with vampiric splendour, held a platter on which rested the severed head of Orpheus. The look in his eyes was his own doom, not hers.

' "I've always liked a happy ending," she said, as she saw me looking at it.

'My memory looped back once more to the bar, words penetrating through the all-enfolding stupefaction of my drunkenness. She had stood there, suddenly stripped of her mirrored force field. It was a sight both terrifying and compelling.

'Her voice sounded disembodied. "You looked back," she said, partly in wonder, partly in what sounded like reproach.

"I had no choice."

' "Nevertheless," she replied, "you're the first to do it."

'Something fatal lurked in her gaze, or in mine, or between the two. That night I dreamt of angels dying, their wings torn from their backs.

'Outside the birds continued their artificial chorus, their chirping like the spiralling sound of electricity in the tube train line.

' "Out there", she said, "they're building their Utopia, but you and I are afflicted by the fear of heaven." And she was right; all around us the mirrored cells were regenerating. They were building heaven in concrete and glass, leaving us trapped in the streets, our horror-stricken reflections staring back at us from every turn.

'I dreamt of angels stripped painfully and fatally of their wings, I dreamt of a city recasting itself in pursuit of perfection,

I dreamt of my mother's face as it appeared as she bent to kiss me as a child, waiting for sleep, during our first days in the city, its powdered surface glowing blandly, the pursuit of perfection. The flames of her eyes were doused in misty sentiment – "When Celtic eyes are lying".

'I opened my eyes and saw Petra. She seemed in her sleep to be falling, spiralling somehow out of the random orbit of my dreams. I reached out to her face, which raised to my touch.

'Revolving once more into sleep, I dreamt that three men came to my bedside. It was their duty, they informed me, to deliver me to my death. My protests of mistaken identity were of no use. They took me to the door of a room. My death, they told me, was beyond the door, then they abandoned me to my fate.

'Deciding not to linger in the antechamber, I opened the door. Inside, the room receded in a sharp and impossible perspective, marked by statues of broken marble, graven images eaten by the years, faces blasted by the sands of ages.

'Between these figures strolled a magnificent panther, its coat a deep glossy black, its footsteps silent as the air. It approached me slowly, baring teeth like needles. Awe-struck with wonder I reached out my hand to this beautiful creature, feeling no fear.

'The panther fell miraculously calm. It came to me softly, nuzzling my face. And then very slowly, and very tenderly, it tore out my throat.'

Cipher (2)

J looked at the lighted windows that lined the pathway of the train, each one leading on to some minimalist drama in a yellowed, peeling room. He could hear a chorus of telephones, their rings undulating against each other like the sounds of crickets on a tropical night.

Over the darkened bomb sites his memory crawled. Across the back yard, through the piles of rubbish scattered festering around the bins, he could see himself, through the window, picking up the phone. The simple motion seemed infinitely diffracted across time, viewed through a cracked window pane.

He could see himself as a passing tramp might have seen him, his expression stony, his gaze distant, his mouth moving without expression. He could even hear the emotion which rattled the flaking window frame . . . .

In the room, last night's cigarette smoke was settling on the carpet and the curtains. A beam of sunlight from the window illuminated the dance of the dust particles – human skin hanging in the air. The television flickered silently.

He picked up the phone and the remote control switch of the video in rapid succession. Pressing the search button, he said hello.

Answering the phone was like being transported into some parallel world, a world where the air was as thick as blood, movement slow and breathing difficult, a world of uncertain memory and dysfunctioning emotion.

The voice on the other end of the line was faint, like the final flapping of a fish landed on a wooden pier. J felt the hook tugging at himself, as if something in his stomach had torn.

'Hullo,' a flat slap against the wood, the water filling its hollow dryness, 'it's Karen.' The sister's voice so like Petra's in every pause, every enunciation. Drowning in the air. A thick red line rimming the rippling gill. The expression one of fixed and stark terror. 'Hello . . . ' In the silences, deep and impossible, he could hear the echoes of other conversations.

'I miss you.'

He could hear words spoken to Petra dropping through the telephone line into the pool on the other side. He heard the ripples.

Sitting on the train, J tried to refocus his memories, to return to the conversation with Karen. He could see the images of his day-dreams – a diagonal column of cloud shearing across the perfect blue, leading to the far shore. He could hear the crackle of her words.

As she had spoken, J had looked at the television, the video of last night's programmes. The railways of Britain in thirty minutes – several train journeys filmed and speeded up. With the video on search function, the images flashed past even quicker.

The speed was quite dizzying, lending a strange exhilaration to their conversation.

J had heard the words coming over the line, but found it hard to relate them to anything, they wheeled elegantly across their own horizon.

'It's like a soap opera,' she had said; in the end the only reality is televised. The countryside reeled past on the screen, blurs of greens and scarlets, the clear, identifiable, circular spots of rushing light playing on reeded water. Unaffected by the speed of the televisual images, J's daydreams unravelled slowly behind his eyes: the fish floundered. The line of the pier stark and splintered against the rippling blue of the sea.

'Oh Christ . . . .' J heard his reaction resound from a distance, an echo from the other side of the bay, a yelp across the bomb site with an edge that prevented it being taken for amusement.

His reality had undergone the shuddering diffraction of shock, each moment a discrete wavering frame, flickering into black space. Now re-running the sequence in his memory, panning in from the viewpoint of the window, he found the blank had invaded the space where his face should have been. He could see the hand holding the receiver, the slow-motion progression of the rippling images on the television behind, but his own face was concealed by a dark spot, like sunblindness.

What *had* been his reaction? The question worried him – every now and then, with a start, he'd find himself looking across a barren landscape at the image of his own face breaking into a morbid grin, while his voice maintained a note of horror, perhaps too even to be natural.

A hand picked the fish from the pier, folding around the soft form, flecks of salt lining the fine hairs; it presented the underbelly to the point of a narrow knife.

Suicide exerted its own peculiar fascination. J had often found himself involved with people who played with it, the white and livid scars standing out on thin arms as testaments of moments of self-hatred, strategically placed pill bottles . . . the cut, clean and regular straight up the body, the tough cartilage, the drip of red on the dry pier – perfunctory puncture.

He'd always thought of that as a different matter, not the cry of help of popular truism but a masturbatory dry run on death, neither better nor worse than the real thing, but definitely different.

'I've often thought', one girl had told him, 'how soothing it would feel, the sensation of a gun barrel against my temple.' As if the mere touch would release the tension, the power and release of orgasm.

It was an elaborate game they played and nothing more, he and the succession of thin girls in love with death, and in love with J because it hung on him like stale smoke. This had been quite different.

He looked deep into the rush of images on the television set and entered their speed. He saw himself as the train driver, watching the light point of the station at the end of the tunnel, turning the brake handle and feeling the slow, satisfying deceleration, scanning the figures on the platform. Then in repeated frames, he saw Petra's face as she threw herself in the path of the train's motion. He felt the last eye contact. And did his mouth break out into an involuntary and inexplicable grin?

It was a long way from well bandaged wrists and minuscule overdoses. For this is my body, offered up to mutilation, at best.

J reeled back through to his first sexual encounter with Petra; he felt the reverberation in his head of the blow she'd struck him. He saw her stretched naked beneath him as he struck back, her hair flicking across her face as the full force of his hand had struck her cheek.

She just laughed, flicking her hair back, raven black. He had run and re-run the sequence in his mind as he'd listened to Karen's monologue of private disaster. The body was now all that was left of Petra, lying taped to a life support machine, finally broken.

The black punch line was that she'd pulled off a draw with their appalling patriarch of a father against whom she'd raged with such a wild and brutal abandon. When he heard the news, he deepened his natural colour of puce, choked a few times and promptly yielded to a seizure. The pair of them still existed, probably even yet, if it could be called existence, on the same corridor, a pretty pair of vegetables.

'You know the funniest thing,' Karen had continued, her voice crackling with hysteria, 'the man who ruled his family with an iron rod now has to have his shit drained out through a glass tube.

Her laugh echoed over the red of the water. The fish lay open on the pier. The sun played on the sea, and the seaweed stretched out to feel the change in temperature.

Sweet Sickness

J's words continue, drily tracing pale images that flit across the perpetual sound of the train on the rails.

'Disease was something which she mirrored in me. Prone to cases of *petit mal,* a minor form of epilepsy, she would occasionally, quite literally, lose her grip on reality.

'It was all a bit like the cartoon figure who's annoyed his illustrator. You know the show – bit by bit, the scenery surrounding him is removed, leaving him stranded in blankness. Except in Petra's case it was she herself who became the blankness. Instead of the colour draining from the surroundings, it would drain from Petra's face. The only thing that drained from the landscape, as far as she was concerned, was the meaning.

'I remember once trying to imagine what it might feel like to see cars passing but to feel, genuinely, that they were coming from nowhere, going to nowhere, tower blocks and wilting parks holding their form but looking as foreign as an alien landscape. I think recently I've begun to realise.

'I'd always know when it was coming. I can still feel now the particular force with which she used to grab my arm when an attack came on. She used to say that the one thing that remained constant during the attacks was me; she would always know me, always trust me. I was the one familiar figure that held her back from the vortex that is the death of memory.

'For a few moments, every month or so, I was literally the centre of her universe. Realising that was a dizzying feeling.'

Drifting

'Forgetting', said the walrus, 'is a science, a science of intricate precision, with rules and laws of its own. Its mastery is the study of a lifetime.

'The important point to grasp, as by now you'll have gathered, is the metaphor of the railway, the drain of memory, the outer orbit of the spiral of forgetting.

'Now the important thing to grasp here is the principle of the drift. No doubt you'll have experienced the effect of it already. Drift is the force that draws your thoughts out beyond the window and through the landscape, the landscape of your own imagination and your memories. The problem here is that by the time you've worked out where you are you're already somewhere else. All of which means that, even if you wanted to, your chances of getting back to where you started from are virtually nil.'

'But hold on a second.' J at last summoned up the energy to pull the walrus back. Listening to his conversation was in itself like getting caught in the drift. All of a sudden J would find himself somewhere that seemed, both to the walrus and to himself, to be of some significance as a landmark, but with little or no memory of precisely how he had got there. 'If the railway is the outer orbit, where is the nucleus of forgetting?'

The walrus's laugh was sudden and bruising, though free of malice. J imagined that through the murk of the carriage he could see the glint of amusement in his eyes.

'Oh, come now,' said the walrus, 'where's the centre you can get to from the railway and never have to leave the system?'

Realisation crept in on J. He was grateful for the darkness in which his blush went unseen.

Suddenly J felt uncomfortable in the company of the walrus. There was the sense that had provoked his petty irritation at first, but which seemed to have taken hold more firmly and painfully now, that the walrus knew much more than it seemed he should. The feeling was familiar, like an alien hand probing his flesh.

Memory flooded in the wake of the sensation. Fighting it

back was like trying not to vomit, an uncomfortable delay at best. He looked towards the window. The only thing he could see was the shadow of his own reflection against the bleak darkness of the landscape.

His voice was dry.

'The London Underground,' he croaked.

The walrus's laugh bubbled away in the background.

The Wings of Morpheus

The sound of bombers hung above them as J looked once more towards the window. Dark shadows paraded past the periphery of his vision.

What was out there? He felt he could no longer be sure – beyond the window, buried in the darkness, skag-faced harpies fluttered through urban labyrinths. Their faces, the maggot-white of the pupae from which they had burst, reflected back in horrendous magnification on the glittering mirrored cells with which the flesh of the nation was regenerating.

He remembered nights spent in strange cities, searching for subterranean dives – 'tis now that psychopathic time of night, when the doors of Mecca ballrooms yawn and hell itself spews out contagion all over the marbled mosaics of shopping precinct floors – and pursuing these minions of Morpheus through the half-light of the street lamps.

It was the sort of light that only seemed to drizzle through the darkness. Perpetual twilight and a doubtful sky, and beyond the pools of liquid, dripping, dismal light, just a skyline diminished by decay and ruin, the stubs of burnt-out buildings planted into the hillside, dripping concrete fragments into the gutters.

He remembered one, a hollow face staring up at him, the lines of her cheekbones only underscoring her vacancy. Her voice came thin and faint, the spiral of forgetting coiling behind the paper-white mask of her face.

'Just tek me home, pleeeease.' Her voice, despite its flatness, betrayed a note of desperation; her hand hooked into the crook of J's elbow and gripped with surprising force. 'I don't want to go wi' 'im.' She pointed to a boyfriend, his limbs flapping, drowning in a cone of dark-orange light. A foghorn voice sounded from beneath an ill-shapen moustache. 'Julie,' he shouted. She insinuated herself towards J. The boyfriend flapped his arms desperately, going under. J's initial fears of mutilation were allayed. The creature's ability to break from the cape of the street light was sapping by the second.

He looked at the girl. Her presence induced a feeling of sickness deep in his stomach, proportional to how close she stood, but there was a promise that quavered on her voice. 'Tek me home, ' she pleaded, 'I'll give you some smack.' Her eyes rolled up to his, protruding from the putty of her face, her mouth was misshapen with need.

The boyfriend wilted finally, his head dropping onto one extended arm, lying slab flat in the grime.

She took J by the hand, the brittle tendrils of her hair shining in the lights, glow worms flickering in front of him through the night.

It was all out there still, beyond the glass that rattled with the motion of the train. Looking through the window, J could see the reflection of the flame applied to the tin-foil, tasting the richness of the sleepy smoke of forgetting as it spiralled up the tube and coiled around his mind, seeping into every corner with its visions of the sable antechamber of death.

The deep black of the window flared as the walrus torched a cigarette. His eyelids drooped in the light of the flame, then flickered, revealing for a second the glitter of his eyes. The lighter's after-image traced patterns of gold on J's retina. The walrus's face glowed briefly as he took a deep drag on the cigarette and then faded, leaving J to flounder back towards consciousness amidst a waft of the aromatic smell of exhaled smoke.

Cloister

J looked back once more to his reflection, pale and gaunt; it already looked like a ghost. Its insubstantial form made only a faint impression on the window. As it seemed to fade he was drawn outwards, in pursuit of his own image. He felt himself pulled into the frame of his own face, the flesh fading, dissipating like mist, leaving him stranded in the ruins of his own features.

He was struck by a sensation of silence which seemed to trigger remembrance, as if, just as sound can take us back, so its strategic absence can transport us into the mythical realm of memory.

Through what gate had he entered this picture? The ivory gate of illusion, or the horn gate of what will be? Or through the rotted, rusted iron gate of the railway, the gate through which myths seemed to chase his memories, and his memories seemed to mould around the shape of myths.

Returning briefly to the carriage, he surveyed the scene. The pale light of dawn on the horizon, catching a tinge from the falling mist, had cast a shade of blue across the seats, the table and the face of the walrus. He floated now in sleep, the shadow of a dream rippling occasionally over the face, whose lines had fallen once more into peaceful furrows.

The image projected itself backwards, returning J to the memory of this same sleeping face as he had seen it, through the dusty film of a waiting-room window, somewhere, sometime, so far back along the line.

Still the sense of silence seemed to fill the carriage, pervasive and peaceful as the blue light. The sound of the rails that had surrounded them for hours, days perhaps, comforting as the pulse of blood in the womb, had faded entirely, and yet the motion continued, like a film whose soundtrack had been lost.

J found himself feeling suddenly alone. Perhaps his hearing had failed – he tried to rouse the walrus, but found the power of speech, or the effort required to raise a sound, also beyond him. He looked back towards the window, the landscapes seeming to flicker through time and space. The fading light glinting off the glassy black surface of a gas cylinder, the silent floodlit vigil of a single radar dish, a line of large crows, standing in wait on rolls of hay, a barren wasteland in the setting sun. He looked once more and saw that he was bound again by the lines of his own face.

Still there was the silence, richly textured, drawing him back. He found himself circling through a childhood visit to a ruined abbey. His memory swooped through the lines of its skeleton, reconstructing a plan, like a sequence of computer graphics, flickering on the television set of his imagination. He saw a swoop through its silence from the point of view of one of the wild, dark birds that wheeled through the arches, as if to emphasise the degeneration of its structure.

He had revisited the abbey some years later with Petra. A visit he'd expected to be a tawdry footnote to that moment of childish fascination, imagining he'd find the geometry of the abbey's silence invaded by shouting children, drowning the cries of the birds as they came in to roost.

And yet, inexplicably, they were alone once more inside the boundaries of the arches. Once more was how it seemed to J, although it was Petra's first visit to the ruin.

The abbey had the reputation of being haunted, but what J had sensed on that early visit was the strangeness of the absence, not the presence of a ghost. His return with Petra seemed to complete the picture somehow. The sense of causeless yearning he had felt the first time was somehow magnified by the geometry of her face and the remaining lines of the abbey's ruined architecture. Both seemed somehow to trace the outline of some inexpressible sadness, the silent shadow of some disaster, lingering or imminent.

He smiled with longing as she walked through his memories, past and present. Her eyelids were lowered as she traced patterns with the point of her foot in the sparse patches of grass that flecked the dust of the ruin.

A beam of light fell from the empty window of the far wall, casting a perfect diagonal across her face. She turned to move towards it as if drawn. She walked like a ghost.

Later, they had sat high on the ridge above as the light fell and the birds swooped in to rest in the arches. The latest of her projects at the time had been to learn ancient Greek, and she sat tracing the intricate shapes of the letters in the summer dust.

'Last night', she said, 'I had the feeling that as I fell asleep my body was forming the shapes of some impossible alphabet. My nightmare was that you could read my thoughts, by reading the letters.'

Wild cranes traced the spirals of memory through the ruins of J's reflection. Their paths traced a story, one that ran parallel and unread, the same distance away from J as his pale image in the darkened glass.

The train crashed through a tunnel, and the noise broke through once more, as if a barrier of soundproof glass had been shattered. The walrus's eyes flickered and opened. His expression, as always, looked strangely knowing.

Poppy Fields

'There are many trails of forgetting,' the walrus began once more, the echo of the rails drawing his words in their wake like scattered leaves, 'and all of them end in silence.

'That', he continued, his eyes finding a point of marvel somewhere in the space behind J's left shoulder, 'is why there's such a strange silence hanging in train stations, despite whatever bustle they may be bursting with. The silence inhabits the peak of the arches, like the shadow of some watchful bird.

'Around stations is where I pick up the scraps of memory, swirling amidst the litter trapped in the wind. There where the toothless men of my country perch in the dark and dust of the bars. Their misty eyes hover above overspilling ashtrays, resurrecting the embers of their charred and crumbled pasts, like tipping out the ashtrays and watching the visions in the spiralling patterns, as speckles hang in the stale old light. And they watch and they trace the shapes of their dying dreams in the reeking snowfall on the floor, the sight of a sunrise in a foreign land still hanging in the mists of their eyes. They sit and wait for death, which follows soon.

'The last rails of their imaginations follow the tracks of the railway lines. The tracks, endlessly trying to shape themselves after the ripples of the Lethe river, the river in which terror drowns, in which memory dissolves.

'You know by now, I take it, or perhaps you may have

dreamt, some time in a better heated carriage, lulled by the sway, of the Lethe river. It ran from the kingdom of Pluto, from the nether world, to the realms of sleep, where shadows decked in poppies urged venturers to silence. Always it ended in silence.'

Ragged and garlanded figures followed J through the back streets of his dreams.

'The shadows', the walrus continued, 'were the spirits of sleep and death. The spirits of death held funeral urns, while those of sleep held inverted torches.'

In the window J saw again the flame beneath the tin-foil, the look of sickness that penetrated and soaked the dead flesh of the girl's face, the moth returning once more to the inverted flame as he would return to the darkness when the gold in his blood dissipated.

As she raised her eyes to the ceiling, he looked out of the window and into the back yard, where the soft orange of the light brought a grainy, snow-like texture to the rubble. The rents in the brickwork of the opposite house looked like seeping wounds. Poppies spilled from every crevice, roots in the soft flesh of the crumbling brick. He had a sudden vision once more of the gangling boyfriend, his body supine in the seepage of light, slowly dissolving into a liquid of corruption, dark-red flowers coiling through the black of his blood.

The walrus appeared once more in the light of his cigarette.

'The cave', he spoke at last, his voice thick and drowsy, as though filtered through some thicker air, 'was the realm of Somnus, god of sleep, who drenched himself day and night in the juice of poppies, despatching his son, the winged and bleary Morpheus, to touch mortals' brows with sleep, the state he believed was the ultimate in bliss.'

J remembered her skull-like head turned upwards towards the ceiling. He envied her her blankness, for him the harpies still gathered in the corners of the room.

'In the shadows', the walrus continued, 'lurked Mors, the god of death, forever cadaverous and hungry. And in the air fluttered marbled dreams and horned nightmares.

'There were two gates through which the dreams and nightmares passed into the world. Those that left through the gates of ivory were shimmering delusions, while the ones that left through the gates of horn were true dreams of what would come to pass.'

The sound of screaming seemed to echo disembodied in the distance, behind and beyond the clash of the train on rails.

'Now your dreams of silver and shadows', the walrus droned on, 'have come through the ivory gates of your imagination. The dreams that smell of burning flesh come through the gates of horn, filtered through the silence of the station arches.'

He remembered the scene from later that night, as she had squirmed and sweated beside him, tangled in swathes of sheets and tortured by the horned pets of the god of sleep. He had looked out of the side window of the bedroom towards the tower blocks in the distance. Only a few cells were activated, the rest had fallen into darkness.

He fell briefly into dreams of tube stations infested with moths and carpeted with poppies.

Tunnels

'Dreams', the walrus said, looking quizzically at J, 'are the strangest things.'

'Ivory or horn?' asked J.

'This dream', said the walrus, 'didn't come from the realms of Somnus, although it seemed to come, I must confess, from somewhere fairly similar.'

J had the sensation once again that his entire history was something merely dreamt up by the walrus for his own amusement. 'Don't tell me,' he said, determined to prove that he knew his part in this predestined drama, 'this is a dream that howled its way through the darkened tunnels of . . . '

'The London Underground, exactly,' said the walrus, 'and being the clever little bastard that you are, you'll already have worked out that the Underground . . . '

'Is the centre of the drift.' J finished.

'You see!' exclaimed the walrus, his face beaming with enthusiasm. 'Now, I knew from the moment I saw you in that waiting-room that I wouldn't be wasting my time. The dreams and the memories that are drained from the railways are drawn by the drift into the underground, which becomes . . . '

'The vortex of forgetting.'

'Ah! You see I knew your mind wasn't idling as you were looking out of that window.'

'If only', answered J. 'I managed once to set it to rest, amongst the poppies in a rotting terraced house, but the respite didn't last for long. I woke to find my hostess strangled in the sheets, while I lay there and shivered, finding, in the inverse of the hypnotist's promise, that I remembered everything.'

J broke off for a moment; once again some old scene seemed to flicker in his pupils.

'The bit about the underground wasn't my own discovery,' he admitted. 'I heard it one day in the time I spent haunting its tunnels, even before I got as far as the outer orbits of the railway system.

'It was from another wanderer. He asked me the time, I told him I had no idea, but he picked up on my accent, a familiar strain in a strangely empty station.

' "You're no English!' he said in celebration. I shook my head. "How long you been down here?"

' "Ten years, twenty years," I answered, thinking of course he meant London. "It all seems to blur after a while. Longer, anyway, than I care to remember."

'He laughed. "No," he said, "I meant how long down *here*, how long in the underground?"

'I told him the answer was still longer than I cared to remember. His gaze, which so far had drifted, met mine with a sudden force. There was a look of recognition in his eyes, and a sharpness behind the slur of his voice.

' "It'll be longer still", he said, "before you'll be able to forget." He went on to tell me the story of the underground and forgetting.'

Fortune's Tracks

The lights outside, the floodlights on factories and on the

science-fiction implants of modern war technology, made arches across J's eyes as he relived the heat of a summer past in a damp, unheated railway carriage.

'Outside, as I remember, one of those becalmed airs hung over London. The cranes on building sites swung slowly through the heavy, bleached heat. The city's reconstruction struggled to wake itself, a behemoth shaking off bad dreams. People clogged the gates of the underground, like the sour particles rising to the necks of neglected doorstep milk bottles.

'In the depths of Baker Street – one of the few stations I had found, after lengthy investigation, where it was still possible to dream – all was strangely calm and serene. The people came and went as if passing through some Continental cathedral, and the soot glistened as though touched for a moment by gold dust. The tourists and commuters around me orbited the nucleus of my dreams with comforting regularity.

'His appearance was immediately a threat, not for the reasons that it might have been for those that pursued the plotted routes around me, but because he was identifiably something outside, an unknown quantity. Having cast for myself a role of mystery, the last thing I wanted to see was someone who could stare beyond my front. A simple can of lager was enough of a mirrored shield to protect myself from the gorgons of the general public.

'He carried on looking, there was after all nothing about me that could alarm him. His eyes peered, restless and alive, from beneath brows that arched with a misplaced elegance. He scratched for a moment at a baggy trouser leg, belched and pulled at the string by which he held his dogs.'

'Dogs?' asked the walrus.

'Alsations,' J continued, 'two of them, great mangy creatures that sniffed around his ankles and panted and drooled all over the platform. They both wore ugly muzzles, although they looked like cowering, docile beasts.

'He was, he claimed, a fortune teller, preying on the gullibility of the tourists. He had the sort of look to his eyes that would send the average American running for the sanctity of the nearest museum, but then it's difficult to tell how wide the boundaries of charming poverty are cast these days.

' "A con trick?" he asked me. "Well, that may be how it seems. Sometimes when I'm feeling lazy that may actually be how it is." He looked back at me with that alarming gaze. "But occasionally", he went on, "you may just have the urge to tell the truth."

' "And what mood might that be?" I asked him.

' "Oh, a particularly malicious one usually," he said. "You see," he went on, "we all like to feel that our actions are under our own free will, which of course they are, if we decide to be ourselves. But the problem is that, even if we wanted to, most of us just wouldn't know where to start. So we follow stories, lay out the paths for ourselves to follow. But the point is that our glimpses of the story come irregularly, if at all.

' "My skill," he said, "is to guess the story. After that it's just a matter of remembering the plot, which I confess I don't always manage with the greatest accuracy nowadays."

'He smiled, one of those smiles that feels like a slap in the face. "I get a tremendous kick you know", he said, "out of sending some poor bugger off to live out some tragedy, just because I've had a particularly bad morning."

' "But surely," I tried to interrupt.

' "But surely he doesn't have to live out the fate I've selected for him. Oh, not in the slightest, but in the end the myth is usually his choice, not mine, and often he'll live it to the death. Strange, don't you think?"

'I asked the inevitable question in that particular tone of voice that people employ for questions to which they don't really want to know the answer. "Why the underground?"

' "Why?" he laughed. "Why, as your mother used to say to you, do you spend a lovely summer day like this sitting in the darkness?

' "Dreams, as you know very well, circulate here, they seep through the voltage, echo through the sounds of old songs, floating through the stagnant air, they congregate and conspire in deserted tunnels.

' "There are two undergrounds, the prosaic one, which is a means of transport merely, and the underground of the imagination, a place where destiny hangs heavy in the atmosphere. What better place for a fortune teller?"

'As he spoke, the dogs' heads moved around him in perpetual motion, coiling their necks like a couple of serpents. Occasionally they would catch a scent on the air as a tube train approached and raise their noses to the rising wind that rushed from the tunnel, whimpering with excitement.'

'Ah,' said the walrus knowingly, interrupting J for the first time, 'remember what I told you about the smell of burning flesh.'

J looked straight at the walrus, his face a blank, simply the reflection of the passing lights and of the ghost of a deranged figure, one day deep in the dankness of the underground system.

'He told me', J continued, 'that the underground had become the centre for what he called "the shifting tides of memory", tides, he said, where the past drained from the future and the future ebbed and flowed into the past and present.

'Memories, he said, drained into the underground, and here they took on their own life. He claimed it was possible to be caught in a tunnel by a tidal wave of memories, to drown, unseen and unheard in a torrent of alien remembrances.'

He looked at the walrus, but it was another ravaged face that he saw, the words of another time he heard. He looked deep into the carriage and he saw the wild eyes of the fortune teller.

'You must have heard,' he had said, 'the stories about people who live above the major points of intersection of the underground claiming to lose their memories? You've heard that the tube can have the effect of wiping clean magnetic tape, that it can drain images from a video tape.

'Those images, those memories, those fictions and those dreams, revolve around the underground system. Sometimes, on a day like today, for example, you can almost breathe them in the atmosphere. For people like me, who feed on them, that makes this a powerful time. People like you . . . ' He had trailed off, staring towards the rails and the rapid scuttling of the rodents scurrying to their holes in the face of the advancing train. 'Well, you'd better be careful.'

In J's eyes, the lines of a tube train platform could be seen, diminishing in sharp perspective. Along its surface stood a scatter of strategically placed passengers, staring at the lines as if looking towards them for some answer.

J stares into the distance, beyond the walrus; as he speaks his voice sounds drained and dead.

'I looked into his eyes,' he says, 'and saw familiar scenes unfolding, looped in endless repetition.

' "The tunnels of the underground", he told me, "are intricate, more intricate than you ever imagined, there are networks of disused tunnels, networks also of dreams. People such as me can disappear into either at will. Sometimes even I can be amazed at what I find there." As he spoke, his words tumbled in patterns, like some mesmeric incantation.

Prey (2)

Karen put the phone down; the ring that signalled its replacement on the cradle resounded in the rich timbered hall. Through the thick glass of the outside door, the blur of her black clothes undulated, the amorphous shape of figures in flames.

She walked up the stairs, a hand trailing dead and white along the dark rail of the banister. Above her, beyond the first floor and up a second set of stairs, her father's apartment, on the attic level, creaked, deserted. His pen lay diagonally on the desk, the collection of leather-bound volumes standing in a simple line of replication on the plain white of the bookshelf.

Petra had always disparaged her father for his devotion to Freud:

'He sits up there like some self-righteous, pompous old goat, poring over books about sex and incest – the last time he fucked he ended up with you.' Never one to miss the chance of a cheap shot she continued, 'Not that that isn't enough to put anybody off.'

Recalling the line caused a flinch to ripple across Karen's face. Her features, usually a blank screen of calm, as if the world had not yet impinged upon her virgin flesh, seemed to be changing imperceptibly but definitely, her passive beauty giving way to a certain troubled energy.

From above, from the vantage point of the door of her father's study, her face, broad and pale, could be seen through the slats of wood that bounded the upper staircase.

Clouds moving quickly across the moon. A razor through the eye of innocence.

The movements of her legs flicker in the spaces like old film footage. Every now and then the raising of her short skirt offers a view of the dark material of her underwear, the inside of her thighs a rare quiver of fleshiness on her starved body, the small mole clearly visible just before the bulge of her pubis. Her body is simply the intersection of the angles of its observance, dark birds watching her from the grain of the woodwork that surrounds her.

This house is old, its owner dead; only its dreams survive.

Karen found it strange that Petra should see her father as a goat; she herself had always pictured him as an old bird, his feathers rumpled, his beak flaking. It was his dark and penetrating eyes that did it, and the hooked shape of his nose, giving the appearance of some taloned predator, but one now past its glory days, its tail feathers trailing a reproachful sadness – an old eagle, still surrounded by an aura of pride, but with the broken air of some unwanted old pet-shop parrot.

She glanced through the open door of her own bedroom and looked at the ugly old chest of drawers that stood by the head of the bed. She'd always like the security it had given her, leaving her head on the pillow, enclosed on one side by the wall and on the other by its wooden surface. When ill in bed she'd played the game of inventing shapes in its grain. That, she remembered, was where she'd first dreamt her father as the hawk. She'd seen him there, raised quite clearly from the dark, flawed surface – a slight chip in the wood had given her the idea of the peeling beak.

It was funny – funny how all her other inventions seemed to disappear once more, seemed to fade back into the mystery of the grain of the wood. Her father never did, he was always there, a dark bird brooding over her sleep.

She was tempted now to walk towards the bed and lie down with her head facing the chest. Somehow she had the feeling that by doing so she could reach her father, in his floating state between death and life. But something stopped her. She turned back towards the door, ignoring the part of her mind that wondered – was the dark bird still there?

This house is old, its owner is dead or he is alive – it has ceased to matter. He lies in a hospital bed, the fluids of his body orbiting their host through tubes. Every now and then his muscles twitch. Only his dreams survive.

From behind, Karen could be seen, her short skirt twitching as she walked down the corridor, the cleft in her buttocks just visible underneath the material.

This house is old, in it the pink buds of desire have grown. Few have flowered. Its undergrowth is dense and infested with the creatures of dreams. A dark bird, caught in the tangle of briars, flapping desperately, the drops of its blood, heavy and dark on the snow.

This house is old and its voices linger; the resin of its wood is soaked in them.

'My family, Jacob, my daughters, they do not respect their father's wishes.'

Old telephone conversations ooze from the wood of the banisters. Her hand trails as she ascends the stairs, feeling their cold substance like the slime of fresh fish. She glances through the open door of her bedroom and looks towards the ugly old chest.

Her mother, cold and impassive as the bedroom wall. Her father, as dark and dream-laden as the old rotting wood. The fold of cloth below her buttocks rolls as she walks down the corridor, into the room of her sister.

The Beat of Distant Wings (1)

J's voice hovered in the carriage, a thick and dreamy blur, scarcely louder than the fluttering at the windows. The train seemed to be running the gauntlet through shadowy forms, occasionally visible in startling silhouetted shapes, distinguishable, faintly, from the darkness beyond.

'Through the blind of her window, the shapes of birds could be seen. The sound of their wings beating on the window was soothing, like the sound of rain.

'We were surrounded, softly enfolded in their feathers as we slept, their spirals coiled through the ruins of our dreams. The sound of angel wings, or the fluttering of harpies.

'Strange how we give wings to our dreams and nightmares. Time, our ultimate fear, we say has wings.'

J broke off and listened for a moment. Beyond the sound of the train's hypnotic rattle he could hear something else, a perpetual soundtrack of alarm. It was the sound of sea birds, apparently closing in on the train.

He looked over towards the walrus, whose eyelids seemed to be drooping involuntarily. As the walrus seemed to be fighting to stay awake, so J felt he was fighting to breach the distance between them. His words felt like neap tide waves, falling ever shorter.

'All these things', said J, shaking his head in despair, 'seem like dreams, and dreams of dreams, memories, old predictions, futures discarded. It seems impossible for me to fight my way back through the ghosts. I can no longer find the original sound, although I suspect that it was a scream, a scream as usual, so perfectly cinematic.

'Or alternatively the tube station carpeted with poppies, her fall a silent, if permanent, lapse from consciousness.'

J started, thinking for a second that he saw a twisted face appearing at the train window. Looking again, he realised it was one of the sea birds, pinned by the motion against the window, its beady eye a black hole of alarm. Suddenly the birds were hitting the windows from all angles. It was like being under siege.

J's voice rose in frustration.

'It's all so hopeless,' he spat. 'Images seem to loop back to images, pictures fall upon pictures. When I look back I no longer see the simple shape of the tracks disappearing to a vanishing point, I see a pattern, a pattern that turns in perpetually on itself.

'You know the illusionist Mauritus Escher, he did all those engravings of impossible staircases; he twisted a dimension, took liberties with perspective, to create a four-sided stairway where each one meets the other. Your eye can follow the figures around as they seem to be ascending, or descending, or doing something, but nobody seems to be getting anywhere. I had a friend who was convinced that he had designed the London underground.

'Sometimes I think he was the architect of my memory. I seem to follow path after path, but each time I return to my own reflection, pale against the procession of the sodium lights.'

In fighting his way back, J was struggling through the corpses of sea birds.

'I remember one Christmas we spent in Brighton. A friend of hers had entrusted us with a flat for the week – an attic, facing down towards the front. You couldn't see the sea, but by leaning out of the low skylight you could sense it, the rain falling on your face and shimmering on the slates on the roof.

'It was perhaps the happiest time we spent. She had got some money from somewhere, I didn't ask where, nothing outside the realms of her presence with me seemed to matter at the time.

'The room was warm; suffused with a golden drug-induced glow, we lay and watched one another, and the sleety snow falling on the skylight and fading into drizzle. The light changed from blue to grey and back to black, the only change in a frozen picture. The room was in an orbit of its own, suspended there magically by the force you could feel in a walk along the dark front.

'For three days the dim walls of the flat and the slow and cyclical transformation of the skylight were our only parameters, our soundtrack the slow and yearning themes she selected from the small selection of records. As they played, over and over, we both stared deep into the sadness of the sound that filled the room.

'Finally we ventured out for the first time, and walked through the streets, still deserted, towards the front. Windows flickered with the ghostly light of telelvisions. We sat in a bar, watching the mist swallowing one by one the lights along the promenade. The world was fading, just as we had decided to re-enter it, and isn't that always the way?

'She turned her gaze towards the television in the corner, and its silent images of lurid technicolour. In *The Wizard of Oz*

Dorothy and her companions were sinking once more into the field of poppies.

' "This has always been my favourite scene," she said. "I've often thought it would be happier as an ending, before they discover that the emerald city is just another citadel of illusion."

'Later that evening, as we walked along the shore, the silence hung in every crevice of the old pier as the mist descended. "It should be wrapped in polythene," she said, "so it won't rot any more, preserved perfectly, frozen right at this point in its decline."

'From somewhere, hidden in the mist, the sound of an old waltz began. Still that refrain wheels through my memory, a structure less certain than the old pier, a citadel of illusion with the wind whistling through its rusted holes. And I come back once again to the same image, of her falling towards the lines, passive and dreamlike as Dorothy, lapsing into sleep in the field of poppies.

'Of course it was neither tidy nor romantic nor in any way beautiful, but she wrote her own ending, at least across my imagination.'

The shadows of the sea birds played across J's vision, like a flurry of snow between him and the sleeping walrus.

Cain's Room

This house is silent. Pausing at the door of her sister's room, Karen listens; the only sound is the blood rushing in her ears.

She enters the room slowly. Had someone passed along the dark corridor from her mother's rooms at the far end, they might have seen her form visible through the partial opening of the door, her calves bulging slightly, straining against the dark mesh of her stockings, her thighs tense. Feeling a ripple on the flesh of her back she turns, but the house is empty; only its groans breach the silence.

The mist of her breath falls lightly on the surface of the mirror; she runs her fingers through the sleek black of her hair, letting one hand fall to her side and the other come to rest on her shoulder, slipping down across her body and along the veins of her other arm.

Still the silence, still the blood rushes.

'I care nothing for ties of blood or ties of shit . . . '

Her sister's words fade into the silence as the mist on the mirror dissipates, traceless, and still the course of her own blood continuous and settling. Her handprint, wet and cool on the glass of the bedside table, the oily, polished texture of the black and blandly modern ashtray. Her hand slipping from the table as she lies on the bed.

Silence falls easily on this house, a dusting of snow on a supine figure and on the bowed head of the crucifix hanging provocative and in this house sacrilegious above the bed. Silence flows from the ink drawings that line the adjacent walls, dripping from the dreamy self-portraits.

The black Bible her sister kept by the bed lies like a dead thing in Karen's hands, limp, broken, its pages fine like butterflies' wings, its binding dry and cracked, a lover's lips in wintertime.

This room is silent, adrift in a silent house, and yet it is possessed by words.

'I don't want your sisterly sucking any longer.'

Petra heard her own voice shouting back, over the silence, over the blood.

'The Lord looked with favour on Abel and his offering, but on Cain and his offering he did not look with favour.'

Her voice could have no effect on the sounds that haunted this silent room.

'You and your parasitical fucking lifeless feeding on *my* talent, stealing the life out of ME!'

Leaning her head back, Karen could see the images flickering against the inside of her eyelids with the uneasy motion of a malfunctioning neon light. She could see herself climbing the stairs, but her face – why could she not focus on her face?

The tube train approaching

a blank

and the tube train closer

movement straining the periphery of her vision

She could see herself lying in her own room between the wall cold and impassive and the warm, rich rot of the dresser's wood.

Her father's voice spoke deep and resonant.

'Sin, it crouches at your door.'

From the viewpoint of the doorway she saw her own face, its image unstable, a television rippling between the channels.

Sounds travel through the silence of this house like bubbles rising from the bottom of the sea; they break with surface turbulence.

She holds her hands out to the mirror, her face in disarray, stretching to hold on to her own image. Hands reaching out . . . the eerie sound of electricity on a tube train line.

This house is silent, the sound of a scream is painful to it, the sound of breaking glass shatters its dreams.

Propelled back from the mirror, she finds herself grasping for the ashtray. Spinning she screams.

As the silence breaks, the words of the living join with the words of the dead.

'And Cain slew Abel.'

Her hand is outstretched; pale and limp it follows the trajectory of the ashtray, its round shape forming an undulating oval as it flies through the air.

This house is old, the fragments of its silence lie in treacherous shards on the thick pile of the carpet.

'But I'm alive and you're suspended somewhere in limbo, sister dearest.'

In a bubble of silence somewhere a body revolves, its shattered form taped with tubes, tubes of blood and tubes of shit.

Lying on her sister's bed, Petra's body squirms. She reaches for the packet of razor blades placed ostentatiously on the bedside table. The edge glistens against the dull metal, the glass fragments on the dark carpet reflect the last brightness of the twilight. The cut in her arm is superficial but the pain enfolds her questions. Her blood is warm and heavy as it drips on her legs, seeping through the viscose of her stockings, the drip a whisper's breath away from constancy.

This house once more is silent, its only sound is the sound of the blood.

Prey (3)

'And today, tell me where is today, sometimes it seems to be the place that I'm fighting through the sea birds and the drift, fighting to return to; other times it's the place that I'm trying to escape.

'Today is the clanking of malfunctioning machinery, bruising the edges of my dreams. Or perhaps that was yesterday. It seems so difficult to tell. Perhaps I'm just one of those people who lives a number of times all at once, never quite present in any.

'Right now, looking through the corpses of the seabirds towards the first flutterings of the dawn, I feel as if I am already an old man, somewhere in the damp of a threadbare sitting room, watching my life on video tape. The screen, inevitably, is cracked, its fragments lying strewn across the floor. To each shard a separate scene, another glimpse of treachery.

'In my mind I rearrange the fragments, casting them as she threw the tarot cards, laying another and yet another vision, each one no more satisfactory than the last. As for myself, I can no longer tell the difference between my present and my future. And the past? I suspect I am the man who failed to learn its lessons and who is condemned to relive them endlessly. Perhaps that's no bad option, as futures die around us. Disneyworld has blown a fuse.

'The narrative of my life was determined one day on the Circle Line; I've been re-enacting it ever since, watching it flickering on the darkened window of the train, any train, anywhere; the motion merely serves to determine the pace. I can watch these films of my life endlessly, their dust and grey fusing with the musty smell of the memories in tear-stained waiting-rooms, the glare of the technicolour flaring in a moment's blur of neon.

'Sometimes I feel these memories keep me sane, because I know so well that beyond these windows is the madness, there, crawling belly downwards across the broken glass of cider-bottle precincts. The madness that hangs heavy in the fumes of the poppies. The madness that lights in the eyes of little children because, yes, Daddy's home again, with the present that you never asked for, never wanted, the only present that isn't broken by the next day, although you, little girl, could so easily be.

'I have held her throat in my hand, fragile as the skeleton of a bird, and looked deep into her eyes, hoping for a trace of fear. Every time I see that scene, once more I hold my breath and will the sequence to change. Perhaps if I recast these fragments once again, I can put some expression in the deadly blankness of those eyes, something which will save me from being dragged once again into their blackness.

'If I can conjure up her face, why must it always be a photograph, an image beyond my control, a face in which I can cause no reaction. That darkness is always there, a darkness which says "You are my death, I know this, I offer no resistance."

'I have seen the madness, the madness that lies beyond these images. I have pursued it through countless cities, countless streets, I have seen my friends raging with it and against it, climbing the walls, only to land amidst broken fragments of sadness. I have stood beneath the city lights and screamed at the top of my voice, the echoes of my shout rising and ringing through the alleys, harmonising with the sound of the madness.

'Death, for her, wasn't something that came with sudden and definite finality; it hovered and threatened like a thunderstorm before finally breaking. Like a tube train, it signalled its arrival well in advance.

'I used to dread those days when it had made a premature advance, when it hung around her jowls – grey, dead flesh. I would wake in the half-light, it was never much more than half-light in that cellar. She would be brooding over my sleep. I would come round, just to be pinned to the pillow by her stare. The clouds of madness hung in her eyes, and the room echoed with the sounds of the birds, seeping through the walls like the cold. She would stare straight into my eyes, while my sinews still twisted through the final strand of some sensual dream.

'Within seconds my flesh would be crawling, twisting on the hook, the hook on which she intended to gash herself open.

' "The pelican", she once said, "has always been seen as a symbol of sacrifice. The legend is that it tears out its own heart to feed its young." She broke off, the blankness of her face seeming to crack for an instant. Her life leaked through once more, through the death mask that had fallen on her face. She looked at me and the film formed once more over her gaze. "Sometimes I look down", she went on, "and all I can see is a row of mouths making hungry noises at me."

'The sound of the birds echoed loud through the cold of the room. I said something cruel, as usual. So you want me to tie you up in a tangle of emotion and lash you with words, OK, so I'm ready now to play my part in this charade, this sad parade. After all, I realise that once we've seen the madness we can expect nothing but torture, hope for nothing that will prove our existence except that pain.

'That first night she had asked me to cut her, producing a sharp dagger from underneath the bed. Cold steel breaking through the flawed, milky white of her skin. J loves Petra 4 Ever, like one of the juvenile scrawlings that crowd the walls around the railway tracks. I wouldn't do it at the time, although since then I've longed so often to etch my loneliness on her skin. But the loneliness, of course, precludes the offer.

'I remember holding her throat in my hand, fragile as the skeleton of a bird. "Sometimes", I said, "I hate you so much." I watched the pulse as it stood out, beating on her neck, soft as the sound of birds' wings, flapping at the window.

'The signs of her withdrawal from me, from life, from everything, were scattered all over the flat by the end. It was even reflected in the titles of the pulp novels she devoured by the day, *The Last Good Kiss, The Death of a Thin-Skinned Animal*. That was how she saw herself, a thin-skinned animal, a frightened little creature, paralysed by the cry of a swooping owl.

'The obituaries to our affair lay scattered on screwed up scraps of paper on the bare floor. When drunk or drugged, she would scrawl her destiny on pieces of paper. Her destiny, or mine. These epistles, or epitaphs, would lie amidst the fallen tarot cards.

'I remember once picking one of them up. The words hacked across it pierced my skin. "Dead love," it read, in erratic capitals, and then "Kill him, or kill myself." Perhaps they were questions rather than statements. Questions answered by the inexorable fall of the cards.

'As I let it drop, as the paper spiralled towards the floor, my mind looped back to the cold insistence of her voice. "Cut me."

'The legend of Orpheus and Eurydice is a myth of sunset and sunrise, Orpheus perpetually chasing Eurydice, Eurydice following Orpheus as night follows day, day follows night, just as our scenes are re-enacted between the angles of my reflection. And the sun rises again, even in my absence, across London, to which I shall never return, to which I return every day, every hour, every mile, every station waiting-room.

'I stare out of the window, watching the corpses of sea birds as they strike the window, and I return once more. I stare across these scenes of desolation, and my gaze continues over the horizon, chasing the light, running from the darkness, but finding it inevitably and unavoidably in the depths of the underground, where the sound of her voice floats on the sentimental themes that haunt the tunnels.

'I am the tube train driver; as her body falls from the platform I see her last look, despairing, relieved, alarmed, in limbo, in terror. In memoriam. In perpetua. Petra.'

Reflections on the Rails

The sound of the sea birds had stopped, the brief calm before the final breaking of the dawn no longer tortured by their cries. In this interlude of unnatural silence J's thoughts continued to revolve, disconnected in the darkness.

Somewhere, always waiting for the dawn, her body continues to trace the infinite contours of the night. Reaching towards her limbo was like clutching for a formless shadow.

Beyond this window, there in the darkness, is a scene of desolation. The wing of a gull, coiled in rusted barbed wire, stretches out to its full extent, it feathers catching the wind, which blows the shifting sands in drifts around its form, now still. The scene is etched in a clouded, silver grey against the rippling darkness of the sea.

J's thoughts, running before the light, return to all those matronly Europeans, collapsing on the marbled mosaics of museum floors, in front of the hanging form of a naked man and the tension of his musculature, straining above death. Was it, he wondered, a sudden realisation that caused the grip to loosen – that there was no hope, no resurrection, no light, allowing them to lapse into darkness on a tragic sigh.

Looking into the grey, J could see the corridors receding, marked by the declining figures of bone-white classical sculptures and the bodies marking the distance of the huge and empty floors. And he watched as the sands rose knee-high to the statues.

Beyond this window is the first fluttering of the dawn, sweeping across the skyline. The dawn too has wings. As the light struggled to life, J could feel his spirit rise to meet it across the sands.

This last night had seemed like a journey in itself, a journey through a landscape bounded by uncertainty. Even the carriage itself, now visible in the cold light, seemed to have degenerated. The lattice of the luggage rack now drooped down towards the shoulders of the walrus, like some rotted fish-net, the shadows of sea birds trapped in the tangle of its fabric.

The table between them had lost its laminated surface, revealing beneath a deeply gashed rough wood, erupting in splinters. The covers of the seats sagged with damp, spilling foam stuffing into the puddles on the floors. It was as if the train itself had taken on the cast of the rot through which they had travelled.

In the midst of the decay the walrus seemed to be the only constant. J looked deep into the vortex of wrinkles that formed his mysterious expression. Sometimes the depths of the walrus's understanding seemed comforting, other times it seemed like the most profound threat, but always there was something about his face that dragged J in. This time resisting its force, he dragged his gaze once more towards the window. By now his reflection was a mere shadow, a transparent mirage, playing on the surface of a marsh, now rippling with light.

He shuddered, partly with the cold, partly with the memory

of the sound of the corpses of the seagulls as they had struck the window, hollow and empty. He could still see the image of those fragile necks, twisted cruelly out of their natural grace. As the train picked up momentum, crashing through the light now with exultant speed, J felt himself pursued by the wake of the night, a wake whose sound was the echo of a gull's last cry.

As usual, his reverie was interrupted by the walrus's voice. 'Well,' he said, as if in conclusion to a silent conversation, 'every Narcissus must have his Echo.'

As he replied, J felt himself caught once more in a loop of time, using to the walrus the words that she had once used to him. 'You see too much.' As he heard her voice chorus with his own, he saw once more the time he had lain, his forehead against hers. Foreign images of her father flickered uninvited through his mind, a white face looming large over a camera. He saw her dancing in the peep show, that cinematic image undulating over her body.

'Echo?' asked J.

'The reproachful sound left to haunt Narcissus as he pursued his reflection to his death, the only reminder of the nymph who died of loving him.'

'So Narcissus, in love with his own reflection, was in turn loved by an echo?'

'Exactly,' said the walrus, 'and I'm glad you didn't make the usual mistake of saying that Narcissus was in love with himself; it was for love of his reflection that he died. The two things, as I'm sure you of all people know, are entirely separate.'

'The mirror', said J, 'has been since childhood the realm of my freedom, the locus of my death, in certain hope of resurrection.'

The walrus, in his turn, looked puzzled.

J felt pleased with himself.

'Just another echo from the past,' he said.

Beyond the window, the first rays ripple on the water, their pattern blurred by the motion.

Sunblind

As the light finally rose, it filled in not a landscape but a stretch of water, extending on either side of the train as far as the eye could see. The effect, in the cascades of sunlight, was like travelling through two banks of light.

Across the shimmering water, far in the distance, the birds could be seen once more, tracing mournful spirals against the sky. Watching J felt, although he knew that it was impossible, that he could hear their plaintive cries. Their wheeling paths wove through the patterns that the sunspots traced across his vision.

In the intricate shapes of the sunblindness, J felt he could distinguish the lines of the stories that clouded his thoughts. Like the patterns in the dazzle, the walrus's tales seemed to etch their own trails between him and what he saw, grouping and re-grouping, casting themselves around the sordid reality, yet more shimmering illusions.

He looked deep into the flickering of the sunlight, and once more towards the distant birds – the flames forever licking at the wounds, the Phoenix forever rising from the flames, and the dawn rising once more.

'I dreamt,' she had once said, 'that my body swelled up and burst, releasing hundreds of winged creatures. The people around me screamed, because they believed them to be harpies, but I remained as the ghost of a contented knowledge, realising they were angels.'

He had thought of that as he had seen her body in the hospital, white under the unremitting light of the neon, a body no longer connected to reality, in a state of dream, dreaming of flight.

J looked at the walrus; the circles around his eyes seemed to trace the shape of an infinite sadness.

'The birds, of course,' the walrus spoke, looking up towards the sky, 'are the warning, the warning and the witness – the warning of the storm, the witness . . . well, sometimes the witness of murder.

'Now take Sisyphus, the poet, torn to pieces by thugs in the woods, a crime observed by no one but a flock of wild cranes who traced their spirals above the carnage. Some months later, the murderers sat in an open arena, watching the terrible scene re-enacted by the Fates. "Look," they cried, pointing into the sun, towards an empty blue, "the cranes of Sisyphus!" A senseless statement, perhaps, but one that awoke the crowd to their guilt. They were hanged, of course.'

Feeling the harsh burn on his skin of sun filtered through glass, J swooped in his mind through the cool of a tube station. He saw a line of figures, motionless and statuesque, looking down towards the lines. He saw the hand placed firmly between the shoulder-blades, and he saw Petra fall. He looked down towards his own hand, resting on the train table. Removing it, he saw the traces of perspiration fade rapidly from the surface. He looked up towards the birds.

'Of course,' said the walrus, 'if you were hoping for a resolution, you have a problem.'

'Oh yes,' said J. 'And what would that be?'

The walrus waved a hand towards the distant spirals.

'They may shadow the entire railway system, they may even roost in the arches of the stations, but they have never been known to penetrate as far as the underground.

'You see, I told you that the underground was the vortex of forgetting. It is the dimension without witness.'

The Beat of Distant Wings (2)

J stood, a lone figure on an empty platform, watching the train disappear towards the light. Why, he wondered, is there always something sad about a departing train? As he looked, the walrus travelled further and further into the realms of memory. Already the lines of his face, which only a few hours ago had seemed to shape the contours of J's story, were beginning to fade into the mists. Only his eyes, swelling with sadness, seemed to linger as his after-image on this deserted platform.

Then there were his words, falling like feathers around J, spiralling through the sunlight, the aftermath of some winged battle. And here, amidst them all was J, alone once more, his reality defined by the parameters of some placeless station, a lost island in a pool of playing light.

On this silent station the echoes of their words were the only sound.

'Just who the hell are you anyway?' J had shouted across the table.

Alarm was a reaction foreign to the walrus; he had looked calmly back at J, across the mêlée of crumpled cans and empty miniature bottles strewn across the table. The lines rearranged themselves around his features, their beneficent tranquillity seeming to enfold and diffuse J's burst of frustration. Looking into their depth, J had the sudden illusion of being able to read the walrus's words before he spoke.

'A storyteller,' he replied, the levity of his tone raising him somehow above the dripping squalor of the carriage, 'a dealer in lies and predictions. Take me as you will, as someone who might venture to suggest where you might be going, or as a clown, whose antics might just make your journey pass the quicker. The choice, my young friend, is yours.'

The walrus's eyes glittered briefly, the light reflected on a passing railside window. 'And so, come to that,' he added, 'are the stories. Think of them as places you might glimpse through the window, the landmarks that define your journey.'

As the walrus spoke J had felt the anger bleeding slowly from him. Despite the heat of the sun, now charging every one of the carriage's myriad dancing particles of dust, he felt a sudden chill. Drawing his crumpled jacket close around his neck, a long and bony hand clinging around his own throat, he looked out towards the terrain of rushing light.

'I wonder where we are,' he said. It was the first time the question had occurred to him.

'Close, I suspect, to your stop,' replied the walrus, 'time, perhaps, for one more story.'

In the brightness, the tangle of the walrus's hair took on a glow, an arch of light around the ruined features.

'Not so much a story, perhaps, as a picture, with which I leave you as a parting gift.

'The land of limbo, outside the gates of heaven, is a landscape of decay, where memories are left to rot. Crumbling arches, strangled by ivy, lead the way into deserted passageways from forgotten shopping malls. Beams of light flood through star-shaped holes in disused launderettes, illuminating the dust, while childhoods rattle, trapped in rusted machines.

'The ruler of this realm, where ancient pillars recede into the cracked paving stones of shopping centres, is an angel known as Jaluha. The sound of his wings can be heard, above the echoes of sirens from long-since abandoned docklands.

'Jaluha's job is to greet the souls of the sinners as they come to be judged or purged. He welcomes them with the cup of oblivion, from which they drink and forget all the places through which they've passed.

'As these places slip blissfully from memory, they become a part of Jaluha's realm, where they themselves decay slowly into oblivion. They say that for those who pray for the release of death the sound of the beating of Jaluha's wings comes as the first welcome sign that their deliverance is at hand.'

The walrus's last words were wrapped around J as he closed the door of the train, and as the fresh air of the platform diffused the staleness of the carriage in his lungs.

As he watched the train disappear he listened carefully, but there was no sound. He had passed the shadow of the beating wings much further back along the line.

Station of Angels

In the shapes formed by his own sunblindness, J felt he could see the shapes of the walrus's mythical creatures, which in turn seemed to be the shape of his own visions and fears. Yet now the walrus had gone the train now disappeared into the dazzle.

J screwed his eyes up against the daylight, looking down the tracks, perhaps for some trail, some proof of the train's existence, but no, in whatever direction he looked, he saw nothing but banks of light rippling on water, the dazed reflections of his imagination.

He shook himself, like some disengaged lover trying to cast off the harpies of a humid night's nightmares. He allowed the warmth of the sun to play on his face, the heat bringing a flicker of life to skin that had felt dead for too long. He could feel the flow of the blood through every tiny capillary, and with it the rush of memory.

Whatever else, he could remember where he had been; the memory of those slowly unfolding landscapes, he felt, would never leave him, despite the times he had strained to hear the sound of Jaluha's wings.

Even now he found that in calling up Petra's face he saw mirrored in her eyes his journey through the twisted landscapes of England. He remembered trails through moors, honeycombed by the memory of shallow graves, the light from heavy clouds filtered through the dark translucence of hooked wings. Darkness breeding.

He remembered the tracks that wound through the shadowy outskirts of London, where murder grows like mould behind cracked window-frames and the flowers on the wallpaper mutate strangely in the cold, unnatural damp. Spores bursting through the paintwork.

Sometimes the journeys that unwound beyond the window were not his. Sometimes what he watched was the internal landscape that had flickered behind some other pair of eyes. He would find himself tangled in the dreams of the moors murderer, Ian Brady, a Scot with a personal war behind his eyes, taking the train from Glasgow Central to Manchester Victoria. Still he could see the pale-faced descendants of Lesley Ann Downey flitting past the windows, ghosts of innocence that inhabited the nether world between suburbia and the echoing graveyard of the industrial wasteland.

Often he would find himself opposite a newspaper headline that testified to the continuing fascination that those murders had, as if the haunting newsprint faces of Hindley and Brady in their endless replication might finally give form to the features of evil. And J's mind flew back to the predatory owls that would sometimes settle in the upper reaches of Petra's room, their glowing eyes peering reassuring and constant from the dark corners, the cooing from their throats a comforting sound in the darkness.

So all those winding landscapes, all those lengthening shadows had led him here, to this strange station in a sea of sunlight. He looked up, where just the fluted line of an overhead shelter separated him from the perfect blue. Over to the left three ornamental lamps led off in a line of sharp perspective towards the end of the platform, their shapes softened by generations of regulation colour paint. At the top of each stanchion there was a winged cherubim figure holding a globe of light. As J watched, one by one the globes extinguished.

As if in a wave of sound breaking on the station, J heard the cries of the gulls mourning their dead. As they passed, their wails seemed only to emphasise the silence of the sunlight, glistening on the water around him. He felt his eyelids droop. Here, at last, in the bright limbo of this floating platform, he felt as if he could be touched by sleep.

As he closed his eyes, the dance of the light echoed the flurry of the images behind his eyelids. He saw fields of stubble erupting in flames, like some oblique prescience of future war, he saw the empty pathways where weeds twined through the shadows of disused railway lines, now torn up, escape routes closed. He saw the deathlike figures of families, standing by the lines, looking up with expressionless faces. And as he passed them again, and once again, he saw their flesh degenerating, falling off their faces, leaving only rows of blankly grinning skeletons in a mire of putrefaction.

And once more he returned to Petra, the voices buzzing in her ears, like words crackling through the static of a malfunctioning loudspeaker system. Petra drowning in the peep show, while behind the panels old men cling desperately to feeble erections.

'The thought of their presence never bothers me,' she once said, 'the thought of all those burning eyes, smouldering behind my image. It reminds me somehow of my childhood. The first awakenings of sex I remember were standing naked in front of my bedroom window. The curtains were open, the window black, and beyond were the lights of the distant, neighbouring houses.

'I used to fantasise about shadowy figures watching me from beyond the glass, while I traced the shapes of my own reflection. I began to evolve a routine that became the root of some childish ritual. I continued to develop it, not out of pleasure, but because I felt trapped in the steps of some morbid dance.'

Often he would walk into the room to find her crouched by

the mirror in the corner, staring at her own reflection. In front of it she looked suddenly vulnerable, as she so rarely did in life, except, for similar reasons, when she faced J.

The mirror itself, although huge, was jagged at the edges, as though it was a mere fragment, broken from a much larger one. Misted with age, it gave the impression of staring into a different dimension, a crack diagonally across it caused a diffraction of the image.

He could picture Petra now, reaching out towards her splintered reflection. He could even place himself in the picture, his own image in itself a reflection of hers, the hair black and coiling over the pale of his forehead, the fullness of the mouth. And yet somehow the tension that crackled between Petra and the mirror was lacking in his case. There seemed in this vision, this bubble of the past, floating through the sunlight of this lonely situation, less distance to breach.

She ran her hand across the crack in the mirror. He winced as blood appeared on her fingertips. She remained expressionless, absentmindedly putting her fingers to her mouth, the red drops standing stark on her pinched lips. It seemed as if the contact with her own mirror image had wounded her.

All these reflections in the blur of a crowded tube station. J, the sister, ties of blood and ties of shit. The world seemed to mirror Petra back, exclusively to expose her own incompetence, her inability to survive.

J could see the image again and again of her falling towards the tube line, every time it seemed to be soundtracked by the sound of reflections shattering. She was the Narcissus feminine falling towards her own image. The mirror was the locus of her own death, her death in her own image. It was the only end of the love of Narcissus. The 's' that transforms the singular into plural, when reflected in a mirror, is a serpent swallowing its own tail.

He remembered standing with Karen, the sister, looking down at Petra's body in the hospital, a body that no longer responded, a dead mirror image, its heart still beating.

And here he was, her Echo, a disembodied voice, haunting the railways of England, remembering the sight of her body inert, recalling the sensation of waiting for flowers to burst from her flesh.

In his dreams flowers burst through the concrete of the tube train platforms, like weeds breaking through the cracks of haunted ruins. Their heads were bent over, staring mournfully towards the lines, like the flowers of Narcissus over stagnant pools.

Dreams of Flight

J looked at the glittering water; in his fatigue the finer detail of the pinpricks of light blurred into a shimmering haze. Deep within the slow evolution of the patterns it traced on his retina, he saw his return, tracing through the network of his dreaming imagination the intricate pathways that might take him from this island of a platform, back towards the malfunctioning metropolis.

He could see the city now, flickering in the dark shadows of sodium lights, the city whose labyrinths replicated the closed circuits of his brain. He could see his own future as a read-out, looping around neon information strips. He could see it in orange dots of light on the train announcement sign at Piccadilly Circus tube station, where the ghost of London's sexuality haunts the tunnels, hopelessly trapped and hideously malformed, its presiding spirit moved to aid the traffic flow.

As J's imagination circled the statue of Eros, he watched its wings ripple as, deserted by his shadowy minions, he prepared to leave this shopping-mall culture. As always, the winged creature was expressing the desires of those who huddled around him – but now the secret yearning of the faceless crowds was tensed not towards sex but towards escape.

And once again J's story rolls around in the neon information strip above the circus, but once again it falls prey to a visual illusion, the words falling into gaps in space, leaving a read-out of disconnected dots, spiralling into nothing.

Hovering briefly back to consciousness, J looked into the mocking play of the sunshine. It seemed, as he swooped back through his vaporous dream world, as if he could see the same light dancing on the waters of the Thames, a pathway criss-crossed by the tracks of memory, lined with museums rising cavernous above the ripples. The daylight neon cast watery reflections.

As he dreamed, the banks of the river unravelled before him, slow as the drift of thick smoke. Its length seemed infested with the winged creatures of myth, all of them apparently making ready to make their escape. The great bronze eagle on the north bank was poised for flight, beginning slowly to strain against the gravity that held it to this base of tawdry glamour. The air was suddenly dense with the sound of beating wings.

An old Arab, sitting in quiet contemplation of a weak and watery foreign sun, is ignominiously tipped from his bench, as the winged sphinxes that form the stanchions raise rusted wings and swoop above graffiti'd concrete and fly-overs. Their wheeling and uneasy path can be traced over past the City to the Isle of Dogs, where they alone can already see the sons of Albion burning in their cars.

Gliding down, their ugly and splendid reflections flicker on the glittering mirrored cells that are regenerating, shiny, brittle parasites, breeding from the rot. And they will build Jerusalem. And in every window J, in his terror, can see the reflection of Petra, falling.

Reflected Glory

Her breath, falling on the already misted mirror, and her hand, reaching out to meet the fingertips of her own reflection.

As J pursues the flight of the sphinxes through the East End of London, his vision is blighted by the glare from the newly built mirrors. Mirrors and chrome bursting like shimmering new skeletons from hollowed-out holes of dwellings, as the wounded hulks of rusted container ships sink out to the east, drifting away into the mists.

The new residents were building their dwellings in the cast of airports, as though to display publicly their power over escape, their ability to disintegrate through these mirrors and rematerialise in some perfect form, somewhere on another side of another mirror.

The world, J resolved, was becoming an elaborate system of teleportation. In front of these mirrors it no longer mattered where you were, and, since it no longer mattered, you might as well be anywhere. The mirror was the realm of dreams, within which you might dream yourself away.

The modern world was a conspiracy to undo the curse of Babel, to eradicate the differences in the pressing of a computer key, to replace the gravity of the real world with the weightlessness of reflection and to rise, therefore, unto heaven. 'Fallen angels,' she'd said, 'afflicted by a fear . . . .'

He could see the sphinxes, these gloriously unlikely creatures, spiralling back towards earth, no longer held aloft by wings of belief. The splashes in the water go unnoticed in the midst of the city's reconstruction. In a hundred years, perhaps, the rusted forms will be washed up on the shores of a paradise decayed.

He could see her, as if from the other side of a two-way mirror, reaching towards her reflection, a tentative touching, her fingers pulling back as if pierced by the spikes of static, but returning once more with a surer touch. He watched her body closing in on the surface as if falling, her small breasts flattened against the mirror like pressed flowers, the aftermark of her lipstick blending into the smear of her mouth.

As she writhes against the flat surface, her lipstick traces the shape of a spiral, echoing the single curled strand that falls across her twisted face. Her body coils into a ball of arms and legs, and then stretches out once more in resignation.

As the body twitches and falls passive, he hears the music of a distant memory echoing through a hall of mirrors; in the ripples of the water he watches the infinite reflection of an old scene. He could see himself, slouched in the corner of some party, as he in turn watched Petra, clutched in the grip of some deathly tango. He could see her body falling as if broken over the strong arms of her partner. At each twist she stumbled, as if to fall, held only by his insistence. He could see his own face, looming from the corner, held spellbound by the strange perfection of the scene.

He watched as the surrounding figures disappeared, leaving only this staggering rag doll. Against the mirror once again the body strained, as if to break through the skin and into the pool of reflections.

J watched, waiting to trace the path of the ripples.

Excuse Me, Odysseus – Isn't This Your Stop?

J came to consciousness once more with the jolt of movement, his head falling and striking a window. Beyond the glass the sun was now at the peak of its arch, playing on a sea now distant, falling off beyond a fringe of rocky green.

The train in its forward trajectory bit deep in the rails, projecting J forwards at a startling speed, very different from the lurching progression his stomach still remembered from the night before. He sat up with a start, looking towards the seat opposite, expecting to be welcomed by a ripple of the walrus's wrinkles. The sight of the empty seat seemed to awaken some deeply buried awareness of the direction in which he was being drawn. These recurrent dreams of return had now become a force as real as the speed which slung him back into his seat.

The light flashed forward in front of him, pulling him in its wake, and yet he felt that something had ended, that behind him he was leaving an intricate tangle of confusion.

He watched the ghostly structure of a deserted station flashing past, the skeleton of its after-image lingering in his eyes, seeming to hold beneath its ruined arches all his dream of decay.

As the train approached the distant sprawling tendrils of London it seemed to pick up speed, as if the suddenly deepening red of the light was drawing them all the faster to the city's intestines. The rays glinting through the empty frames of disused gas cylinders, pouring through the crumbled silhouettes of ruined buildings, seemed almost opaque as he raised his face towards them, letting their warmth bathe his closed eyelids.

He had the feeling, as he always did on returning to London, after however brief a respite, of arriving back in a conspiracy of normality, as strained as the atmosphere in a halted tube train suffocating in a tunnel.

As they reached the Gothic splendour of St Pancras Station the light was finally falling, its last moments flickering through the endless arches as J looked up. From the far end of his carriage his face, with the eyes raised aloft, was touched by the yearning cast of some medieval saint.

He passed through the gates, an uncertain face amidst the trooping faithful, drawn by the magnetism of the underground. Apparently invisible to the belligerent gaze of the inspectors, he continued past their outstretched hands without question, finding himself once more under the neon lights of the underground's tunnels, where the aching tones of buskers met at every intersection.

Here in this realm of unnatural familiarity, as he felt his footsteps drawn into a predestined path, he felt for the first time the pain of her absence.

These tunnels bear their secrets in silence as drab commuters swallow their panic and pass through the labyrinth of its alleys, trying to forget that they walk through the domicile of ragged visionaries, a dimension where illusions and memories glisten.

With This Ring I Re-bled

The ringing of the telephone relocated J within the four dark walls of his room. The familiarity of the surroundings, his sleepy reflection in the mirror above the bed and the lowered eyelids of the Madonna on the dresser – all of it was somehow unexpected. The sickly sensations of his aimless wanderlust lingered, balking at the light that poured through the rotted fabric of the ragged curtain.

In struggling towards the ringing he seemed to be moving backwards through his own dreams, the lazy glow of the motes around him pouring past in a slow-motion rush. Battling through the thickness of the early afternoon air, he felt unable to fix his own image in his mind. As he lifted the receiver the thickness of his voice seemed to join with every other hello he had ever uttered into this receiver – in anxiety, in irritation, in hope.

In its turn, the voice on the other end seemed to be crackling through several dimensions. It sounded lost and somehow scared, as if it had been trapped in the electronic circuitry for some time now, long enough to be suspicious of the wedge of light that promised a possible escape. J replied, but still there was only the crackling and the perpetual questioning: 'Hello . . . can you hear me?' The voice nearly expired on itself. Finally the line went dead.

J, still struggling under the weight of his sleep, tapped at the cradle, succeeding only in adding a series of clicks to the storm of static that filled the receiver. Lost in the white noise, he felt himself transported to previous phone calls. The lost voice of Petra as it would appear early in the mornings, a pale manifestation, reassembling itself across this very system, wailing plaintively from the same receiver.

Somewhere in the endless spirals of the telephone system her voice still existed; 'You're with sombody' it repeats over and over again. J listened to the clickings rippling through the realms on the other side of the handset. Perhaps somewhere in there was a cipher that might release that voice, even with the terrifying coldness of its tone, just one more time.

He remembered one time hearing the voice dying away on the line, surrendering itself to the ocean of static behind. 'I'm bleeding,' it said, the sound of some Ophelia, billowed by a current of electronic interference, a current the mercury-grey of dead television screens.

The line then had also fallen dead, leaving J holding nothing but a buzzing silence, a hand full of emptiness where once her pulse had been. He remembered the train ride across there, the dark shadows of the docklands playing against the reflection of his slowly seething panic. This calm insistence of her words had looped through to the rattling train. 'Cut me, CUT ME!'

Once again, as he looked back, he could see the look in his own eyes, riddled with the horror of doubt. Orpheus-like at a Eurydice. In his memories he could never see himself close enough to act, he was always looking back, from a distance.

In his threadbare passageway the hum of a disconnected telephone line provides the background to a picture of her living room.

By now its decay was complete. Books and clothes lay scattered across the floor, there was something draped perilously across the single-bar electric fire that lent a sickening drowsy heat to the scene. She sat in the far corner of the room, perched bird-like on the edge of the single chair, her head moving with quick, darting jerks, her eyes round, staring, apparently vigilant, as if swelled by panic. She shot her eyes in his direction as the dull crack of a plastic syringe underfoot distracted her attention from the opposite wall. She looked suddenly predatory.

Still perched in the ridiculous position, she proffered two bandaged wrists, held leaking in front of him as a silent reproach for some crime. The crime it seemed to be up to him to invent, not that much invention was necessary. Her hands returned quickly behind her back.

Looking back now, he could see the danger that was inherent in the scene, the glint in her eyes of a destruction that was not self-directed. It was only later, on the telephone once more, that he had realised just how vulnerable he had been, standing watching her. He knew that his protestations of innocence were false; he never knew just how close he came to exacting the toll on his exposed side.

He could hear the voice hissing once again through the static on the line. 'When we spoke' – her tones were clipped – 'I was holding a knife. You were being very nasty to me.'

He could feel the panic at his throat once again, see his left side exposed, see the writing once more. 'Kill him, or kill myself.' Nevertheless, his voice was calm, contemptuous.

'So why didn't you use it?'

He could remember her reply, stark in its simplicity.

'You never came close enough.'

Further Echoes

The receiver choked in his hands and came back to life again, the reassuring purr of the dialling tone bringing him back to present time. Despite the similarity he knew immediately that the voice, lost in the system, belonged not to the ghost of Petra, trapped in the lines, but to Karen, the sister, the nearest thing to a living ghost it was possible to get.

J had never known Karen during the time he had flitted around Petra, but it was difficult to reconcile the shadowy figure he met after the event with the 'guardian angel' that Petra had described. If, as we are told, there is a guardian angel for everything in the world, what happens to the angel when that thing is irredeemably broken?

To hear Petra talk, Karen was her mirror image, herself reflected back with a mocking perfection. Where Petra threw herself with brutal abandon against the mirror, Karen, according to Petra, slid through with all the ease of Alice.

The Karen J had seen, shortly after that first, wavering shock of a telephone call, had been a hazy presence at best. She had a lack of substance, like some shadowy figure on an ill-tuned television set, yet she and J seemed somehow to stumble through the same grey dimension. It was as if the energy released by Petra at the time of hitting the rails had provided them both with the force necessary to escape reality, at least in part.

As he rang back, he was greeted by the familiar chorus of replies. Their Hampstead residence was split into five separate orbits, each member of the family connected to the outside world by a separate telephone extension.

Petra's empty orbit presumably remained as she had described it, in this house he had never seen. The line of masks, perhaps even the crucifix, itself a gesture of defiance against her Jewish parents.

Somehow the house had loomed over both their lives, as dark and guilt-ridden as any of Poe's creations. In his vision of the place, J had always added the odd swooping raven. Now, with the father's overarching solar orbit gone, the balance of the place had been lost irretrievably, leaving the mother, Karen and her younger brother spiralling in frantic ever-decreasing circles.

Still the confused caller could be met by three voices at once, each one reaching out with a barely concealed desperation towards this unknown voice, a representative of the life beyond the shadows of the house. It was only after two disconsolate clicks that J found himself alone with Karen's voice.

It seemed vulnerable as usual, faltering, as if it was unsure of whether it might be destroyed by the small amount of air that might travel down the line and into the musty atmosphere of her room.

This dust is not the same as the dust that settles around J. This is the dust of ages, gilded by sunlight, its taste is rich and heavy at the back of the throat.

Karen's voice drifts uneasily on the static.

'J, where have you *been*? I'd almost given up trying to contact you.'

'I had to go away for a while.' Where indeed had he been? His vagueness seemed only to endear him to her.

'I need to see you.'

Behind her J could hear the chorus of ghosts, whistling across the lines.

Drowning

The telephone drops from Karen's hand, settling once more in the cradle. Although cut, this connection lingers for a moment, like the images in a severed head.

She rests a hand lightly on closed eyelids to shadow the stream of late summer afternoon sunlight, glowing red and gold through the tinted glass by the side of the door. For an instant she is possessed by an image of J, still fighting through the dregs of sleep, drowning in the dust of a peeling corridor. But the image fades, leaving her once again alone in this house, where the invasion of light is failing, abandoning it once more to its more natural milieu of shadow.

Her face glows pale amidst the dark wood, as if its resin had drained her colour. She scarcely disturbs the shadows of this house, her figure moving easily through them, pale, like a figure spread thinly across time.

From her bedroom mirror her own face stares back, tainted

by the darkness behind her, movements fluttering in the corners of her vision. Where she expects to see reproach burning in the darkness of the eyes of her reflection she sees only vacancy. She feels, for a moment, as if her reflection is a vacuum, pulling her in. Joylessly she traces an imperfect line of scarlet lipstick around the pinched cupid's bow of her mouth.

Behind her, in the mirror, she can see her bedroom window, and beyond it the tangled foliage of the garden. She turns and walks across the room, the dappled light playing on her dark clothes. She looks out into the dimension of imagination, where her past is tangled in the tendrils of the undergrowth.

From the overgrown corners, the shadows were gathering, deep and green, thick and impenetrable as the water in the ornamental fish pond. She wondered if any sort of life survived in there; the last time she remembered the water being drained she had been a child. She and Petra had stood there, watching fish after fish being dredged from the heavy green silt that settled at the bottom of the pond. She remembered the pale and lifeless bodies, lying on the garden path, scales falling away from the flesh.

She had the sudden image of her own face, pale and round, staring down, a shape dimly visible in the darkness of the window, from the shadows of the garden. Either way, through the glass she was staring into a museum case where her memories were slowly gathering dust.

She and Petra, staring into the murk of the pool, two faces staring back. 'I can see the bottom.' 'No you can't no you *can't*.' In the bottom of the pool, fish drowning in the murk, fighting for a breath. Her face staring down from the window.

She remembered the garden, its verges softened by a fall of snow, her sister and brother playing outside, raking unsightly wounds in the snow with their feet as she looked on. Her face looking down. Her mother had used Karen's fragile constitution as an excuse for her confinement. Such a shame to spoil the snow.

She returned to the mirror to complete her make-up, powdering lightly over the foundation, glorying, as she always did, in the smooth texture it lent to her skin. She looked back defiantly at her own reflection, feeling at last that she could stand her own gaze.

The heavy front door closed behind her as she stepped out into the soundless late sunshine, drawn down the tube tunnel as though by some effortless gravity. The people flitting past her were like shadows of her own sleeplessness.

Golden Rails

As J stepped out of his front door, he could feel the familiarity of the south London landscape seeping through his bones like damp. Traces of the earlier rainfall that had filtered through his sleep could still be seen, although the clouds had broken, giving way to the translucent early-evening sunlight.

Cracked and decaying, the street was a dark expansion of his imagination, shadowed by the ghosts of the mythical winged creatures that had swooped through his last station dream in the sunshine. Echoes of those images circling in the sky above him, tracing the territory for the last time before leaving.

The terrace reduced in perspective towards a dark vanishing point. A single figure, his shadow cast long across the last strip of sunlight on the damp tarmac. Behind the windows violence lurked in the geometry of peeling walls and cracked cornices.

He reached the end of the street and looked down towards the harsh lines of the estate, where the geometry of violence gave way to the geometry of living murder. The sunset seemed premature to J, still drugged by sleep as he watched its gold, streaming like something you could breathe through the towers.

He looked over the bridge and down towards the station, where the broad span of rails curved off towards the West End. The sun turned the silver gleam of the central tracks to gold and even brought a rusted glow to the disused lines at the edge. He watched the ripple of a sudden shower as it swept across the tracks in the distance, a shower composed equally of water and sunset.

These landscapes fall one upon another, their lines bleeding through across time. Through this scene a memory penetrates of a trip out to the fringes of the city, to a special place of hers, where parkland disappeared into countryside. They had sat by the ruins of a summer-house, watching the light settling through its fallen beams.

Black dots had played in the corners of his vision – whether the dying cells within his eyes, or the St Vitus dance of some expiring insects, inscribing their own epitaph in fussy and fanciful script on the air around him. The light panned low and horizontal and couples called to dogs and children to accompany them as the grass mired itself in a deeper green and planes fell away to dock away to the west.

Over in the park beyond the railway station, a group sprang to their feet as the shower swept across. J could see the cans and bottles they left strewn across the grass, like some obscure hieroglyphic language which traced his past. He watched the tower blocks glinting through the rain and in the distance bleeding rays of sunshine falling on the drab spires of the city.

He could remember a time when the sight might have lit within him some private glory, but today it struck a hollow core. The dark fascinations once bounded by the city's rooftops seemed to have fluttered free of their prison and were wheeling in a last triumphant swoop above the squat landscape before etching the perfect and regimented formation of their departure.

He ducked into the station and ducked out as quick, spotting a gaggle of one-time drinking partners leaping over the barriers towards him. All those greetings and explanations and the inevitable invitations to another night in search of oblivion seemed so unnecessary, not to mention undesirable. Perhaps some other time, or then again maybe never.

Pulling his jacket collar up, he slipped down the side road by the station, gawky and skeletal, limbs flapping like some hapless silent comedian, fighting through a wind tunnel.

The last light glints through the broken glass above a dark wall as this figure, bounded by awkward lines, flits past.

The Pool of Narcissus

Skipping through a back alley, over a wall, nimbly avoiding the row of dustbins lined across the other side, J realised with a sudden shock just where he was heading. The crane silhouetted above the roofs of the houses belonged to the building site opposite Petra's. He looked down; somehow even the texture of the road, now drying once again in patches after the showers, seemed to be veined with memories.

Turning the corner, he was in her road. The building work was now fully advanced, the entire framework of a luxury apartment building standing as some presentiment of the future, a future either of bleak rootlessness or of the cosseted environs of the fully mirrored drone cell.

Through the hollow windows the birds could be seen, huddling in the darkness below the skeletal roof. The flood-lighting no longer shone, and their perpetual song had been reduced to the occasional tentative trill. Occasionally they would stretch their wings to their full, majestic extent, feathers bristling as they prepared for flight.

Descending the stairs to Petra's cellar, J found the door swinging on its hinges. At the far end of the room water from a broken guttering was pouring in. As J stood in the middle of the floor it lapped round his feet, seeping in through his shoes. A couple of loose tarot cards, the only signs left of her existence, swirled in the current around the stream.

J waded through the water, his reflection scattering into a thousand ripples with every step.

Spinning

The sky had faded to a light purple as J exited from Charing Cross Station. Even as the darkness approached, the street seemed scattered with light, brought to life by the gaudy colours of the glowing flower stalls. Drained office workers with spanking mags in their briefcases and viral hives in the drab folds of their suits bought blooms to take home to wilted wives. Their faces could be seen, filling the lighted windows that flickered through the iron stanchions of the railway bridge, lurching with the sound of memory towards the silence of the suburbs.

A young man asleep in a doorway groaned and rolled round into another reel of a technicolour cartoon dream, his shirt riding up above his stomach, his flesh smeared with the grease of the street. J skipped neatly over the tendrils of his piss, just as two policemen strolled on past with a nonchalant glance.

Spots of rain on the window of the café soaked up the surrounding neon, each individual droplet swimming in green and red. Inside, the coffee machine hissed with the sound of machinery forgotten. Karen's face loomed through the steam from the far end of the room, pale and moonlike.

The surface of her skin seemed to ripple as J apologised for his lateness.

'Don't tell me – delays on the line,' she replied, her words twisted by a bitterness that diffused just as quickly.

'How are you?'

Their conversation revolved in spirals of banalities around the indisputable fact that was the body of Petra. The body, its connections with life, tenuous as they were, now finally severed, drifted between their words. Not the body as Karen had seen it, in the coffin, lying in a repaired stateliness, but the one seen only by the Narcissi, peering from the station platform towards the rails. The tangle of the limbs was the secret shape of their communication.

Outside tourists passed, heading for the station, struggling under the weight of overstuffed baggage. Karen looked towards the rippling light of the dimension beyond the window.

'London seems to be inhabited entirely by travellers,' she said. 'I sometimes wonder if anyone actually lives here.' In the twilight the hurrying crowds were a blur of flailing limbs against the neon.

'The mark of Cain,' she continued, her sentences pursuing some dreamlike orbit around the twisted body. They seemed to be flitting around some vortex of darkness that was Petra's absence.

"You shall be a restless wanderer on the face of this earth." The flickering of a malfunctioning neon sign played on the calm of her face. It broke into a half-smile. 'His curse and mine.'

Petra's death was a web of guilt that spread in gossamer folds from the memory of a tube station platform to this conversation in a steamy café, draping itself from the chrome of the coffee machines and across the formica tables. Through its tangle, J and Petra struggled to see one another.

'They're selling the house.'

A web of guilt swathes its corridors, now dark, its silken white enfolds the shadows.

'I get a third share.'

'Or your wings.'

'Exactly.' She broke off, her voice falling as if asking a forbidden question. 'You know when you disappeared? Where did you go?' There was a note of tenderness in her voice.

J struggled through the images of fish-nets, snared with hooks. 'Backwards,' he said, 'through some memories. Where are you going?'

'The opposite direction, hopefully; out of England certainly.'

J was struck by an image of Karen under the web in a dusted and deserted room. Fragile but insistent as a new-born bird breaking from its egg, she tore its substance, sending the dust flying.

The Scars of Memory (2)

As she finished speaking Karen rubbed at her arm. The tissue around the razor cut had healed, leaving a pink swelling of scar tissue where the new cells formed. J's hand reached across the table as though by some instinct of its own.

She could feel the sensors of her skin flickering at his touch.

'An incision,' she said by way of explanation, 'an excision, perhaps a final tribute.' The sensation was pleasurable, a reminder of the physical transformation which was growing from the scar, as if the angry glow of the new skin was the heat source from which her new identity was radiating.

J could feel a powerful force emanating from her, one that seemed to enfold him and alienate him at the same time. It was almost as if she was going through a series of minor metamorphoses, slipping out of focus only to return each time in changed form.

He in turn seemed to glimpse reality in ever briefer snatches. Occasionally words penetrated. 'England isn't just sick,' she said, 'England itself is the sickness.'

J looked towards the corner of the café, where an old man sat, the grease spots on his plate clouding, the same dull white as his eyes.

Outside the lights trickled down the streets as they walked out into the flicker of the guttering neon.

Reflections

J reached his fingers out towards Karen's sleeping face. Her mouth had fallen into a serene and peaceful bow, smooth and silent as a sweeping snow drift. The sexless contact of their bodies reminded each of their own substance. As he looked up above the bed to the angled mirror that faced down on them, he could just see their two faces in the meagre blue light drifting in through the window.

Her dark hair rippled across the two pillows, entangling the sensual economy of his closely cropped head, two pale faces strangely haunted.

Pier

The endless days before Karen's departure seemed to be inhabited by the ghosts of travel. Once again he had the sensation of being an observer in an interminable season of reruns. Past moments would flit through the cold corridors of his dwelling, echoes from the entrance-ways of shadowed stations.

He sat and stared at the wall, watching the walrus's face taking shape in a damp patch. As his eyelids dropped, the face broke into a smile of seagulls' wings. Their beating resounded, heavy through the clouds of misted waiting-rooms.

The angles of this house, all of them somehow askew, were their only parameters, he and Karen, as they floated through the disruption of its rooms, only dimly aware of one another's existence. As the light fell once more they would lapse into bed, entangling one another in celibate embraces.

Only once did they break away from the rich, damp gloom of the house, to go on a day trip to Brighton. It had been Karen's suggestion, made with such enthusiasm that J would not have dreamt of telling her he'd rather have taken an away-day to purgatory.

The seafront was all still open, although deserted, and the out-of-season sadness was drifting in off the sea, mingling with the smell of vinegar on fish and chips soaked in old fat. Hardboard figures of the Prince and Princess of Wales stood on the pier, holes where the faces should have been, waiting for the heads of red and bristled fathers, pinch-faced mothers and impudent kids with sticky chins stuck forward. Like latter-day stocks, the contradiction of the image underlines the order.

J saw guillotines slicing down to sever the oh so meekly offered necks, the nervous chord of old England twitching in the damp air as night lights creaked on looming cranes. Was the seafront itself as thin an artifice as the primary-coloured images of royalty? Could its crumbling façade of romance be as easily torn down to reveal some bare and crouching figure behind?

He breathed in the energy and violence of the sea. Karen's eyes shone with the reflections of her own thoughts. From further down the pier the sound of a remembered waltz suffused the dampness, interspersed with the voice of a DJ, cheerfully at odds with the sea-soaking and flaking wood and the salt-stained amusements. Further down amidst the flickering lights of unplayed machines the sound of a punchball being hammered by huge fists irregularly punctuated the tinny sounds of the music. A dull thud, the ring of a bell and the sounds of celebrations.

As they walked on towards the pier, two figures dwarfed by the rotting structure, the ghosts of screaming fights seemed to undulate on the night air.

The DJ's console was situated in the middle of the pier, its glass still marked by the snotty smears of kids clamouring close, requesting songs from the repertoire that holds the uncertain structure together. It was lit but empty, strikingly so in the garish pink neon. Inside, a tape spooled on slowly and miserably, and the cheerful voice echoed over the deserted pier, before another theme of creaking sentiment drowned out the groaning of the wood and the cries from around the punchbag.

J looked up and saw a host of birds, their wingspan magnificent, plummeting slowly and gracefully into the sea.

Odysseus Ascendant

These final flickering landscapes, endless sunsets over a panorama of rot, were the preludes to Karen's departure. She flitted through them, a ghost in his presence. All after this is silence, the last decaying chords of the swan-song of Orpheus, hanging in the stale cigarette smoke.

The days seemed to blur into one another, a lightening and darkening of the corridors through which their pale faces passed, a lengthening and shortening of the shadows with which they shared the rooms. They walked quietly, as though through some precarious scene of desolation where one overheavy step might send a cascade of bricks tumbling across their paths.

When she is gone, J thought, there will be one less pair of footfalls to compete with the creaking of the walls.

Then one day he found himself stepping out of the house and into the early morning. The lines of the street were etched pale against a misted grey. Her bag in his hand, she stalked in gawky progression by his side. The sounds of aircraft echoed overhead, like the presage of conflict.

Accompanying Karen, J felt himself the spectator of the opening of further strands of stories, stories in which he, as yet, could envisage no part for himself. He waited in the wings.

War Zone

As they stepped from the tube train their figures cast inelegant silhouettes against a bank of screens, each one showing the trajectory of a bomb released from an aircraft, followed by a figurative plan of destruction, the pattern of a city continually constructed and destroyed in purples and greens.

J admired its intricate form, a kaleidoscope of coloured dots – annihilation and regeneration in cycles of thirty seconds. In a momentary vision he felt he could see the entire history of Europe mapped out across the screens, its frame consistently shattered and altered, each incarnation casting up a different form, building to a peak of intense beauty.

Still the reconstructions continued, the city recasting itself less and less perfectly, the dots no longer aware of their place on the screen, the molecules no longer aware of the laws that bound them together. Europe, J reflected, was an imperfect teleportation through time; like the figurative city on the screens it broke itself down, but its reconstructions belonged evermore to the realms of the bizarre and the surreal. Like some godless scientist in a faded monochrome fifties movie, it found itself with sections of an alien culture grafted in its mongrel genetics.

The airport itself was an irritant, a silicon culture, regenerating itself in the midst of soft, rotten flesh. He looked at the open nerve endings of the implant, showing full colour, six hundred and twenty five lines of them, twitching. Six screens across and six screens down, six windows into another world, travel without movement.

As the next train pulled in, covering the bank of screens, J's mind travelled in the opposite direction, back to the tube stop where they'd started that morning. Around them people had waited in three dimensions while, across the tunnel, huddled in two dimensions, figures from the past slept, still half-waiting for an all-clear signal.

As the train pulled out again J looked back at the screens once more and saw each bearing a separate image, the history of warfare in fact and fiction – from noble ballets to poetically tragic corpses, settling like snow as a bullet's trajectory disrupts the patterns of the brain. X-rays showing dying cells, and the city disrupting and reconstructing. Around the terminal people wove like antibodies in a system on full alert.

J looked round to find Karen gone. In the grip of one of the attacks of sudden vacancy that used to affect Petra she had wandered off on another quest, one of a parallel dimension to her flight. As he went to search for her he passed by clots of travellers, rooted like the figures in the poster, frail hands pulling garments closer to swathe bodies, struggling to reach the state of rest, movement murdering sleep. Eyelids flickered as tension crackled underneath.

He found her outside, her face blank. A fly, its movement sluggish, its life already prolonged by the late-autumn sunshine, crawled across her features undisturbed.

Petra's death had planted something deep inside her, something which she refused to dig out but which grew silently in the heat of her flesh, transforming her from the inside out.

Watching her, still and troubled, analysing the broken bonds of her blood, he was struck by an irresistible urge to reach his fingers out to trace the soft folds of her face. But something held his fingers back, something like the suspicion of heat on a surface before the warmth is sensed. It was as if the transformation was disrupting the area in front of her face, like sunspots erupting on the outer parameter of her personal space.

Behind her left shoulder he saw the awkward figure he cast in reflection, a hand stretched out in trepidation, falling short of a touch. He looked at his own face and then back at hers. Suddenly the fingers of his hand snapped back as if at the recognition of something, something like a memory, floating up through the murk of a hangover, unwelcome and insistent. He had a feeling of slight disorientation, as if reality had been given a subtle twist, everything distorted in perfect proportion, leaving him alone and out of synch, out of place or time.

Looking into Karen's face, he saw her bubbling back through the density of her black eyes. He raised his hand and hesitated only slightly before touching the side of her face, soothing the pulse that glimmered to the right of her eye.

Final Frame

The sound of aircraft overhead, of squadrons of bombers,

pursued J down the glimmering neon of the tubular passage-way as he returned towards the underground system, ghosts of female crucifixions shadowing his eyes.

As the angles of the underground opened to greet him, he stopped, hesitated and briefly looked back, this wondering glance captured on the yellowed, grainy screen of the surveillance system.

Eat Your Elders

by

Mark Edwards

1 Come into the Alley
2 Memoirs of a Flea in the Cold War
3 A Toy on Blood
4 Our Family Corpses
5 Man-e-festations of the State
6 Drowned Dreams
7 The Quick End

1
Come into the Alley

BIRTH. Where am I? you ask, waking up in the dark. All bruised and cramped. Boy birth's a vicious entrapment. You are hunched up in this tiny little space, your head a-thumping, and no one answers your question.

Shifting about you find a door and push it. Luckily it gives and you fall out into a hotel room, everything a dingy brown. A dreary home. The bed isn't made up and there are no personal effects or luggage evident. The room is unoccupied, you haven't been expected. You've been in the closet.

You clamber out and up onto your legs, wobbly like an ostrich chick taking its first walk. Picking up your shattered brains, you head straight for the door and listen. Nothing.

You poke your head out o' the door, expecting a bump on it. Things go bump in the night. Things that go bump in the night. Ghosts go bump, people get bumped off, battered kids accidentally fall down the stairs and go bumpety-bump.

Outside is a hall, the same dinge as the room. A musical thud-thud is conga-ing down the hall; it takes over from the thump in your head. You trot after it. At the hall's end is a stairwell; the noises of a party rise to greet you. You go down cautious.

SOCIETY. I'd arrived in the lobby of the hotel. A band was on stage, all old and white, dressed in hideous two-tone suits. They were fronted by a black female singer knocking out an old music-hall number about the Empire on which the red sun never set.

The lobby was full of gargoyles in fancy dress, streamers, balloons and bunting. A red coat was in flustered command of this Masque of the Red Death.

I stood on the bottom steps staring at them open-mouthed but no one paid me any mind. I must have fitted right in with them; my second-hand raincoat made me look like a dick.

I spotted the bar way over on the other side and wended through drunken, weaving corpses, shutting my mind to every question except the one addressed to the barman concerning vodka.

Beside me on a bar-stool was sat a middle-aged man in full American cop drag, with an LAPD badge pinned in his heart. Seeing as he was the copper, I asked exactly where in hell I'd located.

'The Pleasure Hotel,' he replied. 'You that drunk you forgot?

'Not yet,' I said, 'but I'll be sure and try. Where's this hotel, then?'

'Venice.'

'Little Venice?' I asked.

'No, big bloody Venice. Italy, you arsehole. It's a good hotel. I'm booked for two weeks. Me and a mate, we came out here on a coach. One o' those ones with a bog on board. Everything's laid on right here in the hotel, anything you'd ever want . . ..'

He went on to list the services available, legal and illegal. The list was comprehensive, but there was one missing all the same. An information service to provide the answers to certain questions. Why I was here, how I got here, and who owned this false cornucopia. I knew he wouldn't know.

'What are you doing here?' the man asked. At last he'd sensed I wasn't one of his party.

'Checking on the state of the nation,' I said contemptuously. 'And it's disgusting. But I don't discuss these things with the ignorant.'

This puzzled him so he shut up.

The girl started to sing 'The Tide Is High'. She wanted to be my number one. A biological impossibility and a bloody liberty. I took in the scenery refreshed by the vodka. It all reminded me of a pop video, which always tediously remind me of bands playing small clubs. Unfortunately I'd spoken this aloud.

'What are you?' the policeman burbed, fiddling with his handcuffs, which had got caught in his fly. 'Some kind of subversive?'

'God, you truly are a jerk-off,' I said. 'Let's have another drink.' I waved two empty glasses before the barman's sullen eyes.

WORK. Five young scruffs turn the corner of an abandoned factory. Their hands are thrust deep into ripped pockets of what's left of fifties suits. Weeds have arrogantly sprouted in the pitted tarmac road and the only street lamp is broken. A little moonlight creeps about. They walk down the factory's side to a flap door they push open and enter.

Inside it isn't dark. Not only have all the windows been smashed, but most of the roof's caved in, leaving a ribcage of steel supports. A dinosaur skeleton, a beached whale. Jonah's too dumb to stride right out through one of the holes in its decaying flesh. The scruffs swagger over the debris, they don't pick their way through.

In the middle of the old machine room is a mahogany desk, polished till it sparkles, behind which is seated a fat man flanked by two heavies. The scruffs come to a halt before him.

'Why didn't you knock, boys?' he asks, not looking up.

The scruffs look embarrassed and one starts to apologise. The Fat Man holds up his podgy hand.

'Only my little joke.' As he speaks he plays with a paper-weight in the shape of a gun. 'Any job is hard to come by these days,' he says. 'Am I right? Or am I wrong?'

'You're right,' they chant.

'And I've got a very cushy one lined up for you, cushy as the finest satin-lined box.'

He sniggers. The heavies snigger. And then the scruffs follow suit.

'I'm glad none of you finds death and its . . . little matters repellent. The job's working with stiffs. Nothing complicated, I just want some moved. Okay?'

He looks up at them for the first time. They all shuffle.

'Sure,' says one, 'isn't it, boys?'

They all raise their hands. Stiffs are cheap in a cheap town, especially a cheap town like this. But cash is cash.

'That's what I like to see, democracy,' the Fat Man says. 'Here's the address you go to.' He hands them a piece of paper. 'Goodbye, now.'

He stands and leaves, shadowed by the heavies. The scruffs hang back.

Outside, an official black car is waiting. A chauffeur opens the door for him and asks, 'Where to now, Minister?'

'Home,' he replies.

THE RAT. As the car drives away a mealy-looking rat sticks its head out of a hole with elephantiasis in the wall. The rat says in its squeaky voice, 'Life's dandy for rats with no cats, but when there's no cats 'cos the cats got ate by the humans, rats got to watch their tails.'

A small kid comes hobbling up on hollow legs with a butterfly net.

'And here goes mine.' The rat ducks back inside.

RAT LUCK. I left by the front door of the Pleasure Hotel. Above my head its glorious name was immortalised in neon, the gargoyles were coming and going their own way and it was raining.

Up the road lights were blazing. Ambulances and police cars pitched like an encircled wagon train against the onslaught of disorder at the dark mouth of an alley. The blue light they spun reminded me of black movies. They say anything can happen in the movies. In the night anything can happen.

Curious, I wandered up there. My body was getting healthy; fear and anxiety were returning.

Five bodies lay on the ground smothered in bullet holes. Five young scruffs. Hard faces with the premature ageing disease of the north. They were my age. Me.

Here's the story, I thought.

They hadn't belonged on this street, and nor did I. I hurried off but not too fast. Not too fast to attract attention.

THE ALLEY. I was pulling myself along, my legs still ached, through the windy cubby-holes of Venice.

There go they who could have been me, I thought. And some fucker's free with his pound of flesh paid off. Kill to live, the dictum.

It shouldn't be me, and it shouldn't have been them, or any of us, that pays up the price for another. That buys off the hunger.

This hunger's monstrous. The poor have it starved and the rich have it in a different manner greedy, and they'll both do anything to assuage it. Get the pound of sausage for it. And the poor, it leads 'em into all sorts of crap and bother, and the rich by hook or crook get some other to pay it for them to live, and the po or pay with their lives to struggle.

And the middlies, what do the middlies have? A small belly and a measly appetite, settling for the bits and pieces, morality and culture and politeness and security, etc., etc. – all false idols, that make up so called civilisation.

For a monstrous hunger, there's a monstrous price . . . and a Tale of Two Stories. The one you think you're in, and the one you are in. These idiots wrote themselves into it, and were written out. They were dumb and they were thick, and they were dead.

I'd come out in St Mark's Square. All around me winged lions held between their paws a book the pages of which I couldn't read.

I had no intention of being written into someone else's story. I decided I'd decide what happened next. Venice is a dead museum, sinister and sinking slow, so I decided to leave and see the rest of the world.

I stole a gondola and set out into the waters of the lagoon.

2
Memoirs of a Flea in the Cold War

Me and my brother Duncan live with two witches, Mummy witch and Daddy witch, who we call Daddy sir and Mummy sir, in our home witch is an old vicarage. All English homes are vicarages because the family is a holy and sacred institution. And so is England. The holy and sacred old cow.

Outside in the garden are the graves of vampires. When someone dies in England, he or she becomes a vampire on the living. The past sucks the blood of the present. When my parents die they'll be voracious vampires. I can see this coming. In bed at night, I imagine them dead, digging themselves out of their slime pits, creeping into the house and howling about after me. Leaving trails of gook on the carpet to hoover. Them dead'll be worse than them living, witch is bad.

All English homes are property. And so is the family. Our home is an expensive and big house. Victorian mock Tudor, red brick and beam. But inside it's a pigsty, and Daddy won't put out the money or Mummy for central heating. In winter it's a knacker's yard.

I have only the one brother, Duncan, and no sisters, but he's a lobotomy. We're made to wear ties every hour of every day in order that Mummy or Daddy or both together can tug us about. That's when Mummy hasn't got her hands in our hair. Mummy and Daddy tug us round Safeway's, they tug us to school, they tug us to the vicarages of our relatives, all of whom they despise, and they tug us to posh restaurants, where they exhibit a Mummy and a Daddy and their two good boys. Where I'm too scared to eat in case I fumble table etiquette and am served a kick on the shins and go hungry.

Duncan and me have to do all the housework because Mummy and Daddy are too good to get dirty and too busy.

Mummy and Daddy have told us if we don't do as we're told and behave ourselves we'll end up tortured in hell, witch could be worse. When we were smaller we had to pray to Jesus to make us good boys. I think Duncan still does. If we do something naughty, do wrong, Mummy or Daddy or both slap us on the hand or on the top of the thigh. Duncan never gets hit. Duncan's learnt from Mummy and Daddy how to pass the blame, so it's only me who gets hit with the palm of their hands. If I do something wrong and lie about it, don't own up when interrogated, then I'm hit once for being naughty and once for lying. Mummy and Daddy have made me pathologically honest. A disease, because honesty's troublesome, lying's social. That's how come I can tell the tale on them.

My brother Duncan's part of the plant life. He wanders about with his tan bod and short blond hair and absent blue eyes being particularly boring, his pert mouth ajar as if he had something to say and he says nothing over and over in the same toneless voice. When I ask him something he always answers 'I guess'.

He's always staring at the TV as if he is having trouble understanding. If that's possible in England. He's always staring at something as if that thing is anchoring him down. This he learnt from Mummy. I heard on the radio that if you stare at the TV for long enough your brain falls out. This is what must have happened to Duncan. He's on the shelf with the rest of the groceries.

Mummy and Daddy are married and so they've never fucked. Not with each other, anyway. Though sex is a gift from God. How did I get into the world, then? Like all

Englishmen, I was born antiseptically. I came in a boil-in-the-bag from the food department of Marks and Spencer's. Mummy and Daddy claim there was something very wrong with that bag and they tried to return me. We still have the saucepan I was born in; Mummy boils Daddy's white shirts in it. As I was boiled and not born, it's very hard for me to get emotional. My emotions have been sterilised, but I do try.

Daddy looks like Blake Carrington. He is the president of the Rotary and a mason and a smackhead. He has puncture marks all up one arm and down the other. From wrist to gold wrist watch. Daddy takes smack 'cos he's terribly intelligent and has to make lots of money. He does it for Mummy and Duncan and me. He has to. We cop the blame. When he's eventually dead and gone to the great blackened spoon in the sky, he'll have done for us. Daddy's terribly bored and this is his way to let off the steam under his skin. I think this also explains Duncan. Some of the smack got into him when he was conceived by Daddy's seed.

Daddy doesn't say much, which is good because I don't have a thing to say to him. If he does say anything to me I agree with him or don't reply at all. He doesn't notice. There's nothing between us. He insists we all eat dinner together as a family. The meals are like his business meetings; and the next order of business is what did you do with your day? Daddy falls asleep on his plate and Mummy just picks at her food. She never listens to any conversation which isn't about her. And no one listens to any conversation that is. Her eyes drift off to the garden and fixate there. We might as well not be here, but it's the appearance that counts, not that anyone's watching. Anyway, Duncan has enough trouble using his knife and fork to be using his vocal chords too.

And if I do say something to Daddy, forget myself and think he might be interested, he doesn't hear. He doesn't want to hear. Once when I was younger and even dumber (is that possible?) I used to gush on and on enthusiastically like kids do, and if Daddy happened to be there, witch was rare, and if he happened to hear, witch was even rarer, he'd turn to Mummy and ask.

'Fanny, what's the boy on about now?' Or,

'Fanny, can't you get him to stop?'

Or he'd look me in the eyes and say,

'You're crazy, you know that?'

As I grew up I learnt to keep my gob shut.

All Daddy thinks about is money. And fame, which is more money for more fixes. He's always saying we're on the point of financial ruin. Mummy's disgusted we're so poor money has to be discussed. Usually he says this when one of us asks for something that costs money, or when we're about to go on holiday. The only thing we can ask for that costs him more than money is time. We don't bother.

Daddy had a strong moral upbringing and it's made him a hypocrite. What would morals pay him? He votes for Margaret Thatcher. He runs his Union Jack up his flagpole. I think because he has an unresolved Oedipal complex. For his mother or his father (he went to public school), or both.

Daddy does exactly what he wants when he wants. Like all men he cares only for himself. Whatever he feels, whatever's in his brain or in his veins, he does. He doesn't care or feel for anyone but his self. Daddy does love Mummy, but that means he can do as he pleases to her and doesn't have to care what she feels. Like it does to all men.

My Mummy is Jane Austen. She's terribly thin, and terribly proper, and terribly dressed and perfectly made up, and terribly mannered, and a spinster, and she'd like not to be. She'd like to let her hair down and go screamy-screamy round the house but she's too scared. She sits in her study with the door locked on her trying to express herself and this mess of her life in high art. Her finger's well up her arse.

All of this and all of us and the dog, Shat, are a terrible disappointment. She's come down so far in the world. She was born in a beautiful house to beautiful parents and had a beautiful childhood. Or so she says. I don't know; our grandparents never come visit us. And then she married Daddy, witch was a terrible mistake and had us, who are all mistakes. Through faulty Durex. And what a let down we turned out to be.

We embarrass her. One summer my feet got badly sunburnt and swollen and none of my sandals fitted. I hobbled about like a cripple. Everyone who saw me pitied me, which made me very happy and very embarrassed. I never get to enjoy anything whole. But the same people looked at Mummy with hate for treating her poor physically and probably mentally handicapped child so cruel. For making me shuffle without aid. They probably thought her cruel for making me live. They didn't look at Daddy this way 'cos daddies have no responsibility for rearing brats. They felt sorrow for him, having such a dickhead for a son. Mummy saw their faces and was mortally offended. As usual it was all my own fault. It was another way I'd invented to get at her. I had sunburnt my feet, not the sun, and she wouldn't let me have the cold cream.

And I made her angry when I got impetigo. I had an ugly scab on my chin that was growing for everyone to see. And rash on my arse; she had to put lotion on it. I had to have my own cutlery and crockery segregated from the rest by sticky plaster. Mummy said it was because I didn't wash my hands thoroughly after shitting. She called me a dirty little beast. She warned me if I ever, ever caught impetigo again I'd have to go live in the garage.

Mummy gets uptight about this mess, and then every few weeks, like clockwork like everything in our house, she just gets tight and goes on a sherry binge. She has crying jags all over the house. Wailing about how she wants to care for us but can't and about how everything has gone wrong for her since she left the Secret Garden. At least Daddy's quieter. Blubbing beside our beds. Moaning on about how we put her through tortures going back to our births, when she had to be slit with the knife for us to pass out. When I'd have been as happy to stay inside and die and miss these invectives. I mean, I would have done something if I'd known.

Why did Mummy have us? Just to torture us, share her torture? She strokes our heads thinking we're asleep, but how can I sleep through this racket? Duncan does. I peek out from under the sheets. And there is Mummy, blind in her own grief. Crying and drooling and she looks like she's laughing. Her lipstick smeared all over her chin and her mascara run down her cheeks, repeating over and over, 'I want this to be a happy home. Hic. I wanted this to be a happy home.'

And I cringe and wish she'd leave me alone and go back to her own lonely bed with Daddy in it.

The witches are weird; I can't tell witch of them is preferable.

Mummy asks me about Daddy. How is he? What's he doing? As if I know. I'm too dumb to understand 'em and too knackered to try. And Daddy'll ask me the same about Mummy. As if I ever know, as if they don't see each other.

Other times they sneak up and tell me things about the other. Like how much they drink, how much smack they inject. How disappointed the other is in me.

They want me on their side. At school the football captains pick the sides. At home I'm to pick. They canoodle to get onside with me.

Mummy will say, 'I love you more than your Daddy.'

And Daddy says, 'I love you more than your Mummy. You know that, don't you?'

They don't care. They don't care what they say. The words and myself mean nothing to them. I don't care.

I say, 'Yes I know.'

Football at least has rules, though I don't understand them. Especially the mystery of offside. But the witches have none. They claim to have morals, but I don't see how they work that one out. Like so much they say it's gumpf and that's why I don't remember much of it. They're both offside.

Their favourite trick is to ask me who I love most. If Mummy asks I say Mummy and if Daddy asks I say Daddy. And then they go tell the other, who comes running up to ask me themselves. And I answer according to who's asking. And they take this back as ammo; they don't care.

I am the stage for their revenge play that began long before me. They stomp over me to lunge at the other.

Here's a see-saw that is a gangplank. There's me balanced in the middle. Mummy and Daddy on either end. Duncan watching.

Mummy and Daddy jump up and down screaming at me and screaming at each other.

They ask me to choose. Who loves you more? Who's the nicer? Who's the good witch, who's the better witch, WHO'S THE BITCH WITCH OF ALL?

And for every mistake I make, for every wrong choice, and every choice is the wrong choice and no choice means doubled abuse, I get banged on the head. They push me off. No wonder I'm dumb, dropped on the head as a kid.

One grimaces and one smiles, one slaps and the other comforts, one holds out a hand holding a pressie. But it all ends the same with the same bad end. I step forward to take it, the see-saw falls to that side and I lose my balance, the other is tipped into the air and spitting, and I tumble. One step forward, the see-saw crashes down, I fall off. They watch.

In the battle between them, my self is caught and through my self the battle is fought. My self is lived out in war.

I'm the land torn by some religious war. In the schism is the cracked earth ploughed in wounds that bleed in corpses. Our family bodies fettered together in our bowels. The plain's an empty quagmire drowned in blood. Agent Orange. All arms and legs are scattered on the ground. I can't even crawl out.

Hanged men on horizon on family-sized gibbets in Dürer etchings.

The see-saw slits me. The witches grab me by the arms. One arm for Mummy and one arm for Daddy. Mummy and Daddy cling to my self as if I were the only thing they had. Frightened they'll lose me. They try to beat each other by taking me for themselves. I am the only thing they have between them. Duncan's anyone's. They tear me apart. By tearing my self apart the witches keep it. Trophies. Chopped-out tongues, chopped-off fingers. Collecting ears and penises.

There was a punishment for criminals whose selves are

all wrong I read of in history books. A criminal was tied by his limbs to four horses and the horses were hit and galloped off in different directions. Each with a quarter. These criminals were torn apart in the religious wars between Prots and Caths as an example to other wrong people. Other punishments. Gouging out buttocks and breasts. Burning the nipples. These were spectator sports.

Their executioners were like fathers that wept as they beat their children. Weeping and still beating.

This is the witches' punishment for me, for my self being young and dependent. Being a child is committing a crime; everything I do is criminal.

My self is wrong, therefore my self is in prison.

When a criminal is in prison, the prison warders try to kill his self, which is bad, by making him do as they say. They rend him.

Maggots crawl through the dead cells till they die and something smaller like bacteria chews on 'em. Smaller and smaller. Wants become sand. The dissolution of stone, of wants. Prisoners are trash cans of bits and pieces, wants and needs unfulfilled.

I'm in the prison of the witches' selves, selfish.

In the prison of their selves I don't move. To move is to be wrong. I move only when told to. I hide away from them. I hide in my room, frightened and paralysed. Frightened of how long this can go on.

Scared of what they'll say next, scared of what they'll do next. Frightened to lose this crumb.

I want them to talk to me. I don't want to have no one to talk to.

I don't want to be alone. No one there on the door's other side.

I'd do anything. But I don't want more of the same. (Even when they're nice I never forget they have the power to be nasty.) They stay silent in their barrage of words. In this penal silence solitude I'm caught and imprisoned.

I want to be forgiven for my crime. Receive the Queen's pardon.

I want them to love me. They're my Mummy and Daddy,

they ought to love me. But I don't want to be hurt. They hurt. They don't care what I want.

I bury into my self, which is this prison. This prison of anger and guilt.

They make me angry, confuse. I can do nothing. They make me feel guilty and stoopid.

In my prison they fill me with their sick. With the nausea of their lives. They want me to be like them. The same as what they understand. Like the religious and prison warders. They want me to be right. They kill my self.

We plough the field and scatter our dead seed on the land.

Mummy and Daddy are damage, danger, disaster. I am their child.

Why do they want this shit? I think they like this shit. Wallowing in the gore, half-living me tied face to face with their putrefied corpses.

This revenge for the horribleness of their horrible lives. For the boredom and hate they chase. They spit out yellowed teeth raising ogres. It's not my fault. The war started before me. Not my fault. And they want to make my life their horrible lives. They want to eat my self.

The world is stupid and you're obscene.

I was them and I was dead. I don't exist. I have no self but this prison. Trapped in their hate, my time is theirs. They eat me. I am a child.

And what do I do in their belly?

Lying in bed I hear the TV from downstairs. *Jack the Ripper* is on. The theme tune terrifies me. I can hear, but not see, the terror's huger.

And what do I do? I fantasise about suicide, revenge. I commit suicide. I imagine the funeral. Each time they suffer, but not enough. I won't give them the satisfaction of my suicide of my self. I'm going to deny them that pleasure, seeing who makes the biggest show, who goes to pieces. The hypocrites. They'd make a box and lock me in it, and that's the end of everything I want. They bury me in the garden and that's all over with. Then they get on with the serious business of squabbling over my corpse like the body-snatchers they are. Judging who drove me to it.

And what do I do? I daydream about the Princes in the Tower, and how their father, their protector, did them in. Again and again I do this one. And again tonight I'm one of the Princes playing in the Tower's yard through the day. At night we sleep in a four-poster bed under a thick feather quilt; the murderers enter and stick it to us once more.

And what did I do? After the hundred-and-twenty-third replay, death, I decided to escape. I'm dumb for sure to want them to love me, but I do. They're my witches. I decided to escape and find someone who'd force them to love me, because if they loved me I wouldn't be in this prison. I want something.

How I learnt to be adult, told in fairy tale.

3
A Toy in Blood

Prince Charles is Safe in the Royal Oak, Hidden and Protected from Blockheads

I bolted from the witches' vicarage in search of aid, out through the graveyard and into the strip fields lying about it.

I ran across their furrows, twisted severely in lunatic fashion, unnaturally, by a ribbon of rises the earth was laced with. Nature versus adult logic. In the twisted fields stood low trees with emaciated trunks, topped by thorny bushes of tiny sharp needles forming icicle patterns. The low trees standing still and endlessly shaking. I ran up into the forest, running on without rest.

Pulled up by stitch hurting in my side, stop to do a few quick touch-the-toes, and then on, snatching up water in a cupped hand from leapt streams and grabbing at berries on passed bushes, fleeing before the witches' supposed pursuit. If they cared. My eyes strained from finding the way through the hurtling trees as I rushed headlong and my ears frantic from searching amongst the loud twilight cacophony of the forest, flights of screeching starlings dive-bombing me from above, for the approach of the witches.

When night enfolded the forest and me under its black cloak, continuing blind until I had to sleep, and then halted, picking to bed in a giant oak, big and hard to climb but engulfing me behind the shadows of its dark leaves and branches. Curled in the crook of a branch, hoping they can't see me, find me, but fearing they can, through the eyes and ears of the animals and birds of the forest, through even the insects and trees and plants.

Hansel was frightened that lost he had gone round and round in circles, remaining trapped by the forest, close to the witches and their vicarage. If only there were a public bus service, he wished. But here, at least, high up in his scraggy castle Hansel would have warning, would wake, at any attempted recapture, would hear their cursing and clumsy ascent.

He slept and dreamt.

Hansel woke up because he was uncomfortable in the crook of the oak. That's how he remembered the dream. Of a knight on a white charger in shining white armour, with the chaste unicorn rampant on his shield. Hansel doesn't know what he's searching for in the forest. As he's searching for aid and knows only fairy tales he looks for, can only look for, white knights. Damning the witches, he climbed down in the dark and sunk again into sleep in the pile of leaves that had collected around the tree's roots.

The Girlie in Boy's Clothing and the Older Boyfiend

Hansel woke in the morning, with a start, into a shadow. This baby under the tree. Someone was kicking his foot.

He looked up at the clearing he hadn't seen before, which he only knew to be somewhere in the forest. He felt disoriented. How did I get to be here? he asked himself. This day he had no time to collect himself that was left scattered amongst the leaves.

A blurred phantom stood above him, before the sun, reaching out its hand, tempting him to rise.

'What are you doing out here in the woods alone?' asked the phantom, which sounded like Denis Healey.

Hansel jerked back with fear at this interrogating tone.

'Don't worry, little mouse,' the phantom said. 'No one's going to hurt you. I just asked a civil question.'

'I'm sorry,' Hansel replied sincerely. 'For a moment I thought you were a gamekeeper, or worse, one of the witches.'

'Me, a gamekeeper?' the phantom chuckled. 'Do I look like a gamekeeper?'

'No,' said Hansel, not knowing what a gamekeeper looked like.

'And you don't look like a poacher either, little fella. But what's all this with witches?'

Hansel explained. 'The wicked witches have been holding me and my brother captive in their vicarage somewhere in this forest. I escaped yesterday, and now I must find the white knight who'll slay the witches and make them love us, because I'm not strong enough to do it alone.'

'Well, well, well,' said the phantom. 'What a sad tale to tell. But you've struck lucky now. I'm the honourable gent's page.'

'Really!' exclaimed Hansel.

'Yes. Why do you sound so surprised?'

'Oh, beg your pardon,' Hansel said, 'but I've never met a page before, I've only ever read about them. Please, will you take me to your knight?'

'Why, of course, seeing as you asked so nice. Anything for a damsel in distress.' He posed heroically. Hansel laughed. 'But what about your parents, where are they? Surely they don't agree with this monstrous arrangement?'

'The witches are my parents,' Hansel told him. 'It's them we need saving from.' And he jumped to his feet asking, 'Can we go see the knight now?'

'Hold on a minute, you impetuous thing you. There's no hurry. The guv'nor won't even be up yet.'

This didn't seem the proper conduct for a knight to Hansel. But he'd already doubted the page once and he didn't want to get on the wrong side of him, so he kept quiet. The page must know his own business.

'You must be hungry', the page said to him, 'if you've been out in the woods all night.' And he produced a breakfast of Mars bars from his pocket and gave them to Hansel, who greedily massacred them while the page watched laughing gently.

When he had finished, which was soon, the page said to him, 'You need a good wash and scrub to get all this dirt off you.' Hansel looked at himself. He did; he was covered in mud from his adventure of the previous day.

'Out of those clothes and into the river with you,' the page ordered. 'We need to be presentable to meet a gentleman.'

Hansel blushed. He didn't like to be naked before anyone, including his mum. He had to be grime-free before a knight would hear his petition? This was a new one on him. Certainly the manners of the chivalric order had changed from those of the age Hansel had read of, but perhaps the stories left those bits out as boring. It had always puzzled Hansel that knights, his heroes, never had to piss or shit, whereas he had to every day. Maybe the stories left those bits out too. As insanitary and unpleasant. Or maybe knights were of a different order of person. Maybe as his own family never mentioned pissing or shitting they didn't, and did something else in the loo. Maybe they just went in there so as not to make Hansel feel odd. Was he the only human who did these things? As usual Hansel was living in a lot of maybes.

Hansel undressed with his back to the page, trailing towards the river across the clearing, finally dropping his boxers on the bank and jumping in. The page followed suit with his eyes and feet, slowly, with a sure smile licking his chops, thinking, 'What a fair lad and how sweet-tempered.' Hansel ducked his head under the water and woke up, and the page pounces on him, leaping from the bank. He had some soap with him which he lathered up and vigorously rubbed on Hansel's thin hard body, its sweet lemon scent rising to his nose.

'This is better', the page said, 'than staying dirty.' And Hansel had to agree.

The river is naked and clean as none in his home town, polluted and sewage-filled. The sun is hot, birds are singing. Willows bend their startled branches down into the river. The bottom is smooth sand; there seem to be no rocks. The weeds swinging caressed against his legs. Water trickles over him. Sunlight plays with the river's still surface, unbroken except for their contorting torsos. The hands of the page wash over Hansel with the soap gently. To Hansel the most affection, contact, he's ever received, starved at the vicarage. His heart, want, and his innocence, ignorance, were hand-in-hand partners in blurred stirrings.

The page manipulates him, washing, turning his body, lifting his limbs, but when he reached between his legs, Hansel half-heartedly resists.

The page pushes away the hand.

'No, let me do it,' he said. 'You don't know how nice it is.'

'I don't know your nice things,' Hansel replied.

'Isn't it nice to have someone do things for you?'

Again Hansel had to agree. The page's hand tickles and Hansel laughs. The page smiles back at him. Hansel feels all warm inside, just like in some slushy story. How romantic.

They dry off on the bank, lying in the long grass – which made Hansel itch – in the warm sun. Hansel is plagued for a moment that they ought to be getting on, that the witches might arrive at any minute. But the river and the page bathing him have made Hansel relaxed and he enjoys lazing about, doing nothing for once, and why shouldn't he, especially after his exhausting flight? Anyway, the page will know when they have to be going, so Hansel waits for his word to be up and off.

Hansel shivered.

'Are you cold?' the page asked. 'Here, let me put my jacket round you.'

They sit up. The page keeps his arm round Hansel's shoulders, pretending to rub him dry. He touches him, stroking his hand over Hansel's hairless chest, and says, 'See, now you're all clean. Not at all dirty. Don't you feel better?'

Hansel's body listens with a credent ear, nodding yes.

Suddenly Hansel's scared. He could see clearly their, his openness. He sees as a passer-by would, stumbling into the clearing, the two of them sat on the grass in the middle, himself under the hands of the page, open to all. And he feels guilty without knowing why. Hansel imagines a big hand descending out of the forest from behind him. The hand of his guardian angel, of obedience, who followed him as a child to ensure he didn't do anything anybody wouldn't want him to. Coming out and hitting him hard about the back of the head.

A tremor runs through him.

The page, thinking him still cold, takes Hansel into his arms, Hansel frightened but tantalised, and pulls him to his chest, hugging him tight, which stops Hansel shaking, making him feel safe. Obliterates the big hand from Hansel's head. His body has more, clearer, stirrings. His cock grows red and comes up. He is scared because the page is sure to see it and he wants to hide under clothes.

(Isn't this always the way. That the inexperienced and the stupid and the lonely are betrayed in their excitement, exposed in their need, rising to the slightest provocation. Or to what they do not even know is provocation or seduction. On the most innocent of occasions, whilst a man's innocuous remains.)

Hansel can't raise his eyes. He stares in fear at his cock. Where will this lead me? he wonders. But the page says nothing. Hansel watches as the page's hand reaches across and wraps itself round his cock.

'You're trespassing on my dad's land,' Hansel blurted out. 'I'll call him, I will. And he'll come a-running with his gun and my dog'll be here before him. A murderous Alsatian.'

The page says, 'But your daddy doesn't love you, you told me that.'

'Yes, I did,' replied Hansel.

'And he's not anywhere near here.' He kisses the boy for the first time.

The kiss and the caresses, and the sun, melt Hansel, make his body pliant. It moulds itself to the page's will. Hansel thinks, 'There's nobody here now but us. I want to stay all the dark and lonely night and do this.'

When the page goes to stick it to him, for these are the far-off days of yore before AIDS, using some KY he had handy, Hansel asks, 'I won't get pregnant, will I?'

'Of course not,' the page replies, and his certainty kills all doubt.

'And it won't hurt, will it?'

'Don't be silly; just lie still.'

But still Hansel tightens up.

The page comforts him. 'I know,' he says. 'We'll take it nice and easy; just relax.' And he sticks a bottle of amyl under Hansel's nose.

And when he poked the big red thing in, it hurts. Hansel lies squirming as little as possible, not wanting to ruin things for the page by starting a coward's commotion. Hansel thinks to himself, there must be something wrong with me.

When he'd finished the page wiped himself off and hurriedly got dressed. Hansel lay on the ground, feeling sticky and stinging between the legs. He looked to the page for some word, but he was leaving. And now Hansel saw for the first time that he was too old to be a page. He was a middle-aged man, slightly pot-bellied, who had seen his best and was now dilapidating. How could I have taken him for a page? Hansel asked himself. Because that's how I wanted him to be, stupid. Hansel asked out loud, timorous for it was all going wrong, about the white knight.

'What knight?' asked the man.

'The white knight who'll help me,' said Hansel bewildered.

'Oh him. He wouldn't help a little boy like you; he likes them well stacked.'

And, giving Hansel a look as though he were a nuisance and a fool, he trotted off, hee-hawing between his yellow teeth, which to Hansel sounded just like the donkeys of his home town, the same braying pride. Hansel said nothing; he was too dejected.

At the edge of the clearing the man shouted back.

'I'm no knight's page, you know. What a silly billy you are to believe in such girlie stories.' He waved. 'Cheerio, easy fuck.' And he loped off into the forest.

Hansel said to himself, must be the black knight's page to be so nasty. But, dispirited, he told himself severely to shut up.

He sat with his knees drawn up under his chin, hiding himself from the world under his jacket. He felt dirty and unclean, and the man had taken his soap with him. He felt everyone would be able to tell what he had done, that he would never be able to wash it away.

Several hours later Hansel stood up, dressed and left the clearing. He was back in the forest, wandering and lost.

Where are the White Knights in Hell?

Hansel disappeared in the sea mists of the forest and the night came upon him. He spends a long and desperate night alone in this wood filled with broken sleep. The night air, come blasting straight from hell, reigns eager, breathes contagion foul as a witch's mouth pit. Hansel haunted by the phantoms of this day and the night that break open their graves, prisons, that lope and loom around him submerged in darkness and attack.

And plaguing him the fact that there is no one for him to turn to in this world, or the next. Hansel has stopped looking for, expecting, men on white chargers. Unconditional, *a priori* faith in mankind is no more possible.

The fragments of the light of the moon caught in the arthritic fingers of the trees – error of the world rather than faithful signals – confuse and misshape shape and shade. Dragons and monsters dating back to prehistory appear instead of trees; shadows have their evil way with him misled by the moon, a full moon that causes madness, whose moonbeams cause blindness.

And Hansel again lost in the ways of the world, the unpath'd wood, flounders in the paths of animals, sheepishly aimless. Plodding Hansel came against bushes blocking, bumps into trees, and falls into stinging nettles.

Nature, our nature, tyrannises. Misshapes him, already torn on the hidden rocks of his need, that has beckoned him into this corner of darkness, and all he has to touch are his fears, the wounds of battle. Hansel knows he's at war.

Trying to cheer himself as he went, went nowhere for though he seeks direction he wants one, he sang a chart hit.

'Killers in tulips, child murderers free;
And in a wooden jacket I shall go to Morecombe beach.'

Why are you laughing? Things are out of wack. Innocence is overthrown here, the expectancy and rose of his fair state, the boy's eye and mind and heart confounded, pounded to nothing. Canker galls this infant of the spring; this violent bloom twisted in upon itself, inverting on its stalk, piercing its flesh with its thorns, fears to open its little petals.

Better nip it in the bud quick.

The looking-glass of youth is distorted and the mould contorted into a narrow place. Thrown down, an untwinned youth is blasted out.

Am I a child?

No, a monster, a monster . . .. Against this I have sworn revenge.

The child of Hansel stolen. Stolen. Call the police, the police. Murder, murder.

Family in Hell

In the morning, dazed from hunger and lack of sleep, from this vigil of vigilance against his fears, too scared to sleep in moonlight, dangerous as the fairies and the witches and all the evil creatures are fond of moonlit nights, still running, Hansel bolted out of the forest and found himself back at the vicarage.

In his fear and from it his anger he swore, 'That bitch and that bastard, I'm gonna fuckin' stick it to em'. I want revenge, I want their heads on poles, his head and her head.'

And he galloped up to the vicarage, lifting his legs high, imitating a horse and neighing, and mightily barged in the door, shouting aloud to all:

'I'm back, and I'm a white knight on my charger. Quake, witches, I bring your death, I've come to save us.'

And he stumbled over the doorstep and fell flat on his face.

'Shut up, you stupid boy,' Daddy said out of the corner of his crooked mouth. 'I'm in the middle of an important phone call, and you're just daydreaming again. No, not you constable . . ..'

Mummy, the zombie English housekeeper, was glaring across the room at Hansel.

'Trouble's back,' she shouted at him.

Duncan was edging himself into a cranny as usual.

Daddy was on the phone; he made faces at Hansel.

'No, it's alright, constable, I've found my lost property after all. . . No, you cannot have the reward, you haven't done anything. . . It seems to me, constable, that the police spend far too much time sniffing after money and not enough catching criminals. . . . Well, really, how dare you suggest some impropriety between the brat and I? I only keep him out of the kindness of my heart and I am certainly not so desperate I have to kidnap young boys, I'll have you know . . ..'

And with this he finished, slamming the phone down into its place.

'That constable thinks far too much of his truncheon, along with money. And you, you little horror, you left us all up shit creek without a paddle running off like that. Is this the thanks we deserve? You might as well have done your poor mother in, do you realise that? But now you are back in my house, don't think you can try any more tricks . . ..'

And so he continued for hours and days, but I couldn't hear him – I was asleep.

My last thought, that drifted across my mind, out of nowhere: 'The key has been taken, and the cupboard is bare, all has been stolen.'

Hope has been stolen. Although I had escaped the witches, I hadn't been free 'cos I was dumb. And now I knew there was no one going to help me but me. I had to take responsibility for my self.

4
Our Family Corpses

Nothing changed for the better, only worse. Nineteen hundred and eighty-seven again. I tried my hardest not to care, but I couldn't freeze out. I still needed to love and be loved, and they were still bastards. I hurt.

I was welcomed with screaming fits from Mummy and stern finger-waggings off Daddy. They said they'd been worried, they said that they cared. They shouted at me. They didn't want to talk with me. Leadership. But then they couldn't talk to each other.

Mummy was worse, always had a glass in hand. Or the glass had her in hand. And Daddy had a funny look in his eyes. He was even more withdrawn than before. Where'd he gone? A big prick, bigger, bigger. The biggest cock round little cunts. Cause pain.

Duncan hadn't noticed I'd run off.

One day I found Mummy standing in the dining room, staring out through the conservatory at the garden. I stood behind her at the door, watching her, listening to her breath shuffling in her throat. She didn't move. And then I asked her what she was doing. She didn't jump at the sound of my voice; she knew I'd come in. She'd been hoping I'd go out.

She said quietly, with too much effort, 'I want to go back.'

Her voice was buried under the booze and the pills.

'Where to?' I asked brusquely, not knowing what the fuck she was on about and only faintly interested. 'To the womb?' I suggested hopefully for the crack.

There was a long pause, too long, that bored me. She fingered herself and then said, 'I don't know, just back.'

'Stupid bitch,' I sneered.

I didn't have any old memories like Mummy to carry around and louse me up, and I didn't want any. I left her with hers rotting.

I go to have lunch with Daddy. I don't want to have lunch with him. I never do, but I do. He keeps me waiting. I don't get angry, it's typical.

In the car on the way to the restaurant he puts a Billy Joel tape on the stereo thinking I'll like it, need I say more? Moans about women drivers and honks his horn.

In the restaurant I'm nice and smile and nod at all his stupid advice, and listen to all his questions and answer correctly, and pretend to be interested in all his words, and my brain falls asleep and we run out of conversation. He stares out the window, eyeing up the girls passing from the convent school. I realise why he picked this table. He gives me a running commentary on their form.

I drink and pour more and more from the bottle, and start chain-smoking to irritate the hell out of him.

Businessmen Daddy deals with – he insures their lives: what are they worth? – drop by our table and chat with him. This doesn't bother me. They all look the same. And it doesn't bother me that I'm only introduced as his boy. They all compliment him on me. They smile at me approvingly; one day he'll work for us, they think. A recognisable product, all the right qualities, the right background. This horrifies me; I smile back through the fag smoke.

I'm surprised at how little Daddy orders and ask him why. He smiles.

'The doc says I'm to eat less and more often. It's the ulcers.'

His wrist-watch alarm explodes. He explains that it's set to remind him to have something to eat – lucky he's in a restaurant. I imagine him on a desert island with the watch, taking mouthfuls of sand good and regular.

'How's your mum?' he asks me.

'Why don't you ask her yourself?' I reply.

'Because I'm asking you.'

'Okay,' I snap.

'Is she?' he continues.

'Yes, she is.'

'Are you positive? You aren't keeping anything from me?'

'No. I'm positive,' I say loudly. 'Why don't you ask her yourself?'

'I'm asking you.'

'I'm positive.'

''Good,' he says. 'And is she still seeing that psycho doctor?'

'Yes, she's still getting the Librium prescriptions.'

''Oh, good,' he says. 'That's good.'

'Isn't it,' I say.

Daddy won't actually ask me if I need any money, I have to raise the matter. And if I don't he won't give. Then he asks how much I need and I have to guess how much he'll give. We haggle. Then he'll give me a little, after lecturing me on how money doesn't grow on trees and how he isn't a bottomless pit. Tramps have sat through worse for a cup o' tea and a bowl o' soup. A full battery of the Sally army.

'Yes, I know,' I say.

'You look ill,' he said as we left.

'It's the smack,' I laughed at him. The first gag of the meal.

'What's that?' he asked.

On Christmas Eve I went into town with Mummy and we had cream teas at the Olde Tea Rooms.

She keeps fiddling with her hair, keeps attempting to smile. I'm surprised what a chore it is to sit with this blank, made worse by my severe hangover.

'What do you want for your birthday, dear?' she weedles.

I was born on Christmas Day, the greatest misfortune for any child.

'Nothing,' I say sulking. I wish she knew already.

'Oh, Pin, you must want something, dear. What is it?'

'A bigger cock,' I tell her. And then I ask what she wants.

She sits dumb, twirling her hair and sucking the ends. I make a few suggestions. A vodka still, a potent husband; a walled garden.

'Oh, I just want us all to have the most lovely Christmas,' she says finally.

'Impossible,' I snap at her.

She goes quiet again and chases a few scone crumbs about her tiny china plate and then states without looking up, 'You look very unhappy, Pin.'

'That's because I am unhappy,' I tell her. 'Everyone is. And I've got the worst hangover.' We could discuss hangovers.

'Why are you unhappy?' she whinges, begining to panic. 'We all care about you, we love you. You do know that?'

Is she scared I don't feel loved, or does she need a drink to forget I need loving?

'Pin, we love you. We'd do anything for you and your brother.'

She stares at me winningly as if I were a date she had to persuade of her love. She desperately wants me just to say yes.

'Pin, honestly, your daddy and I' – a brief moment of parental unity here – 'would do anything for you. You must know that.'

'You do nothing for me, dear,' I squeal.

This shuts her up.

That Christmas Daddy took us to a hotel for Christmas dinner instead of going to one of the relatives. For this special occasion, we're bought new clothes. Normally they come from a jumble sale. They're gross.

The hotel's nondescript. They don't put enough food on your plate, it's not a proper family stuffing, and there aren't enough of us at table to keep the conversation going. Already everyone's jumpy and irritated at having to spend all Christmas together, and alone. No one says anything and no one dies. Slowly everyone finishes dragging out the food on their plates, 'cept for Duncan, who I watch mush his peas so they'll stay on his fork. He stares intently at them, anchored to them.

Mummy and Daddy go through their annual summary of family and friends dead and seriously ill, and speculate on next year's. When they've finished with that we sit and drink and finally we get to the point of the whole exercise: Daddy's boss walks in. He comes in with his family, who are equally glum, and comes over and wishes us all Merry Christmas and a Happy New Year and goes away. Back to his own morgue party.

Daddy says, 'Isn't that nice of him?'

No one answers.

Driving home, I pressed my face up against the window and stared out at the black silent night. I even managed to keep looking when we passed the cemetery despite the fact that Fanny Adams might be wandering about it. All dismembered. I want to see her tonight. I want some company.

My dream starts off realistic. I'm walking home from junior school through the cemetery, and I'm caught in a downpour. I keep walking at the same pace; I can't be bothered running. But the paths get windier and windier and I don't get any nearer home, the ground is sodden red clay and opens up like a cupboard, everything falling out on top of me, and the coffins and their skeletons break out of the soil, and it's harder and harder to walk, and I keep tripping over them and into them and scrambling out. It's just like the swimming pool scene in *Poltergeist*. It ends when I come to the statue of a boy angel over a child's grave that I see going to and coming home from school. One of his hands is pointing down at me, the other points to the sky and the sky is dark. I look into his face and wake up.

In another dream the vicarage subsides into the earth because it was built on a plague grave. I'd read in the paper that 20,000 buried chickens gave off so much gas the earth bubbled, and then erupted. 20,000 buried children. In *Brookside* an enormous hole has appeared in the Close, and the fear is upon them that their houses will collapse. I wake up and wait for my dream to come true.

One day Daddy arrived home early from the office. He said we were broke and that Duncan and me must go to work.

I said I didn't want to. I said I didn't want to go on the fire, it's not that cold.

He said I must. It was my duty. He gave Duncan and me some new clothes and told us to have a bath and get dressed in them.

I had my bath first. Once I was dressed, I looked in the mirror and a teenage businessman stared back, but he didn't see me. I wasn't there.

I'd forgotten to brush my teeth. I went back to the bathroom but stopped at the door. Daddy was in there with Duncan; I could see them through the door which Daddy had left ajar. Duncan's mouth.

Duncan was stood in front of Daddy, naked but for his tacky briefs. Daddy was staring him in the eyes.

'You're a handsome young man, Duncan,' he says.

His hands drop to Duncan's crutch.

'You're a giant of a young man,' he said with father's pride. 'Where it counts.'

Duncan doesn't flinch, he just said,

'Yes, Daddy sir.'

Duncan's shaking but it isn't cold.

Daddy says, 'It's OK Duncan, we'll stop it hurting.'

And he takes his works out of the medicine cabinet.

'You just have to relax, Duncan, don't you?'

'Yes, Daddy sir,' Duncan says.

Daddy grabs Duncan's arm and takes his belt off and ties it around his arm tight. He slaps the skin to find a vein, and I think, 'Already he has to, already veinless like Daddy. What's his shelf life?' And he finds one, and while he's heating up the smack Duncan stands there, not moving, shaking, and I think I should do something, but what? And I just stand there not moving, watching.

Daddy fills the syringe and sticks it into Duncan. Duncan sighs. I walk away.

As we were leaving the house Daddy told us to say goodbye to Mummy.

She was sitting in the living room, curled up in a corner of the sofa.

Daddy said, 'We're going now, dear.'

She didn't react. Duncan waved at her. I wondered if she could see us through the tears of pure vodka and my hand hesitantly gestured to her. I wondered if she was dead. And then we turned and left.

Daddy drove us to a big house out in the suburbs.

Standing at the front door, Daddy inspects us, and straightens a few details, then he pushes the brass bell. It chimes 'Land of Hope and Glory'.

A man opens the door. He nods to Daddy and then he looks us over. As he does this he says, 'Good evening, Dennis, glad to see you could make it.'

'Wouldn't miss it for the world,' Daddy replies. 'How's business?'

'Fine. And who's this?' he asks.

'My boys, Duncan. And Pin.'

'Pleased to make your acquaintance,' he says to us, shaking our hands, testing our grips. 'I hope you enjoy yourselves tonight.'

'I'm sure they will, Paul,' Daddy answers for us. 'Say hello, boys.'

'Hello boys,' Duncan says smiling.

I don't say anything.

'Say hello to the gentleman, Pin,' Daddy sneers, thumping me on the back.

'Hello,' I say.

We were still on the doorstep and the man asks me for a dance.

I look behind him and into the lounge; men are dancing round each other, some of them, the older ones, cheek to cheek.

Daddy thumps me again, this time with his fist closed.

'Answer my friend, Pin.'

'No fucking way,' I say, blankly staring at the man.

He just laughs in my face. Daddy joins him, tight-lipped.

'He will later, Paul, don't you worry. He just needs to get into the mood.'

'Sure,' the man says confidently. I don't know why but I have no intention of changing my mind. 'Why don't you come in?' He gestures for us to do so.

Daddy guides us into the lounge and sits me down in a chair.

'Try and understand, Pin,' he whispers to me authoritatively. 'This is society and, whatever you think, you've got to learn how to live in it.'

Hmm, I think, I'm going to learn something.

'I'll get you a drink, that'll loosen you up. Vodka?'

'Uh, yes,' I manage to reply.

He guides Duncan off. I sit there and stare at my feet; I don't like looking up. All these men keep passing, leering at me. I feel like a job applicant being given the once over. I should have a CV.

I could have said outside I wasn't coming in, that I was going, but I didn't, and now I'm inside.

No drinks come back. It's stifling. I could go, but I don't know where I am. I begin to panic. By accident I catch one of the men's eyes. He comes over and asks rather hurriedly and rather demandingly, 'Are you passive or active?'

I don't know what to say. I'm so surprised. I stare at him incredulously. He seems to be getting angry that I haven't answered him and snaps.

'Well?'

I say, 'I don't have a cock.'

He looks at me with disgust, and then walks off.

I get up and wander around, ostensibly to find Duncan and Daddy but really just to be on the move.

I can't see Daddy or Duncan anywhere, but I don't look for long. I want to hide from all the men, from their glances.

I find an empty room and go to sleep in it. Asleep is safer than awake. Asleep I don't know what's happening. I don't need to think or decide anything.

In my sleep I've been castrated. Actually, I've castrated myself. Afterwards I go to someone who is standing behind a counter. I put the Safeway's placky bag I have with me on the counter and out of it take twin sets of balls and prick. I don't know why two sets. There's no blood or sign of damage; they've been sheared off clean. The castration was an act of revenge and anger. In displaying them brazenly, proudly, I'm saying to the person behind the counter, you made me do this. How far to go. I feel defiant.

I was right, I had been castrated. I hadn't done it to myself, they had done it to me.

Suddenly Daddy's waking me up. As I come to, he sits himself down in an armchair and stares at me. I remember the dream and start crying, I don't feel defiant anymore.

He picks his nose and looks at me some more while I continue crying, and then he asks me something which I don't catch and assume he's asking about my tears.

'I don't know why I'm crying, I . . . I just am,' I blurt out. 'Maybe it's Duncan, he's a deadhead; and this place, and you and Mummy,' as I try to wipe away the tears with the back of my hand. They fly all over the room.

'What about me?' I scream across the room at him, the callous bastard.

'And what about you?' the callous bastard asks back.

'What are you going to do to me?'

'You'll be fine, stop worrying,' he says flatly.

'I'm worried,' I shout.

'Can we talk about something else?' he says, irritated.

'No, talk about me. Me!' I scream, choking on me.

'Don't be boring, Pin,' he says. 'I'll get you a drink. Vodka?'

I don't answer, beginning to blub and splutter again.

He gets up and leaves.

And just after this, while I'm still sniffling, a man comes in dressed like a priest and sits down where Daddy was.

'You're confused and frightened,' he says to me, calm and insistent.

I wonder who he thinks he is.

'You don't know what's happening around you; that's why you're hopeless, helpless.'

I've stopped crying. I'm embarrassed by this idiot, and stare at the floor unable to meet his gaze.

'That's why you feel there's no way out, but Jesus will show you one. He will come to you now.'

He stands up and comes over to me, crouched on the floor.

'You only have to understand the way things are, and not resist.'

Has Daddy sent him? He's standing over me.

'Heavenly Father, fathers are heavenly, you will free this captive. Those who bind themselves in doubt, you will teach them how to receive and to give, to take part in the true communion of society. Celebrate your Lord, my son. Do not worry about those things which you need not worry about. Ask to be forgiven of your sins and your disobediences, and you will feel an unspeakable joy. If you only give in, release yourself into your Daddy's grace. Allow him to deliver you out of your pain.'

I look up. He's got his cock out; I stare at the ugly, fat-veined thing.

'Let your cup overflow,' he says and begins to piss on me.

Stupefied, I sit there, the piss running with the last of my tears.

He shakes off the last few drops and goes away.

At the door he turned and said, 'I hope this has helped you.'

I sit. I wait. Nothing happens.

'What the fuck are you playing at, Pin?' Daddy shouts as he comes in with Duncan.

'Nothing,' I yell back. 'Fucking nothing, now leave me alone.'

'You're acting like an arsehole,' Daddy tells me.

'How else would you want me to act?' I ask.

'Stop the smart-arse crap. I've some very important contacts here, and you're not going to fuck things up.'

'Leave me the fuck alone,' I say. 'Don't bloody touch me.'

Daddy looks at Duncan, who's standing there smiling, and sneers, 'Jesus H. Christ, Pin. Who'd want to touch you?'

'I'm leaving now,' I say standing up, positive I am.

'You're pathetic. You're leaving? Where you going to go? What do you think you'd do without me? You've no choice, Pin, do you understand? What would you do, run off into the night again and come crawling back the next day? Like the last time? Who would you run to? Your Mummy?'

'Shut up,' I shout, knowing all this.

'What can you do for yourself?'

'Shut up!' I scream.

'I put a roof over your head and food in your mouth and clothes on your back; I give you a bed for the night . . .' He's moving in closer.

'Oh, you've made a bed for me to lie in, with one of this lot.'

'I do all this for you and what do you do in return?'

Nothing. I know.

'Shut up!' I scream, choking.

'You're an arrogant, selfish little bastard. What are you?'

'Fuck off.'

He's so close our breaths mingle. He slaps me.

'Don't talk to me like that, you little prick.'

'Fuck off, you arse bandit.'

'Don't you appreciate what I've done for you?' He pushes me.

'I don't appreciate anything,' I say, rote-like.

'No, you don't, I can see that now.'

'What have you done for me, huh?' I stammer out. 'What're you doing to me? What do you want to do to me? You want to whore me. That's right, isn't it?'

'You're a whore already, Pin. And you did it to yourself.'

My face blushes. How does he know about the man in the woods. Perhaps it was one of the men here.

'You're a parasite,' he continues. 'You're dependent on me and you don't even know it.'

'I know it,' I mumble under my breath and malicious.

'You can't do anything for yourself. Even your little escape, you couldn't pull that off; you came back. Who's going to do all the things I've done for you all these years – feed you, clothe you, bed you?'

'No one's going to bed me,' I croak, my face burning, my throat sore. My eyes wet again.

'Men don't cry,' Daddy says. 'Do they, Duncan?'

'That's right, ask Duncan. Duncan's not alive to answer.'

Duncan nods.

'Come on, Pin,' Daddy says, changing tack. 'You know I care for you just like you were my own son.'

Daddy pulls out a hypodermic and reaches for my arm. I try to move away. I cringe into the wall, sliding to the floor, trying to push my way through, sobbing and laughing at the same time as telling him to go away, asking him what he's doing. But he doesn't listen.

He keeps repeating, 'What would you do, Pin? You've nowhere to go, nowhere. There is nowhere else to go, you belong here, belong . . .'

The words ring in my ears. I don't belong here even if I don't know where I belong. I must say something. I have to hear my own voice. I must shut out all the others. I have to impose myself.

I hurt so much. I want to kill him.

'No,' I shout, and lunge out at him with both arms.

He crumples over backwards and in the fall the needle shoots into his vein like a bullet. Blood splashes across me. The priest touches his fingers to the forehead. He rolls, he hisses like a punctured hot air baloon. The needle breaks. He smiles in a brief flush and slumps.

As I leave Duncan and him are motionless.

As I leave the house the men are too intoxicated by their party to notice.

Outside, I let their tyres down.

Night of Deliverance

I am nothing but anger. Anger troops feet down the drive
Grinding gravel under foot, into black country roads surrounded by night.
Possessed. I had to kill them so hungry, unhappy they eat me.
Condemned to burn in this shit. Cared.
To free kill myself. Myself they had trapped. Had trapped me.
Myself is nightmare eating me.
I can do nothing till I hate myself, self filled with pain.
Possessed with anger I hate myself, gouging out eyes, and want to die.
Hate them. Anger drowns fear and guilt kill myself kill them.
Daddy dead, Mummy dies.

You belong here. Nowhere else to go.
I can't live here. No good excuse to stay.
Can't go back. Black nothing future.
I don't know where I am.
I don't know what I am. Anger.
Anger plunges into night, soaking night,
Night air forgetfulness, walking feet erase.
It comes to an end, anger burns prison self.
I have escaped the trap, walked into delivery night

Never ready for what has to be done,
Never know when come. Crash.

'Cos I had escaped slavery, I named myself Lucky. But for how long?

5
Man-e-festations of the State

U-bend to the Capital

Lucky's last hitch was an M-reg Mercedes and it dumped him in the East End, the back door of London.

Wapping. Where the pirates and the sea rovers were hung at the low water mark, there to remain till three tides had covered them. One. Two. Three tides of pus that suppurated from the venereal sore that is London on the crack that is the Thames. The Thames is the urethra of England, which pissed and pussed the shit into the nations of the world.

He walked the Highway through the shanty towns that are the City's outer fortifications. King David Lane. Council blocks, eternally damned in pre-dawn grey, are ranks of rotten soldiers; their cantilevered balconies are medal ribbons cross their pocked chests, are shooting galleries, raining down used syringes, broken second-hand durables and other household excreta on social workers and the police; and, with the soldiers' mortality, they never die, but cling on faded like dried shit about the hole of an arse.

The arse is London, the hole is the City, and this is the toilet, drains and sewage works, taking its shit.

A proclamation of 16 September 1603 ordered the demolition of houses and rooms in the suburbs immediately surrounding the City as a precaution against the spread of plague by 'dissolute and idle persons'. It was actually directed against the numerous brothels and gaming houses of said areas. But the suburban cesspits were rebuilt; the disposal pools of congealing stools. The last remains of corrupted dead matter.

This ghost road, deserted even by the scavenging pigeons in the seasonless famine, cleft through sooted brick, the Estates of England crumbling about it into dust cloying and choking in the throat, is no small blemish to so fabled a City, but bloody enormous, to have such an unsavoury orifice, or entrée.

Above it all the concrete towers of the City rising white and black beckon Lucky on.

This abysmal abyss breaks into an enclosed Park of English, enclosed by barbed wire, and in this Park are many rare species of car and the Fortress. This harridan old dragon that lies on its back has a head that is a square Keep-keep, with a thousand glaring eyes prying on the world, and in its belly, that is a K-nave, its monster babies gestate electronically. It breathes out fire from its anus and farts out dark lorries from this Anti-Oral, Anti-Oracle, its defecatory and only mouth, that descend the ceremonial ramp of its tail out into the world with their lorry loads of festering words to the waiting masses that sleep in beige death.

Below, each lorry is hailed by the crowd caught in the incandescence of the pylon lights.

They hail them with clamour and fireworks, the noise appropriate to the ancient rites given to the Sun in its winter journey beneath the earth to aid its spring ascension. But these rites are hostile to this Winter Sun.

Their chants discordant, they rub against each other and erase the words, smashing together as the sea and the rocks in surges of the crowd spasmodic, filling any crevice and nook in the rocks, the guards that are unmoved, barnacled with helmet and shield, resistant like the council blocks. Calcified and calcifying the land in a white powder claimed to be icing sugar or not to be icing sugar but asbestos dust. What one professes in this debate depends on whether it's tasted, and those who do, don't live long.

This is not ritual, being neither inherited nor seamless. Ancient rites bound a society together, symbolising their unity. These rites symbolise conflict, exploding apart in this St Vitus's dance of the drowning, fallen and bruised on the rocks.

A parked lorry is seized and overturned, blowing to the black night a puffball of flame, a kiss of hate; signalling the guard to lunch out, lurching through the crowd like a mighty juggernaut, each black Bull-dog goring and gouging with his single horn.

A man injured drops out of the tossed mass as if from an automobile collision, and begins to walk up to where Lucky's stood.

Lucky waits, wanting to know what this place is.

To his question the man, or picket, replies:

'The Roman popes had a fortress to guard over their Infernal City, the Castel San Angelo. This is exactly the same principle. The popes maintained the values of society there, a rich man does here. They and he use these values of society to safeguard their positions.'

Lucky didn't understand.

The picket for his injured arm turned towards the City to find for it a hospital, and in silence Lucky went with him.

East Smithfield. Thomas More Street. Some Lady climbs out of a taxi, golden piss streaming down her sheer legs, the colour picked out in yellow street light, forcing her unfelt apologies and crumpled notes on the taxi man. And then slips through the builders' hoarding down a hardboard passage to the luxury appartments of St Katharine's Dock hidden 'hind closed doors. A sign crawls 'Sorry for the Inconvenience'.

At the top of East Smithfield hovers the Tower of London, between the real and the unreal, between history and the present like all England. The Tower of Traitors' Gate and the Bloody Tower, the headsman's axe chasing the Countess of Salisbury round and round the block – the blocks never change, to lay your head down on and go to death – slashing at her geriatric neck. And of the Princes and other executions of power investing meaning for tourists in this ghost. Whole nations reduced to History. A museum exhibit under the glass that will crumple to unrecognisable dust if exposed to the healthy air.

Chimney-pots peer over the Tower's outer guard wall and guttering runs down its flinty bosom. On these battlements

Hamlet's dad bemoans his early retirement. And the Towers of the City of Rome hem in this fragment of Toy Town, the Tower's white stone lit by the City's cash translucent, whilst the VDU'd offices shine forth a bright light from bared windows suspended in the morgues. For the financial market never sleeps, let alone dreams.

The suited ghouls are still working inside, confident and thoughtless for the outside. They do not inhabit this City but are closer in blood to New York, Paris, Berlin, Tokyo. Under their fingers and thumbs whole nations become economics; their fingers and thumbs through wires penetrate national borders, that have melted like Dali's watches, porous and eroding with gorgonzola holes.

The Function of History

The gates of the City were shut against the night.

Lucky and the picket sat at the side of the road to wait for morning, beside a rock which had been beaten senseless and shapeless. Lucky asked the picket about the City and the work to be had within, but the picket kept stumm. Then the rock which had been asleep, but had awoken at the sound of voices, being gregarious, spoke to Lucky.

He said, 'So, young man, you are interested in our ancient city of Rome, and this recreant won't oblige with information? Perhaps I could slake your thirst for knowledge a little? Huh?'

And without waiting for a reply, the rock, or History, began.

History told his story wilily whiling the hours before dawn, thinking for this he would be remunerated.

'In recent years the City has stood against a great threat, besieged as it was by many plagues . . .'

'What plagues?' asked Lucky.

'Why boy, the feverish inflation and the hypothermia deficit, the anorexic overspending and crippling taxation, bloodsucking nationalised industries, an anaemic currency. . . . Why, you might as well have torn money up then . . ..'

'It is only paper, money is,' Lucky threw in.

'Only paper,' History spluttered. 'Only bloody paper, boy,'

he boomed. History had obviously been a schoolmaster, but had been made redundant. 'No, no. It's not only paper. How can you be so irreverent? Were you brought up by Marxists?'

Lucky said nothing, staring at his shoes and wondering who this loony was.

'Try and understand,' History continued his tirade. 'The land was under hard tyranny, the people discontented, denied all opportunity. The devils you know,' he whispered confidentially.

'What devils?' Lucky perked up, aroused by this new piece of strangeness.

'He means the socialists,' said the picket, sarcastic.

'Yes, that's who I mean, indeed,' History snapped, indignant, snatching back his story. 'The very ones, possessing the people with their nonsense, taking authority that wasn't theirs to take, interfering, meddling . . .' – a hysterical tone entered History's voice – '. . . ruining the country.' He paused, and then continued in his factual manner. 'Those that could got over the Tiber, paying the ferryman with their very life savings and their gold teeth, fleeing in a fearful manner, in yachts, a prey to pirates, to the USA . . .'

'Good for the pirates, I say,' put in the picket. 'They were like rats off the sinking ship, having gnawed the holes in it.'

'The only rats', pronounced History, 'were the socialists, infecting the ship with plague. This was the infamous winter of discontent,' History explained slowly. Lucky resented being treated like a total idiot and the picket just sat there shaking his head listening to the old fool.

'The hospitals were closed,' History said. 'There were no ambulances; the socialists left the dead unburied. And the people faced famine. No unclean thing was left uneaten; dogs and cats, horses and rats, and even the church mice were all curious sweeties – although the British are animal lovers and nearly all vegetarian. Thousands died in the streets, which were dying with thousands of bin bags and the untreated sewage . . ..'

'The peasants were revolting,' The picket again dropped in on History. 'And they sure caused a stink. Not to keep working for a few pieces of shit, what do you think of that? Such arrogance!'

'The hunger and the cold of that winter,' History continued right on in. 'And those that were alive – alive? The nation was nothing but a grey shadow of its former self, in the winter of discontent.'

'Whose discontent?' the picket asked. 'The poor? Theirs in eternity. Or a discomfort in armchairs?'

'Brought to their last beds, the people . . ..'

'Which people?' asked the picket, insistent.

'. . . implored the Emperor with piteous mews to end the strife, but he couldn't. To do that he'd have to surrender, and be uncrowned, if not beheaded. And better he lose his life than his legal liberty. Who would respect his power, any authority, after that? Who would petition him, his power compromised so? He couldn't, though some scum say he could have.'

'Oh, the Emperor, he was sorely afflicted,' the picket mocked. 'Sorely afflicted with the public lice, and was busy scratching himself on the Imperial desk and beating his head against the walls of the Imperial office. Isn't that right?' he asked History.

History looked at him sideways, unsure how to answer, and so he pitched in again.

'Then a worthy patriot, Tamora . . ..'

'The internationalist bitch,' the picket added.

'Why's that?' asked Lucky.

''Cos she always takes the international view, also known as the corporational. Or corpustulating.'

'But who is she?' Lucky asked.

'Rather you'd never have needed to know. A descendant of the German Krapps family, famous neutralists.' Lucky looked none the wiser and puzzled. 'They'll sell anything to anyone with enough currency,' the picket elucidated.

'Oh,' said Lucky. 'Don't Huns eat babies?'

'Young man, that is mere gossip.' History doused them with his thin spittle. 'Nothing but lies, unauthenticated in any source. This Tamora was the very man called for by destiny, the only one capable of answering that call. So pay some respect.'

History was getting just a little bit subjective in his judgements.

He glared at the two others and continued. 'She raised an

army . . . '

And was interrupted again by the picket – 'By selling whatever the people owned into hock.'

History exploded. 'I do wish you'd keep your unsubstantiated trash, your unhistorical opinions to yourself. Who's telling this story? Who is the historian here?' He turned to Lucky. 'You must try to forget what this propagandist says. He's only trying to pervert you.' Lucky shrugged. 'Just you listen to me. Now, where was I? Oh, yes, Tamora raised an army and fell on the enemy while they were drowned in beer, scrounging and songs. In confusion, the enemy awoke and tried to rally themselves but couldn't, being desperately charged by Tamora, their leader thrown down from his horse, and besmirched, and, seeing the slaughter so great by the pale beams of the news, fled, leaving the spoils of their rich camp, the stolen wealth of the nation.

'The City heard the confused noise outside, the clashing of arms and the groans and crying of dying men, and was greatly astonished but could not think what it should mean.

'Then the shades of night taken off and the glorious Sun casting forth cheerful light, the porters of the gate, or the media, saw a lone figure approach the gate and knock, and they took up their courage in their pens and demanded to know who it was.

' "I am,' said the figure, 'Your friend Tamora, and I desire to speak with the Emperor, for I bring you good news." '

'Oh dear,' said Lucky, joking about in his boredom. 'The God Squad.'

'And having said this, lifted off her helmet . . . '

'A Hermes headscarf,' said the picket.

' . . . upon which they knew her with joy, thinking she'd come to do them good. They advertised the Emperor of her presence, who came pell-mell from his Palace of Whitehall, and he wouldn't suffer her to kneel . . . '

'Which she made no gesture to do,' the picket smirked.

'I'll thank you kindly', snapped History at him, 'to keep your snide remarks to yourself. Now I hope this is the last time I have cause to reprimand you.'

'OK, OK, keep your hair on,' the picket replied. 'I'll let you get on with your histrionics alone.'

History ignored him. 'And he, the Emperor, embraced her as a brother, proclaiming she would know how to free the land from the barbarous enemy, against whose force the City could not hold out much longer.

'Now Tamora read him the news.

' "To you this night unknown, your fears are banished, for the siege is lifted, by myself and my party." '

'The Emperor rejoiced heartily, but she warned him that their work was far from over, for the enemy still lurked within and without, and held strong garrisons throughout the land, polluting it with their outdated and alien ideas.'

'Alien?' asked the picket.

'Yes, alien,' History said, animated. 'Foreign to England, these imported ideologies, Marxism and its foster brother Socialism. Totally foreign and alien to the English character.'

'So political philosophies are appropriate on racial lines and not on political and economic grounds. Also,' said the picket in a German accent, 'these Englishers are so commonsensical. Vat happened next, English swine?'

'Tamora promised that if the people gave themselves over to her, she and her party would beat the barbarians and their standards out of the country.

'The Emperor's captains, the media, created a big noise informing the people of the City of these developments and their salvation, and such joy appeared in the countenances of the people that even you would find it hard to scoff; and they uttered the same with happy words and trumpet sounding. To speak of the great numbers of people that flocked together in the streets of London at her coming in, I will omit as taking too long; neither speak of the presents, welcomings, lauds and gratifications made to her. But anyway, the Senators assembled with joy and chose Tamora as their general, the Emperor promising her one half of his kingdom if successful. She for whom the land had long ached.

'The enemy having found these fruitful counties pleasant resolved not to give over and sent for fresh forces. But Tamora was not slow in mustering her own, and gave speedy pursuit, gaining many victories, some even by her voice alone. Her voice spread fear like fire through deadwood; she drove them before her as if she were a flash flood sweeping the land, bearing all with her.'

'An ablution as huge as the bleaching of Chernobyl.'

'She took the wives and families of the enemy captive . . .'

'And put them under the slave yoke of poverty.'

History shot the picket with a sharp glance.

'But the barbarians' rebellious slaughter continued over the years, washing the country with blood, whilst they defiled the lanes and fields with their dead bodies, till . . . '

'Till she had brought in her hearth gods,' shouted the picket in anger, 'and the chief among them herself. Tamora, a god of wars, angers, ambushes, and crippling crimes.

'All hate her head which is twofold, arrogant and patronising; all abhor her head, rinsed and set with snakes. Which she plucks forth and sets upon the people, that slide into their bodies and drive them mad and savage, tossing and turning in their bellies, the seat of greed and setting it a-burning.

'She arms brothers of one soul against each other, twists homes with hatred, bringing in here her whips and firebrands of fear, and driving up and down the country before her all who do not get down and crouch at her cracked feet, giving them Death's Alms.

'A true Hun, she eats babies and hangs the young on lampposts at every corner and smothers the old in their beds in their homes.

'She has a thousand names and a thousand ways of wounding, and shake out the folded strategem of her barren cunt and find she breeds acts of war there that break the old peace pact. And in this stink men desire, demand and take up arms . . . '

'Till', History shouted back at the picket, 'she had locked that unholy furore away, with their weapons out of the reach of these children and had enchained them in a million links of gold, in which they can grind their teeth and howl with their bloodied mouths as much as they like, but they cannot break and must live within them, and rot emasculated.'

History and the picket glared at each other in hateful silence, whilst Lucky had a coughing fit and spat up some phlegm, and then addressed History.

'You're really into this shit, aren't you?'

History said, 'It's my job.' And held out his open palm.

Lucky cackled at the hand and asked, 'And they all lived happily ever after?'

'I don't know,' said History, straightening himself up all ornery. 'I only report what's happened.'

'So that's your job is it, reportage?' the picket asked.

'Yes,' History replied tentatively because he didn't trust the man. He elucidated his role a little. 'History by truthfully presenting the past of a nation gives that nation a sense of continuity and unity.'

The blackened picket exploded. 'Like hell it does. Your history moulds the past for the creation of a particular present. And you're in the pay of certain parties.'

History began to splutter indignantly, but also to fearfully shuffle away.

The picket got to his feet and gave the lap dog that History was his boot and Lucky lent his. Lucky understood this.

When they had exhausted themselves they sat down and waited, speaking no more, as History gurgled and dribbled incoherently to himself by their side.

The Opening of their Hearts – Capital

At the hour of the scuzz commuters, two stage-hands bring on a pastel sofa and set it down before the City. Lucky and the picket from their green hill without the City wall watch the pop morning show *Yup Yup Yup*. Presenter-mummies give toddling viewers baby food and dummies to suck on with their toothless brains. It's too early to think, ever too early to think. And too late.

A flashbulb flourish from the sky blanches the Sun and the contestants, two politicians, spread middle-aged and sombre-suited, appear before the nation – one at one door with his followers and one at the other with his, flashing smiles that make the Sun blush.

The flashy and irrelevant Host pumps their hands and invites them to get comfy. Girls flurry with rouge and paint to make them up for the election.

The politician plump on the right in the sofa is Toryador, a red ragged Bull-dog, and the politician just leaning to the left is Laborious, the Emperor's bastard son by Charity.

The Host – or, more formally, the Umpire – from his armchair of justice addresses the champions of the opposing parties.

'Gentlemen, you have just one minute to plead for your deserts.'

The two shout up at the walls, where aloft the battlements are jostling with people named the media, or otherwise advertisers, who pass on what they say to the folk inside.

Or are they on the outside?

Toryador says the banal and cheap words of tradition, personal freedom, the British way of life and others, and Laborious says the banal and cheap words of tradition, personal freedom, the British way of life and others, and I throw. I don't want to hear no more this tired old talk and this tired old con. The same things said a billion times and said again, and there is no point in saying.

Politicians never make a sound unrehearsed, so why do they go on to repeat?

Their voices are prerecorded, cut-ups from the Speech Archives, but they must still display their colours and their sheeny armour.

Now Laborious sweating under the lights claims the people for his friends, and he is theirs, urging them to defend these words against his honorable friend, Toryador, who hates them. And Toryador sallies out that all which he, Lavo, hath said and declared is a lie and that only he is loyal to these words, and in him their Fathers live . . . Vampiric existence in the backbrain, smoky back-boardrooms of the nation. Not in this traitor, meaning his honorable friend, Laborious. And so he pleads for succession.

And La Beau parries, proclaiming Toryador for a traitor, false and disloyal to Emperor and enemie unto the realme, and promise to prove this with his body against the bodie of Toryador and leaps to his feet. And Toryador leaps to his too, and they brandish their ruddy fists, dancing round each other like two walrus-flies.

And Lucky thinks them juvenile and delinquent.

In England we still have the joust and no debate.

The Host shuffles himself between them and mumbles they've got to go over to the jolly weatherman, and Toryador looks straight to camera and begs, 'Choose me.'

And Laborious looks straight to camera and begs, 'Choose me.'

And they both beg and claim in craven fashion, 'This is what the people want.' When the wants of the people are like God's wants, passing beyond human understanding. Thumping their flaccid chests. Claiming it's in their best interest, like a loved one always does. Wishing to enter their hearts. Wheedling like possessing matriarchs scared of losing their one and only paltry possession. Or, in the case of these twin creeps, one and only paltry profession. Same thing.

The profession of politician in a democracy is womanly. Politicians are coached by charm consultancies to look sincere on TV. So where lies right? And who is honest?

Politicians are female impersonators. Is this TV or transvestism?

This freedom that's fought for turns out to be a formalised game, gravely played out with set speeches and stiff gestures, and appalling lack of any human presence. A stereotypical social insititution, a smooth operation, like pop or chat shows, with no balls.

And behind the bland face is an evil intent and before the screen the insidious spread of brain death. And what is the name of this god of bland face? He has no name, they say, for he is no man-created ideology, but all natural. But he has, and it is multinationalist democracy.

The Host interrupts, saying, 'I'm sorry gentlemen, that really is all we have time for. You'll have to leave your fortunes with the peoples' thumbs now.'

And as soon as the camera turns off, Toryador and Laborious collapse back onto the sofa.

The media on the battlements in shouting down Laborious' words reported:

'The loony leftie says . . . mumble mumble mumble . . . . We love Tammy and hate Labour mitherers. Britain's sick of moaning lefties whingeing on at our great country. . . . '.

When Bobo is told this by an aide, he rages on though no one listens, whilst Toryador goes harumpf harumpf and turns back to the Host, who's gripped to his side, hoping for an invite to one of Lady Toryador's house parties.

'Oh speaking on TV and radio', Toryador is saying, 's'a doddle to me. I can talk crap for hours, if it's crap you're wanting. And if you don't, I can read the Tory Manifesto in Mandarin. You know this show, really, honestly, is the best . . . For dropping a maggot in the ear of the nation, you might say. And I do?'

Big Ben goes gong-gong and Toryador and Laborious get off their asses and approach the City gates, led by the man with the Mace, on which they bang-bang with their fists to be let in. The gates to the Capitol are thrown open before them and they go down the aisle between the cheering people side by side, haranguing with hands and voices – though none can hear for the people's clap and applauding of their own democracy – and ascend to the upper stage, joining the tribunes to watch the funeral procession.

Draped in Black

Into view and over the road and through the City gates streamed a funeral procession made in a South Atlantic squall.

Lead on by Glory, a scabrous old bag in her gory rags of Pride tacked together some human sinew and cartilege, sons march and sway somnambulistical carrying coffins draped in black, the colours of the state, and others bring sea shells and penguin skins.

Across the home portals they trudge in the festering marsh mud and sheep droppings, this thin slanting rain shaken out of storm clouds, overbearing clouds that put out the heavenly lights and snuff out the torches. They are the rain of thunder-cracks that salvoes and booms and bursts and cackles at the earth, when powers collide and war. And there is no end to them in their khaki of the karzies, the dust of ammunition and fire on their feet and hands and in their faces, and shrouding their tongues, the vehicle of their brains, and burrowing into their selves and fastening them down. This rain that churns up the earth and all belongs to the rain, as grey and enduring as the English rain, for which there is no cure, this endless river of brown into this brown Shitty.

At the City gates stands the State Herald, the Host in his other official capacity, proclaiming the titles.

'Well viewers, what a beautiful morning for it. Here at the gates, the mood is jubilant, the streets packed with well-wishers, to greet our valiant troops home. We're hoping at any moment to bring you the first glimpse of Titus Britannicus, who must surely be our greatest great patriot, the great hero of this war – our leader described this morning in an interview with me as 'one of the most brilliant achievements of modern times' – a war into which we were forced by those southern savages. Taking up again the flag of freedom – freedom, our strength and our battle cry, which Rome has a long tradition of defending, and which sometimes demands a sacrifice of us all. And now Britannicus is returning to a grateful nation, laden with honour and spoils. I think I can hear the massed bands which are accompanying him on this his last leg . . . Yes, I can . . . It won't be long now. Honestly, there can't be a man alive today not warmed to the very cockles of his heart by this show. Yes, here he comes. Romans, please, make way, don't crowd please . . . .

As he babbles on, the wail of martial music, the usher of Father Titus, grows louder. Before Titus comes noise and after he leaves tears and torn corpses and defoliated trees.

The old war lag himself appears, Old Nick, named Pious, whose butt is tattooed with a roll call of his old campaigns. A crumbling limestone crag, he's perched in a mammoth TV set dragged on stage by captive soldiers, now slaves. (Always travels by some other's broad back.) Embalmed in victory bunting, and with tears of sorrow in one eye and of joy in the horny twin. To see those old White Clits of Dover.

(A tatty old sail ship, with shrouds for sails, returned to her home port with a cargo of bad grain. Grown, the ergot causes the Deliriums and Delusions.)

The Host crawls up to him in his finest gratuitous manner

and shoves the bulbous mike in Titus Britannicus's mug, asking the obvious, obviously for such a lack of brain.

'Sir, sir . . . . Please, uh, purlease . . . . If you could possibly find your way to, ah, grace us with a few words. Tell us and those watching at home how you're feeling on this glamorous day?'

T. Britannicus looks at him and his staring one-eyed million-eyed friend through slow, rheumy eyes and speaks in his dumb tongue.

'I'm, um, glad to be home. . . . Once again we can all live in freedom and . . . '

The Host ever mindful of good TV breaks off, leaving Britannicus mumbling to himself.

The cameras follow the funeral procession into the City, which is crawling in black, into the streets crowded with people in mourning weeds and ashes, the national costume of the poor. The rich can afford homes and videos. In the streets the procession meets the stares of the people who choke on the multitude of coffins. Then, in the deathly silence, a ruffian element saved their goose, clearing their throats with a rousing chorus of 'Rule, Britannia'; and everyone's caught it, breaking out in flags and streamers, and drowning out the chanting of the dead bodies.

Amidst the funeral processed and the camera flitted back and forth across this . . . 'glorious scene' . . .

Amongst them Lucky sang to himself:

'Rule, Britannia, Britannia rules the waves,
Britons never never never will be saved.'

The Brit Rites

Mesmerised, Lucky followed after in the wake of the funeral procession and didn't notice when the picket slipped off. The funeral descended up into the Capitol, through the City and Fleet Street to Whitehall, the Maintainance Capitol, that maintains all this House; past Admiralty Arch and the MoD, Downing Street crouched between the crushing walls of the Treasury and the FO to the spikes of Westminster, Westminster

Abbey, spiritual bride hand in hand with its temporal bride-groom, the Houses of Parliament. The meek and mild nun married to God, this Dog passing beyond human understand-ing, moving in most mysterious ways.

As it had become a fine day, the Capitol's white stone gleams in the Sun and is clean to the eye, but the Scribes and the Pharisees of the Capitol cleanse only the outside of the cup:

Within is all extortion and excess. And filthy and poisoning to drink.

And the Capitol is a whited sepulchre which indeed appears beautiful outwardly, but is within full of dead men's bones and of all uncleanliness.

Blind men, cleanse out the inside and the outside'll take care of itself.

Now when Jesus was at the Temple, he cast out all that sold and overthrew the books of the moneylenders, saying:

'My House is a House of Prayer,

'and you have made it the Den of Thieves.'

And he said:

'The householder planted a vineyard and let it out to husbandmen to tend. And when the time of the fruits came he sent to the husbandmen to receive the fruits of it, the husbandmen took his servants and beat one and killed another and stoned yet another.

'Again he sent and they did the same.

'Lastly he sent his own son, and when the husbandmen saw his son, they said amongst themselves, this is the heir, let's kill him and seize on his inheritance.

'So they caught him and cast him out of the vineyard and slew him.

'Shareholders and DHSS: you say if you had been in the days of your fathers, you would not have partaken of his blood, but they are your fathers and you would.

'Sheep Stealers and Land Seizers: all are witnesses that you are definitely the children of them that killed.

'Men are sent to you and some you kill and some savage and some persecute from city to city and city to country, perse-cuting age upon age and enjoying their fruits.

'Upon you falls the bloodshed on earth. Why else would you

carry umbrellas, ye serpents, ye generations of vipers?

'When the householder comes to, he will ask you:

'"Who makes the House?"

And he will give you the answer:

'Upon your heads and in your guts, he will miserably destroy the rot of you, wicked men, and keep the vineyard for ever to himself.

'But for now the Scribes and Pharisees, the biggest profiteers, the biggest bastards in all the land, have taken the House up into their arms.

'The usurpers have shut up the House against all men, going in themselves and not suffering them that would enter to go in, but to stand outside in the snow and the rain, the dry wind that blows out the blood and the scorching sun that pickles the skin.

'The House should be as the vault of the heavens covering all her creatures, like a hen shelters her chicks.

'You should gather the children as the hen gathers her chicks under her wings, but you will not.

'Scribes of Debt and Pimps:

'You devour the Widow's House,

'Took the House and made it into a WhoreHouse, and the Widow into a Whore.

'The House is made into a whited sepulchre, which indeed appears beautiful outward but is within full of dead men's bones and of all uncleanliness, your bones and your filth.

'The Judges and the Pharisees:

'They sit in the law's seat. And they can do as they wish.

'All they will, you observe, idiots; but they say and do not, their works done to be seen of men, paying to the word of the law and not the spirit, and making the law up as they go, in their tax returns and share applications.

'They omit the weightier matters of judgement, mercy and faith, those that ought to be done and are not. They commit the crime and sell us the punishment; that's the trick of the rich and the powerful.

'Blind guides that they are, blinded by their own lucred fingers, they strain at a gnat of a crime and swallow the camels, obscuring.

'They bind heavy burdens and grievous to be borne and lay

them on men's shoulders, the donkeys, who lay it on their women, the asses, that squelch under them.

'But they themselves will not move them with a single one of their tanned fingers. And yet their fair discourse has been as sugar and honey making the hard way sweet and delicious.

'They make broad their hands and enlarge the borders of their power; they love the uppermost rooms and chief seats of the House and the greetings in the markets of eyes, having an outward face of honour set upon them by flatterers and parasites; and love to be called Master of the House.

'But don't be called Master.

'None are Master, and all are brethren, are beaten. In the end.

'And call no man your father, for none is your father, for you are all bastards.

'Masters, for a pretence you make a long and pious prayer for peace and prosperity, and therefore will get right damnation, if there's a heaven and a hell, and any justice in 'em.

'And you encompass the land and the sea in your Arms and in your mouths, and the whole globe is merely a gobstopper in your gob and you don't stop.

'You make all converts to your Word, and when you have made them all your converts, you have made them twice the child of hell, once in your sin and damnation, and twice damned for swallowing it.

'Elders:

'You take the child and age him with your dribble and suck out the bone and the blood and spit out the skin. And make them in your Money-World either commodity or discommodity, yuppie or dolee in the International Cash-Flow.

'Blind guided, straining at the fly in the ointment and swallowing the fat camels.

'The Scribes and the Pharisees are painted sepulchres, outwardly appearing righteous to men but within are full of hypocrisy and iniquity.'

The funeral procession disappeared underneath the arches of Westminster Abbey, where the blind and the lame came to be healed then, to ask in prayer and receive, and now nothing but a functionary of the State, and Lucky snuck in with it.

Inside, this House is a dumpyard of mortuary sculpture.

The Elders and the Pharisees build tombs in hard white stone and concrete to the prophets and to the righteous, to their own worthies, garnished with memorials of Rome, Republic and Empire (Ally Pally, the ancient home of the BBC, is the best Roman ruin I've seen). These tombs are remnants, historico-traditional clots, such as the stately homes and palaces, the ancestral-portrait-hung anti-rooms and offices.

And our blood is stopped and full of gangrene.

The Elders and the Pharisees build and garnish these tombs in the fashion of Rome for on Rome's they built and garnished their values. Rome, whose values were the State. For the support and survival of their society, for the buttress and foundation of their House that we built and form.

These values and tombs are like unto whited sepulchres, which indeed appear beautiful but within are full of dead men's bones and of all uncleanliness, our bones in their filth born of the masters assisted by us in our blindness. These values are valueless as being wholy dependent on the State which can have no values and these our values are money and money has no value but blood money.

Blind Elders, which say to swear and live by the House, it is nothing; but to swear and live by the gold of the House is binding, and he who does is a debtor.

Which is the greater, eh, fools and blind, the gold, or the House that sanctifies the gold?

But I forget, which House sanctifies the gold – our House or the Bank of England? Or are they the same and we live in Threadneedle Street?

And whosoever swears and lives by the House, it's nothing; but to swear and live by the dry bone of the tomb, or truncheon, it is all, and he is innocent, huh?

Fools and blind, which is the greater – the bone, or the House that sanctifies the bone?

And if a man shakes these tombs, the sanctifying bones will rattle at him Death's arms and grimace within their politician's head.

For the Scribes and the Pharisees are White Devils appearing as angels in great shining light and blinding, and take the

House and make it a white sepulchre and fill it with dead men's bones and all uncleanliness that makes us vomit and disease; and make the House a tomb that sits on our faces so our mouths eat their shit and our tongues clean their anuses, and shall till the proud mountain is cast off our shoulders, and into the sea, but when?

And this is the State of the House. And Jesus said unto them then:

'The stone which the builders rejected is become the head of the corner, and whosoever falls on this stone shall be broken and on whosoever it falls it grinds him to powder.'

But what does that mean?

Tomb

Lucky watched as the funeral procession was greeted by the Emperor.

The Emperor was a wizened old git with no arms and a wrinkled face, shot through with nervous tics, his face torn by the seismic eruptions below of his terrible hunger for power and his terrible fear of withdrawal – tics that are maggots crawling through his flesh. And with him was Tamora and her party, and the TB, Titanic Bureaucracy, or Tea Bags, a disease of nostalgia, in dress uniforms and black dresses, lace veils and tricorns, hanging ropes of seed pearl and curare-scented badges of club allegiance. All stood before the Tomb of the Britannici.

Titus Britannicus solemnly approached the Tomb and turned to address the assembly, as behind him the pallbearers opened its doors and began unloading the coffins of the dead soldiers and sailors onto the conveyor belt, which silently and tastefully slid them, gathered them up, into the crematorium's incinerator. The TBs drawing the flesh smoke deep into their aching lungs. Relief from the present.

He said:

'I bring my sons home to be buried with their fathers. To rest here in peace and honour, Rome's finest champions.

'A man's life ends in death, that is certain. But by his life's deeds he can win for his brothers still in this earth life.

'In this fire their hearts and bodies were consumed; they sacrificed their flesh for this' – he gestured with his arm to the Deadly Company and the Tombs.

'Society exists by this sacrifice. It is Society's Price. The Price is Right.

'I am glad they paid. Let them be rewarded with cash prizes and holidays abroad . . . .'

He faltered and gave up.

His burden discharged, he brushed off the ash on his hands and led the Company out, interrupted by Queen Pug Victoria, who got off her plinth and shook his hand for sending gunboats up and at 'em.

Lucky hung behind to take a closer look at the Tomb.

Back in the gloom, several technicians in dirty cover-alls stepped methodically about the It, checking on the various dials it was adorned with. None of them paid him any mind, concentrating on their ministrations.

One of the technicians, the chief to tell by his tone, straightened up from a dial and flatly stated,

'Temperature drop, we need to burn more coal.'

And bin men began to empty body bags of dead southern savages into the solid-fuel-burning power station. But this was not enough, and with a train whistle, able-bodied men and women, ordinary citizens, began to troop across the stage, singing cheerily 'It's A Long Way To Tipperary', whilst Roman statues, planted on guard, flexed their muscles and welcomed them, saying,

'Hail Caesar, those who are about to die to warm you; Hail Kaiser.'

And then they went into this Tomb, that is the central heating of the City Society . . . . Closing down lives, our stations end, that weird societal fusion, and the smoky fires catch, billowing into the eyes and wreathing, obscuring the barren and windscaled landscape, the stinky whiff of freedom hangs in the air, burnt flesh, and wept heavy water.

When the temperature was up, the supply line was turned off. The technicians went on their tea break, the Tomb churning on by itself and Lucky left in the House desolate and barren.

He wandered over to the statues to give their antiquated miniature packets a looking over.

They were scrubbed clean and shone pearly white like shark's teeth brushed with Colgate in this sooty HellHouse, their eyes scrubbed white and blank, and they all turned on him, and flipping their wrists, said,

'We too understand the Rules of Opportunity Knocks.'

Horrified by this cemetery place and curiosity withered, Lucky stumbled out through the tombs in their gloom and the feminine shadows that ministered to them into the great market-place that is Parliament Square. Where, thinking he'd never agreed to pay a price to live in this Society, which was hardly conducive to him, and never would, especially such a high one, he remembered he was penniless and tried begging off the crowd, which greeted him as the dead are wont.

And then suddenly he found himself outside of the Capitol, as if he'd walked through an open door and it had shut by itself behind him, barring his way back. He was out in the rotting remains of the City.

In Shards

As I was trailing about the City dazed and uncertain as to whether to stay or go, I came across the picket again.

He took me to a pub and bought me a beer. His arm was bandaged in a sling but not broken.

He said once we were seated, 'You don't want to stay here. Be off and quick about it.'

I asked him why.

'Because soon they'll have their hands about your throat and then they'll squeeze until you croak, and give up your body to 'em.

'The City's fallen unto a conker, and smashed. They're busy with decrees, condemning some to death and some to slavery, and ransoming most for their future.

'They've made the boring bee their symbol, emblematic as it is of industry, conformism and extreme organisation. And by law it's laid down that all in this City must be successful, and the law lays down the penalty for failure, the old Death of A Thousand Thousand Rubs.

'Oh, some are successful, but they're putting the poor out in bin bags, more and more each day. You don't want to stay here.'

'No,' I agreed.

He accompanied me back to my gondola, which was tied up at Embankment.

After we'd emptied it of ten tramps who were playing sardines, he shook my hand and wished me luck, but my name of Lucky was beginning to feel tawdry, and once I was out in the river a cannon-ball that I judged came from a cadet training ship, whose pupils I'd been visually sprucing earlier – perhaps this was their idea of a love note, being squaddie heads – sank me and I drowned in the river that was swollen, it was that time of the month for it, and I thought I was dead and finished, poor ol' me.

6
Drowned Dreams

I plunged, deep in a dumb scream, my mouth open, and water gushes in like breath. I resurface and thrash but I take in more water till my tank's full and it's all over, I'm borne under. The river that drains Thatcherite Britain going down resembling some pox-maddened survivalist. The sun setting over Rome and the sun extinguishing into the river that extinguishes me, and my first sense under water of the loss of fear and pain.

Down with yuppies and sharks, amongst the crumpled empty empty cans and sweet wrappers, I drift into a mosaic-shoal of newpapers and become entangled, and through my dead eyes I can read snatches of the tattered and torn. The first words:

'The water is lapping around our necks . . . . There is no more time.'

I twist to see if the quote's mine, but it's not. Some member of President Alfonsin's government dreading in the shadow of a military take-over. I have been overtaken by death.

Tired at a loose end at the end of my day, I settle back into a cushion of gossip sheets, and read to see if these fragments reported, or predicted, my demise.

'The City is most silently belching forth the satisfied sound of the young wearing sensible skirts and blouses, even the males, mostly drowned in talk of money. Sometimes seems like Britain's last ferocity, the young and active in the City, lubricating an empire based on a shrinking isle. An empire of the second wind, post-colonial dinner burped like Hiroshima hidden behind the PR.'

The New Blood . . . . There could be blood in the City? Human blood, maybe? Streets paved with CDs . . . . The murder of matadors wait to enter the pit, suppressing grins and giggling. Salesmen of the Shitty raved over in *Sporting Life* . . . . Have they nothing to give? Gunning themselves up for a fist fight, the last election, which they buy and sell, with an estimated seven million going on trust – adverts, ring up many votes in the cash register. And it turned into a walk-over, voters with walk on. 'They were out there begging to be taken' – I'm out here begging to be taken. I hear 'Three Times a Lady'. Thrice three times. Is this insane? . . . Argues Dave, puts on a couple of thousand pounds and leans back in bed, saying, 'I buy attractions of the West End . . . Café de Paris, Langan's . . . Piccadilly Circus . . . .'

Rent boy looks up: 'Anything for ya, mister. Cash comes.'

Men of the City are walking property, inches of money money muscle. Feel the pinch? . . . 'Is this a million or half a million I see before me? Poker or what? Couldn't find a bigger casino and I tried . . . Rigged? Eau naturelle . . . .'

There are two civilisations – one is where most of us live and another in which we constitute their stage set only. These bastards even talk with different tongues. Nothing has anything to do with people. Ticker-tape tucked straight into their heads. Like computers never have thought, programmed in a sea of bodies drawn to their world. All these funny little manufactured people here, City trolls in the underworlds of finance, of law, godforsaken.

The tourist hides your wealth away – 'You can sit on notes and the next morning everything is worth francs or whatever' – and cleaned up, moved on, left behind. Others left to rot in the gutter as the darkness floods. We were perched on valuables left behind, the cultural rubbish and filth which are the ends in an Imperial Panorama. The patchwork of Britain is edited together from heroic monuments to Britain's name, and I have no name in their world. The flood is filled with the unnamed.

Past clings on for grim death, begins to show its age through the paint of former glory. Crippling constriction on the nation, even dead meat lasts a while. The old stewer likely to burst into a foul stench. I mean sing halitosis-throated at any moment 'Land of Hope and Glory'. Scheduled for demolition.

'The West,' a Jap friend tells me, 'infected with a sense of incredible loss, visible slip towards the fragile American condition.' Around here people always pretending to be Yank. Everybody their own star, director and audience.

Ladies and Gentlemen, speculation is rife.

Floating with the placid fishes, resigned my life? Or could I have resisted? Perhaps the only thing possible was wanking, and now I can't. Limbs asleep, dead and dumb. Like quite numb.

Numb speaks.

It's cold in the water. All I want is your arms. It's cold as the grave in the water, it's snowing outside. Alarming car and shop alarms in the scarred night chased by police sirens in the back of my dreams, the city's full of feuds and dyings. Splitting the atom. Where every hope is deadly nightshade, it's constant war films. Scenes that lie behind the billboards, impossible to say the external landscape is anything but death. Rock 'n' roll à la cologne spray douches the ecstatic, pummelled masses. Sitting watching TV, people click click click. Switch over. Their Coronation Streets hidden behind advertising that at once erases memories of violence, the flat flawless faces of TVGod excommunicates the thought process. Populism is the ticket and when the old soap sewer in all of us bursts out into a foul stench they find the Titanic.

From white wedding to black funeral a mourning. The church organs grind into bells that are tolling. Feast to wake and hymnals to dirges, that old Twenty-Turd Psalm. And posies to wreaths plucked off to hospital dying and withering by bedsides of horny geriatrics held under the flood of old memories in which all the dead come back to life.

In the river red carnations bloom and their petals bleed off. I'm on my back, hands clasped in prayer at bosom. A pretty picture. I begin to feel like the goldfish in the goldfish bowl. Is this my death or a dream? The world is upside down.

A voice out of a sea shell whispers, 'Ophelia ascends, descends; bobbing in the briny with her bloated belly; pregnant with her death born of her love. Clutching at dead flowers, pulling the petals off daisies . . . .'

Ophelia farts.

Juliet who is Hope is lying on her back on her deathbed, crushing the white lillies sewn into her fresh wedding dress and waiting in death. Daffodils have been scattered on her, yellow shadows to walk by in the subterranean as the darkness floods on.

The Musicians and Peter the serving creature haggle over her.

'We like the feel of what sells, what sells is good for you.'

Are they going to fuck her who's fuckless?

Peter requests the Musicians play 'Heart's Ease' and the Minstrel asks why.

Peter replies, 'Because the ol' corny jukebox of my heart has gone and selected 'My Heart Is Full of the Dole'. So please play some twaddle to cheer me.'

The Minstrel tells him he won't because it wouldn't be proper under the circumstances – remember Juliet's dead meat – and Peter gets all narked and refuses to pay the Musicians. Night-club managers never do. Juliet was or had been a hostess in Old Pa Poulet's Friendly and Amicable. And maybe still is. Perhaps they could drum up some necrophiliac trade.

Now it's the Musicians who get angry; they occupy Juliet's bed.

Peter threatens them. 'I will give you the Minstrel in pieces if you don't play.'

The Minstrel threatens him back with a melodramatic chord on his lute. 'You just go ahead and try and I'll give you the serving creature and then I'll huff and I'll puff . . . '

'Pouf, more like,' shouts Peter, squaring up to him obscenely. 'I'll put the serving creature's dagger in your rancid belly.'

Juliet, squashed up in her own death bed, as if she were working still but she ain't getting paid for this, thinks: I, I, I . . . is there no fucking end to it. I can't get to sleep anywhere.

The Minstrel gets out his ugly dirk and threatens Peter with it, whilst a second Musician, who has a wife and three kids in drama school to think of and needs the gig, tries to mollify them.

'Gents, gents, this is just not done. Now please put away your daggers for a Lady's present. Even if a dead whore.'

'Oh, I will,' retorts Peter to him. 'I'll put it away to the hilt in your palsied friend, I'll dry fuck that pansy with my little iron will. Either sing, my cissies, or put up your bums for inspection.'

Juliet thinks: Ai, these straight men. Do they never bore of this, chasing me even into my death with their bullying boasts. She sighs. And everyone's still getting it but me and it's not fair. Perhaps they were right; mutilate yourself into a specific marketable into a market-place, for experience is to the leper denied. She moans, Oh well, it's too late now, I'll just have to keep on reading Genet till my Prince comes.

She makes a hump under the sheets for her fingers to touch her Prince as Peter chases the Musicians round her bed singing:

'When the gripping cramps the belly wounds
And the doleful dumps the anus oppresses,
Then the seamen with their silver sound of semen gushing . . .'

I have hallucinations in this cold turkey withdrawal of life. My eyes can see, my numb lips barely move. I have left a lot unsaid, undone. Please be patient sea and fishes, and leave my lips.

It all ferments inside, poisonous farts.

Juliet comes out onto the balcony, it's snowing. She reaches out her arms into the snow, crying for Romeo. You who are nameless, tell me your name so I can find you. Through the sludge I see Douglas and try to embrace him. Strains of 'White Christmas' drift through, somehow unbowed, untainted. Her arms close around and clasp him, turned by the cruel gods into cold water; her fingers sieves.

Juliet comes out onto the balcony, it's snowing. Rows of the dead look up at her. Through the snow she sees the *Aurora*, thawing flesh. It fires on the Winter Palace and signals the start of the Bolshevik Revolution, bombarding it with red sperm. Kronstadt sailors fuck on the ice, Last Chance. The *Aurora* sits in the icy water, her guns frozen. In which sperm is strung like long lines of ectoplasm. Freezing out the child unborn.

In my grave of dead flesh, I wondered on return what state I would inhabit? What tail? Would I return never slave to anyone again? But these were dream questions and I needed to attend to my health.

My body was falling apart fast; consequently my sanity, my ability to hold together any functioning self, was in effect a non-existent light cord in my bathroom with parts of me disappearing and flushed down the toilet, wash-basin and bath. I need a switch. There is a switch to shed some light on this entropied atrophied mess to let me clean up but it's constantly devolving.

I dragged my remnants round to the doctor's, where we, me and precarious parts of my body, waited in the limbo room with a request for new flesh.

The doctor referred me to some official at the Department of Health and Bodily Integrity.

On the way over I saw myself mirrored in a shop winow. Few or none would know me, disguised in this dead flesh. I had green hair.

I passed through an assembly hall in which a professor of National Identity was lecturing.

'No one amongst us is as they claim to be, however much they may protest. We are rarely in touch with ourselves or our state. We are not who we were yesterday nor are we who we will be tomorrow. That would really be getting ahead of ourselves. Nothing can exist in stasis, please to remember this. No living creature can stand such a condition. Nor indeed any dead. Things are going to fall apart, it's natural. No rest for the wicked, as they say.'

Slobbering laughter moved through the hall amongst the disassociated limbs and thoughts.

He explains: 'Shrink of the world by the hour. UK is at most thirty years behind real time. It's not declining as fast as our minds. Great changes are occurring and will sweep the old ground from under you if you let them. Or it can lift you right out of your seats and if you're lucky get more than just another passing of the world, can be taken with it. Not passed over, as long as the scripts provided . . . ' He chuckled. 'Can do what you want to form a perfectly reasonable and profitable pisspot. People are sold to stories all the time. Buy yours while stocks last. Ladies and Gentlemen, speculation is rife.'

I eventually found the right office in the right building of the

DHBI. The right office depends on the applicant's initials and there was some problem with my classification. Whether anonymous, non-person, nameless, unnameable, corpse, fish, etc., etc. The possibilities were endless. Finally, after trudging round various offices, my classification was decreed stateless. I thought that the state I was in was if anything an extreme state not a non-state but I bowed to their greater experience and departed leaving bits and bobs.

I knock and enter, slurping myself into the designated chair and wait. The official never looks at me direct with his eyes lacking in any trace of human existence, though I can't blame him considering my condition. Instead he chases sheets of paper that float about his desk.

I sit there feeling trapped in this muffled underwater world, cut off from all human warmth and bodily form. Fear and weakness sock me. My picture of me blurs. It's hard to hold it in focus when looking down informs me that I'm blood and mush. More of me is straining out through a thousand perforations and mixes with the aged shit medium of the sea.

When I press the urgency of my case to him, the official's grey gravestone eyes flicker and turn off, going blank like my confessor's. Then he gets up and just leaves without explanation. I want to follow but can't move. I have to remain seated.

I review my case.

I have been occluded from the present. Made dead. Locked out of my own body and homeland as if my parents had bolted the front door on me, for coming home late or some such trivial misdemeanour. Like dying my hair. Any excuse. Perhaps I am too late? To catch the boat. Devoid of any point of intersection, vein, my connection is broken. And I am consecrated to the buried and drowned past.

The sea shifts, rolling me over in my sleep and out of bed.

I walked into the place where I was sure the party was going to be and found no one there. And I didn't recognise the room. Everyone's gone. What can I do without others? Have I opened the wrong door? I question memory. Right street, right house, right door, but everything's wrong, been changed on me. Or memory's down. I'm sure the owner'll come storming in and scream for the police to dispossess me, charging me with loitering with intent to usurp a body and squat in his story. But seeing as I don't know where I am and I don't know who or what I am, I might as well stick around and hope it all comes back to me. Memory'll return. Or more likely I'll find my way into a story. I'm lonely for a story. Character comes out of a story. No character in nothing.

I dissolved in the chair a little longer and a little more. The sea stealing. And suddenly I can move, which means I'm weightless. The last tatters and rags of corporeal substance rustle to the floor. Farewell body, good riddance. England can keep these scraps. Moving down the hall with the current that ends abruptly in a door that opens and closes in silence, I'm blown away. Alone.

The Serial

War and senseless pain are obscene.

Today was a worn-out classic I've seen again and again. Been in the same over and over and slot straight back into place. I want the exit. Jerking off on the screen which is sludged snow on the trodden-down streets. Downcast, head hung.

The film starts rolling. In broken lines of long and sick waiting, the print is threatening. The print is bad shadows splintering, splitting the atoms. My atoms decompose. Black 'n' white and groaning echoes and blurs fall through the soundtrack crackling. Slipping through the letters of the silent. Tenderised ectoplasmic flesh, frustrated howls of swans. BLACKNESS. Are my eyes open, or am I blind? I can't see you. Ever again. I wish my eyes could pierce the petrol-smoke of the sky. Bells chime, ascending and descending, through the drowned cities in cold black currents. I'm without you, I'm without anyone. I'm put out. I have been ejected from Heaven. Is this the doghouse or am I staying at Heartbreak Hotel, alone again in its plush red velvet raw-heart lobbies? All that matters, you're not here. Nobody's here with me. I want someone. I'd like someone to be with me, my body empty.

The guys who are with the greatest bar-b-q in history just supposed to drop out of the skies tomorrow. Just a phone call away, reach out and touch someone.

A bare white room emerges through the flickers smudged. The lighting's atrocious. Drugged shadows shift like black crepe in a dying underwater breeze, a long black thing amongst them, approximately six feet long, hangs. Up in the air. A question mark . . .

Me?

As if a mounted fish suspended from two cables thick as babies' fists that run through winches in the ceiling and off frame.

It's a black hole, and I can't see. See him?

Or me?

Or it?

It's swaddled in black cloth.

From the shorter cable at the highest point are the hands tied back behind the head, tied by thin leather belts. A hood, black, covers the head in blackest stifling night.

I can't see.

The hood is killing you. The blindness opened up in the minds of millions. The hood is pulled back from mouth and chin so it can breathe. How civilised. Crumpled cross nose and eyes that face down, flesh discoloured bluey-grey. But I can't see you.

How far down is it? How far can I fall?

Is there a bottom?

Or a bottomless floor? Or a bare eternity?

At the waist is a thick belt onto which is hooked the second cable, the second cable that takes most of the weight. The legs dangle limp, weighted down on motorcycle boots with buckles; they swing idle circles.

The room. I can't see anyone in it.

Look out the window and nothing out there but scud.

Look at the door and no one here.

The empty room said, 'No one in the room bare.'

'Cept the deserted disaster this icon threatens.

And I slot right back in. I close my eyes and imagine you and open them and the room and no you. Memory fills this huge empty fish-bowl with the palpable. I remember no you and the cable at the waist drops an inch transferring the weight up, and

I remember you dislocating the shoulders and I remember no you. Never look back. Snaps shoulders. At my back, the Arctic. A landscape of blanket white, snow and sky. Blindly, Arcticly white. Muffled sound, paused in a nuclear flash and everything is dead. My scream penetrates the room in agony and dies through the vacuum.

I watch him not here. No one here any more. Him in the print, the words look stark. 'Cos I want him so much I nothing, cuts tumble out of the print. My flesh, slowly blowing apart, stings in the salt water. I scratch irritably at the open cuts and flesh peels off. Dead fish nibble over the ravaged corpse.

Belt at wrists abrasing the skin red like reddened eyes and weeping.

No one on Victoria Station. His hands travelled over my body detailing its landscape, like the sun which gives sight. His words travelled through my body detailing its landscape. They spoke with each other detailing a landscape. Gone.

His body first and now the memory. Memory shuffles pictures through my ghostly flesh vibrating in the immobile air of screwing time. Coy half-impressions that dissolve in the light. Phantom twinges of amputation. No him. The room bare, between me and the walls vacuum. Britain is the walls, the wallpaper peeling off revealing in blotches an earlier one creating a hybrid. Just memory travels through my body like broken glass and burning petrol. Sucking terror from scar flesh, underwater screams mouthing dumb nerves. And then blackness again. No hands no words no landscape no body. Alone in a plot I can't grasp. My voice recedes, siphoned out through an invisible door in my flesh. Expiring grunt. Leaving the empty body to hang.

Looking out the window, nothing outside but sky overcast. Underneath the window, a heap of clothing, rags.

A heap o' dirty old flesh left when he rose out of my bed.

The heap six feet long that hangs in the air.

His memory a heap o' dirty old clothing that wouldn't keep a body warm. But I want the real thing.

Through a gaping hole in the nets, a heap o' dirty old flesh I used to recognise. Fog-horns blast warnings. In the mist nothing's where it should be. Where it's remembered. Outside I don't recognise. Don't bump into things. Covered in grazes. Black and. The red, white and blue. Bruises.

Looking through the window into the room at the worm that hangs by a thread. Useless. No good to me now. Was it any good then? Floorboards stretch out into an overcast wall. This hideous black-wrapped thing hangs solid and black as industrial excrement in the dead air. Smoke that covers the sun and blots out the world, you are blind. The contours of the cloth a hideous landscape, the grooves and ridges of a record buckled in fire, a record of memory. The patchwork of Britain, drowned in stories.

The hood which is crumpled away from brackish lips split in a sick smile – 'I'm hung.'

One vision of Heaven is indivisibility from all else. Then Hell is absence from this. Hell is being God alone before the world seen. Here is the terminus, feel boredom more strongly than dream. The pain of floating disembodied in space, alone and unconnected. The whole vast world hangs trembling inside. Eternally aware of this and all other garbage, I know everything there is to know of myself and have nothing to do, or nothing to do with it. I don't have a community I can act within and with. Which is the same. Hell is an empty house. Me at its centre, terrorised by the silent vacuum. Hell. To be unconnected by words or by flesh or by feet to earth. To have nobody to connect through and no landscape to connect with. To feel nothing, to feel nothing about me having no senses, no smell, no taste, no touch, no sound, no sights, no senses but this one sense of absence. Hell is a sense and a complete absence of sense. Blackness. A colour and a complete lack of colour. One cannot live without the oxygen line of the senses. To float in this river. Better compared to the dereliction where money is the only body. I watch you go. I watched you go through the window. Black the window, the print dim and flickering, cuts falling through slowly blowing apart. As if caught between two films battling for possession of the one screen.

You left . . .

and now dead.

I was alone . . .

killing myself.

It'll end in slaughter, I promise. I promised. A flattened voice from the never-never. Memory on the never-never.

On Victoria Station in front of everybody I can't kiss you. We emulate Continentals and hug and I hope no one's watching and I hope you don't cry again. The train shifts. Pulling away. Through the window I can see you, but you're behind glass already enclosed. Your mournful expression recedes into shades of fractured light. Closed.

You're behind glass; I can see twisting sarcastic scar that's your mouth I used to kiss cross your stained face.

Soon you'll be enclosed under a different sky and I under mine. I wish my eyes were lightning cracks, still too dark. Already you're pulling away from me and I can't move that fast.

I watch you go through the window and the sky. 'From this world,' he said, looking. Pulling away. Death of that world.

People reproduce their homes in that international hotel manner for the illusion of travel, of going somewhere. Destination. See the Great Stars that are the crystallisations of arriving. People offered safe fictional journey back to their birthplace, the 1950s and the fur lined womb. Who would want to go to such a place?

Trains flirt through my blood. Animal howls through my blood. Fire eating out the insides with flame teeth, havoc and wreck tearing and bleeding and feeding me with pain if I can't have the pleasure. Probing for a destination, any destination. Withdrawal puts whole body in need; jumpy, nervous, uptight. Overanxious and constantly horny, hungry, the flesh desperate. I hope to dream into another life. Peeled senses dart about in frenzied exploration for any destination. Heart-breaking need for land out the window. Trains and travel flirt with me, thirst of blood. But outside the train window disaster driving me away. Lost in Albion. Scenes that lie behind the billboards, impossible to say the external landscape through a paint of former glory is anything but an unfavourable sight. As the darkness floods. Scheduled for demolition, listening to the comfortable rattle of hoardings. And these petrol-doused corpses swaying to stadium rock transplanted in roadways. Travelling with the cultural rubbish and filth, outside dizzy rush of landscapes flushed away. Rows of the dead looking up, searching faces for recognition. Wagging their fingers at us from TV. The landscape of the Western world is most artificial. If anything this time is just shadowy photo in our state of psychopathology. Behind all my dreams rises a mushroom cloud. That's the crystallisation, the definite picture of the landscaped Britain. The deserted disaster this icon threatens. With a scream shatter. Capturing our imaginative yearning, emerge from the void onto film.

When the picture slowly jerks itself back onto the screen, there's a shadow of a boy with a sad face and he's smiling before the window like he's illuminated. The sun cures blindness. And beside him a portrait of James Dean looks down junked up on heroin, his flesh operated on in millions of fantasies that rub him out. Fitted for coffin and poster captioned American Hero.

Another boy slightly taller across the room. Both have faces of dumbfounded innocents crawling into focus but not dumb. The print is badly defaced but the lightnings still too dark at these depths of the sullied river. They're both left too far off. Indistinct.

Both are restrained in darkness. Hidden in strait-jackets, black cloth wound about, their legs shackled. When they move they shuffle awkwardly as the ankle cuffs cuff their wounded skin. As the links of language abrase the tentative. And totter, unable to use their arms for balance, stumbling amongst words.

You don't tell someone you love them originally, I'm explaining to him. The language of love is not gold but counterfeit. You use some other's story, speak through another's mouth to some unknown person.

The more I use their words (are any of these words the right words? I had speech therapy, we all did – I begin again) the less I see in them. These words are dirty. Are these words myself? I'm scared I'll dirty myself with these words, shit on myself with these words, and I must be clean, new-born for you. I stumble, fall from grace. Are these words all we have between us? The currents and the fish and the garbage and the protozoa. Lying in the turgid waters. Afterbirth of death, diluted shit and piss.

These words are dirty overcast sky. Soot falls out of the

soundtrack and smutters me. I try to clean myself, stretching my head to rub my cheek on my shoulder, and begin to twitch as if the ticks dead and dry in my clothes have rehydrated. My whole expression sours to disgust. I'm trying to explain that it's not understanding but misunderstanding. That I bring one semantics, story, of that word, and he another. The stories slide off each other, and into, and whirl like cogs at different tangents. We speak at each other, detailing landscapes incorporating many of the standard features. I think of the words of yawning panoramic displays of decay. Heroic monuments. LOVE, an infinite regress of concrete. Morning after the planner's dream. Behind it rises the vision, the deserted disaster this icon threatens.

He looks bewildered. Through a landscape littered with teeth and lips and slippery with blood, dry skins and cast-off clothes, the remnants of people gone dead. And gone away. My face dead mask in grimace of grief. Mourning the loss of my life, the memory print is dim.

The words I say must be the right ones; I battle to find them. Never imagined I'd be so unimaginative as not to be able to hang language back to its bare bones, that fucked with me. As the darkness floods, under the pressure the words crumble. Scheduled for demolition. I battle to speechlessness. The language of love is silent, come back to silence.

And then I say 'Love is a dirty word. Fuck is pristine.'

And I keep repeating this till I say, 'Fuck your freckles. Just get into my body'; and he says, 'You are my voice.' His soft words fall into me like pure oxygen.

Daylight flashes through the room like a horse bolting. Lightning bleaches. Come back to silence.

And I said,

'I want your flesh,
not your word. But I can't reach you.'

Speaking into his head, spilling out the words with carressing digits. And I try walking towards him, my body lurching, and I fall laughing. And the screen blanks out into the floor.

But I continue forward, wriggling. The other drops to a knee and shuffles forward, reaches and leans over dumbfounded but not dumb bestowing a kiss on my lips . . .

breath.

On the print stain mouth of red lipstick.

He says, 'Here's my mouth, here's myself.' And I say, 'Our bodies break open as if long in the grave already. We're safe at last.' 'Here I am, eat.' 'I don't think we're bleeding. I'm in grace. Our blood knows how to course.'

Both voices die in murmurs of breathing. He falls to my side and pushes his lips on mine. He squirms his body up against mine, and I the same, and we affix. He tries to come undone, straying only to awkwardly kiss. Lost voices. Opened mouths, see the tongues dancing together, kiss cheek and neck and nibble jawbone and ear and nose. In these words you have my mouth and my body, and at each he looks bewildered a new red kisses the screen and these begin to swell outwards, drenching and biting over the face, dripping onto chin flooding the cheeks and spilling across the forehead to brush through the hair finally cascading over the neckline like a tidal wave washing over and over, eyes that dripping onto the cheeks, soft pink putty of faces that fusing, shades shift subtly permutating into new reds, they struggled against their restraints, each his limbs do and as they do the restraints fall away, chains drop as a mock the strait-jackets come undone and their limbs entangle, I'm the hands in grace, the black cloth rots under the red, this red colour restricted to the burning horizon squashed between sea and sky between me and him of the rising sun tints these our bodies sea and me where flesh embraces flesh, the rising sun burning through our veins, blood knows how to course the hare, the reds tear off great hunks of the black 'n' white print, the canvas fills like a colour-by-numbers, red drunk by the suction of lonely flesh, and when the screen is full colour, the reds continue, exploding and infusing into each other as they do cojoining parts of the body suck one shade, bursting into flames with silent cries, that smash glass between us, and fucking and falling through the screen, bursting in blood and flame, till the mass of our body is defined, saturated, against the background only, and both are wrapped in our body, and the reds spurt on, the lines stretching, and give out, burst, and breaking open as if strait-jackets, colour falls from the sound-track, becomes one long, blurred breathing, neither in nor out, neither his nor mine, to the sound of the beating jugular, and the screen blanks out in colours, as shape is conquered and obliterated under reds, the river banks and the landscape disappear underwater, and I dive in and become the same colour, and I can't see anything fucking into oblivion, a flame, a bliss.

On Saturday mornings as a kid I sat in the cinema and watched swirling and bubbling colours like lava in volcanoes entertain me with nothing waiting for the main feature. It lasted only a second and then I'm alone again. A fish passes before my eyes. It's dead too in this pus-filled sewer. Flood of pitch black. The excremental smoke hangs black and solid, acid rain kills lakes and forests. And eats at limestone sculptures, eats away his nose and ears and mouth and skin. Erases, leaving nervous system and brain electronics isolated. Short-circuiting on their own. I search for a lost continent. Outside of me. And I wait alone for the main feature.

The main feature.

7
The Quick End

Before anything. CHAOS. BLACKNESS.

First of all things confused mass. GUTS CHURNING.

In the beginning of this, I'm washed up. Shipwrecked. Body washed away. I'm like to a man paralysed throughout, 'cept in the head. Thought alone. And unable. The I's still stirring in the foul, stagnant gunge behind the eyes.

DEAD MATTER IN BLACKNESS. BRITAIN.

I WANT MY WINGS NOW!

In the beginning, the sea hatches. Riding along on the crest of the waves, awoke to their crashing in ears and their swilling, sickening suction.

A great constipated stone shit quaking through the bowels.

Then the waters broke, splashing up in my face, and I spluttered and spluttered for breath and bawled onto the world, and whilst I was spluttering bumped into something solid in the dark and stopped.

I don't want to open my eyes, then the day begins. I want to lie still in the dark behind my eyes and listen to the seagulls' salty voices.

The tide tickles up my legs, and plays with cock 'n' balls,
cock 'n' bull stories
and smacks my arse and expires on my chest,
Mother's breath. Panting.

And slowly it tickle-trickles back down over my skin. But something shifts with it. Something shifts itself under me, as if it wants to get away or slide me back off into the wild blue yonder, whatever it is I am on. Back and arse and legs sink into something wet and grainy, and I fear I've landed in bog or quicksand that'll eat me, or on the hump back of a whale dozing. I struggle to open my eyes. I beat the lids in panic against the sleep dust that seals me in.

The curtain is rent.

I open my eyes and close them on a painful thunderflash.

It is dark and it is damp, prostrate in the cathedral. Cathedrals are places where they manage the unknown, the bogeyman. Masses die in the present against the coming death. Dawn sun breaks through stained windows in yellow particle rays reassembling reality. Pale-blue glass, sandy stone. The dead corpse is warmed up. The worms too.

I peep cautious between the lids of my eyes like some frightened kid over his bedcovers on the nightmare blurs night makes in his room, and slowly work through them one by one turning them back into the properties of the day world. Render them ordinary.

EMPTY BLUE SKY.

I'm staring up at an empty, cloudless sky of faint azure.

Is it painted?

I take a deep breath and belch the ill stench of my insides out. I take another and exhale thanks to my lucky star,

Madonna,

The moon, my guide. The moon translucent as jellyfish is bowing out at one wing of the sky. Must be west, I thought, even in these hurly-gurdy days. The moon was exchanging good morning greetings with the sun, at the other end of the sky, which was welcoming me from the east, also arisen out of the sea. Sore and red as a cock throbbed through a long night's fuck.

And in the sky between them played a solitary puffin.

Puffin. The bird on the spine of kids' books.

As I was saying good morning to the both of 'em, thankful to be out in the fresh air again, the tide passed over my way and whatever I was on top of sifted out from under me and I jumped up to see what it was I had the misfortune or fortune to have landed on top of. And it was a stage piled with gold sand.

Bognor Regis? But where's the seaweed and pebbles?

I was stuck on a beach of golden sand.

Or is it a sand-pit, and my eye enchanted?

Deposited on its edge like any beachcomber's prize, where the stage that stretched out behind me slunk off under the sea. Before me a flat sea emptier than the sky, having in it no puffin, nor any living thing, nor sail, nor island thing. Empty to the horizon where the sky sat on it.

But I didn't sight see long. The biggest surprise was closer to home.

Home?

When I had jumped up, not sure my body could jump to it, I expected my body to be made up of gruesome meats tacked together with a few plasters of skin and what kissed my eye was a brand-new shell and not my old carcass.

A thing of beauty fetched forth.

I had been blessed. I had been borne out of the sea a Surfing Character.

When I came to the New World, I found myself a new.

I was in the body of Young Elvis. Glory. God-handsome.

Sunbaked from the golden sand with that soft submerged muscularity of adolescence; sticky and dripping with sex; and without a blemish of nature or age soured but oyster pearls of drying sea come.

Better than a sun-tanning holiday on Delos. Glorious.

I scrambled to my knees to search between the ebb and flow of tide and amongst the serrating edges of foam for black mirrors to mirror parts of me invisible. I found a mouth, that crack in the lower face. They'd neglected to brush it with milk before poppin' it in the oven and it had cracked into a sneer of dark red.

What a pie, my lecher addressed to it. The lips below curled and blew back silent kisses. So butch, so rock 'n' roll. So buy some.

A New World of things good and bountiful.

And I glimpsed an eye of the blue of the sky, but the other I saw was the black of the night and sea, as was the hair. A black concentrate from their deepest depths where fish and men are blind.

Sight having savoured the other, and touch, I began to wonder what name named this frame, and searched for clues about its person. I lighted upon a tattoo puckered blue on its left bicep that crudely spelt Caliban.

'Caliban,' I said.

I said that name out loud to myself and all the stage in my new voice, and murmured the name of the body over and over, delighted with its sound as I was with its look, and the name meshed with the breaking waves, and I must have zonked out just as I was on the beach, exhausted from my long swim.

The tide woke me, swirling in my armpits and lapping at my throat. It had crept up on me, and was about to pounce into my mouth that hung open in dead sleep.

Blackness stealing upon me.

Half submerged already, I woke with a fright and shuffled my butt up the beach, keeping a suspicious eye on the waves and cursing the sea as an infanticidal mother. But I instantly regretted this. Perhaps, I thought, the sea is only peeved to lose her beauty to the air, and I repentantly swore to swim daily.

Once out of danger and the sea's murderous reach parked on a sandbank, I succumbed to studying my New World again, doubly thankful for my golden hide, since the sun was at noon strength and in my pallid old skin I'd have boiled like a lobster. But in the midst of this thanksgiving thirst and hunger socked it to me in the belly and clenched at my throat, thus transforming this whole New World into Horror.

When I looked about me on the stage, I saw only sand and sea, and the tops of a few high trees behind the dunes on the painted backdrop flapping in the wind. And no food or drinking water.

I had no clothes against the cold nights of cloudless regions.

No tackle to fish with.

No traps for animals, no weapons to defend myself against wild beasts.

I had no implements with which to implement the necessary adaptations of this New World to make it in the meagrest degree inhabitable.

And as my brain leapt flea-like in great bounds from fear to fear the island rose up to be a giant that would squash me without noticing.

And even if I had any of these, I didn't have any know-how. I hadn't ever caught an animal or fish, and my dad had never taught me. I couldn't tell a good root from a poisonous one, so they were all bad. Unless I was to experiment with my life.

I hadn't the tools, or the hands with skill, or even the tool of knowledge. I had nothing except desperation.

And then perhaps the island hadn't any animals or fruit. I couldn't see any.

Home of starvation, I thought. Whoopie.

My life saved save there are any means to live.

The tree tops waved bidding me go but I had no boat and no hope of making one; in this New World of Nothing I fell into such a misery over my unluck being cast here.

Mourning the king my father's wreck and ruin and sinking under.

The loss of my past and all the world it had created with a special place for me in it, that I had gone and abandoned, and now it was covered by the deluge. I was stuck on this desert ark. Looking out I saw a sea prison and I despaired of land. I tied my arms about my knees in a sad knot and shed tears of tiredness and anger like some overtired toddler, which were unrelieving and watered no seed of hope in me or the island, and I was wont to fall asleep again but I was ravenously hungry and parched.

Music. The Fall begin to churn out 'And This Day'.

Its sinister airs lurk about encircling sea and shore.

It sounds no more, 'tis gone, there it begins again.

Sure it waits upon the god o' this island.

Sure.

If music be Shakespeare's image for the immortal, what immortality's this. Britain.

In the end, I, my body, could sit no longer and fidgeted and nudged me till I got off my butt, and went in search of food and water. I hoped in the form of a bottle of Vimto and a few cans of baked beans, and with good luck the props manager would throw in a jumbo box of Swan Vestas.

I walked the stage of printless sand, cursing each grain perfectly in place and praying on some beach huts or kiosk. Instead there enters from the wings a dodo, and then another, and then another one making in all three, which potter obliviously about the stage.

I went up to the first and asked if he knew of any convenience stores in the area, or a chippie.

The dodo sniffed me up and down, and with a huff turned away.

The same happened with the second, but the third did deign to give me an answer.

He said, 'Let me see. There are some restaurants, young man. Cordon bleu. I can highly recommend them, but I think you might find them a little steep.'

The dodo gave his answer with such an insufferable air of snobbery I put my hands to his throat to cook his meat. He viciously pecked at them and I pulled away. He took to the air like a fish, for his flapping wings were barely muscled, because dodos rarely join with the common sort of bird in the sky and prefer a geeky jerk on two legs about the earth. He flopped on for a few yards and came to ground with a bump, still squawking.

Though starving, I decided not to pursue the chase and declared to my hungry belly that dodo meat stank.

The three dodos gathered together in a clutch and clucked in my direction, and I thought to myself, so the island is populated with dodos. What luck to be cast here. And despite them being my only neighbours, I wished to consign them to their world-recognised extinction, which fact they denied.

Seeing as I had no clothes to have pockets to hold a wallet to have any money in to go to a restaurant, I resolved to be getting on in my search and left the dodos to their afternoon walk. Soon they were out of sight, and I saw no one else till the spheres had been moved in the rafters and twilight had come to the stage.

Enter an uneven threesome.

The one in the middle is an oversized ol' git with fuzzy white hair on his chest and brown toupee mat on his head, with a worn Western hide popping cancers, barely wrapped up in a grubby bath robe, and pontificating to the other two.

The one at his right hand is not listening. A delicate teenage boy in the panto costume of a clown.

The third is eager ears. A thin, sinewy man in officer's khaki and sunglasses though the sun is now dying stage right in pools of blood. He is the first to see me, much as I can tell from his shades fixing me a glare. He points me out to the others.

I figured there was no sense running off as they might, however unluckily, be my only chance, and I should face this now, however risky or good. I strode on towards them in brazen nudity, my cock a-swaying before me, heartened by the boy's shameless eye-fucking, till we stood face to face.

'What litter's this?' the old fuck said, derogatory.

'Yeah,' snarls the sidekick in khaki who I could see close up was a weasel, in what could only be phoney American. 'What are you, boy? It'd be better to tell us now, than force us to force it out o' you with a lot of other little titbits like nails and nipples. We have some real nasty methods of doing so.'

'Caliban,' I said as I am a plain man, 'and Caliban's man.'

I wanted to impress with a jaunty ring of confidence, but principally I wanted to indicate to the boy I was untaken.

'And who are you?' I asked as sharp.

'He is a rude boy,' remarked the old goat to the other two. 'As rude and disproportioned in his manners as in his shape.'

'And what's wrong with my shape?' I asked, as I was proud of it.

'It's . . . it's indecent, downright indecent, that's what's wrong with it,' stuttered the weasel. 'Just take a look at yourself.'

I complied with this pleasant invitation and gave myself a looking up and down, and, still pleased with what I saw, said, 'It's all perfectly natural. There're no falsies on me. See.'

And I took my cock in hand and tugged at it. 'Haven't you got one?'

The boy who is otherwise silent giggles whilst the weasel splutters and screams.

'You little pervert, I can hardly bring myself to see. Filth as thou art. You don't deserve to be around decent folk. What if Ma Pru or Pa Bigot saw you? What then, huh? Bet you didn't think o' that when you took our beach for a nudist colony, huh?'

'Do you mean some moth-eaten old dodos? I shouldn't worry, they've seen already. And it's not as if there was anything I could do about it, I was washed up here like this. And another thing, before you go accusing me of being rude, you haven't answered my question yet, which I count as ruder. Who are you?' I asked the old fuck again.

'Despite your impertinence I'll give you the answer,' he said imperiously. 'Prospero's the name, and kingship's the game. King of this island.'

'Hail to the chief,' the weasel shouted. 'Hosannas to the highest.'

'And this quick character,' King Prospero continued, pointing to the weasel, 'is Colonel Ariel, my inestimable aide, and this my fool, Chester.' He gestured to the boy, who curtsied low to the ground whilst Colonel Ariel began to bow and then remembering himself tried to efface it.

'And as I said I am the King of this island and whoever you may be you're trespassing on it.'

'So what do you say to that?' interrogated Colonel Ariel.

'I'm very pleased to make your acquaintance, I'm sure, King,' I answered, all p's and q's and extending my hand.

The King didn't stoop to see it and rattled on.

'May I remind you that you are a villain stealing on my shore, and I want to know your reason for being so.'

'And it better be a good 'un,' put in the Colonel.

'I don't have a reason,' I replied as nice as pie, 'and I don't have to have one as far as I'm concerned. Do the bees need reasons for beeing. No, they don't. I am here just because I am here. I just happen to have washed up on this shore. I assure you I surely didn't elect to.'

'Oh, didn't you? That's so reassuring,' said King Prospero mighty suspiciously. 'Well, let that be as it may, it's neither here nor there, for now you are here, on my island, and I would like to know as its King how you intend to eat.'

'In the usual style, by placing food in my mouth and masticating; and, having masticated, swallowing. Believe me or not, I find the stomach does the rest without me having to give it as much as a thought. Does that answer your question?'

King Prospero gestured to Colonel Ariel who applied his boot to my goolies. I rolled around on the sand, howling.

'Now answer me,' King Prospero snapped.

'Well I was rather hoping you'd tell me, but if you won't I s'pose I'll have to eat off the land. There must be something to eat here,' I croaked.

'Oh, oh, oh,' shouted the Colonel in at my lug-holes, prancing on the sand about me. 'And who do you think that belongs to?'

'Huh?' I asked, confused.

'This island', King Prospero stated, 'and everything on it isn't common property for any Tom, Dick or Caliban who happens along to enjoy. This island and every living thing on it, and that moves on it, and that grows from it, and from the trees planted in it, and that comes from its waters, free running in streams, or pond still, or coastal, belongs . . . BELONGS TO ME. And you aren't having anything without my say-so. Got it? So on what are you going to feed your ugly mug? There aren't any freebie restaurants.'

'We're not Commies,' warranted the Colonel.

'Oh dear,' I said.

'But there again,' continued King Prospero, softening, 'we're not barbarians, we don't let people starve. You can work for your keep.'

'Work!' I exclaimed.

The King and the weasel nodded.

'For you?' I asked.

The King and the weasel nodded again.

'I'd rather scavenge off the island, thanks all the same,' I flatly stated.

'You mean thieve, sonny. Thieve off me, not scavenge.'

'And the penalties are severe,' Colonel Ariel squirmed. 'A first offence means death. The second, death with extreme malice and pain, and the third offence – Well, I'd rather not say.'

'Why?' I asked. 'Your imagination run out on you?'

'You bastard,' Colonel Ariel fumed. 'Let me at him chief, let me kill 'im.'

'No, Colonel, you must restrain yourself. We don't want him damaged any more than he already is.' King Prospero touched a finger to his head. 'I think he'll see his situation aright in a moment.

'I charge thee attend me.'

'No, as I am a man and my own man.'

'Follow.'

'No, I will resist such boorish entertainment till my enemy has more power. OK?'

I start to go but am charmed from moving.

I turn to go and in the sudden movement hunger and thirst get the better of me, and deliver me a double blow. I wobbled on my pins and hit the sand again.

I would have stood against him but the old sorcerer had woven enchantment to control me, for only he, King Prospero, could open the cramp of hunger 'n' thirst, and release me from the tempest whipping up my belly and unpeg my throat left to parch in the sun. King Prospero had all the food and water, and the shelter, on the island, and the guards to protect it, and I knew this and I knew that my situation was padlocked tight.

Before the mighty sorcerer I was helpless.

King Prospero commanded me, 'Come: obey.'

I, my head hung to the ground, nodded weakly.

'You do yourself wrong not recognising what's for your own good. Yes?'

I gave no answer.

'Yes?' he questioned, and kicked me in the shins like all good men do when you're down.

'Yes,' I said.

'You disgust me.'

He stood towering over me.

And I disgusted myself.

This was the diabolical trick by which I was taken into hand and service by King Prospero of the Isle of Dogs and he got for himself slave labour.

This island is lily-livered shape and has a drowsy climate. Stage-hands cover it in groves of limes, pines, planes, and conifers through which dodos snuffle and on whose tops sit grey clouds of discouragement. At the centre of the stage back is King Prospero's home, a deep cave which rambles into and burrows under the rock that sits on the island's green skin like an ugly pimple. Before its gaping maw is a gravel drive, to one side four ironic columns supporting thin stuff, by which I mean airy nothings of Mr Amiss and Miss Brook-Nothing, and all their British Bookers. And up behind the rock the swimming pool where King Prospero hangs out all day with his baddies fixed in shit-eating grins and him in his baggy trunks, chewing over old matters and chilled beers.

King Prospero was an ancient tale teller.

His motto was 'I write the tales that make the world revolve. And jump.'

I thought he arti-fist tales that made the world revolting, and I hoped the world would retch up his stuff that's rich, I mean revolt, for remembering my life I was sick o' these old tales. Prospero the enchanter had with charming words anaesthetised all the island in his mouldy old legends and done a disappearing act with possibility.

Tickets for Shakespeare are as much a mere commodity as a Picasso is.

Shakespeare is venerated whilst contemporary English writing is deceased.

That Was A Pearl Is Now Dodo Shit.

Out there is the Barbican Theatre, with the decor of a seafood restaurant chain. Plump seats and wall lamps betasselled. Surrounded in barbaric concrete like some Aztec sacrificial monstrosity but lacking in myth.

To assist King Prospero in this production he had as stage director Colonel Ariel. Acting on King Prospero's earthy and abhorred commands, the weasel carried out covert operations, taking on pleasing contrivance to maintain the stories and under their cover King Prospero's hold.

Now Chester was the only passable human and all-round fun person on the entire island, and with him I became bosom pals.

Chester, too, I discovered, had drifted to this stage.

Chester was born in New York City. After his birth, as is the custom, his parents had gone to the Oracle to request his future-story. *Time* magazine told them in no uncertain terms to dump the brat, predicting he would bring them NADA OF USA, role confusion and corporate loss. Having sold them this future, the Oracle advised them on the correct thing to do in such circumstances, which was to expose him to rats. Horrified, Chester's parents returned to their Upper East Side apartment, where, being bourgeois sentimentalists, and like all richies hiring executioners, they gave Chester to their Puerto Rican maid with specific instructions to kill him, thinking she being poverty could have no sensitivity. Luckily for Chester she did. Unluckily for Chester he got to be bigger and bigger, and she, fearing someone would question what a Puerto Rican woman was doing with a white boy and be found out, and he growing too boisterous to be shut up indoors, sealed him in a packing case and cast him into the East River to let things have their course, which course they did to the island, where he was salvaged by King Prospero, who reared him as an idle pleasure to be his jester.

Winters passed without summers, and I slaved on for the old goat. With iron manacles at neck and feet I shuffled about my myriad tasks, of making King Prospero's fire and wet bed, fetching wood and gathering food, as pharmaceutical dogs-body in his study with his spells and potions, demeaningly universally I saved.

And every time old Prospero caught me someplace he would say 'Caliban, my boy . . . ' and dribble me some of his stentorian, sententious dribble in the name of reforming me, as if anything I could do could ever make me worthy in his eyes. Unable to run on my shackled legs, I was forced to stand and deliver my ears up to his pompous drone, and would wonder how he made such tedious farts.

Now while I was a humping logs I had a lot of time to think, and my thoughts turned out to sea on which there must be other islands, but I hadn't a boat to sail to them or a hope in hell of building one with them watching over me like MI5.

But even if I did escape it'd be just the same as the rest of my life; I'd jump straight out of one story and flop right into the hot fat of another. Another one written before me, defining my character and role. All terribly passive. I was acting like the poor that get *nouveau riche* and change nothing, not even against the risk of being trodden down.

And so on and on, I thought to myself, you'll be trapped in stories, being ordered around and running away into the dictates of a new director, and what's worse unknown, for the rest of your life if you don't watch out. It was about time I did something. What I needed was a story about me and my needs. I decided I had to stand my ground and hit back for once, but without more fists than mine and Chester's such a stand was suicide.

But then on the other hand it was suicide going on. I could tell I hadn't much time to run, for Old Bones kept me on brackish water and unwashed mussels and withered roots and husks from which the acorn had been robbed by Colonel Ariel, and which I couldn't stomach. I got cramps of hunger, and got weaker and weaker, and it was easier for Old Bones to cuss me as a lazy swine (and so I stank) and my leaning frame got easier for Colonel Ariel to kick from under me.

Through general neglect King Prospero was causing my hair to mat and my body to be besmirched, though Chester tried to help and wash me but he got spanked for it, and I became pig ugly and was cast out.

I was sinking fast on dry land.

In my dreams, as my days. The days shipwreck on dream's shores on which swamp and quicksand lied and in which I stumble, the set of my eye and pallor of my cheeks marking me as a zombie. In this foul bubble I trod water, tiring.

But in sleep's language need began to speak.

A wind rose out to sea and blew into shore, driving away the marsh gases and stirring up the stagnant waters. In the tide the wind brought I began to bob, and feel my limbs again. My arms stretched into a crawl, and in the sickness of my night throes a ship was born out of the fog, my dream boat with fine cannon and black sails sailing the seven seas to deliver me, and from the high cliff of his power my ruler fell.

One morning I awoke to find the ship had leaked out of my dreams and sailed onto the island.

Night gives birth to more suns.

That morning when I looked out the window in the rock, I saw a tall ship that had been cast up on the stage during the night's tempest. Its hull was wedged tight on the rocks and its sails were tattered and torn, but it was my boat. A three-master.

My heart cheered.

Ahoy! A boy!

And I leapt into my clothes and helter-skeltered, stumbling and falling, down to the shore.

The ship was sat idly on the rocks. Most of its mast arms had fallen to the deck in the storm, but its masts stood and its strong timbers were cracked but had not broken up. On its side its name was painted blood red, the *Endymion*. For a masthead it had the figures of Moon and Sun kissing, from whose lips dripped shooting stars.

The good ship *Endymion*, I thought. Wow-wee.

I scrambled aboard in my excitement and searched high and low but could find not a soul. The ship was abandoned like the *Marie Celeste*.

I scuttled off to find Chester. Chester knew more than I did. He'd know what was going down.

'Chester, Chester,' I shouted hobbling up to him. 'What about the ship? What about the crew?'

'Old Bones', he replied, 'had the police down there early, before I was up, and had 'em whisked away in the Black Marias.'

So King Prospero had used stronger magic on them than he had on me.

'Why?' I asked.

'Because they're pirates, that's why,' he whispered. 'Keep your voice down, or a spirit bug'll overhear us. Pirates,' he said, reverential-like. 'I dreamt of pirates all through my childhood.'

'But what do you mean by pirates?' I asked in his ears.

'Pirates, fictioneers,' he replied in mine. 'Bucaneers of the great seas who cross all the boundaries of can and can't as they please, of can't and shouldn't. The absolute rule and the polite rule. Pirate Youth. Anyone who does as they need and not as they should, or as anyone else would have them do.'

'But why's he arrested them?'

'Because to him they're like carriers of the plague. If allowed to go free, he reasons in his small head, they'll soon have the whole island in a fever and him dead. Old Bones doesn't want an example like them about the place. He's gonna use the Colonel in another trick, to bestow on the eyes and imprint on the memories of these simpleton folk, these dodos, a vanity of his power. As he thinks they expect from him. He'll hang 'em. And if we don't hurry we'll miss the trial.'

'Trial?' I exclaimed.

'Yes, trial, donkey. Now get your ass in motion.'

Donkey was his pet name for me.

The stage-hands had set up a courtroom outside the royal cave. The entire population of the island was present saving the newcomers. King Prospero claimed their presence was only likely to be a disturbance of the public order, and thus they were to be tried in their absence.

Once everyone was seated comfortably, King Prospero in his stately bathrobe as prosecutor began.

'This pernicious gang claim to have been wrecked on our shore, but I tell you they do themselves and myself and all our nation great wrong in persisting in this heinous lie. I have intelligence, which I cannot reveal to this court as prejudicial to national security, which suggests that the case is in its entirety otherwise. Basically, and very unfortunately for them, I do not believe a word of it. And I do not believe the jury will either.'

The twelve just and true dodos nodded.

'I think they came here to usurp this island, that they usurp the name of shipwrecked and put themselves on this island as spies with the intention, amongst a mint of other conspiracies I cannot reveal as *sub judice*, of winning the island from me, the native lord on it. I denounce you as liars, thiefs and traitors. What do you say to that?'

Everyone was rather mystified, and not a little fearful of this last remark. But King Prospero had only got lost in his own rhetoric and forgotten the pirates' absence.

He remembered himself and summed up.

'It only remains for the jury to deliver its verdict and the judges their sentence.'

The jury stood to a man and unanimously declared them guilty. Then the judges who were all butcher-dodos brayed for the death penalty of A Thousand Wogans.

King Prospero silenced them with a wave of his hand and spoke waxing kind.

'Although I am with their high wrongs struck to the quick, to the very quick, with their foul conspiracy of beasts against our civilised life, yet I take part with my noble reason against my fury, for it is the better man who shows mercy and not revenge. And thus, they being penitent, the sole drift of my purpose extends not a frown further, and I will be lenient. The sentence is commuted to just death.'

'Oh dear,' moaned the Colonel.

The pirates were lodged in the deep dungeons under the rock, and I was ordered to take them their victuals. On first seeing this motley band dressed in the accoutrements of b.boy, punk and jumble sales, I knew I was no longer lonely, though I cannot say why. Soon friendship had sprouted between us, and I was sneaking down in the middle of the night, when all were asleep, to talk with them.

I would take Chester along, and he would gaze at them rather lovelorn, which made me know jealousy.

One night, I picked up the courage to question them about the vocation of piracy, and it was one named Lee Oblivion who gave me the answer.

'To be a pirate is to rewrite the stories,' he said, being of a literary bent and very critical himself. 'The stories one finds oneself in. That's all you can do. One can't escape them. One can't just make them up out of nothing, no story is wholly one's own. One must rewrite them to one's own needs.'

'Yes,' I said seriously, for I had learnt this at least in my life, and that is the only true knowledge there is. And this is the only true community there is, in common knowledge, which includes language and memory, to assist one another in managing to live on.

'But the real important bit,' continued Lee Oblivion, 'is to know who you are in the story. I mean it's obvious who we are,' he pointed to the bars. 'But do you know who you are?'

I looked at his sickly yellow face reflecting my own, and his compatriots lounging about the cell, and from the other side of the bars I said with certainty.

'Yes.'

There and then I decided to court this star fortune had cast me, even if for the moment it was eclipsed, but I didn't know how. And I was no good at making escapes, as you've seen.

Before sun-up on the morning of execution, enter several strange shapes, men in the uniform of waiters, and set up a long gallows, and exit. Then re-enter, bringing in a trestle table and setting it down before the cave beneath the shadow of the gallows, and set down on the table a banquet such that if I were in Burley and should report it, would they believe me? And if they did they'd swear faith in God, unicorns and phoenix, but that they've seen *Dynasty* on their TVs.

King Prospero and his Worshipful Company of Elders enter in monkey suits. Their faces in the livery colours of drunkenness – ruddy and bloody. After an all-night binge at the May Ball, prancing and strutting with taffeta girls imported cheap from Swiss finishing brothels, they sit down to a late supper of quails' eggs and caviare, and for a morning brew of champagne.

Plus Chester they make up twelve sat only on one side of the table so no one's view of the gallows is restricted.

About them the strange shapes dance with the gentle actions of solicitation, cutting the food on their plates and refilling their glasses, clearing the empties and wiping up dribbled food, picking up bread rolls they've thrown and enduring their jokes and gropes.

The chimps at tea are no worse.

And as they caroused I as King Prospero ordered for a jest had to wash their sore and barnacled feet with my tongue.

Before the sun had arisen, the Pirate Youth were brought on in the midst of a detachment of dodo police, still wearing their nightgowns and slippers as they came straight from bed yawning. The dodos lined them up on the gallows and placed in each noose a young neck, and left them standing as they rigged the pulley lever so that King Prospero could drop the trap without so much as leaving his seat.

All the Company sat panting in anticipation, or indigestion.

King Prospero raised a magnum to them and shouted, 'God be merciful to you. And if he is I'll deal with him next, I swear on the holy book. And now to set you a twitching.'

'Fuck you,' they called back.

King Prospero pulled the lever. The trap door dropped on them and they left the stage.

At the ends of their ropes they danced. Their bodies firecrackers, their limbs possessed with muscular devils and blood surged in their ears and noses and through tightened veins at formula-one speeds. Racked with contractions and shudders beating under their skins and shitting and pissing their lives out, their features swelled out and sharpened, their faces popped and their necks snapped, each snap a firework exploding in silence, their mouths hanging open and echoing.

'What harmony is this?'

'What marvellous sweet music?'

Old Prospero could hardly contain himself as sparks exploded in the Elders' eyes with such an ablution of tension, and the Elders and Prospero sat in surfeit, humming content, sucking in the stink of death.

ARISE

ARISE

ARISE

I arose and stood facing the gallows.

The ropes hung from the sky, the nooses hung on the ends of the ropes, Pirate Youth hung in the nooses like virginal sacks with their little tootsies peeping out, and my mouth falls open.

THUNDER AND LIGHTNING

This ain't what I need.

A scream comes out, and comes back to me. And out my mouth again.

MURDERED ANGELS' BODIES BEDLAM BRAINS BOILED

WIND CARRIES THRU ME SCREAMS HURTLE OUT MILE UPON MILE

SWIRL ABOUT WIND CARRIES INTO THEIR MOUTHS HOLLOW

ARISE IN YOUR STATIC

Pirate Youth start screaming. REVERB DAWN CHORUS

SCREECHING WHISTLES OF BODIES EXPLODING

THE THEATRE COLLAPSES SEEPS ONTO BLACK STREETS

King Prospero desperate calls back the winds.
THE LETTERS DECOMPOSE ON HIS LIPS, HIS TONGUE GOES BLACK
He fixes his eye on me. HIS EVIL EYE'S A CON
YOUR STORIES ARE OLD STORIES, OLD MULE, JUST TOO STUBBORN TO DIE
I DON'T WANT YOUR LIES
DESTROY THEIR LANGUAGE HERE IS THE HAMMER
CRASHING NOISE attends the Elders, they try to wound the loud winds and stab to kill the still closing waters.
NAILS INTO THEIR HEADS US
TONGUES UNTIED EYES EXORCISED
DEMONS OF FEAR AND DOUBT CAST OUT
I SWEAR THEY ARE DEATHS, THAT ARE REAPERS
THEY REAP THE SOWN SEEDS OF DOUBT AND FEAR
CAST OUT THUNDER I HAVE MADE THEM MAD
The Elders' ears pop and spurt blood over their tuxes.
WIND SINGS GUILTY SUN BRINGS THUNDER PRONOUNCING
STEP OUT
HAVE BELIEF IN WANTS DO AS YOU NEED
TAKE MY HAND
Pirate Youth snap the ropes in two with one good body yank, leap down to the ground. BATS OUT OF HELL.
Whipping out cutlasses, hidden under the gallows.
THE PLAY LINES DISSOLVE INTO SLUSH
SENTENCES THAT ARE BLACK CAPS ON JUDGE'S HEAD
THEIR BRAINS ARE DEAD THEY SEE NOTHING NEW
Girlie is hanging and Colonel Ariel is eating her out. She slips her legs behind his neck without he noticing and with a pelvic thrust snaps his spine in two, allowing his dead weight to pull her down, saying,
'We took one look at it, and knew it had to die.'
GLOBE EXPLODES CRASH STORIES MESH INTO ME
SAILING SEVEN STORY SEAS SAILOR MUSCLE WINDS GIVE SAIL TO
THE WORLD IS MADE AND LOST AND MADE AGAIN AND LOST OVER AND OVER
SET UP YOUR SQUATS IN THEIR MANSIONS

SET UP YOUR SQUATS IN THEIR STORIES
DEAD LAND TO BACK OF US
SOMETHING WAITING IN THE NIGHT
SKY RAW FLESH I WANT OUT
PARENTS WAVING FROM THE SHORE
PUNGENT OF ROADS
FROM GALLOW ROPES
DUST IN HIS HEART DUST ON HIS TOES
'YOU'LL GET NO SUPPER'
'I'LL HAVE YOUR BLOOD I'M SICK OF RUNNING SCARED'
FIRES OF RAGE ON BEACH GALLONS AND GALLONS OF ANGER BURNING LIKE OIL
THE MOON FALLS OUT OF PROSPERO'S WORLD
BLACK SMOKE IN YOUR SKY BLACK PUPIL IN MY EYE
I WANT TO GET ON WITH THE REST OF MY LIVES

The Elders run blind in BLACKNESS, their eyes poked out in disbelief.

In such horror men hang and drown their former selves.

Their yellow entrails strangle 'em.

ROCKET SHIP TAKE OFF ANGEL WINGS BEATING
SHAKESPEARE SAYS HARPIES I DON'T BELIEVE HIM
LAY MY HANDS ON THEIR TABLE IT FLIES AWAY
I WANT OUT GANG SPLASH THRU INTER SPACE
NEW WORLD'S EMPTY BOY SAYS
I'LL BE AN ASTRONAUT DON'T NEED AN ASTROLUNG

Prospero is still jabber-running around like the headless chicken, driven mad without his story. They slaughter those Elders still alive who turn into vultures and truss him up. Then they break my manacles.

We all sit down to debate what to do with 'im.

I gleefully suggested that we return his hospitality and hang him.

And we did, though the old devil he dementedly tempted us with every gift, and he took some killing, gasping on his rope. I had to toll his death bell and took him by the legs and swung with all my might. He was boring us.

Chester and I asked to join the pirates.

They had to have a secret meeting 'bout it, but they did agree.

First, though, we had to do two things, and the first was eat our Elder. The thought of tasting Prospero made me bilious but it was worth it.

They cut him down and roasted him on a spit, and then offered Chester and I his cock. Apparently the best bit.

We took one bite and razzed. We were both embarrassed for being soft and disappointed hangdogs for spoiling our chances.

Sam The Man clapped us on the back.

'Don't worry,' he said, 'it was only a test, and you passed. No one could keep that down, and if they could, devour human flesh, they'd have to be Elder.'

He shook us by the hand, as did the others, toasting our luck in vodka.

Now we had to choose our own names.

I thought for a while and then remembered my eyes; I decided on Black Eye. Chester had settled on Riton in a minute. And then we partied, and when we were good and drunk and collapsed about a campfire made of the gallows, a single spotlight in the black night, Miranda broke into one of her Shakespearean recitals.

'O, wonder!
How many goodly creatures are there here!
How beauteous mankind is! O brave new world,
That has such people in't!'

And so she would have gone on if someone hadn't bawled for her to shut it, and she did, saying it was only a jest, but perhaps she meant it more serious than it was taken.

And, later even, our actors leave the stage one by one, carrying away the light with them little by little, slipping into the darkness surrounding and disappearing.

Leaving you looking at blank space.

EAT YOUR ELDERS, AND SICK 'EM UP.